### Praise for the Novels of C.A. Belmond

*A Rather Charming Invitation*

"The third installment in Belmond's *Rather* series is every bit as much fun as the two previous books. The writing is leavened with just the right dash of tart wit, the romance between Penny and Jeremy is sweetly satisfying, and the search for the missing tapestry includes some fascinating historical details and intriguing tidbits about the perfume industry, French history, and coins. *A Rather Charming Invitation* is a deliciously old-fashioned story that is guaranteed to charm both mystery and romance readers."

—*Reader to Reader*

"Writing well in the first person from a singular point of view must be difficult, but Ms. Belmond pulls it off beautifully. And with fascinating glimpses of Europe past and present, and a gentle romance between a likeable pair, she has produced an enchanting read. I highly recommend *A Rather Charming Invitation* for its combination of charm, liveliness, and suspense."

—*Romance Reviews Today*

"C.A. Belmond's entertaining duo of Penny Nichols and Jeremy Laidley are back in the spotlight . . . a wonderful cozy mystery."

—*Night Owl Reviews (Top Pick)*

"A simpatico duo!"

—*Publishers Weekly*

"Written in such a fascinating way, with characters that will both charm and entertain, *A Rather Charming Invitation* is a book that you don't want to miss."

—*Chick Lit Club*

"*A Rather Charming Invitation* is a lovely reunion with American Penny Nichols and her English fiancé Jeremy Laidley, along with their assortment of English and French relatives . . . There's old-fashioned sleuthing throughout . . . along with some wonderful European locations and a bit of old-fashioned glamour . . . I'm happy to say that this book captures me as much as did the first novel and I am glad to know that Belmond is already hard at work on the next adventure for Nichols and Laidley, Ltd."

—*DearAuthor.com*

*continued . . .*

*A Rather Lovely Inheritance*

"A spirited heroine."

—*Publishers Weekly*

"An entertaining yarn with family drama and intrigue aplenty."

—*Booklist*

"Utterly charming . . . excellent characterization and dialogue [with] a sweet touch of romance. If a novel can be both gentle and lively, surely this is one . . . *A Rather Lovely Inheritance* tantalizes and entertains with its mystery and skullduggery . . . Penny [is] a perfectly lovable heroine. It's a rare gem of a book that leaves behind a feeling of pure pleasure."

—*Romance Reviews Today*

"I haven't read anything like it in quite a while, and I thoroughly enjoyed myself . . . Penny is a delightful heroine . . . Who wouldn't enjoy the unexpected chance to rattle around London and then fly off to the sunny Côte d'Azur?"

—*DearAuthor.com*

"Combines suspense, romance, and crafty wit. The protagonist is a character to cheer for, and the mystery subplot will keep readers turning the pages."

—*Romantic Times*

"[Penny] hooks everyone . . . with her klutzy optimism. . . Fans will enjoy the lighthearted breezy storyline as the Yank takes England, France, and Italy."

—*Midwest Book Review*

"[Has] everything—mystery, romance, [and] a whirlwind tour of Europe's hot spots."

—*Kirkus Reviews*

"A return to the golden age of romantic suspense! *A Rather Lovely Inheritance* weds old-style glamour to chick-lit flair. You just want to move into the novel yourself—on a long-term lease, with hero and snazzy sports car included (villains sold separately)."

—Lauren Willig, author of *The Mischief of the Mistletoe*

OTHER NOVELS BY C.A. BELMOND

*A Rather Lovely Inheritance*

*A Rather Curious Engagement*

*A Rather Charming Invitation*

# A Rather Remarkable Homecoming

C.A. Belmond

 NEW AMERICAN LIBRARY

NEW AMERICAN LIBRARY
Published by New American Library, a division of
Penguin Group (USA) Inc., 375 Hudson Street,
New York, New York 10014, USA
Penguin Group (Canada), 90 Eglinton Avenue East, Suite 700, Toronto,
Ontario M4P 2Y3, Canada (a division of Pearson Penguin Canada Inc.)
Penguin Books Ltd., 80 Strand, London WC2R 0RL, England
Penguin Ireland, 25 St. Stephen's Green, Dublin 2,
Ireland (a division of Penguin Books Ltd.)
Penguin Group (Australia), 250 Camberwell Road, Camberwell, Victoria 3124,
Australia (a division of Pearson Australia Group Pty. Ltd.)
Penguin Books India Pvt. Ltd., 11 Community Centre, Panchsheel Park,
New Delhi - 110 017, India
Penguin Group (NZ), 67 Apollo Drive, Rosedale, Auckland 0632,
New Zealand (a division of Pearson New Zealand Ltd.)
Penguin Books (South Africa) (Pty.) Ltd., 24 Sturdee Avenue,
Rosebank, Johannesburg 2196, South Africa

Penguin Books Ltd., Registered Offices:
80 Strand, London WC2R 0RL, England

First published by New American Library,
a division of Penguin Group (USA) Inc.

First Printing, September 2011
10 9 8 7 6 5 4 3 2 1

REGISTERED TRADEMARK—MARCA REGISTRADA

LIBRARY OF CONGRESS CATALOGING-IN-PUBLICATION DATA:

Belmond, C A.
A rather remarkable homecoming/C.A. Belmond.
p. cm.
ISBN 978-0-451-23461-2
1. Cornwall (England : County)—Fiction. 2. Historic buildings—England—Cornwall
(County)—Fiction. 3. Real estate developers—Fiction. 4. Riddles—Fiction. 5. Country life—
England—Cornwall (County)—Fiction. I. Title.
PS3602.E46R39 2011
813'.6—dc22          2011009678

Set in Simoncini Garamond
Designed by Ginger Legato

Printed in the United States of America

*for R. A.*

# A Rather Remarkable
# Homecoming

# Part One

# Chapter One

It was raining lightly in London when our taxicab wound its way around a familiar tree-lined square and pulled up to the front walk of Great-Aunt Penelope's Victorian town house. I still think of it as hers, for the house seems to exist in its own 1920s time warp; an elegant, cozy, sheltering bulwark against twenty-first-century stress and strife. Every time I approach the front double doors with their frosted glass windows and immaculate white pillars on each side, I inwardly bless the mysterious Aunt Pen for her astounding, unexpected kindness in remembering Jeremy and me in her last will and testament.

The cabbie carried our suitcases to the top step, then said, "Thank you very much, sir," as Jeremy tipped him.

"Home at last!" Jeremy proclaimed to me.

We had honeymooned on the Riviera and then gone straight to New York to visit my parents and friends. After that, it was off to California, where Jeremy did some legal advising for an old client, while I worked as an historical set-design consultant on a crazy movie called *Romeo and Juliet—Vampire-Hunters For Hire*, which some friends of mine were making as an independent film.

But now we both were glad to be back in London again.

Jeremy put his key in the lock, pushed open the front door and, without any warning, scooped me up in his arms. "The bride never *walks* in," he proclaimed.

The cabbie looked as surprised as I did, and he drove away grinning.

"You do realize," I squealed in protest as Jeremy carried me across the threshold, "that this is a very barbaric, arcane custom, from the days when pirates and soldiers kidnapped their brides."

"Any excuse to get an armful of Penny is fine with me," Jeremy declared as we passed through the vestibule.

Then he stopped in his tracks. I peered over his shoulder to see why.

Two total strangers were seated on the small black leather sofa in the little sitting room at the right, which we use to receive business clients. They were watching us with an expectant, amused look. Meanwhile, a harried guy named Rupert was standing at the reception desk, with the telephone receiver tucked under his chin, and a sheaf of paperwork in his hand. Rupert, who still worked at Jeremy's old law firm, was keeping an eye on our business while we were away, by fielding clients old and new . . . and dealing with unexpected callers like these two.

"Oh, you're here!" Rupert said to us, looking slightly flustered. He had a new haircut, with a shock of hair that stood up above his forehead and contributed to his surprised look. "Didn't realize the time. Welcome back."

With an infinitesimal nod of his head, he indicated the young man and middle-aged woman seated on the sofa, and said, "This is Harriet Fieldworthy and her son Colin. They are here from Cornwall at the, er, suggestion of the esteemed personage I e-mailed you about," he added meaningfully.

My jet-lagged mind struggled to remember Rupert's e-mail and to pick up his subtle cues. Cornwall. Yes. As in, the Duke of Cornwall—i.e., Prince Charles, heir to the throne of England. Or, to be more precise, *His Royal Highness The Prince Charles Philip Arthur George, Prince of Wales, Knight of the Garter, Knight of the Thistle, Knight Grand Cross of the Order of Bath, Member of the Order of Merit, Knight of the Order of Australia, Companion of the Queen's Service Order, Privy Counsellor, Aide-de-Camp, Earl of Chester, Duke of Cornwall, Duke of Rothesay, Earl of Carrick, Baron of Renfrew, Lord of the Isles and Prince and Great Steward of Scotland.*

While we were away, His Royal Highness—or, H.R.H., as we peasants like to call him—had sent us an elegant, intriguing note about a possible assignment for our new company, Nichols & Laidley, Ltd. But the Prince's office, upon discovering that we were on our honeymoon, had assured Rupert that it could wait until we returned to London. Now here we were . . . and so, apparently, were the people that the Prince wanted us to meet.

Jeremy was staring dubiously at our callers, who hardly look like palace courtiers. Colin appeared to be in his early twenties, and wore a black rock-and-roll T-shirt paired with traditional kilts (yes, that's right, a man-skirt); whereas Harriet, his mum, was shod in a countrywoman's boots and wore a fairly masculine tweed suit, and the kind of Alpine wool hat that you'd wear while hiking in the high country. I couldn't help wondering if the whole thing was a massive hoax from some wiseguy at Jeremy's old law office. But then I saw Rupert mouth the words *They're for real* to Jeremy.

By now Harriet and Colin had risen to their feet, and probably would have shaken hands, except that Jeremy remained rooted to the spot, with his arms still full of "new bride". So our guests paused, awkwardly waiting.

"Darling," I said, with as much dignity as a gal could muster in such a position. "I think you can put me down now." Jeremy awoke from his shock, and obliged.

"I'm Penny Nichols Laidley," I said to our guests, trying to sound as dignified as my English mother might, even though my husband had just deposited me into the room like a sack of mail. "And this is Jeremy Laidley." Rupert flushed, realizing he'd failed to formally introduce us.

"Oh, we know, we know!" the woman said, beaming at us while shaking my hand vigorously as if it were a water pump. "Our *friend* says if anyone can help us, you can. He thought you might be willing to take our case, because, you see, we believe it's of vital personal interest to you as well. When we heard that you were coming back to England today, I thought, mercy, we'd better grab your attention straight away, before you two go off on another case."

Gazing at her, I saw that Harriet's green eyes had interesting crinkles around them, and her cheeks were a healthy, ruddy color, which hale-and-hearty folks get from spending every day outdoors in all kinds of weather. Her cheerful face was rimmed with unruly brown hair flecked with strands of grey.

"You see, it's all got to do with your grand-mum. And her last wishes before she died," she added. "Dear me, I did put that rather bluntly, but time is of the essence."

"Grandmother Beryl?" I said with some surprise. My mother's mum had died decades ago, so it seemed rather late indeed to speak of Grandma's "last wishes" . . . and I wondered how time could possibly be of the essence.

"Why don't we all have some tea?" I found myself saying, hoping that my travel-weary brain would catch up to all this after a "cuppa".

Jeremy shot me one of his *Watch out!* looks. Because, Prince

Charles or no Prince Charles, in our short time in business together, we've gotten into some tight spots at the behest of wealthy and powerful clients; so shortly after our wedding, we made a second set of vows to each other, this time regarding our work. To wit, we agreed on the following points: *One: No more cases involving relatives*; and *Two: No more accepting weird invitations from the big movers-and-shakers of the world.*

This case had the dubious distinction of killing both rules with one stone.

But Harriet looked at me gratefully now and said, "Oh, yes, tea would be lovely. It was a long drive from Port St. Francis."

"I've just had some take-away food delivered," Rupert said to Jeremy, as if relieved to be able to be of some help now. "Cold meat and sandwiches, and scones and cake."

"Got any beer?" Colin asked. Both he and his mother had an accent that sounded slightly Scottish. Harriet nudged him. Jeremy looked as if he would be only too happy to pop open some ale, but Harriet shook her head firmly.

So we all adjourned to the study, which is a nice big room smack dab between Jeremy's office and mine. It's where we meet up at the end of the day over a glass of wine. Jeremy's butterscotch-colored leather chair and matching ottoman sit across from my paisley wing chair, right in front of the fireplace, with a round table beside us. Opposite the table is a horsehair sofa, and I gestured for Harriet and Colin to sit there together. Harriet patted the sofa approvingly, like someone who's been around horses and farms all her life.

"Shall I light a fire?" Jeremy suggested, resigned to the idea that these guests would be here awhile. Although it was June, the room was chilly from the damp weather as evening descended. I helped Rupert arrange a large tray with the tea things, and then he murmured that he had to head back to his office. With a nod to me, Rupert slipped out of the room.

"Now then," Harriet said briskly when everyone had filled their teacups and plates. "You'll be wanting to know what this all about."

She took a hungry bite of a dainty chicken sandwich, and a sip of her tea, then she sighed with relief and began. "I am the president of the Port St. Francis Legacy Society," she explained in a matter-of-fact tone with a touch of pride. "We are responsible for the preservation and protection of our quality of life in the village, and the welfare of our citizens."

"Which, these days, means that Mum and her crowd have to pick up all the slack for what the ruddy government doesn't do," Colin translated, slicing a scone in two and using his knife to spread whipped cream on one side, and jam on the other. Then he closed the scone as if it were a sandwich.

"The Legacy Society is *not* just a bunch of little ladies who feather-dust old landmark houses," he declared, popping half the scone in his mouth. When he was not quite finished chewing, he continued. "Mum's group has rescued everything and everybody in town, from the post office to the hospital."

"True on the whole," Harriet said with some humor, "except I *do* own a feather duster as well."

In a maternal but unsentimental way, she had quietly patted Colin's bare knee where it stuck out from his kilts, as if she were soothing a skittish horse or a lost lamb. Colin, for his part, was tough-looking and rough-edged, with his spiky haircut and his black T-shirt blazing with red and gold lettering in a language that I couldn't comprehend. But I could see that he was one of those wild boys who are exceptionally tenderhearted when it comes to his mother. I couldn't help liking both of them.

"Penny," Harriet said, "perhaps you already know that your grandmother, Beryl Laidley, once owned a house-by-the-sea in our little village on the northern coast of Cornwall?" There was an affectionate twinkle in her eye as she mentioned my grandmother's name.

"Oh, yes!" I blurted out. "We know all about *that* house. It's where Jeremy and I met, years ago when we were just kids."

"Did you really?" Harriet asked, looking from me to Jeremy. "How nice. Your gran's property does have the most wonderful view of the sea," she said to me.

"I remember," I said softly, thinking of the lovely stone house with its old-fashioned parlor, where, during one magical summer, I'd spent hours ensconced in a window-seat reading a strange book of dark fairy tales while listening to the far-off whispering sound of the sea.

And in my mind's eye, just as if it were yesterday, I could see myself as a nine-year-old, with my copper-colored hair in a pony-tail, shyly walking into the garden to meet Jeremy and his parents for the first time. He was thirteen, a bit gangly but a good-looking fella even then, with dark hair and rebellious blue eyes, and the impeccable good manners of a boy who'd been raised with "all the advantages".

Jeremy's stepfather was my Uncle Peter, who was my mom's brother. So, although Jeremy had no blood connection to my family at all, he had a special place in my childhood. When we first met as kids in Cornwall, Jeremy had already heard many curious things about this American girl called Penny Nichols, and, as he later confessed to me, he was eagerly awaiting my visit.

He'd been told that my English mother, who'd defiantly moved to America as soon as she graduated, was a children's book illustrator, and she and my dad had written a series of picture books together featuring a little "Girl Detective" based on me. When I arrived in Cornwall, Jeremy was already convinced that I was some sort of American sleuth and celebrity.

Typically as kids, Jeremy and I quickly teamed up in our attempt to resist the grown-ups and create our own world of play. We went swimming and biking and spent hours listening to our favorite music on the radio. Behind the house, facing the sea, there was a beautiful garden where we'd cautiously confided our hopes for the future to each other, while making our way down the narrow, pebbled garden path and the flight of steep stone steps that led to a small, hidden sandy cove.

Running along the shoreline and darting in and out of the waves that summer, we could scarcely have known that we would meet again . . . let alone become partners in our own eccentric investigative firm, Nichols & Laidley, Ltd. Even in my wildest dreams, I couldn't have foreseen the exciting cases we'd work on together. Using my art history skills and Jeremy's legal background, we pursued other people's family histories and mysteries—as well as our own—to uncover priceless lost treasures and works of art.

Nor could we, in our youthful chats, ever imagine that we would end up married to each other! Still, as we like to remind ourselves, the little seeds of our future life together had been planted in Grandfather Nigel's garden, long ago, during that very sweet summer in Cornwall.

Jeremy was grinning at me now, making me blush a little, so I knew he was revisiting the same memories. But when he turned to Harriet and Colin, his manner was more businesslike, and a bit protective of me. Ever since the inheritance from Aunt Pen, we've had to fend off our share of aggressive kooks who come knocking at our door with "business" propositions that are chiefly designed to relieve us of our windfall.

"It seems to me," Jeremy told our visitors calmly in his Barrister's Voice, "that Penny's Grandmother Beryl sold her house quite a long time ago . . . in the early 1990s, I believe. Were you the buyer?"

"Not exactly," replied Harriet, unruffled by his slightly suspicious tone. She turned to me with a gentle air and said, "Penny, your grand-mum was a founding member of our Port St. Francis Legacy Society. She was very passionate about protecting our village, long before it became fashionable to do so."

"Really?" I glanced up curiously, for, although I didn't know my English grandmother well, she'd struck me as a very conventional woman, unlikely ever to have been a firebrand, especially compared to her brilliant and dramatic older sister, my Great-Aunt Penelope, who had outlived Grandmother for many years.

"Oh, yes," continued Harriet. "Beryl was very forward-looking, and she could see what was happening in Cornwall . . . low wages and sky-high housing prices driving our young people away, because they can't afford to stay."

Harriet glanced a bit worriedly at her son, then went on. "So, toward the end of her life, when dear Beryl was forced to move back to London permanently to be near her doctors, she decided to sell her country house to the town of Port St. Francis at a very reasonable price, with the stipulation that they lease it to our Legacy Society for twenty years, giving us the first option to buy it if the town ever needed to sell."

Harriet paused now to let this information sink in, and to sip more of her hot tea. "You see, back then, we all agreed that this was the best way to give our Legacy Society time to raise funds to buy the house," she explained. "Beryl could easily have sold it outright to a private buyer, and I daresay for more money. But your lovely grandmother said she'd rather count on our group to do good things with the place for everyone in the community. I am proud to say that the house has been used as a woman's shelter, a seniors' and veterans' center, a day-care nursery, and it was even where we launched the town's organic farmers' market."

Colin interrupted now, taking a great big gulp of tea, which he drank "black".

"And if it weren't for Mum's group, there'd be plenty of babies and old folks who wouldn't be alive today, that's the God's truth of it," he said, eyeing Jeremy more keenly than his mother had.

"For awhile, we really did your grand-mum proud," Harriet said to me, her eyes shining. "To the locals, it was a place to go in good times and bad."

I had been listening attentively, noticing that every time Harriet mentioned Grandmother Beryl, it was with the warm tone of someone who deeply missed a close friend, and who had, against all odds, kept the house as a shrine to their shared good intentions. I couldn't help being touched by this.

Harriet said warningly now, "But I must tell you that there are plans afoot for your grandmother's house that we do not like."

"Don't sugar-coat it, Mum. Tell 'em the place is about to be razed to the ground!" Colin broke in impatiently.

I gasped, and Jeremy looked up sharply in surprise.

"And furthermore," Colin said darkly, "life in the entire village as we know it could be totally destroyed! Fact is, everybody in Port St. Francis thinks that you guys are the only ones who can stop it."

# Chapter Two

"Who's going to knock down my grandmother's house?" I demanded indignantly.

"The town," Colin blurted out. "They own it, and they want to sell it to somebody else for more money."

Jeremy regained his composure first. "So, I take it that your lease on Beryl's house is near its end now?" he asked. "And that your Legacy Society is not in a position to buy?"

"Right on both counts," said Harriet promptly, "but I'm afraid it's a bit more complicated than that."

She turned to me. "You see, earlier on, we were able to help the town buy some of the property surrounding your grand-mum's house, thanks to the kindly donations of our supporters, who stipulated that the town give our Legacy Society the same kind of lease on all the new property. Oh, we had some great plans for the house and the land!" she exclaimed, and I had to smile at her enthusiasm.

"What did you have in mind?" I asked.

"Our dream was—is—to restore the house to its former glory, and then, on the new property, to build some reasonably-priced housing for our young people so they can raise their families there," Harriet responded. "We even hired an architect to draw up the plans. We want Port St. Francis to remain a vital place, where folks can walk or bike to everything they need—shops, post office, dentists—instead of having to drive miles and miles to other towns just to mail a letter or see a doctor!"

She paused for breath, then continued. "We've got it all worked out. It would all be a very 'green' use of energy, while still making everything cheerful, homey, and beautifully appealing to the eye, to raise the spirits and well-being of the folks who live there. This, we hope, will help Port St. Francis become a new, really self-sustaining eco-village, one that works *with* the environment, not *against* it."

"Ohh!" I said. "An eco-village! Like the Prince's trust, right?"

Now it was all beginning to make sense. I'd been reading about how Prince Charles had, for many years, devoted himself to advocating and assisting in the planning of such eco-villages, and to organic and sustainable farming. At first, the usual naysayers had hooted and jeered and called their prince a "tree-hugger" who ought to mind his own business and just hang around Buckingham Palace, doing only ceremonial things, like pinning medals on heroes and shaking hands with foreign visitors. But over time, even the most cynical Brit admits that the Prince's vision has become a vital step forward to insure the survival of future generations.

"But I don't understand," I said. "Your plan sounds wonderful, and you even have the support of Prince Charles. So, what's the problem?"

Colin leaned forward with a fierce look in his eyes. "Because whenever you get a good idea started, the big-boy bastards from the City wake up and smell the money," he exclaimed, unable to control his fury any longer. "Some hotshot international real-estate developers have blown into our town with plans of their own. They *say* they want to do the same thing as Mum—create what *they* call an 'eco-bos'—"

At my blank look, Harriet translated for me. "*Bos* is Cornish for 'home', basically," she explained.

"Yeah, well," Colin said, "these jackals want to grab the whole caboodle: your gran's house, and all the land Mum's group acquired, and even some other nearby property as well! In a way, Mum's Legacy Society laid out the bait—by attaching your grandmum's house to all that surrounding land—so it's now a big, juicy, tempting parcel for these vultures."

Harriet gave her son a reproachful look, then turned to me. "Our *friend* has helped as much as he can, but you might say we're not the only worthy cause on his dance card," she said, alluding to H.R.H. "You see, part of the problem is that your Grandmother Beryl's house is falling into disrepair," she added with a regretful tone. "You must believe me when I tell you that we really tried to keep it up, but there never seemed to be enough funds, and finally the place was no longer up to code for our group to safely use for our offices and meetings. So the town has put us on notice that they can't afford to keep the house, and they say they must sell it to the highest bidder."

"Which is a total black-hearted lie," Colin interjected heatedly. "The Legacy Society was *forced* to abandon the house," he explained, still looking outraged. "It's all politics. See, years ago, when your grandmother was dealing with the town officials, they were all like-minded folk. But a lot of them got old and died off."

"I'm afraid that's true," Harriet admitted, looking less cheerful for the first time.

"Now we've got some flash new politicians from the City who have 'retired to the country' but they still want to wheel and deal and keep making piles of money," Colin said bitterly. "The rest of the town council is either too corrupt or just too lily-livered. You should have seen the First Minister, and some of the town officials, lapping it up when the big-money developers showed up to wine and dine them and ferry them about in a limousine. Amazing how little it takes for a politician to sell his own ass—"

"Soul," Harriet corrected quickly. "Sell his soul to the devil."

"Well, once those fools on the town council got a whiff of the big money, they saw that their main obstacle was Mum's group and their option-to-buy," Colin went on. "So, next thing you know, the Legacy Society gets a little visit from the building inspector, who tells them that the chimney isn't up to code; or there's termite damage somewhere, or an electric whatsis is a hazard that has to be fixed immediately. Every week, somebody new showed up, looking for another infraction, no matter how minor, as an excuse to bleed the group dry of all their funds. What the officials couldn't find wrong they made up, and it cost big legal fees to fight; so even when you win the case, you lose the war. And finally the town got what it wanted—they forced Mum's group out and declared the house uninhabitable."

"It became a self-fulfilling prophecy," Harriet said sadly. "The house has now lain empty for years, so naturally it's at the mercy of the elements, and we have no more money to fight it. Our option expires at the end of the summer."

Colin had fallen uncharacteristically silent now. The fire in the fireplace sizzled with what sounded to me like moral indignation.

When Jeremy finally spoke, he did so gently but directly. "Would it really be so bad if the big shots got their way? Wouldn't it at least stimulate the local economy and provide jobs?"

"Pah!" Colin said scornfully. "They plan to bring in cheap immigrant labor to build it all. You want to see what the developers have *really* got in mind?" he asked cunningly.

Harriet covered her face with her hands. "Oh, Colin," she said, "some day I fear you're going to get yourself into real trouble."

Defiantly, Colin looked Jeremy in the eye and said, "This is all confidential, right?"

Jeremy nodded. Colin nudged his mum, who reached into her bag and pulled out a sheaf of folded papers, which Colin triumphantly plunked on the table before us.

I peered at them curiously. The plans were printed on a thin, parchment-like paper, and when unfolded, they took up most of the table.

"Exhibit A," Colin said, stabbing at the architectural sketch laid out with a map of the area. "Mum's original plan. Here's your grand-mum's house, which they'd use as an historical inn, with offices for the Legacy Society. On the adjoining new property, working with ecological surveys, the Society would build a few housing clusters right here. All the rest remains public and protected land."

Colin now unfolded a second set of plans, printed on a sheet of translucent paper, and he laid it on top, so that we could see through it to Harriet's plans below, and observe where the differences were.

"Exhibit B," Colin announced. "The plans the developers submitted to the town. Note that Beryl's house gets replaced with a modern, five-hundred-room hotel and conference center including a time-share hunting lodge, and a spa development. Surrounded by a golf course. No conservation area."

"Well, at least it's got a park of some sort, designated as public space, albeit not much," Jeremy pointed out.

"Yeah, right," Colin snorted. "Which brings me to Exhibit C." Now he unfolded another layer and put it atop the others. "Here are the actual, current plans the developer has in mind. Got it right off their computers. Doesn't quite match up with what they're telling the town they'll do, does it?"

Jeremy leaned forward and stared intently. "Did you actually hack into the computer of the development team?" he asked, fascinated.

Colin's freckled nose quivered as he looked up defiantly. "Let's just say providence threw it into my lap, and leave it at that," he replied. He tapped the page. "Now suddenly the developers' monster spa-hotel-plus-convention-center-from-hell has been expanded even more, to eight hundred rooms. Not only that, they also plan to build time-share condos with another one hundred fifty units. There isn't a single condo here that will cost under ten million pounds. And instead of a conservation area, these guys are going to stock fancy hunting grounds with wild boar and deer and birds who will be trapped there, surrounded by electric fencing, like ducks in a shooting gallery."

He moved his fist to another spot and banged it down. "Over here's a heliport! And in the cove, they'll build a marina for all their big yachts. On the remaining scrap of property—where the so-called public park was supposed to go—they've now got a mall with a private bank, shops, medical group and four restaurants. It's like they're building their own private town. So, nobody's gonna saunter into Port St. Francis and support our local shops or our hospital anymore!"

Colin traced another area with his forefinger. "Look at what kind of water wells and sewage this place will need. And take a glance at the security headquarters they have in mind to guard all the entrances. So," he concluded, "what kind of homesteaders do you think will pay this kind of big bucks for bulletproof windows, and basically their own police force to guard them? High-end foreign criminals, that's who. They come out here to play English country squire for the weekend."

"You're going up against the Mosley-Clint Group?" Jeremy interrupted, having spotted the developers' name on the document. When Colin nodded, Jeremy whistled. "I've heard about those guys. The Mosley brothers play nothing but hardball, and they have a rep for being just a shade away from gangsters."

"Not exactly a fair fight, is it?" Colin said dryly.

By now my breath was coming out in short, indignant huffs and puffs as I grew progressively horrified by everything I was hearing. I knew, of course, that the English countryside had been in a state of siege all these years. But somehow I always thought of Grandma's town as a safe, magical place, like Brigadoon. I realized that this was my wake-up call, and I could hear the urgent countdown to do something about it, as surely as I could hear the clock ticking on the fireplace mantel in this room.

Harriet spoke now, still in a calm voice, but sad. "Penny, if the Mosley brothers get their way, there won't be a single brick or blade of grass you'd recognize from your grandmother," she explained. "Meanwhile, many of our villages are becoming ghost towns. Where will we have our babies? Where will our old people go if our local doctors desert us and our public health centers close down?"

This was all too much for me now. "What price is the town asking for the whole place—the house and the extra land?" I asked, ready to elbow out all comers.

Harriet named a sum which, I am sorry to say, would have taken our entire inheritance . . . and then a whole lot more. Sufficiently humbled, I turned to Jeremy pleadingly. "There must be some way to protect Grandma's house and the surrounding property, like, maybe put it into a *permanent* trust this time."

Harriet took the cue, leaning forward on the sofa and looking at me with a lively gleam in her eye. "Well . . . we *do* have an idea," she said feistily. "And our, er, 'esteemed friend' thinks it's 'right up your street'. You see, if your grandmother's house should prove to have some important historical value, well then, it might qualify for Landmark Status or something like that, which would put pay, once and for all, to the Mosleys' dreadful plans. And such a discovery might also open many more doors for us to qualify for donations and financial aid, so we can hold on to it all."

Colin was nodding vigorously throughout this. "You guys have done stuff like this before, right?" he said challengingly. "You dig through history to find evidence that some old thing is worth a lot more than it first seemed."

"Do you have reason to believe that the house has such hidden value?" Jeremy asked cautiously.

"Perhaps," Harriet said with a mischievous smile. "A member of our Legacy Society—Trevor Branwhistle—thinks he's found something that he'd like to tell you about personally. Of course, he'll need *you* to find better evidence to back up his theory. Now if *anybody* could uncover the true historical value of a place," Harriet suggested, "it's the famous firm of Nichols & Laidley. Why, your reputation precedes you! Our royal friend has been following your exploits in the newspaper and he is *most* impressed. So we all think you two are the right team for this noble task."

Now, the English will joke about practically anything, and they are highly suspicious of flattery. But all you have to do is tell them that their King or country needs them, and, well, they get this sober look on their faces as if they're ready to mount a horse, grab a sword and shield, and ride out to battle in the service of King Arthur.

Jeremy had just that look on his face right now. In fact, I think he even gulped at the mere thought of Prince Charles reading all about our latest cases while munching his royal breakfast scones.

Meanwhile, having put the hook in our mouths, Harriet rose as if to leave. Colin, realizing that they were on their way out, quickly reached for a ham sandwich and wolfed it.

But as Harriet paused to shake hands again, she said urgently, "Even if you don't want to take on this case, if you would only be gracious enough to just come out and have a look at the house again, why, whatever advice you care to give would be most deeply appreciated. But do keep in mind," she added, "that we are running out of time."

Colin now nodded shyly to me as they walked out. But when Jeremy shook hands with him, Colin said with a cheeky grin, "Never thought I'd ask the help of an Englishman, but I hear you're one of the better ones."

When the door closed behind them, I said, "What was that all about? Isn't Colin an Englishman, too?"

"Nope," Jeremy explained, "he considers himself Cornish. You know, from the Celts. To him, the English are merely the Anglo-Saxon invaders who forced his ancestors to stop speaking Cornish and to pay taxes to the British crown."

Jeremy now gave me a meaningful look as we carried the plates and cups into the kitchen.

"Don't even say it," I said. "Don't even tell me to butt out."

"I already know that I haven't a hope in hell of convincing you of any such thing," he answered. "I only advise caution. To tell you the truth, I'm pretty curious myself about seeing the old place again."

"Where do you suppose Harriet and Colin are going tonight?" I asked mischievously. "A hotel room—or will the Prince let them crash at Buckingham Palace?"

"Who can say?" Jeremy replied, shaking his head. "But it's not a bad thing to be friends-with-the-friends of the Duke of Cornwall."

"Oh, right, the Prince is a Duke, too," I said. "So a king has a 'kingdom', and a duke has a 'duchy'. That means the 'Duchy of Cornwall' is of very special interest to Prince Charles." Then I said teasingly, "So if we don't take this case, will he chop off our heads?"

"Penny, dear," Jeremy said calmly. "I am more inclined to wonder what will happen if we *do* take the case but we *don't* succeed."

"Who, us?" I said recklessly. "Fail? Pshaw! Never happen."

But that night, I actually had a dream in which strange tribal armies were fighting to the death with clanging swords and shields on the high cliffs of Cornwall. One army was dressed in animal skins; the other side wore clanking, indestructible metallic armor. Below them, the ocean was churning perilously. Above them, the wind was battering the clouds across the night sky as if they were ships at sea about to crash upon the jagged coastal rocks.

I woke with a start, panting rapidly, before the dream had ended. And the thing is, I have no idea which side won.

# Chapter Three

The next day my mother telephoned to report that she and my father had arrived at the villa in Antibes that Great-Aunt Penelope had bequeathed to Jeremy and me. This gave me a chance to tell Mom all about what was going on with Grandmother Beryl's old house. My mother was fascinated by the "H.R.H." connection to the case, but, with her usual English skepticism, she warned me not to be too hopeful.

"Everybody thinks their grandmother's house deserves landmark status," Mom said in her droll way. "I don't recall my mum ever indicating that there's anything particularly special about that house. But if you want to pursue it, then do give it a go, darling. I know you like this sort of thing," she added vaguely, still a bit unable to believe that my career is really a serious occupation.

"Everything okay at the villa?" I inquired.

"It's raining cats and dogs and tigers in the entire Riviera," my mother replied, almost accusingly, as if I'd deliberately lent her the villa now because I somehow was prescient enough to know that there would be freak storms this summer.

"Rain never lasts long on the Côte d'Azur," I consoled her. I am an optimist by nature, but I certainly didn't inherit that quality from my mother. My French father lays claim to that, and he popped onto the extension right now.

"Hallo, Penn-ee dear," he said warmly. "Don't listen to your mother. It's paradise here and she knows it. The air is sweet, the season has barely begun, but ze market is already bursting with ze first peaches and roses."

I could not only picture it, I could almost smell it. "Mmm," I said. "Have a wonderful time. We'll catch up with you in August."

"Hey," Jeremy shouted from the kitchen, "tell your father I'm making his pot roast recipe."

My father, who is a retired professional chef, heard this and chuckled. "Tell him not to forget the *roux*," he admonished. "That and the *bouquet garni* make all the difference."

"Okay, Dad," I said, "see you soon."

"Happy eating," he said affectionately, as if he could imagine the meal already.

"What's a *roux*?" I asked Jeremy when I got off the phone. "Dad said not to forget it."

Jeremy was already busily browning the onions. "It's the flour and butter mixture," he said. "Makes that smooth sauce you love."

"And *bouquet garni*," I said, "that's the herbs, right, pal?"

"Of course. Think you're dealing with a total amateur here?" Jeremy inquired. "But as long as you're sniffing around the kitchen, make yourself useful. Hand me the pepper mill."

So that afternoon, once the pot roast was slow-cooking, Jeremy and I packed our bags for our visit to Cornwall.

"Now remember," Jeremy warned, "we're just going to look around, and listen to what Harriet's group wants to say. But none of this indicates a commitment on our part. Even if it's a worthy case, we still might not be the right team for this."

"Here's your socks," I said. "And if it's a worthy case, there's nobody better than us to take it on."

"Did you pack your Wellies?" Jeremy said.

"My whats?" I asked. Jeremy went to the closet to fetch them, then held them up. "Oh, galoshes," I corrected. "Rubber boots. Why can't you English speak English?" I teased him.

"The weather out there is wildly unpredictable," Jeremy warned. "Better bring a warm jacket. Remember, summer doesn't really start till July."

"That pot roast is starting to smell really good," I said hungrily. "When's it going to be ready?"

"Another hour," Jeremy said cheerfully, and I groaned.

A short while later, someone rapped the knocker on the front door so vigorously that it seemed to shake the very bones of the house.

"Yoo-hoo!" came a voice through the mail slot, as our visitor tried to peer inside.

"It's Rollo. No use ducking him," Jeremy said resignedly. "He's surely seen the lights on through the windows."

Rollo was standing on the doorstep with a broad grin. "Welcome back to London!" he said, clapping me a bit too heartily on the shoulder as he gave my cheek a peck of a kiss. "Am I interrupting dinner?" he asked with undisguised hopefulness.

"Cocktails first," I said. "Come on in."

He brightened so enthusiastically that I had to smile. Rollo is my mother's cousin, and her family always considered him the black sheep, but he used to be a lot more trouble in the days before I met him. Compared to his past exploits (drugs, scary gambling debts, and the kinds of legal problems where you have to pay somebody off to keep them from killing him or getting him arrested) his antics of late are pretty tame.

Nowadays Rollo's shady skills are chiefly employed in "borrowing" the occasional antique in your house if he fancies it (he's actually a very knowledgeable collector); or timing his unannounced visits to whenever he figures he can mooch a meal or a drink—not because he's cheap (he is) and not because he's a drinker (definitely), but because his mother, my Great-Aunt Dorothy, is a cold fish who can't bear to dine with her own son. Even when she's trying to be nice (which is once in a blue moon), she can't help insulting you. Dorothy is the only other American who married into the Laidley family, but that's about as far as my kinship with her goes.

"Mum sent me over to see if you two are still in love," Rollo said bluntly as he accepted the whisky that Jeremy already started pouring for him.

Good old Dorothy, I thought to myself. Sitting there in her London mausoleum, just like a spider in a web, spinning her ill will against all comers. Some things never change.

"Every morning at breakfast she *will* keep reciting the divorce statistics to me," Rollo said obliviously as he settled into Jeremy's leather chair, careful not to spill his drink. "Dreadfully boring; but then she turns round and tells me I ought to be married by now. Can't see the logic in that, can you?"

"Well, I hate to disappoint her, but we're still married," I said, as Jeremy handed me a glass of sherry and poured one for himself.

Rollo beamed with genuine pleasure. "So glad to hear it," he said. "You're both looking well," he observed, gazing keenly first at me, then Jeremy.

I glanced back at Rollo, trying to size up what condition he was in since I'd last seen him nearly a year ago. Not too bad this time, actually. He's the sort of man whose clothes telegraph what's going on in his life. When he's in trouble, he dresses like an arms-dealer in a shiny sharkskin suit; and when he's on an upswing he appears like a well-rested man of leisure, as he did today in his pale cream-colored flannel trousers and navy-blue blazer, quite dignified for a man in his mid-sixties.

With a trace of maternal concern, however, I noted that his grey hair was a bit shaggy and needed a cut; and the pouches under his eyes indicated that he wasn't getting enough sleep, which probably meant he was still hanging out late at nightclubs picking up girls. These days, women are more dangerous to Rollo than loan sharks, because when Rollo starts buying rounds of drinks, he attracts the kind of gold-digger on the prowl for an easy mark.

"What's for dinner?" Rollo asked, sniffing appreciatively.

"*Pot-au-feu,*" Jeremy said proudly, "and it's ready right now."

Rollo rose happily and followed us into the dining room. He paused to notice the suitcases we'd packed, which were standing in the hallway waiting to be loaded into the car tomorrow morning.

"Going on a trip again so soon?" he asked casually. "Heading for the villa in Antibes, perhaps?"

"Not till August," Jeremy said as he passed me the plates. "Penny's folks are staying there through the month of July."

Rollo could not hide his disappointment. "Ah, too bad," he said. "I was rather looking forward to catching up with you—and perhaps being a houseguest this summer, seeing as I've got some business to conduct in Monte Carlo. How about the yacht? Is that available?" he asked hopefully.

"Honorine and her family got it for July," I said apologetically, referring to my French cousins.

Rollo looked crestfallen, and as we sat down to eat I worried about this Monte Carlo business. Of course, it could simply be that he was sheltering his money in Monaco as a tax dodge. Rollo has lived most of his life receiving a monthly "allowance" from his father's estate, which is tightly controlled by his mum, and she won't give him a penny more. So, Rollo tends to "supplement" this income with gambling. Sometimes he wins, which is fine. Sometimes he loses, big, and this usually results in a hasty departure in the dead of night from his Monte Carlo hotel.

"So where are you going this time?" Rollo asked, his mouth full of roast potato.

"Cornwall," I said. I paused, since Jeremy and I had sworn confidentiality about any further information on this case.

"Really?" Rollo said with interest, taking a healthy slug of his wine. "Been a long time since I've gone to Port St. Francis. Nice house Beryl had. Can't imagine what a place with that view would go for now. Loved it when I was a little kid. Didn't see much of it once I grew up. Must have changed a lot."

Something in his face indicated to me that Rollo was perfectly aware that the family elders considered him *persona non grata*. Well, it's hard to remain a welcomed guest when you constantly harass your old aunties for money. Poor Grandmother Beryl and Great-Aunt Penelope used to dread Rollo's arrival, then breathe a sigh of relief when he disappeared. But until now, I hadn't realized that Rollo actually knew how his aunts felt about him, and why they had stopped inviting him to visit.

"Frightful long drive, Cornwall is. That's why I didn't pop over to Beryl's house more often," he said lightly now, as if it had been his choice to stop summering there. "Got friends there now, do you?"

"Right," Jeremy said noncommittally.

"Which route will you take?" Rollo asked, and they launched into a spirited guy-discussion about which highway is best for driving out to "the West Country" for the weekend: Take the busy

M5 . . . or take the A303 to the M3? I have seen people come to near fisticuffs at dinner parties over this debate.

Allow me to weigh in here. I say, a road is a road is a road. And a highway is a highway is a highway. So no matter what route you pick, the final result after hours of driving is the same: a physically challenging, slightly nerve-wracking haul, which in traffic jams can become the true test of a marriage. But I was still keen to go.

Finally, when Jeremy had yawned enough times, Rollo took the hint and rose to go home. As I walked him to the front door, he whispered conspiratorially to me, "Off on another case already, aren't you?"

There was no point in denying it, so I just smiled mysteriously.

"Remember, I am on e-mail if you should require my services," Rollo advised in a low voice so Jeremy wouldn't hear. The truth is, Rollo has actually been extremely helpful to us on previous cases . . . in those dicey moments when you need a thief to catch a thief.

"Simply say the word, my dear girl, and I'm 'in'," Rollo whispered with a grin. "After all, life in London has been so very dull without you."

# Part Two

# Chapter Four

Cornwall once belonged to the Celts, who arrived from Europe in the Iron Age with their mysterious culture of Druid high priests and their strange rock formations like Stonehenge. Some folks say that the map of Cornwall resembles an inverted map of England: that is, if you could take the western tip at Land's End, pick it up and plunk it north where Scotland is, then Cornwall itself is practically the same shape as England.

The Romans, however, thought Cornwall was shaped like a horn of plenty, which may account for why they called it "Cornovii" from the same root for "cornucopia" or the horn of plenty. And the Romans certainly got "plenty" of tribute from the Celts, but somehow they all managed to do business together for awhile—until the brutal invasion of the Angles and the Saxons, who contributed the suffix *wealas*, which means "foreigner"— hence, the name "Cornwealas" or Cornwall. The Danish and Viking invaders came next, until the Normans from France took over; and finally, after fierce struggle and strife, Cornwall came under the rule of the English kings.

So the Cornish people have seen foreigners come by land and

by sea, with torches blazing, arrows flying and flags waving. I, however, arrived singing.

> *"Over the river and through the wood,*
> *To Grandmother's house we go;*
> *The horse knows the way*
> *To carry the sleigh*
> *Through the white and drifted snow, oh!"*

"Pardon me," Jeremy said, interrupting my enthusiastic, if slightly off-key, singing, "but there is no snow. What *is* this little ditty you're singing?"

I stared at him in disbelief. "You're kidding," I said scornfully. "I realize that you grew up on this isolated, sceptered isle of ye olde England, but surely you've heard of a little American holiday called Thanksgiving, have you not?"

"Is that the one where you rogue Puritan colonists were invited to a nice dinner with the natives, after which you all behaved like very bad guests and took all their land?" Jeremy inquired wickedly. "And anyway, wasn't that November? It's only late June, dear girl."

"Forget Thanksgiving," I advised pityingly. "It's about *To Grandmother's house we go.* All my childhood friends sang it whenever they went off on long car drives to visit their grandparents, no matter what the season. I was always wistful because my grannies lived in England and France, so I never got to drive to their house singing this song."

"But one fateful summer as a little girl, you finally hopped on a plane to England," Jeremy reminded me, as if I were the heroine of a fairy tale. "Whereupon you met your future husband, alias *moi.* You promised to love, cherish . . . and feed me. What say we dig into one of those sandwiches now?"

"Are you kidding? We've just barely gotten out of London," I objected. "If we break into our stash now, we'll never even make it to Bristol." We had pulled away from the great wheel of highways that surrounded London, reaching out to every corner of England.

"If I were a horse you'd feed me," Jeremy objected. "How do you expect me to run without fuel?"

"Okay," I warned, "but don't eat all of it, or you'll be sorry later when we're only halfway there, driving through the moors with nothing to eat for miles, and the ghosts of Heathcliff and Cathy wailing to each other across their *Wuthering Heights* all night."

I rummaged around in the cooler and handed Jeremy a wrapped turkey sandwich.

"Thanks, navigator," Jeremy said enthusiastically, considerably cheered. "Let me know when the next exit is coming. Because if we take a wrong turn, we could end up in Scotland."

I dutifully studied the map, and did my best as co-pilot. Jeremy is a good driver and he steered his way heroically through the big city hubs, beginning with Bristol and its old stone buildings juxtaposed with modern high-rises; then the next major switch at the cathedral city of Exeter, after which things got more rural, with sheep grazing unperturbedly along the green fields near the highway.

"Keep an eye out for a sign that says Kennards House," I announced. "That'll take us right past Dartmoor National Park."

"Home of *The Hound of the Baskervilles*," Jeremy announced in a nasal tone like a bus tour guide.

"Oh, of course!" I cried ecstatically. "I *thought* I heard Sherlock Holmes telling Dr. Watson that the game's afoot."

Jeremy gave me an affectionate smile. "Who knew that you and I would end up being a team of English sleuths ourselves?"

he said. "To think it all began as kiddies in Cornwall pretending to be international spies."

"And you taught me Morse code," I recalled. "You tap-tapped to me all through dinner. Boy, that really annoyed the grown-ups. I was very impressed that you knew the code."

"I was just showing off for you," he confessed. "Until you came along, all I had to look forward to was getting car-sick when Mum hauled me out there every summer."

"How sophisticated the grown-ups seemed, with their cocktail parties in the garden," I commented nostalgically. "Grandmother Beryl and Great-Aunt Penelope did love to gossip, mostly about their brother. Wish I'd met Great-Uncle Roland."

"No, you don't," Jeremy advised. "Rollo's father was a strange duck. Always sidling around with a furtive look, sneaking extra drinks when nobody else was looking. I always thought he would pocket the family silver if it weren't for Beryl's sharp eye."

"Sounds like Great-Uncle Roland was a lot like Rollo is today?" I asked curiously.

"Yes, without the redeeming qualities, I'm afraid," Jeremy said frankly.

"Did he look like Rollo?" I asked. I'd never really known about Rollo's relationship with his dad. Great-Uncle Roland had died much earlier than his sisters, Beryl and Penelope.

"Yeah, Rollo and his father resembled each other," Jeremy replied.

"Maybe that's why Rollo's mum is so mean to him—because he reminds her of her ne'er-do-well husband?" I suggested.

"Dorothy's rotten to everybody," Jeremy responded. "As you well know. Mum and I always avoided going out to Cornwall on the same weekend that Rollo's folks were scheduled."

I yawned noisily. "Go to sleep," Jeremy advised. "I'll wake you when it starts to get interesting."

I must have slept for quite some time, because when I awoke, the light was beginning to fade, and I could feel in my very bones the strange new open expanse of sky. Immediately my nostrils picked up a distinct scent of seaweed in the air, and a tingling from the salty sea, and other earthier smells I couldn't identify—heather, bracken, gorse, moss, peat?

At the same time, my ears were adjusting to something unusual— the absence of traffic. All that relentless whoosh-whooshing was gone, replaced by the somewhat ghostly sound of the wind rolling off the sea and across the open farmland, downs and moors.

Jeremy, stoic as ever, had been driving steadily the whole time, drinking tea from his thermos. He smiled at me gently now, saying affectionately, "Welcome back, Sleeping Beauty. We're very nearly there."

I sat up excitedly, rubbed my eyes and peered out the window, occasionally catching glimpses of pretty old stone farmhouses with silos, and cottages with thatched roofs. The roadside hedges and shrubs were scrubbier now—the tough, scraggly kind that know how to dig their roots in deep and hang on against fierce gale-force winds that blow in off the North Atlantic. It reminded me of America's northeastern coastline, like Nantucket Island in Massachusetts, and Montauk in Long Island. But this terrain was even wilder than that.

"Where are we?" I asked, fumbling for the map that had slipped from my lap to the floor.

"Just passing Slaughter Bridge, where they say King Arthur was killed," Jeremy replied.

"Wow. Really?" I said enthusiastically, straining to get a look out the window, half expecting to glimpse castle turrets and knights jousting, but seeing only the passing roadside.

"We'll be in Port St. Francis shortly," Jeremy said.

We had reached the northern coast of Cornwall, not as far east as the castle town of Tintagel, but not as far west as fancy Padstow with its trendy gourmet restaurants. Port St. Francis was one of the little villages in between, perched on a cliff above the rugged shoreline where the Atlantic Ocean comes pounding in. I couldn't see the water yet, but I could already sense it in the wind, and feel its mighty presence crashing somewhere below against beaches and ancient craggy rock formations along the coast.

Now things were happening very fast, as we made a quick turn and a loop, and suddenly there we were, right in the center of town. It was really just one long main street with impossibly narrow country lanes springing out of it like vines climbing up into the hills, all crammed with whitewashed and slate-roofed houses that looked just like huddled ladies putting their bonneted heads together to gossip on market day.

The main street itself was lined with only a few essential shops and public buildings, most of which were closed for the evening and only dimly lighted, so I strained my eyes to peer at the weather-beaten signs rocking slightly in the breeze. There was a town hall, a bank, a very old post office, a hardware store, a hairdresser and barber, and a few typical tourist shops, all closed at the moment.

Farther along was a stone church with its grey-shingled rectory sitting quietly beside it, and an old graveyard beyond that. There were a few Edwardian houses with white fences and tiny immaculate gardens, but there were no lights on in any of them, indicating perhaps that they were owned by "second-homers". And there was a venerable but worn-out theatre whose street-level windows were boarded up, its marquee still bearing the traces of letters from some long-forgotten theatre troupe's appearance.

Then suddenly there was a brief, clustered spark of life: two very grand Victorian houses sitting side by side, the larger one with its lights ablaze and a grand wraparound porch filled with welcoming old-fashioned wooden chaises longues, and gliders and rockers.

"That's our hotel!" I said, pointing to the painted wooden sign that read *The Homecoming Inn.*

Jeremy steered the car around the corner to a well-lighted parking lot behind the hotel, where there were only a scattering of cars. He turned off the ignition and we both let out a sigh of relief.

We trundled our suitcases up the walkway and across the hotel porch. The heavy front door had a small window covered with a white lace curtain. We pushed it open and entered a dark, old-fashioned parlor with formal chairs and a grandfather clock whose grave *tick-tock* was the only sound echoing in the hotel. The lobby was a smaller room at the foot of a staircase with paisley carpeting. Behind the stairs was an elevator; but we stopped at the broad reception counter and waited.

A young girl in a white blouse and black skirt was sitting sleepily behind it. When she saw us she straightened up, rose from her chair and attempted a professional smile. Jeremy gave her our name, and she consulted her computer, clacking away for a time, until she finally handed us our key.

"You're all set," she said shyly to Jeremy. "Do you need help with the bags?"

"I can manage. But can we get some supper?" Jeremy asked.

The girl hesitated, then said, "Well, the restaurant is closed. But I think I can send you up a cold plate."

"Thanks," I said, and we headed for the elevator.

Our room was on the next level up, and the polished but ir-regular floor boards creaked beneath our tread as we went down the corridor. Jeremy had booked the biggest suite, and we entered a small but cheery sitting room where we deposited our bags.

"Got a fireplace in the bedroom," Jeremy reported, for he was in there ahead of me, and was already wandering around in search of a corkscrew for the bottle of wine he'd brought with us.

"Mind if I shower first?" I asked.

"Go ahead," he said. "They've got nice bathrobes in there. But no corkscrews anywhere!"

"Open it with your teeth if you have to," I joked, as I stepped into the big old-fashioned tub with the shower overhead. I was so grateful for the reviving hot shower, even if the plumbing did groan alarmingly and the pressure rose and fell without warning.

By the time I emerged, pink and moist in a fluffy bathrobe, Jeremy was busy in the sitting room, arranging the table with the help of the girl from downstairs, who'd brought up the supper tray herself. She reached into her pocket for the coveted cork-screw, and handed it over to Jeremy with another admiring smile.

As soon as she left, Jeremy poured out the wine and we clinked and took a sip before he darted into the shower. When he reap-peared in his bathrobe, we collapsed gratefully on the sofa to ex-plore the tray of food.

"Smoked salmon, some ham, assorted cheeses and pickles, and a few odd greens and tomato," Jeremy reported. It was all service-able enough, and I was so weary that I was just glad not to be in motion anymore. My head was still whirring.

"Let's sleep till noon," Jeremy advised.

"We have an appointment with Harriet to see Grandma's house tomorrow," I reminded him. "Harriet's a busy lady, you know."

Jeremy was still slumped against the back of the sofa and said nothing. "You're falling asleep sitting up!" I exclaimed solicitously. "Go on to bed. I'll clear up."

He was too weary to do anything but trot off obediently. A second later, I heard a plaintive, exhausted snore. I couldn't help but smile in sympathy.

"My hero," I said softly, turning out the light.

# Chapter Five

I woke to the sound of gulls cawing in the distance above the harbor, and for awhile I just lay there, absorbing the feeling of the sea and the cliffs all around me. Then came the usual bustling sounds when innkeepers politely but deliberately wake you from your slumber: the rapid tread of the maids as they set about their work with clattering carts, and the other guests hurrying to get to breakfast, showering and rushing out of their rooms and slamming doors.

I turned around in the bed and stared at Jeremy hopefully. His eyes were slammed shut.

"Poor guy," I murmured aloud. "He's plumb worn out from all that tough driving he did to get us here. He's entitled to sleep late, I suppose."

A good wife would just let him snooze and have his breakfast later . . . wouldn't she?

But I couldn't help shamelessly bouncing onto the bed beside him, hoping he'd feel my eager, impatient presence. He did, and opened only one eye.

"You awake?" I said pleasantly in a daytime voice.

He shut the solo eye. "No," he sighed.

"Aw, c'mon," I said encouragingly. "It's another rare and wonderful sunny day outside. Everybody else is up and at 'em already. Breakfast is buffet only. Let's not be last on line."

Jeremy rolled over and, still without opening his eyes, said, "What time is it?"

"Nine fifteen," I said severely. "We're supposed to meet Harriet at noon. That doesn't give us much time for sightseeing."

"S'all right. Seen it all before anyway," Jeremy mumbled.

"Well, *I* haven't," I said. "*Some* of us didn't spend every privileged summer of our lives out here. Some of us don't even know what a Cornish pasty tastes like. Some of us want to see the fine bone china they make out here. And the fishing boats hauling in their fresh catch. And the cheddar cheese that is actually made in a real place called Cheddar. And the local ale from pubs that still brew it on the premises—"

"All right, all right," Jeremy groaned, sitting up now with both sleepy dark blue eyes wide open, and his dark brown hair appealingly rumpled.

But he didn't exactly jump out of bed. So now I nudged him for real.

"Get *up*," I said. "They'll stop serving breakfast soon."

Jeremy sighed heavily, then rolled out of bed.

We took our coffee in the downstairs parlor, which was nearly empty, then we hurried out to the parking lot, which was fairly deserted. Jeremy pointed out that the smaller Victorian house next to our hotel had been recently turned into a restaurant called *Seaside with Toby Taylor*, a celebrity chef we'd seen doing frequent guest appearances on television.

As we drove down the main street of Port St. Francis, I could see more of the town, now that it was daylight and the sun was shining brightly, burning off the white morning mist that had drifted in from the sea. Directly across the street from our hotel, the old theatre with its ornate trim, large heavy-timbered front doors and faded sign was actually quite beautiful. Nearby was a dusty-red storefront that said *Donnegan's Wines and Spirits*; and a tiny pizza place, and a doughnut shop where the doughnuts were made on the premises with a copper machine displayed in the storefront window, so that fresh doughnuts came sliding down the copper chute right in front of you.

Farther along was a tiny yellow building called *Susie's Ice Cream Parlor*, which was not opened yet. There was a shop full of vintage items called *The Frantic Antique*, which seemed to offer everything from prized period furniture and sharks' teeth to hand-painted glass kitchen jars decorated by Cornish painters from the 1920s. Nearby there was a village green with a bandstand and climbing roses.

Sprouting off from the main street were those delightfully funny, crooked lanes that twined up into the hills dotted with tiny whitewashed houses, which had an absurd, perky attitude, as if they had been built to be the homes and workshops of elves, instead of fishermen, shopkeepers and local artisans. As we drove by, I peered up these little side streets and saw signs advertising a bakery, a grocer, a pottery studio and some funky little dress shops.

Once we passed the main street's wall of buildings, we could see the open expanse of sky again, and I realized that the entire town overlooked a modest harbor crammed with small fishing boats. From here we finally had a breathtaking view of the great and mighty sea, tumbling upon itself as it rolled from the horizon line and came crashing against the shore.

Already the fishermen were hauling in crab and lobster and

other marvellous fish. On both sides of the harbor were cute little pebbly-and-sandy beaches flanked by astounding black jagged rock formations that had been carved by the last ice age a gazillion years ago B.C. Farther out to sea, a few isolated big black boulders sticking up out of the waves looked like silent, watchful mythological sea-giants who'd surfaced to stare back at the new invaders.

"I forgot how rugged it is out here!" I exclaimed, twisting around in my seat to take pictures of it all. Gazing at the far-off headlands that jutted out into the misty sea, I could picture ancient tribes of hunters and gatherers chasing rhinos and mammoths and other bizarre animals, leaving behind strange stone markers and arrowheads and flinty tools and animal bones.

"It's funny," I reflected aloud, "but somehow in Cornwall the prehistoric past seems more in the here-and-now than our own present-day does. Why is that?"

"Because out here, you can't really control Nature," Jeremy announced gleefully, accelerating his Dragonetta and veering noisily down the kind of open country road that such sports cars were made for.

"Did you know," I said, "that it's basically all because of Napoleon that these fishing villages became tourist hot-spots?"

"Why? Did Napoleon hang out here in the summer?" Jeremy asked skeptically.

"Nope. But because of his wars, the fancy English ladies couldn't go to France or Italy for their vacations. So they came to the English seaside instead," I said.

"Okay, Joséphine. We don't have much time. What do you want to see first?" Jeremy asked as we passed signs for the hospital and police station, which were just outside of town.

"There's a maritime museum that's got real plunder from genuine shipwrecks," I said enthusiastically, scanning my guidebook. "Apparently the villagers used to lie in wait for ships that were foundering at sea, hoping the boats would crash against the rocks, so the locals could pounce on the cargo and steal it the minute it washed ashore!"

"Remind me not to turn my back on the villagers," Jeremy joked.

At that moment my mobile phone rang.

"Harriet here," the voice chirped. "Did you find your way into town okay last night?"

I told her that her directions were excellent, and she went on to say, "I know we're not due to meet until noon, but I've just found out that the developers' men plan to inspect the property then," she said, and now I sensed something urgent underneath her usual cheery manner.

"I wanted you and Jeremy to have a chance to look things over privately," she added in a confidential tone, "because some of your grandmother's things are still here, and you might want to come earlier to view them without these guys underfoot."

I relayed this to Jeremy, who merely swung the car away from the tourist area, and wheeled it in the direction of Grandmother Beryl's house.

"We're coming right now," I told Harriet, and hastily hung up.

Soon we were driving along a quieter country lane that wove through pastures and farms on the left side, and coastal property on the right. Here the roadside shrubs and hedges were juicier and prettier and rose very high—with hollyhocks and honeysuckle and other colorful flowering species I couldn't identify. These, I knew, had been planted by the wealthy Victorians and Edwardians at the turn of the century, who adored gardens filled with exotic plants from Asia and other glamorous corners of the empire. Their proud houses still stood overlooking sequestered bays and sandy coves.

"This is starting to look familiar to me," Jeremy announced.

"Me, too," I said excitedly, consulting my map again. The left fork of the road veered sharply away, following acres of rolling hills, meadows and farmland.

But Jeremy slowed the car down and said, "Don't tell me. It's a right turn . . . right?"

The right fork of the road ended quickly here, at a private driveway that we both recognized.

"This is it!" I announced. "Say hello to Grandmother Beryl's house."

# Chapter Six

The first bad sign was the driveway. There must have been stormy weather recently, because the front yard was littered with fallen branches from old trees, and the drive itself was choked with so many overgrown roots that Jeremy had to stop the car midway and leave it there.

We got out on foot, but neither my eyes nor my feet could actually find Grandpa Nigel's fine pebbled driveway, which I'd once pitter-pattered over so delightedly on a bicycle when I visited long ago. It must be buried under there somewhere, but it was completely caked with hardened mud, rocks, twigs, wandering roots and piles of rotting leaves.

It only got worse as we drew closer to the house. The beautiful roses and rhododendrons that had once neatly and fastidiously bordered both sides of the drive, had by now gone completely wild, becoming a mass of tangled, angry-looking gnarled shrubs, which, when stirred by the wind, seemed to be shaking their blowsy, unkempt heads at us like the three witches of *Macbeth*.

"Good God," Jeremy said in a voice low with fascinated horror. "Look, there's the house."

I stared dead ahead. "Oh, no," I answered, shocked. "It can't be."

Jeremy took my arm so I wouldn't stumble, and, very carefully, we made our way up the cracked and broken front path. My horrified gaze focused on the roof—for it was sagging right in the middle, as if it had buckled a bit from backed-up rainwater, and now was collecting acorns and leaves in there as well. Elsewhere, the roof had several missing and broken shingles, like an old man grinning at us with a mouthful of cracked teeth.

I stared at the peeling paint all around the doors and the windows, whose panes were dark and dusty, as if the house itself had closed its eyelids in despair. Moss was creeping up like a green tide against the shady side of the house, and on the sunny side there was a thick rope of ivy twining like a boa constrictor around the chimney. Everywhere else were tendrils of vines resembling Jack's beanstalk gone amuck, threatening to pull down the remaining shingles. Squirrels scampered back and forth across the roof with audacious impunity.

I wish I could tell you that we'd got the wrong place. But the worst of it was that, underneath all this horror, I could vaguely make out the house of my memory, with its elegant cream-colored stone exterior, and bay windows on either side of the white front door, which had a window at its top that resembled a king's crown.

"Is it me?" I asked in a hushed voice. "Do I just remember it wrong? Did I paint this place into something better than it was?"

"No. It *was* beautiful once," Jeremy said, "but now it's as if it's got a veil over its face."

"Exactly," I said.

"You know about antiques and stuff," Jeremy said. "Is it too far gone?"

I pulled myself together and made a more professional assessment of its condition, based on what I'd learned from my historical work on the sets of period films and TV costume dramas. As a kid, of course, I hadn't known much about history or architecture, so I did not realize that the house was such a pastiche of architectural styles.

"Looks like it was originally built in the late 1500s," I told him. "But I would say that it was redeveloped and extended in the mid-nineteenth century, because there's a definite Victorian influence here in the windows. But it's all made of very good materials—local stone and wood that would have been precious even back then. So, no, it's not too far gone."

"Thought so. Foundation looks solid," Jeremy said, walking across the front of the house, squinting.

Suddenly the door opened, and a moment later Harriet stepped out, smiling encouragingly. "Hallo there!" she cried out. "You made it!"

Jeremy was still standing in the tall grass, looking up at the house with a typically English expression of horror mixed with hilarity at the sheer awfulness of the situation.

"Watch out for vipers," Harriet teased him. "Haven't seen one yet, but they do exist in the West Country, and they love tall grass." Turning to me she said cheerily, "Don't be put off by the 'wear and tear'. This house is still a gem and we can't wait to fix it up again." I found myself wondering if she was, perhaps, a bit crazy after all. I took a deep breath of apprehension as we walked inside.

"Now, mind the floors as you come in," Harriet warned, still cheerful, "for the interior *does* want a bit of looking after. But fear not. The Legacy Society has restored bigger wrecks than this."

We paused in the entrance hall, where I had an even stronger sensation of having been here before, yet in some ghostly, parallel

world. For there was Grandmother Beryl's central staircase, and
to the left was her dining room with its mahogany swinging door
in the back that led to the kitchen; and to the right of the stairs
was the beloved parlor and the window-seat where I'd curled up
with a book on that rainy day when Great-Aunt Penelope found
me teary-eyed over a sad story. Yet now, everything was covered
in a film of cobwebs or spiderwebs or ghost-webs, making it look
truly haunted, as if someone had done this on purpose to entertain kids for Halloween.

It was when we reached the parlor that Harriet said to me,
"Your grandmother sold the house with these furnishings in it. I
don't know if anything has sentimental value for you, but if it
does, better let me know soon," she advised. "Because the town
administrators are already talking about getting rid of the furniture to make it easier for whoever buys the house."

I suddenly pictured a bunch of house-hunters pussy-footing all
over the place, snooping in Grandma's cupboards and laughing at
her old-fashioned curtains and possessions. Despite the ram-
shackle condition of the house, something inside me felt fero-
ciously protective and I wanted to barricade the doors and
windows, and fire back at all invaders with a rifle, like a hillbilly
refusing to vacate the old homestead.

So, Jeremy and I dutifully examined the pieces of furniture
that Grandmother Beryl had left behind. I recognized the teak-
wood credenza in the entryway, and the faded chintz sofa in the
corner where the ladies had congregated to gab after dinner by the
fireplace. Grandfather Nigel's favorite sea-green upholstered club
chair was worn out quite beyond the pale, but I admired the
matching beaux arts globe lamps that stood on either side of the
parlor's doorway. Still, everything seemed coated in sad-dust, and
smelling vaguely of damp.

"We just couldn't pay for the heating of the place," Harriet said apologetically, as if reading our thoughts. " 'Specially in the winter, when the north wind blows in from the cold sea, well, you can't keep office workers warm with only a fire in the fireplace."

"So, where are your group's headquarters these days?" Jeremy asked. He sat down on the window-seat cushion, and a *poof* of a dust-cloud rose in response, as if it were part of a magic act and he might disappear. Warily, he got up again.

"In town," Harriet answered. "In the old theatre."

"Oh, yes, we saw it on the way in!" I exclaimed.

"The theatre's been closed for years, but we use the offices upstairs," Harriet said. "In the mid-1800s it was mainly an opera house, where the world's finest divas and tenors came to sing. Now we've got sparrows singing in the rafters, doing Hamlet's soliloquy, I expect," Harriet said, laughing at her own joke. Jeremy and I exchanged a look of amusement mingled with despair.

"Right this way, there's more to see!" Harriet trilled determinedly, leading us around the first floor's rooms. Jeremy wore a deliberately neutral expression which he maintained for the duration of the tour.

As we continued, I noted that the long hallway leading to the back of the house had good hardwood floors, but a few of the panels had buckled, like the roof. At the end of this dark corridor was the sitting room, with Grandma's old-fashioned black sewing machine still parked in the corner; but this room more than the others bore signs of being an office for Harriet's group, because there were now metal file cabinets that I had never seen before, and a rickety desk and chair and lamp, and a disconnected telephone so old that it required dialing instead of punching in the numbers.

We paused at the last room in the back of the house, the kitchen. I recognized the matching cream-colored stove, refrigerator and dishwasher that Grandma must have bought all at once, circa 1965. There was even an old tea towel, neat and unsoiled but coated with dust, folded as Grandma had always folded it near the sink.

This little item suddenly brought back my grandmother's presence with a force I didn't expect, and now I vividly remembered her standing at the table, holding out a basket of assorted berries that my grandfather had picked in honor of my arrival. I could see myself as the little girl I'd been, eagerly reaching out and gobbling the fruit, with the juice dripping on her floor; I had expected a scolding, but Grandmother had only laughed and patted me on the head.

So without warning I found myself winking back the tears that had taken me by surprise. Jeremy saw the expression on my face, took my hand and squeezed it.

Harriet either didn't notice or tactfully pretended not to. "Things really look a lot worse than they actually are. The plumbing is still intact," she offered. "The electric isn't so bad now, but of course it's been turned off. There's a small basement, but it's empty." I was only half listening to her; my eyes were taking in all the signs of mice in the corners, and the sound of those impudent squirrels on the roof above us.

Then I heard another noise—the voices of men calling to each other. Harriet peered out the window and grimaced. "The surveyors," she reported. "For the developer. They're here early. Well, let's ignore them."

But I couldn't. All through the rest of the tour, I peered through every window I passed, watching the men carrying their surveyor's tools as they tromped around, setting up their tripods and squinting into their instruments, shouting out measurements to each other.

When we ascended the staircase, it creaked but held firm. On the second floor there was more evidence of spiders spinning their own complicated tapestries in various corners of the two bathrooms and six empty bedrooms. The big green-and-white bedroom was where Grandmother Beryl and Grandfather Nigel had slept in a huge four-poster bed that was no longer there; the two yellow guest rooms were where my parents and Jeremy's had stayed; and the very feminine violet-colored bedroom with the poufy gauze curtains was where Great-Aunt Penelope had often smoked into the night.

That left two remaining bedrooms, one pink and one blue, which were little wood-panelled affairs, tucked into opposite sides of the house, each with sloping ceilings since they were both under an eave.

"I slept in this one," Jeremy said, smiling as we paused at the blue room where there was a very big, charming, old-fashioned rocking-horse and a complete wooden croquet set. "Penny, you were way down the hall in the pink room on the east end of the house. I used to lie here at night thinking that you would get to see the sun rise before I did."

Finally, we went up to the small attic, which contained only some wicker furniture that was too far gone to keep. As we went back downstairs, Harriet said brightly, "Let's go outside so I can show you the property we added on to this parcel."

We walked out the front door and back down the driveway where the surveyor's car was now parked near ours. Directly across from Grandmother's original property were green, gently undulating meadows dotted with old, disused stone outbuildings, barns and silos. In the distance was a long line of tall dark evergreen trees, to which Harriet was now gesturing.

"We helped the town acquire this parcel all the way to those evergreens," she explained as we tromped forward to get a better view.

It was an impressive amount of land, and Harriet gazed at it with some pride. "We wanted to build our new-home clusters 'way over there, where you see the barns and silos," she said, pointing east.

Jeremy had been sizing the whole thing up, and now asked, "Who owns the property to the west, on the other side of the stone wall?" He indicated an area just beyond Grandfather Nigel's free-standing garage that was half hidden in the trees, near a low, crumbling farmer's wall that seemed to mark a boundary between the end of Grandmother Beryl's property and someone else's fields.

"Ah!" said Harriet. "The earl! Actually, for centuries, ALL of this property—including your grandmother's house, Penny—and most of the other houses up and down this part of the coast were part of one great estate belonging to the earl's ancestors. Goodness, they were a long line of earls. But over the years, bit by bit, each earl sold off parts of the estate."

Jeremy said slowly, "I remember now. Isn't there a manor house out on the headland?"

"Exactly," Harriet said. "And it still, to this day, has an earl in it."

Something about the way she said that struck me as funny, as if the earl was an owl stuck in the rafters of some drafty old stately home. "He shows up at county fairs," Harriet mused. "Likes to see the animals. He's about thirty-four years old."

"But I remember a much older man living there," Jeremy said, puzzled. "He rode his horse across the meadows. He carried a whip, and if we crossed his path he was pretty terrifying."

"Ah, that would be the *tenth* earl," Harriet explained. "He was the grandfather of our current earl, but the old man died years ago. The current earl—he's the twelfth—has his hands full just keeping the manor going, because the upkeep is staggering. I hear that he lives in only one small suite of rooms, and rents out the rest of the manor house to movie companies, big corporate events, and weddings whenever he can. And, the main floor of the manor is open to the public once a week."

Harriet pointed to the section of the earl's property that abutted Grandmother Beryl's area. "The Mosley brothers want to buy a serious chunk of the earl's land, too, for their development. They want to combine all this"—Harriet made a grand sweep of her arms to indicate Grandma's house, the town's land and the earl's meadows as far as the eye could see—"to make one big real-estate package. They won't buy it in bits. They want it all, and everything at once. And I must tell you that we fear the earl is very close to signing on the dotted line."

"Ohh," I said, finally understanding what was at stake. I glanced apprehensively at the surveyors, who were still marching around with that annoying proprietary air.

"Would you like to see the backyard?" Harriet asked, moving us away from the land at the front of the house and back toward the yard in the rear. "The garden is really still quite lovely."

The area behind Grandmother Beryl's house had a wide lawn and garden, bordered at the far end by a much higher, more decorative stone wall. I instantly recognized this lovely spot where we once all gathered in the afternoon to have iced tea and play badminton and croquet. But now the patio was carpeted with fallen leaves and branches, and the iron chairs and table were rusted.

"Grandfather Nigel would have a fit if he saw this," I whispered to Jeremy, who nodded.

The lawn was no longer the neat, fastidiously clipped yard of my memory, and the grass had grown so tall that Jeremy had to gallantly hack a path across it with one of the fallen branches. Ahead, a short flight of stone steps led to a lower, terraced area where Grandfather Nigel had kept his flowers.

"Look!" I cried. "Grandpa Nigel's garden."

For, despite all the neglect and time gone by, and all the storms and animals and insects that had overtaken some of it, a tangle of honeysuckle had survived, and I could make out masses of climbing roses and shrub roses. The azalea and forsythia was already flowering, and there were promising buds on the hollyhock and hydrangea. Hazel, hawthorn, bluebells and elder were still growing sturdily here.

"There's Grandfather Nigel's gardening shed!" I said nostalgically, pointing to the little hut at the right.

"Actually," Harriet said, "that was originally a kippering shed. To cure or smoke fish."

Now, as we walked to the very edge of the garden and peered over the wall, we could see the little private sandy cove below, and the great grey-green-blue sea that came crashing in, depositing foamy curls of water that swirled around the rocks and skittered across the patch of sand, looking like white lace. Gulls were swooping overhead in the open sky, which was bright with streaks of blue and milky white clouds that muted the yellow sun. I inhaled deeply and tasted the invigorating salty sea breeze that rippled my hair teasingly, like a friend.

"See that house over there?" Harriet said, pointing to a white Edwardian structure sitting high atop a distant hill to our right. "That belongs to our resident theatre expert, Trevor Branwhistle. He's a wonderful actor who worked for years at BBC radio. What a voice that man has! Anyway, he's the man for you to see about the history of your grandmother's house. He says that, way back in the late 1500s, Beryl's house had some interesting tenants—a group of performers known as 'The Earl's Players'," Harriet said with a twinkle in her eye.

My bloodhound instincts were instantly aroused. "Harriet," I said, "is that the reason that you think we might turn up something historically significant enough to save this place?"

Harriet's eyes widened hopefully now. "Well . . ." she said carefully. "I wanted Trevor to be the first to tell you, but . . . it just so happens that William Shakespeare may have slept here!"

There was a long silence, during which Jeremy now gazed at her with undisguised disbelief. Harriet pretended not to notice this. "It's all very exciting," she continued, "but you must let Trevor explain it when he returns. He's doing a series of lectures in Ireland. But he'll be back on Monday, and he's agreed to meet with you then. You will stay on here through Monday, won't you?" she asked, and for the first time a note of anxiety crept into her voice.

"Yes," I said. "Trevor e-mailed me, and we've already set it up."

"Great!" Harriet said. "Then I must be getting back to town. Take your time here, have another look round, think about whatever furniture you want to keep, and let me know as soon as you can. I'll have Colin pick it up for you in his truck and we'll hold it for you at the theatre."

She smiled at us now. "Goodbye, then. I'll leave you two alone now with your memories!"

# Chapter Seven

After Harriet departed, Jeremy and I made our way along the narrow, pebbled weedy garden path. It was here that, long ago as kids, we had confided our hopes and dreams to each other . . . while dodging the summer's bees.

"You were very defiant when you told me you wanted to be a rock guitarist," I reminded him. "And I wanted to be a painter. It didn't quite work out that way, did it?"

"At least we found each other," Jeremy said. "So, I've got no regrets."

"Me, either," I said.

Cautiously we descended the steep flight of stone steps leading down, down, down to the tiny cove, where the water came lapping up to the sheltered beach. We took off our shoes, rolled up our pants, and walked on.

"Wow," I said as we picked our way across. "The cove is so little, tucked away like this. Somehow it loomed larger in my imagination."

We paused at the shoreline, gazing at the sea in silence for a bit. "Do you think there's really any chance that William Shakespeare slept here?" I asked.

Jeremy rolled his eyes. "I don't think there's a bookie in London who would take odds on that," he said. "Which leaves you and me between a Cornish rock and a Celtic hard place."

"Just wait till we meet Trevor Branwhistle!" I said, for it occurred to me that we had stepped into a party of Mad Hatters who possibly had spent too much time out on the Bodmin moors with the constant wind whistling spookily in their heads, while they told each other outrageously tall tales.

We resumed walking, moving beyond the cove to an area of shoreline that was flanked by a big blackened horseshoe-shaped rock formation, like an upside-down letter "U" that was jutting out into the sea. We would have to pass under it to continue our walk.

But here the tide was suddenly crashing more wildly and raucously, and I instinctively paused even before Jeremy said, "Tide's coming in. We can't go much farther, or we'll get stuck."

Slowly we made our way back, and when I shivered, Jeremy put his arm around me to shield me from the brisk wind that was chillier now that the sun was setting. Climbing up those stone steps was a bit more strenuous than coming down, and I could feel my leg muscles getting more of a workout.

When we popped back up into the garden, Jeremy, seeing that the surveyors were coming into the yard, said, "Let's take the shortcut to the road. I don't feel like seeing those stupid guys."

"What shortcut?" I asked, intrigued. Jeremy leaped up onto the top of the tall stone wall that rimmed the edge of the garden, then took my hand and said, "Follow me."

We proceeded like tightrope-walkers along the wall as it curved around and then joined the lower, more jagged border that marked the property line separating us from the earl's land. Grandfather Nigel's garage was a hop, skip and jump away, and we landed with a thump on a more wooded area at the back of the garage, where the scent of pine was strong. I saw a neat stack of firewood that must have been waiting here for ages.

Jeremy was staring at a row of overgrown hedges smack against the garage, nearly ten feet tall now, which had become wild and so took up most of his "shortcut" to the front of the property.

"Hmm. Let's see if we can squeeze in between there anyway. Walk sideways," Jeremy advised, taking my hand and leading me, just as he had when we were kids that summer, pretending to be spies and deliberately sneaking into tight spots as if we had enemy agents after us in hot pursuit. With our backs to the hedges, we inched along the rear wall of the garage.

"Ouch," I complained as my hand scraped something round and metallic on the garage's wall. "What's this?"

Jeremy peered closer, then laid his palms against the wall, tracing his hands around a wide rectangular area. "Looks like there's some kind of door here," he noted. "A little one. It only comes up to my chin. It's got waxy stuff all around it. What you touched is a metal ring, like the kind that pulls open a trap door. Look. Can you stand back a bit? I want to see if this thing actually opens."

I had to scrooch myself even flatter in order to slide by Jeremy's chest. As I brushed against him, he murmured, "Mmm. You feel good," and he kissed me.

"No smooching on a caper," I said with mock severity, kissing his shoulder as I passed it.

Then I waited as he beamed his pocket flashlight beneath the metal ring and discovered a padlock. It was so cheap and worn that he could use his keys to break the thin loop of metal. But he had to tug hard at the recalcitrant door, which did not want to swing open on its rusty hinges. He couldn't make it swing all the way open, because of the hedges, but he got it just far enough so he could squeeze inside as he shone his flashlight there.

"Watch your head," Jeremy advised when I sidled through the opening like Peter Rabbit, stooping down under the low doorway.

Immediately we were faced with a narrow wooden staircase. I followed him up, mindful of the kinds of critters that do not like to be surprised or disturbed after years of peaceful solitude in dark, dank places. The area smelled musty and claylike, like a tomb, I thought. We had to remain hunched over while climbing the stairs so we wouldn't bang our heads on the sloped ceiling above the steps.

"This staircase was made for pixies," I muttered, gingerly touching the cold, damp stone wall as I ascended. When we reached the top, the stairs simply ended in the middle of a very large, open attic area, and we could now only just barely straighten up to our full height.

Jeremy made a sweep of light so we could take it all in—three little school desks, the kind with a flat writing surface at the right arm; two bookcases with three wide shelves each; a very big chalkboard with fat broken pieces of colored chalk still in the rim; a double easel so that an artist could paint on either side, both having round wooden wells for pots of paint. On the wall nearest the stairs there were two small shuttered windows that would overlook the garden if opened. There was a tiny sofa, and even a small tea table, with four little chairs and a girlish tea set of china pot, cups, creamer and pitcher.

"It's a playroom!" I exclaimed delightedly. "A perfect secret hideaway for kids. Maybe Grandfather Nigel made this for his children. Do you suppose my mother and your stepfather played here? Mom never said anything to me about it."

Jeremy said, "No, Peter never mentioned it, either."

We moved farther inside, still crouched like two hunchbacks wherever the ceiling sloped. I peered more closely around the room.

"Here's an antique hoop," I noted. "But Jeremy, it's much older than our parents' time. It's the kind that little girls used to run with, carrying sticks to make them go, just like Louisa May Alcott did."

"Who?" Jeremy asked.

I ignored him and continued prowling around, examining everything I found.

"Old roller skates," I reported gleefully. "The metal-and-leather kind you have to strap on to your shoe, with those metal wheels that make your feet go numb when you skate."

"Ha-choo!" Jeremy responded, having kicked up dust when he pried open the shutters, which had only a simple wooden board that slid across them to keep them closed.

I was grateful for the whiff of fresh sea air that wafted in, and the spill of sunlight that made it easier for us to see. Dust and sunbeams danced together in the shaft of new natural light.

Jeremy was now examining the three desks, each having a little cubbyhole to stash schoolbooks beneath the writing surface. He poked around inside them and found an old, dried-up fountain pen, and dust-covered erasers.

I had drifted over to the bookshelves, which had simple wooden-and-glass doors, and I discovered a few worn-out children's books and piles of old magazines and newspapers.

Carefully I pulled down a stack of papers, shaking off the considerable dust. I tossed them onto the sofa and stared at the newspaper headlines, squealing as I read each one.

"Jeremy, look at this!" I exclaimed, holding them up:

*Charles Lindbergh Lands Safely in Paris, Sets New Record in*

*World's First New York to Paris Flight . . . "Black Friday" in Germany as Berlin Stock Exchange Crashes . . . Isadora Duncan dies in Nice, France at age 50, strangled by her hand-painted Russian silk scarf . . . First movie talkie "The Jazz Singer" to open this fall.*

"Know what?" I demanded. "These are all from the summer of 1927."

"Interesting," Jeremy muttered distractedly.

"It's more than interesting!" I said. "It means this room *definitely* wasn't made for our parents, because Mom's not that old." As I perused the newspapers, I found a notebook hidden in the fold of one of them.

"Let me have that flashlight," I said.

"Torch," Jeremy corrected as he gave it to me.

I beamed a circle of light on the thick, faded ruled notebook, a kind that kids wrote their school lessons in. But where a student was supposed to put his name I saw only one word scrawled in bold, childish black capital letters: *PRIVATE*. I actually hesitated a minute.

"You're not going to let something like that stop a nosey Girl Detective like you, are you?" Jeremy demanded, peering over my shoulder.

The notebook cover flapped open easily enough. On the first page, three lines contained a firm declaration written in a careful schoolgirl script:

*Herein lie the Articles and Minutes of the*
*Cornwall Summer Explorers' Club.*
*Private. Do Not Disturb.*
*This Means You.*

"Keep going," Jeremy prompted.

The lined pages inside were so yellowed and old that I had to handle them as carefully as a museum restorer does. I touched only the edges, using just the tip of my fingernail to flip to the next page, which contained a dramatic pledge that I read aloud:

*"We, the founding members of the Cornwall Summer Explorers' Club, do hereby solemnly swear to be loyal, fearless and true, and to never, ever reveal the secrets of this society to anyone else, especially grown-ups. We will keep all secrets and reveal no tales of the C.S.E.C., no matter how old we become. We mark this occasion with a signature in our heart's own blood . . ."*

And sure enough, there were three childish signatures, signed in fountain pen, but each accompanied by a little brownish smeared fingerprint.

"Holy cow," I said, taken slightly aback. "Is that—?"

"A blood oath!" Jeremy said, fascinated, gazing at the names below:

*Penelope Laidley, President*
*Roland Laidley, Sergeant-at-Arms*
*Beryl Laidley, Treasurer*

"Ohmigosh!" I exclaimed with glee. "It's a secret society founded by Great-Aunt Penelope, and Rollo's father, and Grandmother Beryl!"

"It means this house belonged to Beryl's family when she was only a little girl," Jeremy said. "I never knew that."

"Just look at all the notations. Pages and pages of them!" I said admiringly. "Some bright little mind really spent a lot of time on this. It's full of oaths and secret passwords and very meticulous entries for a whole summer, like a diary."

I rapidly scanned a few random pages, and saw that these were not so much diary entries as they were rather formal "minutes" of the club's meetings. It seemed to me that there was something about the handwriting that was familiar; yes, it bore a strong resemblance to Great-Aunt Penelope's adult script that I'd seen in her letters. These "minutes" were all written in a tone of great solemnity and pride, recording whatever daring-do adventures, outings and escapades that she and her siblings had experienced— jaunts into town by auto, or treks with bicycles across farms, even a special boat trip to an island area where the "club" watched schools of dolphins leaping like well-coordinated ballet dancers up and over the ocean's waves.

I could just imagine the plump, girlish hands and earnest face of Aunt Pen as a child, busily scribbling all of these passages.

"Oh, Jeremy, it's so cute!" I said, reading choice bits aloud and showing him some of the funny doodles and drawings that illustrated a few of the entries. "Can't you just picture Aunt Pen and Grandma Beryl and their brother Roland scampering around? Look, here's an inventory of the seashells they found, and a record of who won a local archery contest," I enthused. "Boy, they explored all up and down the coast. They put you and me to shame! We just *pretended* to be international secret agents when we were kids. Listen to some of these headers: *An Adventure by the Seashore; A Voyage into the Woods; The Mystery of the New Neighbors; The Secret Garden of the Summer People.*"

"It's a snooping society, all right," Jeremy said. "Apparently being a nosey-Parker is definitely in your genes."

"It's very clear that Great-Aunt Penelope was the ringleader of this outfit," I observed. "Let's see," I calculated quickly, "she would have been thirteen then. The same age you were when I visited."

"Then Rollo's father would have been eleven," Jeremy mused.

"And Grandmother Beryl was eight," I said.

We spent the afternoon exploring the little room, but every-thing else was just ordinary playthings. Finally Jeremy glanced at his watch. "We should head back into town," he said. "I booked us into that restaurant for dinner."

"Good," I said, tucking the notebook into my purse. I glanced around the room again.

"Anything else you want from here?" Jeremy inquired.

I hesitated. "Somehow I don't want to tell Harriet about this secret room yet," I said, looking around. "I would feel as if I were ratting out the club."

"That's okay. But, I think we should keep the croquet set and that rocking-horse that was in the bedroom I used to sleep in," Jeremy said.

"And the teak credenza," I said. "That's a good piece. And those beaux arts lamps."

We turned and made our way cautiously down the wooden staircase. Once outside, Jeremy heaved the door shut behind us. He had a small combination lock that he carried on his keychain for his health-club locker back in London. He used it now to pad-lock the door.

"That way nobody else can go sneaking in there," he said.

We made our way around the garage, which was empty, except for a fastidiously arranged rack of saws and hammers and other hardware tools that Grandfather Nigel had left behind, some hanging on hooks, others fastened securely with leather straps, all of which had not been disturbed ever since he'd left them there.

"Gee," I noted. "I never realized how well-prepared Grandfa-ther Nigel was for any disaster made by man or nature. Look at these old-fangled whale oil lamps! And what's that contraption?"

"A homemade short-wave radio," Jeremy said in fascination,

turning the knobs; but it remained silent. There were also plastic jugs of distilled water, and boxes of big candles and matches, and even an old horse-harness and a pony cart. But Jeremy couldn't remember ever seeing a horse on the premises.

We followed the low wall until we emerged at the end of the driveway, and I saw that the surveyors' car was no longer there, so they must have packed it up and gone home.

We climbed into Jeremy's Dragonetta, and as we pulled away from the house I leaned my head against the headrest and sighed.

"Oh, Jeremy," I said wistfully. "Wouldn't it be great if we could spend the whole summer here again?"

"Are you kidding?" Jeremy said. "In that house? We'd get trapped in all those spiderwebs. Years later someone might find us here, like a couple of dead flies." He put an arm up and froze with a dopey look on his face, as if petrified in a web.

"We could rent one of those sweet little cottages people always talk about out here. We could eat fish and drink ale and explore up and down the whole coast! Who knows? Maybe we *will* find out something wonderful about Shakespeare."

Jeremy tried to hide his dubious look. But the thought of that developer arrogantly sending his men over here to measure it up left me with a new sense of urgency, and I flung one more backward glance over my shoulder at the dark hulk that was Grandma's house.

"We just *can't* let them sell her home!" I declared stoutly. "That house needs plenty more generations to love it. We can't let it go down on our watch!"

"Steady on," Jeremy said as he steered the car toward the village. "*Come not between the dragon and his wrath.*"

"Shakespeare," I said.

"*King Lear*," he replied smugly.

"Oh, yeah?" I said. I racked my brain, then emoted triumphantly:

*"Our doubts are traitors,*
*And make us lose the good we might oft win,*
*By fearing to attempt."*

Jeremy looked chagrined, and I said, *"Measure for Measure,* baby! So wipe that surprised look off your face and buy me the best dinner you can get here tonight!"

# Chapter Eight

Well, he did. Buy me a great dinner, even though at first the evening looked none too promising.

"Holy smokes!" I exclaimed as we rolled back into town and approached the hotel parking lot. It had been nearly empty last night and this morning. Now it was jam-packed with cars. Not only that, but every parking space along the street was taken, and not just in front of the restaurant, but all up and down the main street.

We had to hover about, until finally Jeremy managed to swoop in just as a car pulled out of the space on the corner. "You landed on it like a duck on a June-bug," I said approvingly.

All along the sidewalk, as well as inside the restaurant, chic-looking people were noisily thronging as they waited for a table. Every available barstool and small table in the bar area was occupied. The reception desk had a long line of hungry customers, all trying to charm or bully the harried but intractable staff.

"This is a fierce crowd!" I murmured.

I peered beyond the maitre d' into the large dining room, which was ringed by a wall of tall glass windows and doors leading to a spacious deck that overlooked the harbor, and was used for outdoor eating in the warmer summer months.

Tonight, however, the weather was too chilly even for hardy English folk to sit out on the deck drinking in the gusty wind. So all the weekend visitors were crammed indoors, with everyone jockeying to get a table with a view.

"We're going to be here all night," I groused.

You know how it is; even the most civilized among us can't help staring at other people's food as it goes by on a tray, and the longer you wait, the more you feel like snatching it right off their plates in your teeth like an alley cat.

"Don't worry, just follow me," Jeremy murmured, straightening up to his full height and assuming an attitude that I call his Important Person Look. Without seeming the least bit pushy or arrogant, he simply moved forward with so much grace and confidence that the crowd actually parted respectfully for him, as if he were the Duke of Cornwall himself.

"We have a reservation," Jeremy said quietly and calmly to the maitre d', giving him our name as guests of the Homecoming Inn and as friends of the Port St. Francis Legacy Society. I recalled that Harriet had advised us to "mention our group's name anywhere" when she e-mailed us the directions to Grandma's house.

And perhaps because of all the publicity we'd gotten on our previous cases, the reservations-desk attendant seemed to know who we were, for the maitre d', a tall, elegant Frenchman with a pencil-thin moustache and a tough attitude, snapped into gear.

"Ah, yes, Nichols and Laidley, of course!" he said briskly, selecting two menus and leading us past the envious, bejeweled crowd and into the dining room, with me at his heels and Jeremy following.

All the while, I steadfastly avoided catching anyone else's eye. I heard only one faint objection, which was some guy who muttered, "Nice to be somebody!" I tried not to look surprised as we were escorted straight through the noisy part of the dining room and up to one of the coveted tables with a view.

As waiters pulled out our chairs and dropped snowy napkins into our laps, Jeremy told me, "I hear the local lamb is incredible. But of course it's the fresh Cornish seafood that most people come here for. Want to order both, and we'll share?"

"Perfect," I sighed. "How nice of you to offer to share you dinner. I *do* like being married at times like this."

"Hmmm. Which times *don't* you like being married?" Jeremy countered teasingly.

"When people address my mail to Mrs. Jeremy Laidley," I said frankly. "I love your name, but there's no sign of me in there at all! Some people just refuse to write Penny Nichols Laidley."

"What people?" Jeremy asked, amused.

"Great-Aunt Dorothy does it every time," I said promptly. "On the wedding gift, her Christmas card, all her charity invitations when she wants us to be donors. No matter how I sign my replies, she keeps addressing me as Mrs. Jeremy Laidley. I swear it's deliberate, as if to tell me to know my place."

"Oh, well, phew, at least it's not something that's my fault," Jeremy replied.

A waiter approached us and said, "Before I tell you our specials tonight, would you like a cocktail or a glass of champagne?"

Jeremy smiled at me encouragingly, so I said, "Definitely champagne."

A short while later, as we were drinking our bubbly, there was a mild commotion at the front of the room. This was due to the arrival of a dining party led by two men who looked almost identical, even though they were of different heights and wore different suits. Each had close-cropped sandy-colored hair, a pallid oval face, deep-set pale blue eyes, a protruding lower lip, and rather large ears that stuck out a bit and were pointed at the top. They wore an identical cold, veiled expression, so that if you happened to catch their glance, which I did purely by accident, you instinctively felt something in your gut freeze warningly.

Theirs was a party of six diners. This included a bevy of tall, leggy girlfriends-for-tonight teetering on spiky high heels and clad in competing tight dresses, flashy necklaces and elaborately coiffed hairstyles; and they all left a heavy trail of cologne in their wake.

The group was showily escorted to the largest table in the house, right in the center of the room so that no one could miss their arrival. As they all took their seats, I saw that the two hosts of the party wore big, glittering diamond cuff-links.

"And who's-them-when-they're-at-home?" I whispered with a fake cockney accent to Jeremy.

"That's the Mosley brothers," he answered in a low voice. "A pair of fairly sinister bookends."

I gasped. "The developers?" I asked in disbelief. Jeremy nodded. "*Those* are the guys who want to wreck Grandmother Beryl's house?" I hissed in indignation.

"Yep," Jeremy said in a low voice. "I've seen their photos in the press. And, see those men and women who are joining them now?"

I followed his gaze and saw that the Mosley party had indeed been joined by six other people who frankly looked like poor relations—three women wearing dresses with too much shoulder-padding, and three men who laughed a bit too loud the way guys do when they're insecure.

"Those are the local town council people that Colin told us about," Jeremy explained. "The ones who willingly signed on to the development. I looked them up before we came here."

"If you've already done this kind of research," I observed, "then you must think we're in for a serious fight."

Before he could answer, there was a new buzz of interest among the diners; and all heads turned in a chain-reaction across the room to stare at the famous TV chef himself, Toby Taylor. I watched as he nodded and smiled, pausing here and there to greet an old friend or a special client along the way. But despite his casual attitude it was perfectly clear that his destination was the Mosleys' table, where the conversation had already reached a lively hum. When the chef shook hands with both brothers, the chatter at their table rose to a higher pitch, with even heartier guffaws from the men in his group, while the women simply gazed at Toby in flirtatious admiration.

Toby quickly signalled the waiters, who hurried over with large trays of appetizers. The sommelier appeared with more waiters in tow, and soon several corks were popped open at once. Toby leaned over to listen attentively as one of the brothers spoke to him, then the chef nodded vigorously, conferred quietly with a head waiter, and moved on.

As if to prove that he was as interested in the peasants as well as the big shots, Toby now stopped at one small table to pour wine for a beaming, touristy couple; then adjusted a napkin at an empty table, and nodded to a group of elderly diners, before finally landing at our table.

"Hallo! I'm Toby," said the chef, turning his full-wattage smile on me and shaking hands with Jeremy. "What a distinct pleasure to have the famed team of Nichols and Laidley at my table!" he added, affably and easily, as if we were all old friends. Yet I got a creepy feeling that we'd been pointed out to him by the Mosley brothers, both of whom were now staring in our direction.

"May I tell you our house specialties tonight?" Toby asked, and a waiter approached the table respectfully, his pen poised above his pad. Toby began to reel off the list as if he had just cast his line into the sea and was gently bringing in the day's catch before our eyes.

"Our appetizers tonight are bay oysters sautéed in farm-fresh sweet butter and organic parsley; Dover sole meunière; scallops with serrano ham; mussels from Torbay; local Padstow lobster; freshly-caught langoustines from Scotland on ice . . ."

I gazed at him mutely, forgetting the Mosleys altogether as I contemplated this dizzying choice.

"Or," he said, smiling, "a mini sampler of everything."

"That's the one," said Jeremy decisively.

"Excellent," Toby said with a smile, and Jeremy ordered the lamb as a second course.

Toby chatted about the wine, seeming just as he appeared on TV, joking and laughing while exhorting the joys and benefits of local, organic farming. He was dressed in his trademark attire of blue-and-white striped shirt and black pants. His hair was blond and he was not especially tall, but he was powerfully built, resembling a rugby player. He had an aura of down-to-earth alertness and confident skill; yet, there was just the slightest trace of a thuggish businessman that made me wary.

Finally he bowed, and moved across the rest of the room, shaking hands and greeting people as he retreated to the kitchen.

Soon the waiters began moving quickly and quietly around us, arriving with our food and wine. Jeremy and I clinked our glasses and drank, and we laughed and joked all through our meal.

"When we were kids wasn't there a folksy restaurant here?" I asked. "I seem to remember this dining room and deck, but it looked much different, like something out of the 1950s, with waxy checkered tablecloths, and food like mutton stew and macaroni-and-cheese."

"Yeah, I remember," Jeremy agreed. "It was a menu for grown-ups who'd already gotten drunk on scotch and simply wanted big portions of food. But the fish was quite good then."

Just before dessert, our meal was suddenly interrupted by the appearance of a waiter who presented Jeremy with an unopened bottle of champagne, which we had not ordered. With a flourish, the waiter told us that this was a rare vintage from their cellars, "compliments of the Mosley brothers". The waiter held out a small silver tray to Jeremy with a note on it.

Jeremy took the note, read it, and then said firmly to the waiter, "Thank you. But send the champagne back."

The waiter actually turned pale. "But—but sir," he stammered.

Jeremy gave him the fisheye. "Send it back," he repeated. "With a thanks-but-no-thanks."

And I could swear that the whole restaurant watched as the waiter, who had flushed beet-red, carried the champagne back to the Mosleys.

"Any idea how much that champers cost?" I whispered to Jeremy.

"In the neighborhood of two thousand pounds," he said. He shoved the note toward me that had come on the silver tray. It said only, *Perhaps we can do business together.*

I stole a look at the Mosley brothers, whose faces betrayed nothing as one of them spoke to the waiter. However, only moments later, our waiter re-appeared at our table, bearing the gift of two glasses of a more modest cognac. He looked petrified now. But Jeremy diplomatically accepted it this time, and raised his glass to me.

"If I drink it, does it mean I have to work with the Mosleys?" I asked, as the two brothers nodded briefly to us.

"No way," Jeremy replied. "It only means I don't have to do pistols at dawn with one of them."

We sipped our cognac, which was smooth and warming, and a great companion to our coffee and a dessert of mixed berry fruit *tarte* with Devonshire cream.

"Well, apart from the little Mosley drama," I sighed contentedly, "this was a wonderful dinner."

As we rose to leave we passed through the bar again, and it still had a sizeable throng of people waiting to eat. A few sated diners lingered on the front porch, chatting in the cool dark night.

"Hope there's some room in the parking lot behind the hotel now," Jeremy said as we walked down the front path to the sidewalk. "I want to move the car there—" Then his tone changed completely. "Bloody hell!" he exclaimed.

I followed his gaze, and saw that Jeremy's Dragonetta, which was still parked at the street corner where we'd left it, now had an ugly, strange splotchy shadow over the windshield. As I drew nearer I saw what it was.

"Eggs!" I cried. Someone had thrown a couple of them, *Splat!* right on the glass. The broken yolks, cracked shell fragments and gooey white had formed one drippy, hideous pattern of hostility.

While we stood there stunned, I noticed that the Mosley brothers had come out to the porch, and one of them strolled down the front path to light up a cigarette. As he flashed his lighter, I momentarily saw his pale eyes shining in the dark night, with a look of chilly amusement that I did not like.

Toby Taylor had come out, too, saying goodbye to another group of finely dressed men accompanied by slender ladies wearing gold jewelry that flashed at their throats and hands. But when

Toby saw the look on our faces, he quickly realized what we were staring at, and then broke away from his other guests with an expression of genuine sympathy.

"I'm terribly sorry, Mr. Laidley," he said quietly. "The local vandals sometimes get a bit out of hand on the weekend. Egged on by their elders, no pun intended. Some people can't stand progress. Don't worry, I'll have one of the valets clean it up for you in the morning. But for now, let's get it off the street. It will be safe in our garage."

Jeremy wordlessly handed his car key to the valet. I simply wanted to get away from the stares of the other guests, who were probably wondering why we'd been singled out for this abuse. After all, Jeremy's Dragonetta was a beautiful car, yet there were many other cars parked all around us on the street that were far more expensive and showy.

We went into our hotel next door, where the front parlor was quiet and consoling, with its low lighting from pretty lamps, and invitingly upholstered chairs. I saw that a white-haired elderly couple sat on a sofa, happily doing the crossword puzzle together.

We climbed the wide, old-fashioned staircase, and I absently ran my hand over the smoothly polished banister. Then Jeremy unlocked the door to our room, and tossed the key on top of the chest of drawers. I switched on the lamp nearby and stole a look at him to see if he was still scowling, but he only smiled ruefully at me.

"Who the hell are these so-called vandals everyone blames everything on?" I demanded.

"Local kids with too much time on their hands, I imagine," he replied.

"I don't believe it," I said stoutly. "It had to be the Mosleys, I just know it."

"Maybe, maybe not. These villagers do resent newcomers who roar into town with fancy cars," Jeremy answered ruefully.

"And why name them after the Vandals?" I mused. "Why not the Visigoths?"

"Vandals is easier to say," Jeremy offered.

"You're winging it," I scoffed. After a moment I said, "Why would anyone attack us? We haven't done anything yet."

"We're here," Jeremy said. "That may be enough." He smiled at me. "Don't worry. We'll soon figure out who our friends and foes are," he said calmly as he took off his jacket and deposited his wallet on the bed-stand. I could see that tonight's events had only strengthened Jeremy's determination to fight back.

Struck by the quiet strength of his attitude, I interrupted his appealingly male routine of undressing by flinging my arms around him, and I planted a particularly loving kiss on his warm lips.

"You're a good egg," I said daringly. "That's why I married you."

He put his arm around my waist and pulled me closer with mock ferocity, then helped me unbutton my dress while kissing the back of my neck. "You," he said, "make me feel happy to be alive."

# Chapter Nine

The next morning was a Sunday, and I awoke to the dolorous sound of church bells clanging in the cool morning air. They had a very measured, solid tone, as if they had been tolling for flocks of villagers all down the centuries on mornings just like this one.

Jeremy and I walked over to get our breakfast at the farmers' market, which was set up in the big parking lot near the harbor. Each vendor had his own small white tent and metal tables heaped with fruits, flowers or vegetables that had just been picked. One farmer had a goat for kids to pet; and a beekeeper displayed a buzzy, busy hive inside a glass bell. The baker's table, with its fragrant, fresh-baked bread and muffins was especially popular, as was the booth with locally made cheeses and sausages. And the fishermen had their own prominent section with piles of newly caught fish on ice.

Because the day was fine, we spent the rest of the morning watching the fishing boats coming in and out of the harbor. In the afternoon, we hurried back to the Homecoming Inn to pick up the car, so that we'd be on time to meet Trevor Branwhistle. Jeremy gave the valet our room number. The valet, a local Cornish lad of about seventeen, bolted off with alacrity, and a second later Jeremy's Dragonetta came roaring around the corner at breakneck speed. The kid pulled right up to us, and jumped out with a smile of pure pleasure as he stepped aside for Jeremy.

"Great wheels, dude," the valet could not help saying with undisguised admiration.

I noted that the windshield sparkled in the sunlight, and the car looked as if it had never been sullied. Jeremy gave the kid a tip, and we drove off.

We headed away from the harbor with its fishing boats bobbing on the sparkling sea and the sound of the waves lashing the sandy, rocky shoreline. Today we were climbing a bit higher inland, where the houses perched near dewy meadows.

"Trevor Branwhistle, here we come," I said.

Now, when you're out in the country, the English play fast and loose with the word "cottage". I suppose it's all relative to the main building and the original reason that the first owner had for scattering other houses on his estate, as if they were little plastic pieces from a Monopoly board game.

So sometimes a "cottage" truly is a cute little abode like the ones that hermits inhabit in fairy tales. On the other hand, an English cottage can be a house that most normal folk would consider rather grand—from awesome castle-like residences that were once an abbey or rectory; to stone "farmhouses" that look more like winery châteaux, to an elegantly built mansion.

Trevor Branwhistle's "cottage" fell into this more imposing category. It was a white Edwardian structure that sat very proudly in a clearing on the flat top of a high hill, overlooking a meadow with fluffy grey sheep grazing placidly. Several acres separated the property from Grandmother Beryl's house. Although he had a view of the sea in the back of his property, Trevor's house was higher up, and did not have direct access to a cove or shoreline as Grandmother's did.

"Wow, I didn't know working for the BBC paid so well," I said, duly impressed.

"No, dear. Houses like this are inherited. I imagine the BBC pension merely helps pay for the expenses. Where's the front door to this ruddy place?" Jeremy muttered, steering the car around a gravel drive that surrounded the house, and parking beside another car in an area edged with a white fence.

"Over there. See the big door with the balcony above it?" I told him, pointing at the main entrance.

The front door was opened by a plump, middle-aged housekeeper in a grey dress and white apron. She had a pleasant smile as if she were expecting us, and she led us through a cool, dark reception hall, directly into a study that overlooked the meadow.

I liked this room immediately. The wall opposite the entrance had four tall windows and a French door that was opened wide onto a terrace with balustrades. The other three walls were covered with floor-to-ceiling bookshelves, which housed an extensive collection of tall, leather-bound volumes. Peering closer at the spines, I saw from their gold-lettered titles that many of them were collections of famous plays. Others were actually BBC sound recordings of Trevor doing Shakespeare or being interviewed about the English theatre.

Jeremy was wandering around examining four busts mounted on white pedestals reigning over each corner of the room. "They're all playwrights," he noted. "Here's Shakespeare himself."

"Isn't he wonderful?" I whispered, stepping across the square red-and-green wool rug in the center of the room. *To be or not to be . . ."* I intoned, poised before the marble bust.

"This one's Ibsen . . . this is Shaw . . ." Jeremy said, staring at the other noble faces. Then he paused, searching for the identity of the last one. I drifted to his side, studying the bust of a man whose hair was worn in long curly ringlets, and whose face had heavy-lidded eyes, an elegant nose, a well-shaped wide moustache, an intelligent brow, and a mouth that indicated a trace of humor.

"Not sure who that is," Jeremy murmured.

"I am Molière, sir!"

The booming voice seemed to come right out of the statue itself. We both jumped back and stared at the stone face, as if awaiting its next word, which came soon.

*"We die only once, and for such a long time!"*

It really did seem as if the statue had spoken—in a French accent, no less. This time I whirled around, searching for a human presence. Then, out of the corner of my eye, I saw a figure on the terrace just stepping out of the shadows, and coming into the study.

Trevor Branwhistle had a lion's mane of silver-and-black hair with a matching, very pointy beard and moustache, which made him look as if he belonged to the seventeenth century rather than our present one. He wore brown tweed pants, a corduroy olive-green jacket with mustard-yellow patches on the elbows, and an olive-green knitted vest. His face was not so much wrinkled as leathery, and I judged him to be about sixty.

"You are fortunate, young lady," he said to me with a mock-severe look, in a normal voice which was Oxford-educated. "Monsieur Molière rarely converses with visitors before he's had a proper introduction."

"I'm Penny Nichols, and this is my husband, Jeremy Laidley," I said, delighted to play along with his whimsy. He took my hand and kissed it with the kind of theatrical gesture that only an actor can get away with in such ordinary circumstances.

"You're a very good ventriloquist," Jeremy observed.

"An actor must have many tricks up his sleeve," Trevor said, reaching out to shake hands with Jeremy, but at the last moment he flicked his hand instead, and appeared to pluck out a card from Jeremy's sleeve. It was the King of Hearts. "However I am less a magician and more a Jack-of-all-Trades," he added, flicking the same card again, so that it seemed to have now become the Jack of Clubs. With a flourish, he handed it to me as if it were his calling card.

"Would you care for a glass of port?" he asked. Without waiting for an answer, he went over to a tall table in the corner and poured the ruby-colored port from a decanter into three narrow glasses. He handed the first to me, then another to Jeremy. We all clinked.

"To your grandmother Beryl," Trevor said in a more respectful, less jocular tone. "She is sorely missed."

"You knew her, then?" I asked, as eager to hear the answer as I was to continue listening to that deep, resonant voice that was as silky as the port.

Trevor gestured for us to sit upon the green velvet upholstered sofa. "Certainly. After all, she was my neighbor, and a true patron of our local theatre. Beryl had her own special box seats, and she was a devoted fund-raiser," he said, sipping his port. "More conventional than her sister Penelope, mind you, but a real brick when it came to defending the village. Beryl was content to remain backstage, if you know what I mean; whereas her sister Penelope adored the spotlight and even once trod the boards right here on our stage, performing as a song-and-dance gal."

"When was this?" Jeremy asked, amused.

"For a benefit, back in the 1970s!" Trevor boomed, sitting in a brown leather chair opposite us. "She brought her old partner down from London, what was his name?"

"Simon Thorne," I said, delighted.

"Yes, yes. They did a Noel Coward and Gertrude Lawrence music-hall-style number," Trevor recalled. "Quite a hilarious routine, called *Red Peppers*, where they played sailors who'd stayed ashore too long and missed their boat," he said, and hummed the song *Has Anybody Seen Our Ship?*

Well, after that, it wasn't hard to get Trevor to tell us all about himself and his own career. He was a genuine ham who enjoyed attention so openly that I couldn't help giving him the bright smile he craved. "What made you decide to do radio?" I asked.

"Money!" he intoned, stretching out his long legs and gazing off in the distant land of memory. Then, resuming his normal voice, he added, "I taught acting in London for awhile, and when the BBC radio heard about my classes, they engaged me to do an on-air adaptation of some of my lectures. But after that, I tired of London—vastly overcrowded these days—and now I've 'swallowed the anchor', so to speak."

At my blank look, he translated, "That's seamen's talk for 'retired'. So here I be, in Port St. Francis, and at the end of a good day, you can find me wherever there's a decent game of darts and a pint of home-brewed ale. Not a bad finale, I assure you." He fell silent.

"Mr. Branwhistle," I said eagerly, "I suppose you know why we are here."

"To rescue your grandmother's house!" Trevor declaimed, looking amused at us. "They say you are a pair of newlywed sleuths who dare to delve into history where angels might fear to tread. I believe you look promising. So, where shall we begin?"

"Shakespeare," Jeremy said.

# Chapter Ten

Realizing what a wild detour a guy like Trevor might take with such a huge topic as the Bard, I added hurriedly, "Harriet says you've discovered some connection to Shakespeare and my grandmother's house?"

"Why, only that he lived there!" Trevor announced, gazing at us watchfully for our reaction. "And possibly left a fragment of a long-lost play of his in your grandmother's attic."

I gasped, but Jeremy said with equanimity, "Are you saying you've actually seen this document?"

"I have, sir," Trevor said with exaggerated dignity. "I sent it on to a colleague of mine at Cambridge University. He is an expert in this field. However, I did retain a copy."

I sat transfixed as Trevor rose from his seat and walked over to one of the bookshelves, which had a row of thin drawers beneath the bottom shelf. From this he extracted a document, and he carried it over to the table near me, where he dropped it lightly, but with a flourish.

"We know that in 1613, a London actors' group called the King's Men performed a play by Shakespeare entitled *Cardenio*," Trevor said in a more serious tone. "Many believe that *Cardenio* was about an episode in the life of Don Quixote, since Cardenio is a character in the Cervantes novel. But some scholars think *Cardenio* might have been a children's play about King Arthur."

Trevor gestured at the document on the table. "If this fragment is authentic, it may prove firstly, that *Cardenio* was indeed about King Arthur, and secondly, that Shakespeare worked on the play much sooner than we thought. The man who wrote it was a lodger in your grandmother's house in the summer of 1592. This was during a period of history that just happens to be a tantalizing gap in time when Shakespeare vanished from sight. In other words, there is no known record of where he was and what happened to him. Until perhaps, now."

Jeremy and I abandoned any reserve and pounced on the document. It had only about five lines on it, because the top part had been torn off. And I must say that the handwriting was so terrible that I could scarcely make out a letter, let alone a word.

"But I can't tell what it says!" I exclaimed.

Trevor smiled. "That is because in the Bard's day, English grammar and punctuation were less standardized than in our time. But let me translate for you."

He paused, then read aloud:

*"Because the lady fair loved tales of knights,*
*My songs of valor set her heart alight.*
*A hazard of new fortunes I did make,*
*And in the dawn her virtue I would take."*

"Is this his signature?" Jeremy asked, pointing to a messy scrawl at the bottom of the page.

I saw that the first name said *Willim*, spelled without the usual "a" in "William". But it was hard to tell what the last name was; to me it looked like *3hurByjre*.

"It is indeed a signature," Trevor said. He copied it onto another piece of paper for me and it looked like this: *Shakspere*, which was still missing the additional "e" and "a" of our modern-day spelling of the name. When I pointed this out, Trevor said that back then, they often used more than one spelling for a word.

Jeremy asked cautiously, "What was Shakespeare doing way out here? His home and family were in Stratford-on-Avon."

Trevor puffed his chest dramatically and intoned, "Sir! You obviously are not aware of the many theories of the Lost Years of William Shakespeare. The theatrical and academic world are rife with speculation as to where our Will disappeared during this gap. Many theories are based on the notion that he got into trouble of some kind. Some say he fled Stratford to avoid being prosecuted as a deer-poacher. Others say to escape religious persecution. Still others believe that he needed money and therefore worked as a schoolmaster in the country shires. But, because his plays have so many allusions to the sea, some believe that he went off as a sailor—perhaps even voyaging with Sir Francis Drake himself!"

I tried to imagine Shakespeare working as a deck-hand on the infamous pirate ship.

"However, many believe that Shakespeare was travelling in Italy," Trevor continued, "because afterwards he wrote so many plays set in Italy—*The Two Gentlemen of Verona, The Taming of the Shrew, The Merchant of Venice, Romeo and Juliet.* I also once believed this myself—but, no more!"

His raised his arm, with his index finger in the air as a dramatic flourish. "I am not a naïve man, nor am I given to ephemeral fantasies. Yet I have become convinced that the crucial link to Shakespeare lies in the history of your grandmother's house."

Here he paused for effect, until I said, "Please go on."

"Back in the late sixteenth century, Beryl's house, like mine, was part of the earl's estate. Well, after all, the earl pretty much owned everything, and therefore everybody, in Port St. Francis!" he exclaimed. "The villagers either labored in his copper and tin mines or else lived as his tenant farmers. Sometimes an outbuilding was used as a lodging house or a coaching inn."

"But Harriet told us that my grandmother's house was occupied by some performers in Shakespeare's time, right?" I asked.

Trevor said, "Correct. During the year in question, Beryl's house was the residence of a troupe of actors whom the earl sponsored, so they were called, appropriately, 'The Earl's Players'. In those days, musical or acting companies would often perform in private homes. They were known as 'household players'. The earl's estate kept records of what he paid people, and the Players were listed on salary all year. It seems that during this particular summer, a travelling actor was hired to replace a member of the troupe who'd fallen ill. And the name of the vagabond actor who was hired was none other than . . ."

Trevor tapped the document where the signature spelled out the name.

"I see. So, that explains why this document was found in Beryl's house?" Jeremy observed, staring at the manuscript fragment.

"Yes, in an old barrel in the attic. Harriet and I uncovered it quite accidentally while sorting through the place when we were told to prepare Beryl's house for sale," Trevor answered. "There's no doubt that the man who wrote and signed this fragment, was, for the entire summer of 1592, a member of The Earl's Players and therefore a lodger in your grandmother's house. The question remains: was he really the Bard of Avon?"

Trevor seized my hand and held it in both of his. "Can you understand how utterly seismic this discovery would be if we can prove it? Not only would your grandmother's house be designated a landmark—with all the protection that that would afford—but we would have astounding new information about Shakespeare and his work."

"What does your friend at the University think?" I asked breathlessly.

"He is subjecting the document to the most vigorous tests you can imagine!" Trevor said, releasing my hand and pacing the room impatiently. "Handwriting analysis. Chemical tests of the ink and paper. Academic tests of language and usage. Records in London—although so many, alas, perished in the Great Fire of 1666."

Trevor paused to take a deep breath. "I must say, I am not a Shakespeare historian," he admitted. "So I feel that I have come to my scholarly limit. That is why, when I chanced to hear about you two at a party, I thought it was time to pass the baton and see if you could reach the finish line with this."

"Do you think your Shakespeare expert would talk to us?" I asked eagerly.

"He said he would be glad to," Trevor said. "I think it's best you see him in person, my dear. You are such a charming young woman and he would perhaps be more forthcoming if you paid him a visit." Trevor wrote down the name and address for me on the back of one of his own business cards.

"This is all well and good, if he declares that your fragment is authentic," Jeremy said. "But what if your expert says the evidence is inconclusive?"

Trevor gave him a knowing nod. "That is where you and Penny

come in," he said challengingly. "Any supporting evidence that you can unearth might 'Save Our Ship'! Though, I must tell you, we've been through the entire house with a fine-toothed comb, and found not a single scrap of additional evidence to help us out. So whatever you discover will have to come from somewhere else, I'm afraid."

I gazed at him, dumbfounded. What on earth did he expect us to do? Find a personalized quill pen out on the moors, autographed by the Bard himself?

Trevor had risen to his feet now, and moved to the doorway, signalling that our conference was at an end. We followed him outside.

"And now, I must 'away'. Duty calls," he said with a proud gesture, pointing toward another building on his property, which I hadn't noticed until now.

"What a beautiful old house," I said, admiring its stone structure and antique windows.

"It is actually the old Priory, where, long ago, clergymen were trained," Trevor said, pleased at my interest. "I'm surprised Harriet didn't mention it to you, because, thanks to fund-raising by our Legacy Society, we have managed to turn the Priory into a seniors' home for old actors. And you would be surprised at how many of today's London performers have already contributed money to our Actors' Home, in order to insure that when they reach retirement age they will have a place there! I won't name any names, of course," Trevor said with a sly smile. "Would you like to take a look before you go?" he asked so eagerly that I had to nod, even though Jeremy was making faces trying to signal me to say no.

By now Trevor was insisting that we just "pop in" for a moment. I don't know if it was because he just automatically sought to recruit new donors, or if he was simply so proud of the place.

"The Actors' Home is actually my own brainchild, because my fellow thespians need a special place to retire to," Trevor explained. We entered the fine old three-storied stone house.

"It's gotten an excellent rating, with quality medical care provided by good doctors from the local training hospital. And the food here is first-rate. So, we are nearly full to capacity," Trevor said as we went upstairs. "We rely on nursing students from the hospital to work here. Ah, here is Nora. She is one of the best."

The bright-faced young nurse was busy with patients, but she gave us a warm smile as we passed her.

"But if we can't continue to keep our local hospital thriving, then student nurses like Nora will have to abandon us for some big city," Trevor said.

We had been politely walking down the corridors of the second floor and peering in at rooms that actually looked quite attractive, since they were furnished in an old-fashioned way, not only with brass beds and cozy-looking upholstered chairs, but with desks, tables and lamps. The desks, I realized, gave the rooms more dignity, for the occupants were not forced to be bedridden, and they wore regular clothes instead of hospital gowns. As we passed the large common room on this floor, we heard theatre music from the 1930s and 1940s wafting out, and when I peered in I saw groups of residents sitting there, playing cards and viewing old movies.

"Nice music," Jeremy commented, looking amused. "Not what you usually hear in a care home."

"Yes, well, that's all part of what makes this place so special," Trevor said with a pleased expression. "Recent studies show that elderly people retain their mental capacity and zest for life when they live in an environment that recreates the atmosphere of their youth," he explained.

Trevor ushered us into the elevator and continued, "Here in our Actors' Home, each floor will be devoted to a different era, outfitted with the music, movies, books and furnishings of that time," he explained as the elevator door reopened, and we crossed the first-floor lobby. "We hope to soon convert this floor into our 1950s and 1960s wing."

I watched Jeremy struggling to keep a straight face as we passed a common room that already had large framed photos of Elvis Presley, the Beatles and the Rolling Stones.

Near the front door was a main office. Trevor paused there and said, "Everyone in town is very excited about this Shakespeare find. Did Harriet tell you that we're doing a big benefit show for the hospital later this summer? We're re-opening the old theatre in town, and some of our residents here are going to come out of retirement to read scenes from Shakespeare. May I put you down for two tickets to our Shakespeare Festival?"

"Of course," I said, pausing at the office anteroom where a plump, pleasant woman took my credit card to charge the tickets. I idly wondered if Trevor had conducted this entire tour for the simple purpose of selling a couple of tickets.

"Thank you so much," Trevor said as we all shook hands. "And do please call me the minute you return from London. I can't wait to hear what you learn about our Elizabethan lodger."

Jeremy didn't say a word until we were safely in our car in the parking lot and heading for the winding country road that would take us back into town. Then he said in a deadly tone, "Okay, Penny, when I get old and go dotty, I want to be put in the 1960s wing. Have you got that? I want to go where the Beatles are."

"But that's not your decade," I reminded him. "Your misspent youth was in the 1980s, right?"

"Oh, please!" Jeremy exclaimed. "Punk and New Wave are okay when you're young, but I don't wish to spend a lifetime there."

"By the time we're as old as these folks are," I said, "we'd be lucky to get into any wing at all."

Jeremy pondered this, then said quite vehemently, "Well, whatever happens, do *not* stick me in the 1970s. I will *not* spend my last breath hearing Donna Summers. Do you hear me? I HATE disco!"

"Okay, okay!" I cried. "Stop talking about it. I mean, why do you keep telling me to park you in a home in the first place? Don't I get to stay with you?"

"Right," Jeremy said, calming down a little. "We'll go together, listening to *Rubber Soul*."

"Never mind all that!" I cried. "Are these Legacy Society folks totally crazy or what?"

"The Cornish are known to be an eccentric lot," Jeremy told me. "But, this is beyond any of my expectations."

"Well, what do you think? Did Shakespeare hang out in my grandmother's house?" I asked.

"I think that bloke Trevor is such a compelling storyteller that he's got everybody out here mesmerized," Jeremy said frankly. "But all he really has to offer is a scrap of paper and a lot of theories. No hard evidence that I can see. I mean sure, we should go to London and see what his expert has to say. But I have to tell you, I'm not particularly hopeful."

I sighed gustily. "I know," I admitted. "I did plenty of research on Shakespeare for that silly vampire film I worked on. And the more you search, the more you find out how little we really know about old Will. *But*," I said determinedly, "if there's any chance that Trevor is on the right track, I say we go for it. After all, there *was* an acting troupe in that house, and there *was* a man who signed his name that way, and Shakespeare had to be *somewhere* that year, so why not here?"

# Chapter Eleven

"I don't know about you," Jeremy said as we drove back toward town, "but I could go for a nice tall ale, and a plate of fresh-caught Cornish seafood."

He looked as if he was already picturing the scene, and he held up one hand and mimed grasping a stein of beer.

"Hey," I said as we entered the hotel parking lot, "plenty of spaces tonight. Isn't that great?"

"Hmm," was all Jeremy said as he slid easily into a prime parking spot.

The front porch of the restaurant was empty as we clattered up the wooden steps, and I could sense that things here had changed drastically, even before we tried to push open the locked doors of the restaurant.

"It's six o'clock. What time do they start serving dinner?" I asked, bewildered.

"They don't," Jeremy said, pointing to the white placard that listed the restaurant's hours. "Not tonight. We're still in low season, so it's closed Monday through Thursday," he announced, "until next week. Then they're open every night."

He sighed. "Damn. I had my mouth set for that turbot *à*

*l'anglaise in hollandaise.* This is what comes of counting one's chickens before they're hatched," he concluded philosophically.

"Please don't mention chickens," I objected. "What I wouldn't do for a roasted one! I'd even settle for an egg. I mean, they can't *not* feed us . . . can they? This restaurant is connected to our hotel. There has to be *some* kind of room service, right?"

Jeremy snorted. "You want that cold plate again?"

I shook my head emphatically. "Well, maybe our hotel can recommend someplace else, so we don't have to drive around for hours," I coaxed. "I think I saw a stack of menus on the reception desk. Monday's always a tough night to eat out, though."

We hurried over to our hotel. The lobby was empty and there was no one standing at the front desk. But the door to the little office behind it was open, and as we drew nearer I could hear a rustling noise that clearly indicated someone was definitely back there, ignoring us, even when Jeremy said, "Harumph!" a couple of times.

"Yoo-hoo!" I called out finally.

There was a creak of a chair, and a thin old man, with only a few strands of grey-white hair over his otherwise bald pate, peered out at us. He had wire spectacles perched on the end of his long, skinny nose, and there was a napkin tucked under his chin, which he now reluctantly removed before emerging.

"Where can we find a good dinner tonight?" Jeremy said bluntly, for he sensed that subtle good manners would be wasted on this fellow, who behaved more like the kind of night watchman that takes such a job because he prefers not to have to talk to people.

Without answering, the man reached into a drawer and pulled out a stack of well-worn menus from local restaurants. The old fellow flapped them on the counter, then turned as if to shuffle back to his little mouse-hole.

But Jeremy, refusing to glance at what he knew he'd find on all those menus, said authoritatively, "Which one is open tonight?"

The old man paused, and gave us a slight smirk of amusement. "There's nuffin' open tonight round here," he said definitively. " 'Twere all the same, these fancy restaurants. They run on the exact same hours, like a herd of sheep."

"This guy's great for hotel P.R.," I muttered to Jeremy.

"We could send you up a cold supper," the man said without enthusiasm.

"No thanks," Jeremy said shortly. He was ready to walk out, but I nudged him.

"We should let the hotel know we want to stay on longer," I murmured, for we had agreed that we were going to need a base out here, even if we went back and forth to London.

"Do you handle reservations for the hotel?" Jeremy asked the man doubtfully. Without a word, he shuffled into his office.

"Back to his pickle-and-cheese sandwich," Jeremy muttered.

But a short moment later, a middle-aged woman emerged. With a determinedly bright expression, I told her we'd like to keep our room for awhile longer. And although I didn't exactly expect her to leap with joy at the prospect of having us around for an extended stay, I surely wasn't prepared for the definitive way she shook her head, as if dealing with two foolish children.

"Not possible, dearie," she said. "The 'igh season begins next week. We're booked solid till October."

There was a stunned silence. Jeremy's expression remained deliberately unflappable because, being English, he resolutely refuses to ever let anyone see him looking crestfallen.

I just thought that she was simply trying to drive a hard bargain to ratchet up the room rate.

"Are you completely sure about that?" I asked. "You haven't even looked in your reservation book," I added pointedly.

"Don't have to, darling," she replied, but, as if to prove something to us, she opened it, and flipped page after page, shaking her head, as if somehow we could read upside-down and this therefore made her case beyond a shadow of a doubt.

"Who else around here can you recommend?" I asked, feeling cranky now. "Hotels, or cottages—?"

But this only produced a short, incredulous laugh from her.

"Sweetie, every decent little shack in Cornwall and Devon goes rented by March!" she declared. "So-o-sorry," she sang out, attempting to sound a little regretful. "I'll ask around tomorrow morning, and if I hear of anything I'll definitely let you know."

Which meant, of course, that tomorrow we were out on our ear.

"Let's go," Jeremy said abruptly, steering me back outside. The street was quite dark without the bustle of the weekend crowd's automobiles.

"We could drive to Padstow," Jeremy said dubiously as we stood at the curb. As he spoke, the first fat drops of rain plopped on the pavement beside us.

"Swell. We'll probably skid off the roads to our deaths whilst trying to score a meal," I said.

"Want to just go to bed?" Jeremy said stoically.

But I am part French, and no matter what the circumstances I simply cannot treat eating as if it's merely a pastime, like playing bridge.

"Can't do it, sonny," I replied. "Surely we can scare up some take-out joint, or a food mart?"

"This isn't London, darling," Jeremy said. "Out here we must hunt and gather for our meals, just like the Celts."

Just then a bright red pick-up truck came roaring up, and ground to a sudden stop right in front of us. The driver peered out. Recognizing us, he inched forward, and rolled down the window.

"Hey," Colin shouted in greeting. "What are you doing standing out in the rain?"

"Looking for dinner," I said. "Nothing's open."

Colin said dryly, "The gas station in Rock sells caviar and champagne. That goes over well with the second-homers."

The image of tinned caviar standing on a shelf next to cans of motor oil nearly turned my stomach, and my face must have reflected this, because Colin laughed and said, "Care for a pint? The only place open tonight is the old pub, but it's not easy to find in the dark. Follow me," he called, then went roaring off.

"Great. We can surely get something to eat there," Jeremy said excitedly.

"Lord, don't lose him!" I cried. We hurried into the car, and Jeremy tore off after him.

Colin led us down one dark street after another, swinging around the turns and hills at breakneck speed. We drove past the railroad tracks, and then careened up another very steep hill where some dark warehouses dwarfed a few remaining old nineteenth-century brick buildings. It looked as if this street had once been a residential part of town, and I imagined that many other such brick houses had been torn down and replaced by these grim-looking warehouses in the twentieth century. But from the sight of things, most of these warehouses were now empty, too.

"So, all the hotels and restaurants like Toby Taylor's posh-nosh—they only cater to the wealthy weekenders," I said aloud. "What happens when the locals want to eat during the week in the off-season? The only place they can go is here, in this old part of town that's been half abandoned."

"This is what Harriet's been trying to tell us," Jeremy said. "And even in the high season, most of these local kids never even get to see the beach, let alone eat out. They work long hours for low wages in the back of hot, sticky restaurants and hotel kitchens—and they still can't pay their rent."

I looked up in surprise, for it was unusual for Jeremy to display personal feeling about such a subject. He caught my glance and explained, "I had friends from out here who played in my band but they weren't as fortunate as me. They were smart enough to qualify for good schools, yet couldn't afford it, so they never saw the inside of a university."

Colin slowed down in front of one of the brick buildings—the only one that had any lights on. He rolled down his window again. "Go on inside, and tell Joe at the bar that you're with me and you'll be wanting a table," he instructed. "I have to go through the back door to haul in my stuff."

"What stuff?" I muttered to Jeremy as Colin drove away.

"I think tonight it's best to ask as few questions as possible," Jeremy advised, parking the car under a street lamp in front of the pub. "We will be lucky if this car is still here when we come out."

"Colin wouldn't tell us to park here if it wasn't safe," I said optimistically.

"Let's hope so," Jeremy said. "Meanwhile, I suggest we go inside and case the place out."

# Chapter Twelve

Although *Ye Olde Towne Pub* was on street level, the interior felt as if we'd entered a basement or rathskeller. A very long bar was flanked by high stools, all of which were occupied by big, beefy men who had bushy beards, or long wild hair, or arms covered in tattoos . . . and some of them had all three of these features.

On each side of the bar were many big, antique dartboards at which several clusters of men were hurling darts. Each time a dart landed, a derisive or appreciative roar came up from some of the audience at the bar.

The entire floor was covered with sawdust. Across the room, opposite the bar, was a huge working fireplace with carved wooden gargoyles on either side. I thought I spotted a brick oven as part of this fireplace.

The center of the room was tightly crowded with tables, most of which were already occupied by groups of men, or groups of women, but hardly any couples. The diners were of all ages, from teenagers to old grizzled folk, with practically everybody wearing jeans and sneakers and other casual attire.

A surprising number of waiters were working tonight, each

wearing butcher's aprons over their jeans and T-shirts, all very busy hustling about, balancing big trays of beer glasses, which, when necessary, they hoisted over their heads to better navigate the crowded room. There was a jukebox going with rock-and-roll blaring out, and this caused the diners to raise their chatter to a level that was very nearly deafening, which perhaps explained why there weren't many signs of couples looking for quiet conversation on a date night.

At the farthest wall of the bar was a very dark cavernous area, where a number of scraggly-haired young men seemed to be moving furniture in the shadows, probably making room to set up more tables there for more diners, I thought.

"Looks like they've got plenty of chow here," Jeremy shouted to me above the din as we were escorted to our table.

He gestured toward a buffet with an enormous straw cornucopia in its center. Spilling out of the horn of plenty was an assortment of cheeses and fruit; and the rest of the table was occupied with carving boards that were manned by more waiters, who stood brandishing big knives over large roasted hams, turkeys, venison and beef.

I gazed about in amazement, watching all this cheery, convivial activity in the midst of the abandoned side of town. When I glanced up at Jeremy, his smile bore some affection as he said, "It's one of the last of the authentic neighborhood pubs. Now you see what England was . . . and what it's losing."

We studied the chalkboard menu, then Jeremy suggested that we try the shepherd's pie. He had to shout our order to the waiter. "They brew their own beer," he said happily, and soon our waiter returned, carrying our glasses aloft on one of those big trays.

Now, shepherd's pie can vary wildly, depending on the pub

and the type of meat used. Tonight we were served one of the very best—a fine homemade piecrust filled with a stew of ground beef, tiny perfect onions, carrots and tender green peas; all massively topped with whipped mashed potatoes that had been browned with butter. The tart green salad that accompanied it had sliced apple and radishes.

We ate and drank so gratefully that neither of us said a word, which was wise in this deafening din. Then, suddenly, the jukebox went silent. A few moments later, the entire crowd did, too. And then, a flood of lights came up on the darkened area where I had supposed that the younger men were moving furniture.

Only now I saw that it wasn't furniture they'd been fussing with. It was band equipment, erected on a platform. There was a full set of drums at the back, and a keyboard on a stand, and guitars and a bagpipe, and other instruments that I couldn't quite identify. Several men picked up their instruments, and then the drummer walked in and took his place.

"Jeremy!" I cried. "The drummer. It's Colin!"

At that moment one of the waiters, a stout man with a bald head and one earring, hopped onto the platform and spoke into a microphone. "Ladies and gentlemen, it's my great pleasure to present Port St. Francis' very own 'Tor Nation'!"

"What's a tor?" I whispered.

"A Cornish word for a rock formation," Jeremy answered.

The crowd broke into wild applause as the band members stepped forward. All of them were dressed like Colin—in kilts and black T-shirts with gilt design and lettering. Colin picked up his drumsticks and tapped them together to give the band the tempo, then they burst into what sounded like a strange sort of sea shanty with a rock-and-roll beat. The combination of the *"Eee-*

*eee"* of the bagpipes, the *"Wong"* of the electric guitar, and Colin's steady beat somehow all blended together in a harmonious, fascinating way, mixing rock motifs, traditional Celtic folk music, and ancient troubadour songs.

"I get it. It's folk music with drums," Jeremy said, watching closely with respectful appreciation.

As the band progressed through their set, the crowd started to keep time with the music, tapping their hands against the tables. Finally, when the band took its first break, Colin climbed down from the platform and headed toward us, nodding at a waiter who brought over an extra chair for him at our table. A big glass mug of beer quickly appeared in front of him.

"Well done!" Jeremy told him, clapping him on the back. Colin ducked his head in embarrassed pleasure.

"Celt rocks!" Colin said, raising his fist in the air. "But after the break, we're going for straight rock-and-roll."

"Thank heaven you told us about this place!" I said. "We would have starved to death tonight."

"It's the last holdout, apart from the sailors' bar at the harbor where the food is terrible," Colin said frankly, after thirstily drinking his beer. "When this place bites the dust, we're done for."

He smiled appreciatively at me, as if, now that I was in this lively bar-room setting, he was seeing me as a woman for the first time, instead of a married-lady visitor to his mum. With a good-natured trace of flirtation Colin said teasingly, "So. How do you like Cornwall, heh? Gonna stay on a bit this summer and dig up some history for us?"

"We'd love to," I answered, "but we're being thrown to the wolves. Our hotel has informed us that there is no room at the inn until autumn!"

"Bullshit," Colin said. "We can find you a place to stay. Ah!" he said, suddenly inspired. "See that guy over there holding the bagpipes?"

We all turned to study a very tall man in the band who had a brown ponytail and beard.

"He's Geoffrey, my brother-in-law," Colin said. "He and my sister Shannon have a cool farm, and I bet they could put you up in one of their cottages if they knew what you were working on."

"But we wouldn't want to impose," Jeremy said quickly.

"You wouldn't be," Colin said, waving to a table of women who appeared to be about my age. One of them had straight, straw-colored hair that was so long it went down past her waist. "Shannon and Geoff are a couple of New Age hippies," Colin declared, as if that explained everything. "They're off the grid," he added. "They grow their own food, they produce solar energy, the whole works. They got sheep and all. They make the best damned cheese you ever ate."

I thought the idea was fascinating, but perhaps to change the subject, Jeremy began to talk to Colin about music, with the two of them enthusiastically discussing all the unusual instruments and songs that the band had in its repertoire.

"Jeremy had a rock band when he was in school," I told Colin.

"No kidding?" Colin said. "Guitar?"

"Right," Jeremy said. Now it was his turn to look embarrassed.

"I thought so," Colin said, leaning back in his chair with a grin. "Can you handle a bass?"

"I suppose . . ." Jeremy said warily. "But I'm out of practice."

"Ah, nothing to it. It's like riding a bike," Colin said. He rose from the table now as his band members signalled for him to re-join them. His chair made a scraping sound as he did so.

When he reached the stage he spoke briefly to the other band members, then stepped up to the microphone, saying, "Attention, everybody! There's a friend of mine in the audience who plays guitar. He's from London, but don't hold that against him. Let's invite him to join us, shall we? Jeremy, come on up."

And he aimed a drumstick at Jeremy, who looked thoroughly horrified as the audience cheered and everyone turned in his direction, smiling expectantly.

"Shit," he said under his breath to me. "This is all your fault."

"It is not," I objected. "You were begging for it, whether you realize it or not." Then I smiled gently and said, "Do it for England, my boy."

Jeremy put on his stoic face, and rose and went up to the stage, where he was handed a cherry-red electric bass guitar. He adjusted the guitar-strap around his neck, while the other guitarist plugged it into the large black amplifier, which momentarily rumbled with feedback. The band members had a brief discussion with Jeremy, plinking a few test notes and chords while they worked out an arrangement. Then suddenly they faced the audience, Colin slammed his snare drum, and the lead singer shouted into the microphone, in a perfect imitation of Paul McCartney-imitating-Little Richard, singing *I'm Down*.

I was nearly bursting with pride and pleasure. I'd never seen Jeremy perform before an audience. Even during that very first summer here, despite all his thrilled talk about rock-and-roll, he'd never shown me what he could do.

When they finished the song, the group bowed deeply, and Jeremy, with a wry grin, replaced the guitar in its case, nodded to the other band members, and quickly left the stage. The waiter, smiling, brought him another beer "on the house".

I waited a few seconds for Jeremy to settle back down into the anonymity of the audience before I whispered to him, "You were great!"

"Yeah, well, you'd better say that," he growled at me with mock ferocity.

"Honestly, I swear," I said. "If I weren't already married to you, I would have fallen in love tonight."

Jeremy laughed and rumpled my hair, now finally convinced of my sincerity.

"To tell the truth, I hit a few bum notes," he admitted cheerfully, "but nobody seemed to mind."

The room was emptying early tonight, because it was a work night. Colin's sister was on the way out with her group when she stopped by our table and said to me, "Hi, Penny. I'm Shannon. Colin said you're looking for a place to stay? My mum has told me so much about you two!"

She signalled to her friends to go on without her, then she took the seat the waiter had planted there earlier for Colin. Shannon looked nothing like Colin; she was very tall, and wore a wheat-colored jacket that looked hand-embroidered with purple and russet-colored flowers. She was so eager to show us photographs of the cottages on her farm that all I could say was, "Oh, sure, love to have a look."

The cottage she had in mind for us really was quite lovely, painted a pale blue, with clusters of flowering shrubs and a white fence. Inside it had a good-sized kitchen, a big brass bed in the lone bedroom, a parlor with a fireplace, and, in the backyard, a small patio and a private vegetable garden. The rent she cited for the month of July was so reasonable that I knew she was giving us a special deal as a favor to Colin.

"The fact is, I hope you succeed in getting landmark status for your grandmother's house," Shannon said eagerly. "You see, our farm and wells abut some of the land that the Mosleys plan to develop. I can't begin to tell you the impact their toxic runoff would have on us. And that would be a real violation of Nature, because we just know that there are ancient ley lines running through part of our farm there."

At my mystified look, she nodded vigorously and said, "Ley lines are like ancient highways, and the magnetic energy is just fantastic! I don't know why, but everything we plant in the path of the ley lines grows twice as tall as it does anywhere else. It's the right confluence of sun, earth, air and water."

I glanced at Jeremy to see how he was reacting to Shannon's comments. He had that tolerant but skeptical look that I knew so well whenever people get what he calls "too blissy". Yet I found Shannon to be quite serious as she showed me more photos of the farm, where, in addition to growing organic fruits and vegetables, she and her husband Geoffrey raised chickens and sheep, and they even spun their own sweaters and blankets, which they sold at the farmers' market and on their own Web site.

Geoff had left his bagpipes with the band, and he joined us now, dragging over a chair from a nearby table. Shannon concluded her pitch by saying, "So please . . . will you be our guests?"

Geoff gave us an encouraging smile, and said, "Frankly, we have selfish reasons to keep you guys around. The Mosleys could put a lot of folks here out of business. So, whatever we can do to help, just ask."

Something about the generosity and conviviality from everyone here in this folksy pub tonight must have gotten to me. After all, these people had fed us when we were hungry, and they'd offered shelter when we were about to be turned out on our ear, and, well, I just liked them. So, somewhere along the way, with visions in my head of a great summer of sun, sea, fabulous beach walks and great food, I caved in.

"Let's do it, Jeremy!" I cried.

Jeremy squeezed my hand and said, "Sure, Penny. If you really want to."

"Great! I'll e-mail you a map the farm," Shannon said, and she rose decisively and went out the door. Geoff shook hands with Jeremy and, just like that, we had rented ourselves a cottage in Cornwall.

I beamed at Jeremy, who said to me wryly, "Did we just agree to go live on a sheep farm?"

"Guess so," I said with a grin.

Jeremy signalled the waiter for the check, just as the front door was flung open, and a bunch of new arrivals burst aggressively into the room.

They were obviously students from London, quite formally dressed, with top hats and tails and expensive shirts. I could not imagine American college boys ever dressed this way, but these privileged kids seemed perfectly at home in clothes that reminded me of the millionaire cartoon guy from the Monopoly game. I half expected to see one of them wearing a monocle, yet they were young.

And very, very drunk.

They staggered over to the bar shouting their drinks orders in the loud voices of plastered guys who either don't realize or don't care to notice that their volume is higher than anyone else's around them.

"Give us your finest whisky, my good man!" bellowed one.

"And a keg of ale, sir!" shouted another. I thought they were posh students on holiday, or perhaps they'd recently graduated. I couldn't quite tell. They were different from kids I knew at high school or university. These guys walked and talked like the kind of older men who would be in a private club somewhere in London, ordering around their butlers. One heavy-set lad even had a cigar in his mouth, which seemed so incongruous with his chubby-cheeked, youthful face.

Warily but resignedly, the bartender began to line up shot glasses for them. These were downed as quickly as they were filled. None of the locals spoke to these guys, and I could feel people around me stiffening with apprehension.

"Time to go home," Jeremy warned me.

The newcomers had embarked upon a loud game of darts, but were flinging them wildly in all directions, even making it necessary for some of the waiters to duck out of harm's way.

Over the din, I heard one of the interlopers suddenly shout, "I love the sound of breaking glass!"

This seemed to be a signal, for they each picked up a glass and hurled it at their own reflections in the mirror above the bar.

I can't even tell you what happened next, because everything seemed to erupt at once. Suddenly more glass was shattering, and bodies were flying through the air as the locals leaped upon the offending invaders. The waiters tried to pull them apart and ended up partaking in the fracas. Chairs were hurled across the room before I could even see who had flung them. Several young men—some locals but mostly the newcomers—went skidding into the sawdust across the floor.

Ducking the flying debris, Jeremy quickly yanked me away from the chaos and toward the musician's platform. "Come on," he said to me urgently. "Colin says there's a back door this way."

Colin had already kicked open the door, which led to the small parking lot where his truck waited. He was running back and forth with his drum equipment, stowing it safely in his truck.

"Last time, one of those jackasses tried to play the drums and punched a hole in it before I could get to him," he told me darkly. "Want a ride to your car?"

"Oh, geez, the car," I said to Jeremy. We hopped into the passenger side of Colin's truck. The upholstery on the seat was so worn that I could feel the springs under my rump. He quickly drove us around the corner to our car, and Jeremy and I hopped out.

But just before Jeremy started the engine, the front door of the bar was flung open. A few of the posh young men were literally chucked out on their butts, but several of them came out walking. They paused in the light-spill of the open front door, dug into their pockets and suddenly began to fling paper money and coins onto the floor of the pub. There was quite a pile of cash when they were done.

"For any inconvenience we may have caused!" shouted one of them contemptuously as they staggered off into the night. A few of them paused by a street lamp to vomit. As we drove off they waved and yelled something incomprehensible.

"I suppose, because of your car, they think we're 'their kind'," I said disgustedly. "Who the hell are these creeps?"

"Tomorrow's leading politicians and businessmen," Jeremy muttered.

"Where are the cops?" I demanded.

"Oh, they'll show up, but people here undoubtedly settle their own scores," he replied somewhat ominously. "One way or the other, these kids will surely be gone before the night is done."

And indeed there was a general screech of cars roaring off. As we pulled up to the hotel, Jeremy said gently to me, "I suggest we head back to London tomorrow. I want to see what I can do about getting some kind of injunction to put a temporary stop to the sale of Beryl's house and the land that Harriet bought."

"I could check out Trevor's Shakespeare scholar," I agreed. "Maybe we can finally get somewhere with this Elizabethan lodger who calls himself Will!"

# Part Three

Part Three

# Chapter Thirteen

Trevor's Shakespeare expert was from Cambridge University, but he arranged to meet me at the famed British Library in Bloomsbury. His name was George Blendale, and apparently he had enough "pull" to have secured a private conference room so that he could show me some of the library's collections, and, of course, the original fragment that Trevor found at Grandmother Beryl's house.

From the outside, the library surprised me, for I had expected a venerable, old-fashioned landmark building. Instead, it was a "modern" structure designed in the 1970s by an architect who basically went bust before the job was done. It took about twenty years and hundreds of millions of pounds to complete. Even so, it is said that Prince Charles described the architecture as, "A collection of brick sheds groping for significance."

Furthermore, when I crossed the courtyard I was confronted with a strange, gigantic bronze sculpture of poor Isaac Newton all crouched and hunched over a compass, just like some depressed geometry student. I would have much preferred to see Newton sitting back, relaxed and contemplative, under a tree with an inspiring apple plopped in his lap.

However, once inside the library, I was delighted. For here were zillions of books in old-fashioned bookshelves; but instead of being crammed into dusty, dark archives, these shelves stood grandly in big open rooms made with white travertine marble, where wonderful windows and glass domes let in plentiful streams of light.

"Penny Nichols?" said the man sitting all alone in a quiet conference room that I peered into. "I'm George Blendale," he added, awkwardly rising from the table behind which he'd been sitting. Instantly a sheaf of papers slipped off his lap and out of their folder, scattering to the floor.

When I stooped to help him recover his lost pages, he seemed embarrassed and quickly said, "These are just my notes. The archival material is on the table."

George Blendale was a tall man who appeared to be both athletic and gawky at the same time. He had thinning brown hair, a beaky nose like an intelligent bird, and small, wire-rimmed eyeglasses. He wore a brown suit with a vest, and I noticed that his shoelaces were a bit askew. His manner was perpetually nervous, but as we conversed I realized that this was just his normal way of being and had nothing to do with me or the subject at hand.

"Now then, shall we get right down to it?" George asked, and then, as an afterthought, added, "We can't bring coffee into this room. Do you want to stop in the cafeteria before we begin?"

I told him I was fine, and he seemed relieved. Then he said, "Trevor of course told me about your interest in the fragment that he gave me. I thought I'd begin with a brief overview for you. You see, there is really very little that we know for sure about Shakespeare. Actually, you can pretty much say it in a sentence: he was born in Stratford-upon-Avon, journeyed to London where he became an actor and playwright, went back to Stratford, wrote his will and died."

"And married Anne Hathaway," I reminded him. I've noticed that for some reason, scholars are a trifle unkind about Shakespeare's wife, usually pointing out that she was a bit older than he was.

"Hem, yes," George said, opening a few large folders and tall bound books, and passing them to me to illustrate his speech. "Well, although we believe we have handwriting samples of his signature, we do not as yet have a single page of play manuscript in Shakespeare's handwriting. We have other documents to compare it to, some legal, for instance."

"The fragment Trevor gave you has a signature," I pointed out. "Does it match?"

"Ah!" George said, and now he opened up another folio and took out a single sheet. I instantly recognized it from the copy that Trevor had shown Jeremy and me.

"I didn't realize how different the original paper is," I marvelled, gazing at it.

"Indeed," George said. "In a way, we are fortunate that this fragment was not written on the sheepskin of his day, where the ink is more easily rubbed off. What we have here is definitely authentic sixteenth-century paper made of rags. It has no acid in it, which accounts for its durability."

"So, the paper is the real McCoy. Is our signature a match?" I asked curiously.

"Hem, well, you must understand that Elizabethans were not as consistent with their handwriting and spelling, which makes it much harder to definitively say yes or no," George explained. "Actually, even among the documents that we are fairly sure of, Shakespeare seems to have spelled his name differently on various occasions. So, I would be willing to entertain the possibility that the signature on yours could be real."

This was hopeful, but hardly a ringing endorsement. I don't know if it was simply George's droning voice, or his abashed manner, or just the way he kept hedging his bets, but I found myself feeling uncharacteristically impatient. "Has anyone examined the signature besides you?" I asked bluntly.

George had been gazing meditatively at the fragment, and now he seemed to be jolted awake, as if he'd been giving a lecture on a somnolent afternoon and the recess bell had suddenly rung.

"Oh, dear me, yes," he said. "I have, at Trevor's behest, called upon a panel of experts to examine this, and they are still in progress. We have consulted a handwriting analyst, various esteemed senior archivists and Shakespeare scholars who I assure you are the very best in the field. We have called upon the most renowned museum curators and language experts."

"So," I prodded, "what does everybody think? Does this seem like Shakespeare's verse?" I asked, pushing beyond the whole signature question.

"To be honest, the verse is a bit rough," George admitted, "but then, that is the very meaning of a first draft, is it not?"

He seemed to find this funny, but I didn't. He saw that I was a bit annoyed, and he quickly went on, "I could not definitely say if this was or wasn't written by Shakespeare. I do agree with Trevor that it is of interest, for it does seem to hark back to *Cardenio* and Don Quixote. Particularly the line about *the lady fair loved tales of knights*. Also, the line *A hazard of new fortunes* is a phrase that Shakespeare used in the play *King John*. So, there may be some validity to it . . . or else it is a cunning forgery."

For one wild moment I envisioned Trevor in his lair, devilishly and laboriously writing out the verse himself. But then I dismissed this picture.

"And there is the aspect of The Earl's Players," George was

saying, "which I find intriguing. It could perhaps lend credibility to the story."

"When do you think we'll have some kind of conclusion about this?" I asked eagerly.

"Oh, ho, you must understand, there are so many people involved who hopefully will come to a consensus, which is not easy to achieve in the world of Shakespeare scholarship in particular, and academia in general. They will doubtless end up framing their answer in terms of 'probability'." At my blank look he patiently explained, "That is, they will probably express their conclusions by saying: Is it *more* likely or *less* likely to be authentic?"

Now I was getting the gist of what he was trying, or perhaps not trying, to tell me.

"You don't really know, do you?" I asked.

"No," he admitted. "But in time, perhaps in a few years or decades, we may at last find out the truth."

# Chapter Fourteen

"I think Mother Nature is going to be our best ally," Jeremy informed me on the telephone.

I had been walking to the Tube station when he rang me on my mobile. Now I was standing right outside the University of London at Bloomsbury. Jeremy had been working all morning with his law associate, Rupert, on getting an injunction against the sale of Grandmother Beryl's house and the town property around it.

"If we can find some endangered species or a vernal spring or something that would be affected by development, we might possibly hold up the sale while our environmentalists do an impact study," Jeremy explained. "At the very least, that will stall things for a time."

"Thanks," I said. "You're my knight in shining armor."

"Of course, milady," he replied. "So how did you make out with your Shakespeare expert?"

"The good news is, he was impressed with the manuscript fragment and what Trevor told him, enough to start assembling a panel of experts to look into it," I reported. "The bad news is, he says that many egos are involved, and it could take—and these were his parting words—'years or decades' to come to any definite conclusion."

"I imagine that's true," Jeremy answered.

"But we haven't *got* years," I said passionately. "You and I are just going to have to come up with more evidence to clinch this thing."

"That won't be easy," Jeremy warned. "So let's not get Harriet's hopes raised too high. Whoops, Rupert is signalling me now. I gotta go. I have a meeting with a judge and I'll have to turn off my phone for awhile. Just wanted to give you an update."

"Thanks. Bye," I said quickly.

I put my phone away and continued walking down the street. It was a soft, pretty day and I felt like getting some air. When I turned the corner I came upon a little square that looked suddenly familiar.

"Of course! This is where Simon Thorne lives," I muttered to myself.

It was here that I'd first met Aunt Pen's music-hall partner. The kindly old gentleman had helped me to literally connect the dots in my family tree. He'd patiently explained my Aunt Pen's life to me, in a way that no family album or genealogy research ever could. That was how I figured out the whole story behind not only my inheritance, but Jeremy's family secrets.

Now, as I approached the charming green park, I smiled in recognition at the pretty gnarled sycamore trees whose arms reached out to one other overhead, like old-fashioned dancers doing a minuet. The park was ringed on all four sides by neat old houses with brightly painted front doors. Simon had told me that the homeowners rented bedrooms to dignified but cash-strapped lodgers, mainly students and, in Simon's case, working actors. It was a magical little square, one of the last quirky holdouts of bygone times, a cozy storybook place from another century, quiet and elegant.

I went up the short flight of steps to Simon's front door and rang the bell, tentatively at first; then, when no one answered, I rang a second time. I frowned. The last time I was here, the door was painted a bright purple. Now it was a mild-mannered beige.

I heard rapid, forceful steps, as if someone were rushing down a flight of indoor stairs. A moment later, the door burst open and a man in his twenties, dressed in navy-blue sweatpants and matching jacket, came barrelling out. He looked as surprised to see me as I was to see him.

"Hallo," he said briskly as he locked the front door behind him while still jogging in place. "Looking for someone?"

"Simon Thorne," I answered, forced to follow as he jogged down the stairs. "Doesn't he live here?"

"Sorry, no," the man said definitively, and he bounced away.

I stood uncertainly on the sidewalk, for I did not have Simon's telephone number on my phone's address book. I would have to go home to dig it up and find out where he'd gone. I'd hoped that Simon, with his knowledge of the theatre and his endless Rolodex, might be able to help me in search of Shakespeare. Now I found myself pushing away the dreadful thought that he might have died.

Just then I had an odd feeling that I was being watched, and I glanced around in time to catch sight of a woman staring at me from the house across the square. There was an aspidistra plant in the window, which the woman hastily retreated behind. This, of course, was absurd, for I could still see her behind it.

A moment later, her front door opened, and she came out with a leashed miniature bulldog. The dog was dressed in a plaid sweater that matched her own, and he had such little legs that he had to walk very, very fast to catch up with his curious mistress.

"Can I help you?" she called out in the sort of tone that always has so little to do with being helpful and everything to do with being a busybody.

"I'm looking for Simon Thorne," I said. "I'm a friend of his. Do you know where he is?"

"Simon? Oh, he's gone," she said with a certain smug satisfaction. "Took ill and collapsed right here on the sidewalk. They carted him off to the hospital and he hasn't been back since. His nephew came and took him to a care home, and sold the house. *My* daughter visits me every week," she boasted, and at first I didn't get the connection, until she added, "Sorry to think of Simon all alone now. It's what comes of never marrying nor having children of his own." This, I suspected, was her way of criticizing Simon not only for being gay, but for being an actor and, worst of all, just being *different.*

"Do you know the name of the nursing home?" I asked quickly, not wishing to encourage her to volunteer anything more of her esteemed opinion. Without hesitation she gave me the name, and I used my phone to locate it. The home wasn't very far from here; if I took the Tube it would be only a few stops away.

The nursing home was on a street of several depressing grey concrete buildings that had been erected decades ago as public housing and designed by an architect who clearly never expected anyone he loved to occupy any of his creations. It was a utilitarian series of identical, dreary structures, which would serve only to remind you how hopeless your prospects for happiness were. The care home took up the three biggest of these buildings.

Some of the other buildings were apparently still residential units, for they displayed a few halfhearted attempts to make them bearable; one even had a series of concrete balconies, which sported folding chairs and a couple of barbecues. There were signs on the corner indicating that a hospital was just around the block, so I imagined that this was why the nursing home was located here. The ground floors of the buildings across the street housed the offices of a radiologist and an osteopath; and it also did not escape my notice that there were two competing funeral parlors there as well.

"I suppose it could be worse," I thought to myself. "The home could overlook a graveyard."

Things did not improve inside. It began with the smell, which reminded me of my high-school biology lab that reeked of things pickled in formaldehyde. The walls were painted a peculiar shade of institutional green, which makes you think of the worst pea soup you ever tasted. The lighting overhead was both glaring and yet cast a limited brownish-yellow glow that left parts of the corridors quite shadowy. I had to walk past two metal counters that looked as if they were meant to be reception desks, yet no one was there to greet me or stop me.

Finally, halfway down the long hallway, I came to another reception desk, this one occupied by a security guard in a grey uniform. He was on the telephone and did not put it aside when he saw me. I took this as permission to walk right past him. That roused him.

"Sign in, Miss!" he shouted, gesturing toward yet another steel-grey desk where two nurses' aides were having an animated discussion over a lunch take-out menu. When I approached and gave them Simon's name, they shoved a grubby guest book at me, where I had to sign my name and note the time of my arrival. They told me Simon's room was number 302.

As I stepped into the elevator, I was joined by an aide pushing a wheelchair containing an elderly woman swaddled in blankets who was moaning incoherently and non-stop for the rest of the ride. I was glad to escape at the third floor, but now the corridor stank so strongly of antiseptic that I felt myself choking on it. I wondered how on earth anyone could bear to be here for an hour, let alone an entire workday or for life. As I hurried onward, I passed a janitor with his cart of dirty mops and buckets; and beyond him were several laundry trolleys loaded with soiled towels and bedding.

I turned the corner to another corridor, which was lined with various elderly people struggling to make their way with the assistance of metal walkers. One or two patients were accompanied by a nurse, and a few were attached to various feeding tubes and bags. There were some residents in wheelchairs that had been parked into corners, and as I passed, the poor souls looked up at me hopefully and then became visibly disappointed upon realizing that I had not come to see them.

I kept peering at the numbers on the doorways until I finally reached Simon's room, which was actually a ward, filled with about a dozen metal beds. Each had a simple foldable chair for visitors nearby, and a small metal table with the kind of cheap lamp that has a bendable neck.

I did not recognize any of the sad grey faces that looked back at me with limited interest. A few occupants lay on their sides, resolutely asleep. As I passed the beds, I saw that several tables bore plastic cups with plastic sippy-straws, and the occasional tiny vase with wilting visitors' flowers, and some half-eaten trays of a lunch that most of us wouldn't feed a dog.

And then I spotted a figure at the far end, in a bed tucked into a corner. He had dozed while reading, so a book lay across his

stomach. His reading light was still on, and there were two other
books on his table, which lent him a dignified air, as if he had
somehow, against all odds, carved out a little quiet world for himself. As I drew nearer, I saw a small paper cup of pills that had
been left there, untaken. Hesitantly, I peered closer at his face,
just as he stirred.

"Simon?" I whispered hopefully.

The eyes fluttered open sleepily, then widened in surprise, although he did not move a muscle when he whispered tentatively,
"Penny Nichols? Can it be you?"

Then a tired smile spread across his wan little face. He had
always been a thin, wiry man of medium height; but lying here in
bed he seemed more shriveled, as if he weighed nearly nothing at
all. Still, those hazel eyes were alert with intelligence, and his long
narrow nose, high forehead and neat, balding head made his face
seem extraordinarily long and soberly thoughtful.

"Little Penny Nichols!" he sighed, turning as I came closer and
took the visitor's chair beside him. "I haven't seen you since your
wedding, right, darling? How do you like being a married lady? Is
Jeremy treating you well, I hope?"

He was teasing me as always, which I found reassuring. He
clearly had all his marbles in place and had not been drugged into
an alternative personality. But his voice was weak, a little tremu-
lous, and I didn't like the pallor of his skin. He'd always looked
healthy and suntanned from his brisk walks around London; he
was the kind of elderly gentleman who prided himself on being
vigorous and self-sufficient. The mere fact that he'd gotten on a
train to France last year to attend my wedding had won him the
admiration of many; so I surmised that whatever happened to
him had weakened him in a rather short period of time. He was,
after all, in his mid-nineties, and perhaps he'd been more delicate

than any of us knew, for he was the kind of man who carefully hid his ailments from his friends instead of complaining about them.

"Jeremy's great, and I'm happy," I reported, then asked tentatively, "and how are you, Simon?"

"I'd like to sit up," he said instead of answering. "Can you get the pillow up against the headboard for me?"

I reached out behind him and arranged the pillow, managing to discreetly help him raise himself up without offending him by an offer of more assistance. He saw me glance at the cup of pills and he said wryly, "The new nurse is a bit dim. She's supposed to wake me when it's time to take those. Darling, do you think you could get me some water?"

I took my own unopened water bottle from my handbag, and poured some water into his cup. He quickly swallowed his pills.

"Good water," he said when he was done. "You can't imagine what the tap tastes like here."

"Yes I can," I found myself saying, and he glanced up at me with a more sharp-eyed smile of complicity. Simon is one of the few people I know who prefers the truth to a lie, despite his life's long work in the artificial atmosphere of the theatre. "What happened?" I persisted.

"The old ticker, of course," he replied, lying back on his pillow and coughing a bit, as if the mere thought exhausted him. "And naturally all those cigarettes from my smoky past didn't help."

He paused, then said thoughtfully, "I always thought they'd find me dead in my own parlor, in that nice chair by the fireplace. But no, they picked me up off the sidewalk like yesterday's trash."

"I ran into your neighbor from across the street," I said forthrightly.

He rolled his eyes. "That poor creature has never had a single original thought of her own," he sighed. "She and her wretched daughter. Mercifully the pair of them were not at home when I hit the deck. I at least deprived them of the pleasure of that spectacle. They had to get it all second-hand."

While he was attempting to entertain me, I was covertly sizing up his situation. Despite his cheerful attitude, I sensed that he was depressed and a bit nervous, which was unusual for him. He'd always been full of high voltage in the way that actors often are—in fact, he was the kind of man who put energy into a room, not the type who drained it out.

But now he himself seemed drained in the way that a flower or an animal is when they haven't had any nourishment or sunlight. I knew that Simon's former tenants, who were mostly acting students, were what really kept him going; he'd often told me he leased rooms on a month-by-month basis just in order to see the new talent come and go, and to hear the theatre gossip. Stuck in this nursing home, I saw that he'd been deprived of the very things that, for him, made life worth living. And I wondered who could have thought that this was a good idea.

"Simon, are you very ill?" I asked, wanting to give the nephew the benefit of the doubt in case Simon was worse off than he appeared and required vigilant care; although, judging by the cup of pills that had been dumped here, I didn't see that he was getting much useful supervision.

"I'm stuck here because I can't walk," Simon answered. "The minute you are unable to shower on your own, you're done for. Make sure you and Jeremy go to the gym every week, darling. You want to stay ambulatory as long as possible."

At this moment, a nurse entered the room. She had what I can only describe as dark-grey skin and a dour mouth that did not once attempt a smile, even when Simon introduced me to her as "the great-niece of my old dancing partner".

Very perfunctorily, she took his blood pressure and his pulse, listened to his breathing and heart with a stethoscope, and noted a few things on his chart.

"When has he last seen the doctor?" I asked quietly. She didn't answer right away and at first I thought she hadn't heard me. "Nurse?" I said, rolling my eyes at Simon when she didn't even look up.

It was the first time that Simon didn't look amused; instead, he looked frightened, and even shrank back against his pillow when the nurse finally fixed him with a beady stare.

"Doctor will be in tomorrow morning," she said shortly, and went on her way to her other luckless charges in the ward, most of whom appeared drugged into a stupor.

"She's new. She won't win any personality contests," Simon whispered to me when she was out of earshot, "but at least she doesn't give you the wrong pills or the wrong shot. You should see what the previous nurse did to the fellow who had that bed across the way last week."

"Simon, what about your nephew?" I asked.

"What about him?" Simon said grimly. "The boy lives in Canada. He showed up when he thought I was at death's door and on the verge of leaving him something. He talked me into selling my house because it would be too expensive for me to get home care. Said this is the best I could afford. That way, I still have a little bit of money left from the sale of the house. I call it my mad money. I'm sure my beastly nephew is hoping I'll kick off before I find anything to spend it on. The boy won't be back here until it's time to bury me."

His voice trailed off. "What brought you here, Penny darling?"

he asked finally. When I told him about Trevor Branwhistle's theory, Simon perked up for the first time today. He had met Trevor when he performed with Aunt Pen in Port St. Francis that one time in the 1970s, and Simon had enjoyed listening to Trevor's radio shows on the BBC ever since.

"Shakespeare a lodger at Beryl's house!" Simon breathed in awe. "Could it really be true?"

"I'm trying to find out," I replied, just as the nurse returned.

"Simon Thorne?" she said, as if we all hadn't even spoken before. She was checking a sheaf of printed-out computer pages and, without even looking up, said, "They're moving you to the first floor tomorrow. Do you have any things you want sent down there?"

"No!" Simon cried in distress. "This is a nice bed. I get good light from the window. Why should I want to move? The first floor is all dark."

"Orders," said the nurse.

"But why?" Simon quavered. "I'm all right. I haven't done anything wrong."

"They need to put someone else here," was all she would say. I saw that Simon had begun to visibly tremble now. The nurse did not appear to notice.

"Why can't you put your new arrival in the bed downstairs?" I asked bluntly. I didn't want to get Simon in trouble with the people he must live with on a daily basis, but this was just too much.

"Because the new patient needs more supervision than he can get on one," the nurse said incredulously, looking at me as if she were about to finish that sentence by saying, *stupid!*"

Then she went off, her rubber-soled shoes squeaking on the dirty linoleum. Something else in motion on the floor caught my eye—it was a silverfish slithering across the linoleum until it disappeared into a crack in the wall. Simon hadn't noticed.

"They have bedbugs on the first floor," he said fearfully.

"Right. That's it," I said decisively. "Simon. That mad money. Are you mad enough yet?"

# Chapter Fifteen

Okay, look. When I started that day, I had absolutely no inkling that I was going to spend the latter part of the afternoon busting an old friend out of a nursing home. It's not the kind of thing you plan. It's the kind of thing you do just as I did . . . in a sudden burst of outrage.

So, first I told Simon about Trevor Branwhistle's home for retired thespians.

"It's a nice old Priory with a lovely garden, and they've got young student nurses from the nearby hospital," I told him. "The actors there seem to be doing very well, and some of them are even able to perform this summer. But it's way out in Cornwall. Would you want to leave London?" I asked, knowing how much the city's venerable theatres meant to him.

Simon pondered this very carefully. Then he looked up at me so trustfully that I nearly wept. "Do you think it's a good place for me, Penny dear?" he asked.

"Yes," I said. "It's got fresh air and better food and nicer people. I don't even know if I can get you in, but I'll try if you'd like me to."

Simon took a deep breath. "Yes," he said decisively.

"Should I speak to your doctor first, to see if you're up to such a trip?" I asked.

"My regular doctor died a year ago. That's how I ended up with this crowd," Simon said. "I don't like the doctor who replaced him."

"Want me to call mine?" I asked. Simon nodded, looking suddenly too scared to speak.

"Will they let you?" he whispered. "They don't like inconveniences here."

"Too bad," I said, hitting my speed dial.

I have learned that there are times like these when the inheritance I got from Great-Aunt Penelope comes in handy, and part of it is being able to get a doctor to show up when *you* want him, instead of when it's convenient for him. I am not ashamed to say I used all the influence I possibly could that day. I didn't even have to actually remind my doctor of the contribution Jeremy and I had made to his new wing at the hospital in Belgravia. He just heard it in my tone when I said, "This is critical," and he answered briskly, "I'm on my way."

While I was waiting for him to come, I called up Trevor and told him that my good friend Simon Thorne had fallen ill. Could he find a bed for him? When he heard the name, Trevor quickly consulted with his staff.

"If he doesn't mind sharing a room, it will be all right," Trevor said. "Bring him as soon as he's ready."

My doctor arrived quietly, as if he were an ordinary visitor. After he examined Simon and consulted the charts, he stepped aside and told me in a low murmur that although Simon was quite seriously ill, he could certainly make the trip to Cornwall, if he wanted to. When I mentioned the name of Branwhistle's Actors' Home and the hospital in Port St. Francis, my doctor looked them up on his computer and said that they had excellent facilities for Simon.

"May I make a suggestion, off the record?" the doctor said to me quietly. "This place he's in now has a reputation for not being very agreeable at discharge. They use protocol to try to keep their occupancy level high so they can continue to qualify for funding. I am willing to sign any medical and legal papers necessary, but I suggest you get the patient all dressed and ready to go the moment I give you the word. Have a car ready, too. Don't depend on this place to help you or make it easy to get out."

That was all I needed to hear. I trotted right back to Simon's bed, where he sat looking like an alert little bird in a nest. "Okay, Simon," I said. "You got the green light. The doctor's gonna file some papers for you, which you'll need to sign, and the minute he does we're out of here. Are you up for a caper?"

Simon's eyes were bright with excitement. "Certainly," he whispered with that trustful look.

"Where are your clothes?" I asked. He nodded toward a scuffed set of old lockers at the far end of the corridor. They were all half-size, and couldn't store much. He handed me a key. I opened the lock and pulled out his pitifully small bundle of personal items, including clothes and a pair of shoes.

"Simon, where are all your other possessions from home?" I asked.

"My nephew sold most of them. The rest is in storage," he said.

"We'll get it later, okay?" I said.

"Okay," he whispered.

"Want me to help you dress now?" I asked.

"There's a nice aide—that fellow over there," Simon said. "His name is Omar. He'll help me."

I found the young Pakistani man assisting a patient who was

trying to make his way back to bed with a walker. Once Omar heard that Simon needed help, he asked no questions and hurried over to him. I stepped out into the corridor to arrange for a car.

Because Jeremy had warned me that he was going to be in a meeting with a judge, where all mobile phones had to be off, I could only keep checking to see if he had e-mailed me back yet. But there was no news from Jeremy.

The one new message I had was from Rollo. It said: *Hello, Pen. Agent Rollo here. How goes it in Cornwall? Always loved that house. Got any new and dangerous assignments for me?*

I hesitated, then phoned him. "Hey, Rollo?" I said. "I'm in London. A friend of mine here needs a ride. Remember Simon Thorne, the song-and-dance man at my wedding? Right, Aunt Pen's pal. Well, I'm busting him out of a nursing home today. Can you pick us up and drive us to my town house?"

Now, the advantage of having an eccentric cousin (who's more the age of an uncle) and who has lived a rather roguish existence all his life (in which he owes you, and your husband, a favor or two), is that he can be counted upon to do a strange deed with little or no questions asked. It is one of the things I like best about Rollo. There was only a brief pause and then he said easily, "Right. Will it be as dangerous and profitable as the last escapades?"

"No, not nearly," I said.

"Hmm. Does Jeremy know about this?"

"Nope."

"Delightful. What's the address?" Rollo asked. When I told him, he said, "Ah. I'm actually not far from you at all. Be there in minutes."

"Thanks." I rang off, and while I stood there in an alcove of the corridor answering other e-mails, the doctor returned, saying the papers had been properly filed, and he'd given Simon some copies. So now Simon could go.

I thanked the doctor and he said briskly, "Not at all." Then his beeper sounded, and he rushed off.

Moments later, two nurses went by without noticing me, just as one was saying, "There's a strange woman around who's trying to take a patient out. See if you can head her off while we assess the situation," she added meaningfully.

Hastily I got off the phone and rushed to Simon's side. He was sitting in his guest chair, fully dressed in the one suit of clothes that his nephew had left there for him. It looked incongruously formal to me. Simon allowed himself a faint smile.

"I think my nephew imagined I'd be leaving here with an undertaker, instead of a friend," he explained.

"Well, screw him," I found myself saying, surprising even me. Simon only chuckled.

"Did they bring the wheelchair, like Omar asked?" I said, looking around.

"Of course not, darling," Simon said. "His supervisor went off in a lather about it."

I glanced across the room, where an elderly gentleman was being wheeled back to his bed by a young female aide. I barely waited until the patient was in bed. Then I swooped down on the aide.

"Thanks, we've been waiting *hours* for that," I said, taking the wheelchair so forcefully from her that she only stepped back and then said in bewilderment, "You're welcome." Apparently she wasn't in the loop . . . yet.

"Come on, Simon, your chariot awaits. Get in," I said, offering him my arm and helping him.

"They made me take a sedative," he confided in me. "So if I doze off, don't be alarmed. Just keep pedalling."

I wheeled him down the hallway so fast that I didn't even stop when the elevator door opened. A laundress was arriving with fresh towels as I barrelled toward her. Upon seeing me, she hastily pulled her cart out of the elevator. Which proves that there is some value in having a lunatic look in your eye. People do tend to clear the way for you.

I shoved Simon's chair inside, groped for the button and closed the elevator doors just as I heard a nurse's indignant voice saying, "Miss! Oh, Miss!"

Simon looked as if he was still a bit afraid of the personnel here. "She's whopping mad," he whispered.

"We don't care," I said. But the truth is, I was worried about what I'd find in the lobby when the elevator doors re-opened. An array of security guards with a cop waiting to arrest me? I pulled out my mobile and dialed Rollo again. He said he was just turning on to the street where we were.

"Great. We're approaching the lobby now," I said to him. "Get yourself right in front of the main door."

"Check. I'm here already," Rollo replied.

The elevator landed. The doors opened. No army yet. I pushed Simon's chair out and headed speedily through the lobby with a nonchalant expression on my face.

I got about halfway across when one of the guards noticed me, but he didn't make a move until the phone rang at the reception desk. A nurse and another guard came running toward him. They conferred hastily, then the three of them headed my way, and the guard called out, "Hold on, there!"

I steadfastly ignored him and I never stopped wheeling. They didn't catch up with me until I was very near the front door.

"Miss, stop! You can't do that," the nurse declared accusingly.

I looked her straight in the eye. "Oh, yes I can," I said. "You've got all the paperwork you need. But here is a copy, just for you."

Right on cue, Simon handed me one of the copies of the release letter from the doctor, which Simon had signed, and which had been properly witnessed. I snatched it now and thrust it at the nurse.

"Read it and weep," I said as the automatic doors slid open. I shoved Simon forward, gliding out and giving him the first gulp of fresh air he'd had in months. I trundled ahead determinedly, having immediately spotted Rollo, who was standing by his car with the back door open, just as I'd asked.

As soon as I waved to him, Rollo leaped forward. Simon handed me his little bundle, and then Rollo scooped Simon up in his arms and deposited him into the back seat. He shut the door, and Simon locked it. I hopped into the front passenger seat as Rollo rushed around the car to the driver's side, and we locked those doors, too. Rollo turned on the car and floored it, just as if we'd pulled a bank job.

Believe it or not, the security guards had chased after us, and one of them even pounded on the trunk of the car as we pulled away. But it was all for show, because they hadn't called the police, which meant that we must have done it right.

When we were already halfway across the city, and heading for my town house, I got an e-mail from Jeremy: *What's up? Signed, Devoted Husband.*

I e-mailed back: *Absconded with Simon Thorne. He's coming to Cornwall with us. Love, Your Outlaw Wife.*

# Part Four

# Chapter Sixteen

High season in Cornwall was a completely different world from the one we'd left. Those nice, empty highways were now clogged with summer traffic that barely crawled along, with cars full of shrieking kiddies and frazzled drivers. People handled this in different ways. Some stuck their bare feet out the window, even up on the dashboard, while their radios blared. Other drivers darted in and out of each lane, as if somehow this would enable them to fly over the traffic jam. And then of course, there were the vacationers who *did* fly over everyone, in private helicopters and small planes. It all made for a great deal of startling noise and soot in a land that had been so austere and quiet.

Meanwhile, tour buses and ferries plied the coast, disgorging day-trippers who were out seeking quick, cheap thrills in a couple of hours until they were summoned back to their group to move on. Mercifully, Port St. Francis wasn't considered a hot spot, but even so, the traffic on its main street had practically come to a standstill, making it almost a pedestrian-only zone; for even here, the roads were thronging with clumps of tourists who'd straggled off the beaten path.

Ensconced in the Dragonetta, Jeremy and I inched along in the traffic as we were returning from the Priory, where we had just left Simon Thorne in his new surroundings.

"Hey, Simon seems to like his new home," I said proudly.

We had already spent the morning arranging Simon's books and possessions in a room he would share with an actor who'd once done a costume-drama TV series. I'd put flowers in a vase on Simon's bedside table, and presented him with a nice mahogany box where he could keep his personal things—eyeglass case, pill-box, mail, etc. Then I unpacked his theatre scrapbook and put it in the drawer there.

Simon watched me do all this with a grateful and amused smile. Nora, the young nurse, personally escorted Simon on his tour of the grounds' pretty patio and gardens. I'd glanced apprehensively at Simon as he took in his surroundings, for he looked a little pale from the long ride and from the whole upheaval. I had a moment's worry of whether I'd done the right thing to uproot him from London, which had always been his home.

But for most of his life he'd been a travelling trouper who'd played theatres in all the far-flung corners of the British empire, so he seemed to take this as yet another role for a working actor. He waved regally at me as he was wheeled around, and I watched his expression change from wary to highly pleased when Nora informed him, "I must tell you that I'm *very* impressed with your 'C.V.' Penny says you have a great scrapbook of those wonderful gigs you played. Did you really meet Noel Coward?"

Simon's face looked like a small boy's as he beamed with abashed pleasure. "Certainly, young lady!" he said with great dignity. "Mr. Coward told me my rendition of *Red Peppers* was, and I quote, 'bright as a button'."

By lunchtime Trevor Branwhistle was on hand to personally

welcome Simon. Both men immediately engaged in a very animated conversation about the latest version of *Hamlet* currently in London. They invited Jeremy and me to join them in the dining hall for lunch, but we were eager to head back into town and get some supplies for our stay at Shannon and Geoff's cottage.

So I gave Simon a kiss, and told him I'd be back to visit soon. He seized my hand, squeezed it, and said with bright eyes, "Darling Penny, you are a treasure."

"Simon will be just fine," Jeremy assured me now, as if reading my mind. We were driving away from town and heading for Shannon and Geoff's farm.

"Good thing we found Simon when we did," I said grimly. "I don't think he was going to last much longer where he was."

"So what kind of bargain did you have to make with Rollo to get his help busting Simon out?" Jeremy asked suspiciously.

"Um, well, somehow Rollo got wind of the fact that Grandmother's house in Cornwall is up for grabs," I said, flushing a bit guiltily. "And Rollo really does have fond memories of summering at Port St. Francis as a kid."

"Rollo has fond memories of every freebie he ever got," Jeremy answered.

"Well, he said he could do with 'a bit of Cornish R&R', so I asked Shannon if she had any space for Rollo. She's renting him a small cottage next to ours," I blurted out, then added hastily, "but it's only for a week."

Jeremy rolled his eyes, then changed the subject. "You do realize," he said, "now that we've committed to spending July in Cornwall, we've also committed to solving this case. Otherwise, they'll lynch us. So—the question is, can it be done?"

"Only if we come up with more than I've found so far," I admitted gloomily. "Some scrap of evidence that it was really the Bard who showed up in Port St. Francis, let alone in Grandma's house! Trevor isn't going to like it, but that fragment of manuscript isn't as earth-shattering as he'd hoped."

I sighed. "How'd you make out with the stay-of-execution for Grandma's house?"

"It has to go through a few legal hoops and get signed off by a judge. Even so, it would just be a temporary halt to the sale of the house and property," Jeremy reminded me. "We'll know soon if it's going to come through."

"Okay," I said, leaning my head back and gazing out the window.

We followed the directions that Shannon had given me, and were now passing her farmland, which was sprawled out across a series of lush, green undulating hills. Wooden fences and gates rimmed fertile fields with neat rows of plantings, and a horse paddock and rich pastures for the sheep and cows to graze on. Shannon and Geoff resided at a great big rambling old farmhouse that sat close to the road, beyond which were dirt paths that led to barns, silos and various-sized outbuildings that had once belonged to tenant farmworkers. Our cottage was the largest of these, at the end of its own unpaved driveway. It was tucked away in a nice corner of land that eventually bordered the property which the town had acquired through Harriet near Grandmother Beryl's.

When I got out of the car, I stopped short in delight. Parked on the lawn were two bicycles, one blue, one rose-colored. The blue one had a saddlebag; the rose one had an antique country basket in front. I squealed with delight, and Jeremy beamed, proud of the little surprise he'd arranged for me.

"His-and-her bikes!" I exclaimed. "They're adorable, so old-fashioned!"

"They only look old-fashioned," Jeremy corrected. "They're brand-new, see the gears? The whole thing is ergonomically balanced. Try it out. The guy at the shop in town said you might want to stop in after you've ridden it a bit, and he'll adjust it for your height. You have long legs, but I think this looks like it's right for you."

"Are these ours for keeps?" I asked, drawing nearer, for I saw my name painted on the fender at the front.

"Yep. Best way to get around town," Jeremy advised. "The guy in the grocery store told me there won't be a car-parking space available on the street until September. An exaggeration, perhaps, but why struggle? Just don't forget to lock your cycle when you leave it in town. There are plenty of bike racks in Port St. Francis for that."

I was already wheeling around the front yard to test it out. "This is perfect!" I cried. "I'm on my way to the hall of records to see if old Will Shakespeare got a traffic ticket or something."

"Have some lunch first," Jeremy advised, reading a note tacked to the front door. "Shannon says we can have use of the cottage vegetable garden as long as we tend it ourselves. She says she left us some ham and eggs and goat's cheese in the refrig. We can make a hell of a chef's salad."

My stomach growled. "Okay!" I said, hopping off and knocking down the kickstand.

Well. We ate. And then, we fell asleep from the long drive. And then we said, heck, let's go for a swim at the town beach. And then we collected seashells to decorate the cottage with, and we stopped for an ice cream cone. And if you've ever had ice cream in England, well, that's about as dreamy and creamy as it gets anywhere. My cone was lined with melted dark chocolate, and the ice cream was that pure fresh vanilla with the little bean bits in it, and the whole thing was topped with crushed hazelnuts.

We then went down to the pier where the fishermen were selling the catch of the day, and we bagged a fish for dinner. After that I barely had the strength to pedal back home.

And how sweet it was to return to the quiet little cottage that sat in its lush garden away from the roar of the sea, with only the sound of birds chirping in the trees around us. Jeremy loved the rough wood table in the kitchen where we dumped out the groceries, and he set to work chopping vegetables, making me read aloud to him from the cookbooks that my dad had given him.

We spent the next day working like field hands in our own little garden, which had several varieties of lettuce, spinach, and other vegetable and herb plantings, some still under cold frame.

"Absolutely no pesticides are to be used here!" Shannon warned us when she and Geoffrey stopped by to see how we were doing. She showed us how to use a spray of water-and-garlic instead.

Geoff handed Jeremy a large, beautiful head of lettuce. "No chemicals. The only thing you have to worry about with *my* lettuce is that maybe a rabbit pissed on it. That won't kill you."

"As long as that's all the rabbit does," Jeremy said wickedly. Geoff grinned, and showed Jeremy how to let the ducks wander about in the garden paths picking off some of the pests. While we were strolling about knee-high in vegetables, a curious bird landed on Geoff's shoulder and then flew away again.

Geoff shrugged. "They get used to you," he said.

I had never been on a farm before, so I guess I can be excused for spending the better part of a week learning how to milk a cow, and collect eggs from bossy hens, and herd sheep (Tip: let the sheepdogs lead you, they know where to go) and how to divide the roots of seedlings to plant vegetables in raised beds.

Then I would go visit Simon to make sure he was getting along all right, and after that, Jeremy and I would check out the nearby courthouse. We scoured old legal files about Port St. Francis, hoping to discover that Shakespeare had sued somebody out here or poached deer—anything to prove he'd been around.

In the later afternoon, we'd go down to Grandmother Beryl's cove for a swim, and we'd ransack the house to see if we could turn up anything that Harriet and Trevor may have overlooked, like a diary by old Will, or a letter or a sonnet, or even one of those starched ruffs with his name sewn in the tag . . . I was desperate to find anything that could be linked to him. But there was nothing. Zippo.

We'd bicycle back to the cottage at sunset, where I'd collapse in a hammock in the back garden, and laze about until I got up the energy to help Jeremy with dinner. At night, we lay on our backs together on the patio chairs to watch the stars spread themselves across the sky with stunning clarity, the likes of which you never see in well-lit cities.

"This is a good life. I think I want to be a farmer's wife forever," I declared as we climbed into the big bed and snuggled under the pale, undyed linens and hemp bedspread. We didn't stir until the farmyard rooster squawked about the sun before it was humanly possible to do so.

And thus we were, in our little Eden in merry olde England . . . until one day when the party came to an unceremonious end.

# Chapter Seventeen

"The earl has gone bung!" Harriet announced on the telephone the next morning, in a strange, unusually urgent tone. "He's finally agreed to sell that big plot of land adjacent to the town property at your grandmother's. He's been waffling back and forth on this, but my sources say the Mosley brothers got to him at last. So, the pressure on the town to fast-track this deal is enormous. If you're going to come up with something, it's got to be now."

She really sounded rattled, so I said promptly, "Okay, we'll put it into high gear."

But when I hung up, I had no idea what we'd do. Jeremy had just come out of the shower, toweling his hair dry, and I filled him in. "We can't just wait around for some injunction to come through," I said, adding dramatically, "this train has left the station and it's got no brakes."

"Steady on," Jeremy counseled. "I agree that we've got to do more. But let's not do anything foolish. I'd better head back to London and stay one step ahead of the Mosleys, to make sure they don't interfere with the injunction. You want to come with me?"

"Hmmm?" I said absently. "No, I think one of us had better stay here and push on the local front."

Jeremy eyed me suspiciously. "What are you thinking?" he asked.

"Oh, I just thought I'd check out the local library records," I fibbed. "You never know."

Actually, oddly enough, in the end it wasn't a lie. Not really. I *did* go to a library—but it wasn't the Port St. Francis Library. It just so happened that the day Jeremy left for London was the one day of the week when the earl's mansion was open to the public for a house tour. Now, I certainly couldn't wait for Jeremy to return. I *had* to go that day. Therefore, the library I found myself in was the earl's.

His grand manor house, which looked more like a castle to me, sat serenely facing its own private headland that jutted out to the sea. If the earl wanted to, he could look to his right and see Grandmother Beryl's house and cove. But the earl's property also extended in the other direction, encompassing over a hundred fifty acres of woodland, streams, meadows, farmland and spectacular formal gardens.

I arrived at the earl's place on my bicycle, just as a tour bus was entering the main gate. I followed the bus up the front drive through meticulous parkland, and tucked my bike under a tree. The tour group exited the bus and was herded together in the gravel driveway, where I joined them. Together we shuffled forward like polite buffalo, while the guide, a rather snippy Scotswoman with blonde-grey hair informed us that the house had thirty-nine rooms, not including the "recent" addition in 1802 of a tower. She made us line up like school-kids before she let us inside through the big front doors that were flanked by giant lions.

"This is the great hall," the guide announced, as we stood in a very imposing main foyer. "It was used for important banquets when it was built in 1079. This staircase was built later, in the mid-1800s, of Carrara marble imported from Italy. Above, you see the visitors' gallery, and these portraits are all important family members, extending throughout the centuries."

We all craned our necks to view paintings—which the guide called "pictures"—of various ladies with lace-trimmed white bosoms, and men with pencil-thin moustaches and wary expressions in their eyes.

"Note the green paint on the walls," the guide intoned, "which originally got their color from the use of arsenic. And to your right, we see the first parlor. Note the crimson damask fabric on the wall, which was quite the rage in the nineteenth century."

We continued to shuffle about obediently with sufficient awe, as the guide pointed out a Van Dyck here and a Gainsborough there and a Wedgwood vase over yonder. The dining room was a "saloon" and the music room was "the round room" and the view out of each window was spectacular.

Finally we reached the enormous library. While the tour guide nattered on in breathless admiration of the statistics of the earl's collection—how many books it held (squillions), how long they'd been mouldering there on the shelf (eons), how the loyal servants had rescued the books from a house fire in the 1800s (truly heroic)—I found myself staring across the velvet ropes into an adjacent alcove, where the manor house's ancient books were kept in a series of tall shelves with lattice doors.

While the guide went into the history of the King James Bible, I casually squinted at the volumes in the alcove, and saw that among these books were account records, meticulously kept year by year, down through the centuries. The section on the 1600s was right ahead of me, and as I peered at the spines, one volume in particular caught my eye, for it was labelled *The Earl's Players.*

I stifled a gasp, quietly transfixed for so long that I scarcely noticed the tour group moving on without me. They followed the guide into the next room without ever realizing that I'd been left behind; and I heard their voices successively fading away as they continued from room to room, until there was nothing left but silence, the empty library, and me. And that roped-off alcove.

It was inches away. Quick as a cat, I ducked under the rope and slipped into the darkened cubbyhole. A weak shaft of light came from a very narrow, stained-glass window. I knew I wouldn't have much time, so I grabbed *The Earl's Players* and opened it right there, gently but quickly turning the pages.

In neat, faded but legible columns it listed every payment made to the actors during their stay here. Rapidly I scanned the names of each actor, until I came to the one that I'd been seeking: *Willim Shakspere, being also of the name Rudd Marchman.* After that was a list of his wages for a period of about three months, similar to the wages of the other actors. Then, suddenly, Willim's wages ceased, even though the other players continued to perform for the rest of the year.

I heard footsteps echoing across the ancient floors, and I froze for a moment until they veered away from me and continued down a corridor. But I could tell that a guard was making the rounds. Quickly I whipped out my phone and photographed the pertinent pages of the book.

I snapped and snapped, then softly shut the ledger and slipped it back in its place on the shelf. It happened all in one smooth motion, right up to ducking back under the velvet rope and slipping across the main library to other rooms, so that I could get away from the guard, whose footsteps warned that he was now marching toward me.

From the corridor windows I could see that my group had assembled on the lawn to admire the gardens as the tour came to an end. I caught up with them while they were pussyfooting through the magnolias and camellias. The guide was just informing everyone about the gift shop, and the tea room where we could purchase refreshments. The group applauded the guide, who nodded and said goodbye to each one of us now as we shuffled past.

When I sidled by her, she seemed faintly puzzled, as if she couldn't quite remember me going from room to room, but I just beamed at her and then headed with all good speed for the parking lot with others from the group.

I climbed back on my bicycle and pedaled out to the road that would take me back to the cottage. But as I cycled past verdant meadows, I spotted a strange figure ducking in and out from behind trees. It could have been any member of the earl's staff, perhaps a gardener, yet something in the man's appearance seemed so out of time, simply too leisurely for this world.

He continued moving through the fields and trees, his motions more like that of a cautious deer than a human out for a stroll. Some instinct of mine made me dismount my bicycle and push it off the road, into a shrubby, grassy area, so that I could hide behind a hedge and get a closer look at the man as he emerged from the shadows and into the dappled sunlight.

He was clad in a dusty-green hiking outfit, a jacket and matching pants with a funny brown hat on his head; and his pants were tucked into a pair of knee-high brown boots. The hair that stuck out from beneath his floppy-brimmed hat was reddish brown in color, and he had a growth of matching stubble on his chin.

I continued to follow him on foot. We were very near the dividing line between the earl's land and Grandmother Beryl's property, and when we reached the end of the earl's estate, the man stopped.

A pair of large, very old-fashioned binoculars hung around his neck, dangling on his chest, and he now raised them to his eyes to peer into Grandmother Beryl's front yard.

I followed his gaze to see what he was so intent upon. But suddenly, he lowered his binoculars and made a peculiar grimace. A second later he raised his hands and cupped his mouth, emitting a strange sound, like a whistle through his teeth, "*OO-eee-ooo-ee-whooo!*"

It was a plaintive kind of warble, and I wondered if he was signalling someone or was just plain bonkers. But a second later, I heard the exact same cry come from a bird that was now flickering through that tree. "*OO-eee-ooo-ee-whooo!*"

"Good God," I thought. "I'm tailing a bird-watcher." And something in the man's luxurious manner clicked for me. "Why, I bet that's the earl!" I whispered to myself, as if I, too, had stumbled upon a rare species. I was willing to bet that he came from a long line of naturalists and bird aficionados.

I huddled out of his view, watching him as he tromped along the border, not quite crossing it, but gazing raptly at his bird. Then he sat upon a rock, and pulled out a small, leather-covered notebook, in which he seemed to be sketching or jotting something down. He continued doing so, until his bird eventually flew away.

Then the earl rose, put his book back in his breast pocket, and went tromping back into the trees, sounding just like a deer crashing through the underbrush, until at last he vanished from my sight.

I pushed my bicycle back on the road, but paused to quickly

e-mail Jeremy: *Bagged some info on Earl's Players, especially one Willim Shakspere! Seems he was using an alias while he was in Cornwall. The other name he used was Rudd Marchman. Maybe W.S. was on the lam from the law? Perhaps those stories about deer-poaching were true? See if you can find out any arrests, lawsuits et cetera involving someone named Rudd Marchman. Photos attached. P.S. I think I just spotted said earl in the woods. He is one strange bird.*

Jeremy must have had his mobile phone in his hand and therefore received my message right away; for within minutes he shot back with a response: *OK, will investigate the Bard's alias. But please, dear wife, do stay out of the earl's woods and wherever else you were when you dug this info up. I have a feeling it's not exactly public record, is it?*

Well, honestly. Could anyone really expect me to abandon the scent I'd just picked up? I had to find out what it was that the budding Bard was hiding from, or trying to keep secret.

What had Shakespeare done to make it necessary for him to disappear for all those years which historians, even today, can't account for?

# Chapter Eighteen

My next clue came to me in a truly unexpected way. Simon had previously asked me to arrange for his things to be taken out of storage, and sent to him at the Actors' Home at the Priory. Nora, the nurse, telephoned to let me know that they had arrived, and she said it would be a good idea for someone Simon knew to help him sort them. So I had already agreed to come to the Priory that day.

"He's adjusting really well," Nora told me when I arrived. "He loves coming down to the main hall to watch our actors rehearse for the Shakespeare fête."

I came upon Simon where he was sitting in his wheelchair on the patio, with his face raised to the sun just like a sunflower. He already had better color in his cheeks now, and his eyes were bright and alert; and when he saw me he clapped his hands with pleasure.

"Darling Penny!" he said. "I didn't expect you to visit so soon. Hasn't the weather been kind to us?" I gave him a light kiss on the forehead and he gestured for me to take a seat on one of the iron lawn chairs nearby.

"Isn't Nora a gem?" he continued. "She's engaged to be married, you know. But her young man—he's a fisherman—is struggling like so many in Port St. Francis, and they do so want a little house of their own to raise a family. She's been showing me the estate ads, and I can't believe what it costs to buy even a little biscuit box to live in out here!"

"She says you're helping Trevor rehearse the performers," I said as I sat down.

"Yes, there are some lovely young acting students but they are nervous as cats," Simon said.

"Oh, I thought the older actors from the home were doing the show," I said, confused.

Simon's eyes twinkled. "Well, darling, we can't have the whole programme done by geezers like me," he said forthrightly. "Half of them can't remember their lines, and the other half will be up past their bedtime. *Someone* more youthful is going to have to guide them on and off stage. As for our audience—you and Jeremy *are* coming, aren't you?"

"Oh, yes, I bought those tickets ages ago," I said.

Simon wagged a finger at me. "It's not enough just to pay for the tickets," he admonished. "We need the bums in the seats, if you'll pardon my French. We want the theatre so jam-packed that the press will *have* to write it all up. Fingers crossed that the old theatre doesn't collapse on the crowd in the middle of Juliet's balcony scene."

"We'll be there," I promised. I went over the list of his possessions that had arrived, and he told me to donate some of them to the Legacy Society's thrift shop. The rest would be sent to his room.

"And now, Penny dear, tell me all about your latest case. Did you and Jeremy find out whether Shakespeare slept in Beryl's bedroom?" Simon said waggishly.

I swore him to secrecy before updating him about the alias I'd discovered. "If I could just figure out what happened to Will out here," I said, "maybe I'd have a breakthrough. In the first place, why did Shakespeare leave his work in London *and* his family in Stratford for all those years?"

Simon listened attentively, then cocked his head thoughtfully. "Well, let's see. A man hits the road when the creditors are after him. Or, when the law is after him. Or, he's chasing another girl. Or, he's already chased a girl, and her father and brothers are chasing *him* with a shotgun. At least, that's how it works in the theatre."

"I've been all through the local records," I said gloomily. "Nothing to indicate why he came here and joined The Earl's Players. I've found out that it was during a year when the plague was so terrible in London that its theatres were shut down, so actors had to go on tour in the provinces to perform . . . or else starve. Maybe he left London simply because of that. And it's possible he couldn't find a gig in Stratford, either."

"Ah, yes, we thespians always get thrown out of work at the most inconvenient times," Simon observed. "So let's assume that he came to Cornwall in search of employment, and joined up with the household players at the earl's."

"Then why did he leave his nice job here so abruptly?" I said, perplexed. "The players went on performing a great deal longer than Will."

"You know more about this sleuthing game than me, Penny dear, but has it ever occurred to you that we are right at this moment sitting on top of a possible source of information?" Simon inquired.

I gave him a baffled look, and he continued, "We are in an old Priory, darling. And Trevor told me that the basement is stuffed to the gills with ancient church records. Baptisms, marriages, funerals, the works. It may be a long shot, but—"

I jumped up and threw my arms around him, and Simon, looking pleased, calmly told me which staircase to take down to the basement. Trevor was in London for the day, which was just as well. I was fairly certain he'd allow me total access to all these boxes and boxes of documents. Right?

My research took the better part of the day, during which I inhaled the dust of more centuries than I'd care to count. But just as I was going cross-eyed, I finally found a familiar name among the records of summer marriages. It was written in such an archaic scrawl that I had to study it closely for a long time before I could piece it together.

And basically what it told me was that a fellow called Rudd Marchman had married a local girl on the very date that the earl's wages to him had ceased. Furthermore, a month later, his Cornish wife brought her newly-born child to be baptized, naming Rudd Marchman as the father.

"That could be it!" I mused. "He got a girl pregnant and was forced to marry her—which would have made him a bigamist, since as William Shakespeare he was already married to Anne Hathaway! So he used a fake name here in Cornwall, but then deserted the girl and returned to his life in London. What a bounder!"

Well, that's the trouble with history. Snoop too deeply in it, and nobody looks very good. So if you don't want your heroes tarnished, well . . .

Still, I couldn't wait to tell Jeremy my theory. But I discovered that he had already e-mailed me to say he was on his way back to Port St. Francis, and his message was a bit cryptic: *Research ended. Coming to Cornwall. Meet me at cottage for debriefing.*

# Chapter Nineteen

Well, I didn't imagine it. There was definitely something ground-breaking afoot, and from the look on Jeremy's face when he walked into the cottage and set down his suitcase, I knew it wasn't going to be good.

"He was hanged," Jeremy announced without ceremony.

"Who was hanged?" I asked in disbelief.

"Your Rudd Marchman, that's who," Jeremy said, sitting down wearily at the kitchen table as I handed him a glass of iced tea.

"*What* are you talking about?" I cried. "How could he be hanged? He had to go on for years and years and write all those wonderful plays."

"Well, William Shakespeare may have gone on to write those plays," Jeremy said decisively, "but Rudd Marchman most definitely did not. He was hanged in September of 1592."

I sank into the chair opposite him, while Jeremy reeled off the fruits of his laborious research.

"Rudd Marchman was a con man and a scoundrel, and frankly it's amazing that he lived as long as he did," Jeremy informed me. "He may have crossed paths with the Bard at some point, because Rudd was an actor for a time—loosely speaking. He also tried his hand at playwriting—and his handwriting is an absolute match for that manuscript fragment that got Trevor so excited. I stopped by the University of London to check it out with a handwriting expert and another Shakespeare professor."

I absorbed this blow slowly, as if my mind couldn't catch up.

"Anyway," Jeremy continued, "at Rudd Marchman's trial, it came out that he was a bit of an imposter—posing as a nobleman to attract the ladies, or pretending to be a great actor when he went into a pub, just to cadge a pint of beer. He made up fake awards he'd gotten, just to pad his résumé to get acting jobs. So it's not that Shakespeare went to Cornwall under the alias of Rudd Marchman. Quite the opposite. The truth is that Rudd Marchman went around the country using the alias of Shakespeare or, to be more precise, 'Willim Shakspere'."

I digested this, then demanded, "But what was he hanged for?"

"Violating the sumptuary laws," Jeremy said.

I stared at him. "What's that supposed to mean? What did he *do*? Murder, robbery, rape?"

"He wore a blue velvet coat," Jeremy announced, as if that explained everything.

And actually, something stirred, dimly, in my memory. I knew from my historical research for the films I worked on that in Shakespeare's day, what you wore was not simply a personal choice—you were absolutely required to "wear" only what you "were", that is, to dress within the accepted garments of your class. Dressing above your station, I knew, simply wasn't done. However, I certainly did not know that it was a capital crime to ape your betters.

"In Elizabethan times, if you earned twenty pounds a year, you were allowed to wear a satin doublet," Jeremy explained, "but you couldn't wear a satin gown. Now, say you made a hundred pounds a year, well, then you could wear all the satin to your heart's content, but don't even try wearing velvet. Especially red or blue, because those were the colors knights wore."

"So our lodger wore a blue velvet coat," I said. "Talk about delusions of grandeur."

"Yeah, well, actors got an exemption when they were onstage," Jeremy explained, draining his glass of tea. "Which means they could dress like a nobleman during a performance. But woe to the actor who wore his noble costume in the street, to impress a girl. Which is what our man Marchman did. And he got hauled into court and hanged for it. Period, end of story."

Now it was all sinking in. "So, there *was* a lodger in Grandmother Beryl's house," I said, "and he *was* an actor with The Earl's Players. And he *did* sometimes go around calling himself Willim Shakspere."

"Right," Jeremy replied. "And as I said, it appears that he even tried to write a play on that scrap of paper that Trevor told us about, and he may even have met the real Shakespeare somewhere, and therefore used his name. Who knows? But the fact is, Marchman died in 1592, so he couldn't have possibly been the renowned William Shakespeare."

"Zounds!" I cried. "Are you absolutely, positively, completely certain about this?"

"Yes," Jeremy answered emphatically.

"Oh, my God," I said, flabbergasted. "What are we going to tell Harriet and Trevor and all the rest of them?"

"The truth," Jeremy answered, after a pause. "And this means our name is mud at Buckingham Palace."

# Chapter Twenty

I absolutely dreaded having to tell the Port St. Francis Legacy Society the truth—that their "Shakespeare-slept-here" theory was a dud. In fact, it was Jeremy who gallantly did the deed. And as I expected, it wasn't easy.

The meeting was held at the old theatre in town. Harriet's group had a conference room on the second floor, but when we arrived, she was meeting with her "refreshment committee" so Jeremy and I stayed downstairs, where Trevor and his actors were rehearsing their "Scenes from Shakespeare" right on the old stage.

We stood at the back of the theatre, at the top of the sloped floor, and I couldn't help being delighted by the beautiful rows of seats covered with crimson damask. They were old and dusty, but still wonderful. The trim around the molding of the stage, the balconies and box seats were all done in gilt, and there were six fine crystal chandeliers overhead. The onstage curtain was also crimson, decorated with embroidered gold theatre masks of scowling Tragedy and smiling Comedy.

Trevor was onstage with several of the elderly thespians from the Actors' Home, as well as a scattering of the young summer-stock actors that Simon had told me about, and they looked both wide-eyed and amused. Trevor appeared quite dapper with a silk foulard around his throat, and a green knitted vest; and he had his white shirtsleeves rolled up to his elbows.

So there they all were, innocently rehearsing their Shakespeare scenes, totally unaware of the bomb we were about to drop. And maybe I imagined it, but I could swear that the actor who gazed straight back at us over the footlights was delivering these very prophetic words just for our benefit:

*"Thus do all traitors;*
*If their purgation did consist in words,*
*They are as innocent as grace itself.*
*Let it suffice thee that I TRUST THEE NOT!"*

"How do you like our Frederick in *As You Like It*?" Harriet asked, when she came down to find us. "Everyone's ready upstairs," she said eagerly. "We are all on tenterhooks."

"And they're going to hang *us* on a meat hook when this is all over," Jeremy mumbled to me.

My heart sank as we entered the conference room, for Harriet and her ladies had decked out a side table with a red paper tablecloth, upon which they'd artfully laid out plates of cookies and other nibbles, with pots of coffee and tea available. Harriet exhorted everyone to partake of the refreshments.

Trevor Branwhistle joined us now, breathless and eager. The big conference table awaited us, with neatly arranged pads of lined paper and pens at each seat, so everybody could take notes. There were twelve seats, and nine were already occupied by members of the Legacy Society as well as various merchants from town who were eager to coordinate their summer business with whatever Shakespeare findings we could give them. Even the chef Toby Taylor was here, because he was planning a whole Shakespearethemed summer menu to coincide with the "Scenes from Shake-speare" performance in August.

But mercifully, Jeremy had managed to schedule this meeting for when the town politicos were away at a one-day conference in London. While the last few stragglers settled into their seats, Jeremy, as if bucking up his courage, muttered to me:

*"Over hill, over dale,*
*Thorough bush, thorough brier,*
*Over park, over pale,*
*Thorough flood, thorough fire."*

Then he squared his shoulders and stood up before the whole expectant group. He carefully explained our findings, walking his audience through the evidence so they could see for themselves. We had printed out all our research, and now I spread it on the long conference table.

The whole time that Jeremy spoke, the group remained in stunned silence. I was forced to watch the expressions on their faces go from bright hopefulness, to puzzlement, to wariness, disbelief, and finally, fury.

When Jeremy came to the end of his presentation he took a deep breath, then said, "Any questions?"

One of Harriet's ladies turned accusingly to Trevor and said, "But *you* looked at the document and you told us that your so-called expert at the University was impressed. How could this be?"

Trevor, looking embarrassed and horrified, said defensively, "Now, Martha. You know perfectly well that every step of the way I warned you that nothing was certain."

"We all clutched onto every stitch of hope that we could," Harriet said diplomatically, but she glared at Jeremy when she added, "of course, you two could be mistaken. Couldn't you?"

"It is highly unlikely. I cannot advise you to pursue this any further," Jeremy said frankly.

"Well, then it's all a damp squib!" said a neatly bearded man who, I later found out, was the manager of the Homecoming Inn. (I also later learned that a squib is a kind of firecracker. So, you can imagine what a damp one is worth.)

Harriet sat back in her seat and pursed her lips. I'd never really seen her annoyed before. When people have unrealistic expectations of you, then it doesn't really matter if you're right or wrong. They just believed in you, that's all, and now they clearly felt that we had betrayed their trust and let them down.

And then there were the folks who never wanted us around in the first place, voiced by a lady with frosted blonde hair who said, "Well, *I* for one warned everybody from the start that bringing in a detective team from London, who know absolutely nothing about our ways and our people, was a terrible idea."

She glanced around the room with a spiteful smirk of satisfaction, her gaze flickering at me, although she was unable to look me in the eye.

"Always thought the whole thing was a lot of hokum smokum," an elderly gentleman agreed.

Now everyone around the table began grumbling, and a few simply scraped back their chairs, rose and walked out of the room, still murmuring to each other.

I heard Toby Taylor out in the hallway, already on his mobile phone, instructing somebody back at his restaurant, "Kill the whole Shakespeare menu. This is what comes of working with local amateurs."

But Trevor and his theatre group unexpectedly refused to change their plans for the Shakespeare fête.

"The show *must* go on!" Trevor declared, and the others in his group nodded vigorously. "After all, the hospital is depending on us. We'll just have to try that much harder to sell tickets. We must advertise—put a sign in every shop window."

Yet although his group seemed determined as they filed out, they also looked worried.

"Well, you two sure know how to empty a room," said a white-haired man who ran a local tour-bus operation. He reached for a cookie from the tray, then walked out.

Harriet and a meek little lady from her group quietly began collecting the half-empty cups of tea.

"I am so sorry about this," I found myself saying.

Harriet didn't respond, but the meek lady patted my hand and looked at me through her tortoise-shell framed eyeglasses saying, "Don't worry, dearie, this was not an easy job. I think you two are very nice."

Jeremy jerked his head at me to indicate that nothing more could be done. Harriet said casually, "Well, that's that. I'll let my friend know how things turned out."

Oh, God, I thought. She's going to ring Buckingham Palace the minute we're out of here. Once the word spread through London, nobody was going to want to hire us again. At this point, I was so wretched I hardly cared.

"At least that's over and done with," Jeremy said as we got in our car.

The day was warm and all the other creatures on earth were happy—the butterflies were flitting, the bees were buzzing, the birds were singing, the squirrels were chattering. Apparently they were all completely unaware that everything had just gone totally bust for the poor town of Port St. Francis.

"I feel just terrible," I said. "My stomach aches. Does this mean Nichols & Laidley are history?"

"No. Frankly, I'm fed up with these people," Jeremy said. "I mean, they're not children. They ought to have expected that something like this might happen. It's Shakespeare, for God's sake. I don't enjoy bursting anyone's bubble, but they had to know it was a long shot to begin with. And to be honest, I'm getting sick of this entire little tin-pot town."

"Well, that's just fine," I said, "because there's no way we'll be able to hold our heads up and walk down main street anymore anyway. What are we going to do? We're booked into the cottage for a whole month. Geez, I just can't face Shannon and Geoffrey at the farm. They'll hate us, too. And wait till they tell Colin!"

"Let's go to the beach and take a good, long walk to clear our heads," Jeremy suggested firmly, swerving away from the country lane that led to the farm, and instead heading back toward the harbor. "Then we can figure out where we want to go from here."

# Chapter Twenty-One

The sea was a soft blue-and-pewter grey with frisky waves that raced up the shore and splashed across our bare feet as we walked on the beach near the harbor. The air was cool and bracing and tasted of salt. We held hands and just walked in silence, skirting along the shoreline. Once we were farther beyond the sheltering harbor, we collected some beautiful seashells which Jeremy deposited in the pockets of his shirt. This kept us occupied for awhile, and it was all very soothing and meditative.

Had we but gazed out to the horizon line, we might have identified an innocuous-looking, but distinctly battleship-grey row of clouds, as if the Spanish Armada were massing for war. It began as just a painterly streak across the vista; yet it was moving toward land more rapidly than a couple of amateurs like us could guess. But we were so engrossed in examining the marine life, which clung to the rocks on the cove and washed up on shore, that we hardly noticed.

Until that first rumble, like a cannon firing the opening salvo.

"Did you hear something?" I asked.

I moved closer to where Jeremy was peering into a small, shallow cave that was already knee-high with seawater. Now he popped his head back out again, frowning at the sky.

Before he could even speak, a rare, hostile wind came whistling in at us, filling the little cave with a mournful, shrieking sound. A split second later, we saw jagged lightning, breaking into scary-looking branches across the sky.

And then, sudden, swift and decisive, the downpour began.

To say that this deluge came down in sheets would not even begin to do it justice. It was more like a great big cloth whipping about us, as if we were on the deck of a ship whose sails had just collapsed on our heads. Plus, the wind and lashing rain were now driving the tide against the shore, filling up the rock pools in an alarming new way.

"Come on, babe!" Jeremy shouted, grabbing me by the hand and hauling me across the beach, back the way we had come.

But I hardly recognized the coves now; the storm was crashing in so violently that I could barely distinguish sea, sky, earth and air. It was all just one big dark wet mess. As we hurried for the safety of the town, I felt as if we were hurtling ourselves with all our might, and yet we seemed to be struggling in slow motion. My feet and ankles were sinking deeply into the newly-soaked sand with every step I took. By the time we straggled onto solid land, my feet were so caked with sand and mud from the wet ground that I looked as if I were wearing a thick absurd pair of socks.

When we finally reached the parking lot, it was coursing with rivers of rainwater that immediately washed off my sand-socks. Jeremy fumbled in his pocket for his car key, cursing all the while. Finally the headlights and tail-lights flashed as the car unlocked.

"Phew!" I cried as I cannonballed into the passenger seat, struggling to haul the door shut against the wind, while Jeremy ran around the front of the car to get into his seat. The windshield was completely awash outside, and it quickly fogged up inside with our panting breath.

Jeremy started the engine and drove hurriedly away, just as another forked tongue of lightning split the sky. Once he got the windshield wipers going, we could see that the main road of the town was flooding quickly, so Jeremy turned the car away and took a side road that climbed up to higher ground and the country lane that led to the farm.

"Eek!" I cried involuntarily as a new round of thunder bellowed directly overhead, and seemed to rattle everything like chattering teeth, including the car and the ground we were travelling on.

Jeremy's nice little zippy Dragonetta was designed for tooling around sophisticated, *dry* Riviera highways. It was certainly not a car made for plowing through wild and wet dirt roads. The very farm paths that had been so hard and dusty just scant hours ago were now fast becoming sticky mud trenches. But the Dragonetta gamely chugged forth and, despite the gobs of mud that spattered her beautiful deep-green fenders, she got us to the farm just as a fresh wave of rain came hurling down on us.

When we pulled up to our cottage at last, I struggled to shove the car door open and get out. By now my clothes clung to me uselessly like limp old lettuce leaves. My hair was plastered across my face, no matter how I pushed at it. Jeremy had to use all his strength to haul open the cottage front door against the bellowing wind, and then he had to hang on to the door to keep it from being blown right off its hinges.

Once inside, we didn't even have time to catch our breath, for the sky had become as dark as night. I stumbled about, gasping, fumbling around to turn on the lights. The very walls and windows seemed to be shuddering in dismay.

A moment after I'd turned on the lights, the power blew out. But Jeremy anticipated this and had already yanked open the cupboard that contained the lanterns, candles, flashlights and battery-powered instruments which Geoff and Shannon had shown us when we arrived. Back then, the whole thing seemed cute and quaint. Like ooh, sure, how nice, something to know about in case of a storm.

Now we set about planting the lanterns in strategic places—bedroom, kitchen, bath. But it had grown eerily cold and damp as the temperature outside plunged rapidly. Well, you just try lighting a fire in a fireplace when it's raining elephants outside. It was as if Neptune himself was spitting on our fire.

We peeled off our wet clothes, and hastily toweled each other dry, then ended up in bed, snuggling under the extra blankets that were also tucked away for "a rainy day" such as this, when a guy like Noah would be busy counting pairs of animals.

For a moment, we just lay there, panting, silent.

"Wow," I said finally, master of understatement that I am. "It's a whopper."

"Huh," Jeremy answered, shivering. Then he added ruefully, "I get the feeling that even Mother Nature is pissed off at us for screwing up the whole Shakespeare connection."

I giggled, but then found myself quaking at each new roll of thunder. The rain was still furiously lashing the sides of our poor little cottage.

"How long can it last?" I asked.

It turns out that this innocent question of mine was key. Because there was a deep, dark secret that all the sly Cornwall residents had failed to share with us. That nice, sunny summer weather—which had been so pleasing to the many tourists who flocked here, booking every hotel room and cottage in sight for the entire season—was, it turns out, a complete aberration. It had already lasted far too long. The earth must have had some strange cosmic blip, some jolt of its axis, making the Mediterranean countries wet in the past weeks, and the British Isles sunny and balmy. Perhaps the stars and moon had been pulling the tides in odd directions. Or perhaps the clouds and oceans were temporarily distracted, recalibrating themselves in an attempt to compensate for man's contribution to global warming—and thereby permitting a sunny July in Cornwall.

But in any event, Mother Nature had now finally decided to redress the imbalance and put things back the way they used to be. The sun returned to the Mediterranean where it belonged for the rest of the summer . . . and the cold wet weather for which the West Country of England is so famous returned with a vengeance to the land of King Arthur.

And as far as I could tell, this tempest was here to stay . . . for a long, long while.

# Part Five

# Chapter Twenty-Two

Strange things can happen to two people when you're stuck with each other for days on end, in a small, confined space. When you can't even venture outside because the weather is so evil. When you finally get the TV going again and the reception is so awful that you just switch it off. When your Internet connection, which was tenuous to begin with, repeatedly gives up the ghost. When telephones sound so squeaky and squitchy that you think you're talking to someone on Mars.

The first bad thing was that Jeremy got sick. And that's when I came to realize how much I'd grown to depend on him. The sweet guy just does things without complaining, so I had gotten spoiled, often awakening to discover that he'd already made coffee and boiled eggs for breakfast, or that he'd cheerfully chopped wood to feed the little black stove, or that he'd worked in the garden to pick us some nice vegetables for dinner.

But now, here he was, sick as a dog, for the first time since I'd known him. A guy like him doesn't stay in bed unless he really can't get up. At first, all he said that morning was, "I feel weird," and he kept pausing after each chore as if waiting for his energy to return. By noon, he had no appetite for lunch, which was totally out of character for him. By five o'clock, his forehead was burning.

"Take your temperature," I commanded, handing him the thermometer from my first-aid kit, which my mother gave to me when I was eighteen, fully stocked with Band-Aids and all, and which I've replenished and carried with me like a talisman my whole life.

Now, the thing about men who never get sick is that they don't really know how to be sick. So when Jeremy impatiently took the thermometer and stuck it into his mouth, three minutes later he took it out and announced dubiously, "I'm 94, all right?"

"Gimme that," I said, examining the thermometer suspiciously, then shaking it down again. "Only a lizard has a temperature of 94. Try it again," I said, and this time I watched to see what he was doing wrong. "You've only got the tip of it in!" I said incredulously. "Put practically all of it on a diagonal under your tongue," I admonished. "Even a two-year-old knows that."

"Thanks a lot," he mumbled. Sulkily he complied. Three minutes later . . .

"Oh my God," I said. "Your temperature is 102."

Jeremy swore under his breath and then said, "No wonder I feel like death warmed over."

"Don't die, Jeremy!" I exclaimed, running to get him some aspirin. He was sitting in the kitchen, shivering a little, despite the way the old-fashioned wood-burning stove was warming the room.

"Hah-choo!" he said in response. He paused. "That," he said ominously, "was a particularly bad sneeze. I don't think you should come near me. I'd better sleep out on the sofa."

"No, I'll sleep on the sofa," I volunteered. "You need the bed."

He coughed again, too miserable to argue, and he trotted off to the bedroom, flinging himself on the bed, where he fell asleep instantly.

He slept and slept. It scared me a little. I kept tiptoeing in to make sure he was still breathing.

But the next day, despite the aspirin, he still had a fever, which climbed even higher. He was coughing and so congested that I put a little pan of water on the hob, to mist the room.

"Everything aches all over," he admitted, "even my hair hurts!"

"What's the matter with Jeremy?" Shannon asked a few days later, having stopped by to show me some of the new cheese she was making. When I told her, she frowned.

"I know. There's something like that going around; the other farm families had it. Better let Doctor Calthrop take a look," she advised. "He'll come today if I tell him I've got his favorite cheese ready for him."

A few hours later, the doctor rapped on the front door, waking Jeremy from the sleep he kept drifting in and out of. The doctor was about fifty, and had curly grey hair, a fuzzy grey beard, and the sort of tweedy suit that seemed more indicative of an absent-minded professor.

He didn't say much at first, just fell into a sort of tuneless humming at regular intervals between taking Jeremy's blood pressure and pulse, examining his throat and listening to his chest.

Jeremy eyed Doctor Calthrop with undisguised dubiousness. But apart from asking Jeremy key questions, like, "Does your throat hurt more in the morning, or is it the same all day?" the doctor basically ignored Jeremy's gaze and instead talked to me as I hovered worriedly in the doorway.

"Bacterial throat infection. Seen lots of it this summer. He'll be needing antibiotics," he said matter-of-factly.

Doctor Calthrop handed me some pills, and a cough syrup. "He should eat if he has any appetite. Start him slowly, on toast and tea," he advised as he packed up his bag. "Bananas if you can find them. Then some clear soup, and rice. If he's hungry enough for real food, feed him eggs or some plain chicken. Whatever he has an appetite for is okay. Plenty of rest, plenty of fluids."

"What about Penny?" Jeremy croaked from the bed. "What if she gets it?"

The doctor smiled at me. "Call me if you do, but I think you'd have come down with it by now. When he's been on the medication for three days, you're pretty safe from contagion."

As Doctor Calthrop wrote out Jeremy's name for the prescription, something must have rung a bell in his mind. "Laidley," he mused. "Nichols and Laidley? You two must be the ones who screwed up on the Shakespeare, eh?" he asked cheerily.

"Right, that's us," Jeremy said. "Thank you very much."

The doctor chuckled. "Keep quiet and calm, m'boy, and you'll be fit as a fiddle in no time."

Doctor Calthrop had barely gone out the door when Jeremy said sulkily, "He's talking to me like I'm some little kid."

"You are," I said comfortingly, tucking the covers around him again. "Everyone's a little kid when they're sick."

At first, Jeremy was a good patient and I was a good nurse. But as he started to recover, he became a restless pain-in-the-butt, always wanting to get up and about without realizing that he would only teeter and have to return to bed.

Meanwhile, I made tea and toast, and I kept the fire going in the stove and fireplace. Then, whenever the rain let up temporarily, I drove into town to search for everything else the doctor ordered.

The village of Port St. Francis was still thronging with summer visitors, but they, like me, were restless and disappointed with the damp, soggy weather. As with any vacation town, what at first seems quaint soon becomes a bit of a nuisance, once you've bought all your souvenirs and fudge and T-shirts, and all you're really looking for are the basics—bread and milk, soap, can-openers, aspirin, paper towels.

Furthermore, I know I am not exaggerating when I say that I got a fair share of dirty looks from most of the proprietors, who by now knew me on sight, and who'd been counting on Jeremy and me to make them rich by turning Port St. Francis into a Shakespeare tourist mecca.

I found myself darting in and out of the shops as quickly as possible, not breathing easily until I was on my way back to the farm.

The pills did their job, with Jeremy improving enough so that I was able to launder the bedding and resume sleeping with him. Everything was fine . . . until he started to get hungry for real meals again.

"I'll make dinner," he offered, and over my protestations he hurriedly got out of bed, then became dizzy and sat back down on the bed, appearing mightily surprised. "My knees buckled," he said, looking outraged.

"Right, it's called being sick," I said in as bossy a tone as I could. "Lie down."

"You just bought that fresh chicken," he objected, still clutching the bedpost. "It has to be cooked or it will go bad."

"So, I'll cook it," I insisted, tucking him back into bed. "The doctor said plain chicken is best. Like roasted, maybe?"

"A roasted bird is not as simple as it sounds," Jeremy warned, looking sympathetic.

"I can do it," I said stoutly.

And here's the thing. I did everything right. Really. Almost. I cleaned it, I dried it, I rubbed it with a mixture of olive oil, fresh sweet butter and lemon; and I put a small onion and some newly picked thyme in the cavity, and sprinkled some nice cracked pepper and sea salt over the bird. The oven was properly preheated, and I also put in a small tray of potatoes, lightly glazed with olive oil and thyme. And I sat there at the kitchen table and snapped the ends off the green beans that I'd painstakingly picked fresh from the garden, and I put them in a steamer pot on the stove-top to gently cook.

And it all would have made a perfect dinner. Except for one thing. That last essential twenty minutes, which can make or break a dinner.

In which we both fell asleep.

Now, Jeremy was entitled to. He was the sick-o. But I was on duty, and I was supposed to stay awake. Maybe I had a touch of whatever he had, because I fell into a thick sleep, sitting on the parlor sofa. But in any case, we were both awakened by the smell of burning chicken. And I'm not talking barbecue.

"Yikes!" I exclaimed, rushing into the kitchen, stumbling in the dreary darkness of the late afternoon. I raced to the oven door, opened it . . . and smoke poured out.

I grabbed the oven mitts, yanked the roasting pan out and placed it on the cold stove-top. The tips of the bird's legs were charred black, and the wings were total goners. The rest at first didn't look that bad, not black, just mahogany-colored all over, and wizened.

But upon tasting it, I realized that the burned potato pieces which had exploded and fallen on the oven floor, had totally permeated the chicken with the taste of smoke. The potatoes themselves had become little black billiard balls. Only the string beans had survived, for the simple reason that they'd been cooked on the stove-top, and I'd turned off the steamer and set them aside before I fell asleep.

"Good God!" Jeremy cried, hovering in the doorway in his pajamas, looking shocked, his hair standing straight up from days of being in bed. "What's on fire?"

"Dinner!" I shouted, tears of exhaustion pouring down my cheeks. "The potatoes exploded all over the floor of the oven. The bird's a dead duck."

We both started coughing from the smoke, and I flung open the windows, letting in the cold, clammy air. Rain spattered my already tear-streaked face.

Jeremy now added fuel to the fire by stating the obvious. "You have to *watch* food when you're roasting it!" he said in exasperation. Then he flung back my previous remark to him: "Even a two-year-old knows that!"

Later, I had to explain to him Rule #1 in a marriage: If your mate insults you, do not harbor the exact words of the insult in your bosom and then fling it back at her at the first golden opportunity.

"Now you're going to freeze us out and we'll both die of pneumonia!" Jeremy exclaimed, as the wind whistled in through the open windows, dispelling the smoke and all my hopes of a fine dinner.

"You're just *trying* to get sick and die!" I shouted back. "Either put on a robe and slippers and do something useful, or get back into bed."

Rule #2: Never tell a man he's useless. We spent the next fifteen minutes shouting at each other, reminding ourselves of every stupid thing we'd done on this trip.

Then I cried in earnest. Then he sulked guiltily. Then we didn't speak for a half hour. Then Jeremy decided to be big about it, and he insisted on trying to eat some of the chicken, which only made me feel worse. It's true that the meat wasn't technically burnt, but it tasted like it was. It was truly hideous.

But he kept patting my back and telling me that it would have been a wonderful dinner, and that it was an easy mistake to make, and that he didn't care at all. However, after a few bites, he had to spit it out and admit that the whole damned thing was inedible.

"I can't go back into town and shop again!" I wailed, totally exhausted. I'd shopped so carefully, and spent money on high-quality goods, and worked hard to get it right . . . and I simply didn't want to go face those resentful shopkeepers who were still pissed off about Shakespeare. "Look," I said tearfully, "if I make you some eggs, would you feel like eating them?"

"Sure," Jeremy said. He glanced round the kitchen. "You could throw those string beans in, they look okay. Add a little cheddar, and you've got yourself an omelette. Want me to do it?"

"NO!" I shouted. One thing my father *did* succeed in teaching me at a tender age was how to make an omelette. So off I went.

When I was ready to present it to Jeremy on a tray in bed, it must have looked good, because he sniffed hungrily and then said, "We got any white wine?"

"Yup," I said. I poured two glasses, and we both sat there in bed and ate.

"Wonderful," he kept saying.

"And to think it only took me a zillion hours and as many dollars," I said wryly. "Piece of cake."

"Got any cake?" Jeremy demanded. "I want dessert, too."

"Biscuits," I said. "Digestive biscuits. That's what the doctor said."

"As I recall," Jeremy said smugly, "the doctor said I could eat anything I had an appetite for. So bring on the desserts, and a small glass of port."

"Welcome back, podner," I said, immensely relieved to hear him starting to sound like his old, lusty, cantankerous self. "This case just ain't the same without you."

# Chapter Twenty-Three

Afterwards, we settled into bed, and it was quite cozy. We had gotten used to the candlelight at dinner, and sometimes we carried it into the bedroom with us instead of turning on the electric light. I liked the shadows the candles cast, flickering across the room.

Jeremy glanced at the newspaper, then set it aside. He was still coughing a bit whenever he lay down, so he stayed propped up and tired, bored with the television.

Now I ransacked my bag for something to read, and came upon the little school notebook from Great-Aunt Penelope's clubhouse. I started to really examine it, and soon was chuckling out loud.

"Jeremy, listen to this," I kept saying, irresistibly compelled to read to him from the "minutes" of their meetings, which were all written in Aunt Pen's neat, schoolgirl handwriting, with playful flourishes and dramatic narrative. I picked out one of the escapades and recited it:

"*July, in the twelfth day of the 1927<sup>th</sup> year of our Lord,*" I intoned, "*the officers of the Cornwall Summer Explorers' Club infiltrated the Annual Parental Tea whose guest of honor was the vicar,* *the minister of Parliament and the earl and the earl-ess. The raid was conducted at the hour 15:30 when the dining table was still being laid.*

*"Entry was gained through the windows of the north wall, which was scaled by the President, with able assistance from the Sergeant-At-Arms. Upon successful infiltration of the tearoom, the Prez thence collected various items in a basket and handed them down a rope to the Treasurer, without ever being discovered.*

*"The C.S.E.C. thencewith returned to the clubhouse at 16:00, having succeeded in absconding with an assortment of six petits fours, three scones, and a slice each of orange cake, chocolate cake and spice cake. White Tea was smuggled out in a thermos. Devonshire cream and jam were put in jars, which the S.-a.-A. dropped and almost smashed, but which were saved by the Treasurer in the nick of time."*

"Know what that means?" Jeremy chuckled. "Aunt Pen's little club made a raid on the grown-ups' tea party. Why didn't they just walk in and eat with the adults?"

"Are you kidding?" I said scornfully. "Where's the fun in that? Their parents were all in a tizzy because of the illustrious guest list. So," I said, translating Great-Aunt Penelope's high-blown prose, "Aunt Pen—the *Prez*—made Great-Uncle Roland—the *S.-a.-A.* or *Sergeant at Arms*—boost her up to the side window, so she could sneak in and pilfer sweets and tea. She actually slung them in a basket on a rope to the *Treasurer*—Grandmother Beryl. They even made off with milky tea in a thermos!" I marvelled, picturing three kids scampering across the lawn and retreating to the secret room over the garage. "But Great-Uncle Roland nearly queered it all by dropping the jam jar."

"Sound just like his namesake, good old Rollo," Jeremy commented.

All that night, Jeremy listened intently, as, instead of watching television, I continued to read aloud about the further adventures of the kids' club, which seemed to escalate in daring as the summer of 1927 wore on. After rescuing a baby bird that fell out of a nest, they chased a viper out of the garage. They bicycled out to a farm to deliver medicine to an old lady who was ailing. They solved a local "mystery" by locating a neighbor's missing horse out on the moors; and on another day they boldly "recovered" a new wheelbarrow from a town thief who'd stolen it from a neighbor, for which the police commended them.

All their summer "cases", mysteries and discoveries were narrated in Great-Aunt Penelope's utter seriousness of tone, embellished with high drama. After years of hearing about my great-aunt's sophisticated, mysterious adulthood, I loved picturing her scampering around Cornwall as a thirteen-year-old, with her bright, imaginative sense of romance and excitement.

"Don't you just adore her?" I said.

"I adore your voice," Jeremy mumbled sleepily. "You've never read aloud to me before. It's so ve-e-ry soothing . . ."

He tried to stay awake, but soon he was snoring gently. Silently to myself, I read further on until, just around midnight, I reached a passage that was very strange indeed:

*The 21st of August. Officers of the C.S.E.C. discover the Great Lady. Her ghost has haunted these shores for many a decade. We shall give her a proper burial. Only the Black Rod decides where to bring her to her final resting place.*

Below was a verse, *The Song of the Great Lady, Our Mascot*:
*When this you see,*
*Remember me.*
*They say I drowned*

*In the stormy sea.*
*But I am closer than you know,*
*I rest where flowers will not grow.*
*I lie beneath the house of fish,*
*And I will grant your every wish.*
*And with my garden round me now,*
*I watch your father tend and plow.*
*Just hop aboard your trusty steed,*
*He'll give you rightly what you need.*
*And with the keeper of the stone,*
*You'll find your way back to your home.*

After that, there were only these two short entries:

*The 31st of August. All members of club on deck. Secret outing in search of Greatest Treasure Ever.*

*5 September 1927. The great adventure ends for the summer. We seal the door to this room in molten wax. Secrets of the century safe for now, with only those worthy of this trust. Until next year. Adieu.*

There were a few doodles of swirls, whorls and spirals. Then the notebook ended there.

I was truly exhausted by the wild day of cooking I'd just had, and my eyes were bleary. So I set the book down, blew out the candle and tried to sleep.

For awhile I just lay there, musing about the little poem. If the notebook had been written by just any kid, I would have easily put it aside with the thought that these were simply a lot of fanciful jottings to while away a summer.

But this wasn't any regular, ordinary kid. It was my Great-Aunt Penelope. She who had bequeathed her fascinating legacy to me and to Jeremy and to Rollo. I hadn't known her very well when she was alive; but much later, in dogging out her mysterious last wishes, I had certainly come to learn that whenever Aunt Pen wrote that she had something important to say . . . well, it behooved her family members to believe it, and to find out just exactly what it was that she wanted only the "worthy" to know.

# Chapter Twenty-Four

I allowed Jeremy to sleep for as long as I could bear it, but finally, at nine o'clock in the morning, I couldn't wait any longer. I made coffee and sunny-side-up eggs with a bit of ham, and toast and marmalade and orange juice. I figured if the scent of coffee won't stir a man to rise and shine, well . . .

"Hey!" he said, sitting up in surprise when I carried his breakfast to him on a tray. He sniffed appreciatively and peered at it as I set it down in front of him. "That's quite a yeoman's breakfast," he commented. "The only thing missing is baked beans and kippers."

"You English amaze me," I said. I bounced on the bed alongside him. As he ate, I gave him the news.

"Aunt Pen's club had a great adventure!" I announced. "But I can't tell what it was, because just when it started to get good, she slipped into some kind of poem. See? Can you figure out what she's talking about?"

Jeremy squinted at the notebook, reading it carefully with his second cup of coffee. Then he just shook his head. "Nope," he said.

I persisted. "Aw, c'mon. Try harder. You're English. Figure it out, will ya? It says here, *Only the Black Rod decides.* What can that possibly mean?"

Jeremy munched his toast thoughtfully.

"Well," he said, "it's a term from the House of Lords in Parliament, where the Black Rod is basically a sergeant-at-arms. He's in charge of things like security—making sure people behave, ejecting unruly members, that sort of thing. In medieval times, the sergeant-at-arms was more like a bodyguard to a king."

"Aha, the *S.-a.-A.*!" I exclaimed, riffling the pages back to the one which listed all the club officers. I pointed to the officer's name.

"Look at who the club's sergeant-at-arms was," I said. "Good old Great-Uncle Roland. In charge of security, you get it?"

"More likely they put him in charge of the dirty work," Jeremy said, re-reading the poem. "Sounds to me like their dog died and he had to bury it."

I fell silent for a moment. Looking over the whole thing, that's exactly what it sounded like. And yet, I felt I had to pursue this to see if that's really all there was to it.

"I've been wanting to take a drive out to Grandmother Beryl's house anyway," I said. "Just to keep an eye on it. I think I'll go poke around there again." I peered out the window. "It stopped raining," I said hopefully. "The sky is still full of clouds, but at least they're whitish clouds."

Jeremy picked up the breakfast tray and carried it into the kitchen. "I'm going with you," he announced. When I objected mildly, he said firmly, "Let me put it this way—if I don't get out of this cottage today, I will go stark, raving mad."

The sun had peeped out a bit already, which gave me the bright idea of cycling to Grandma's house. Maybe it had to do with Aunt

Pen's club—I felt I had to get into the mind-set of a bunch of kids on summer vacation. Jeremy, who was feeling much better, loved the idea.

So we pedaled down the quiet lane that wound its way around the farm, and then out toward the sea. In the distance I could barely make out the headland and the castle where the mysterious earl was ensconced, counting his shillings or whatever the landed gentry do in their spare time. I guess I had old nursery rhymes on my mind, and I sang one as we cycled along:

*"The king was in his counting house,*
*Counting out his money;*
*The queen was in the parlour,*
*Eating bread and honey . . ."*

When we arrived at Grandmother Beryl's place, it seemed as if the house and grounds were holding their breath, watching us with an expectation that something was going to happen for which they'd long been waiting.

The silence was so deep that I could hear the clunk when I tapped my kickstand and left the bike at the front of the house, and we went squish-squishing across the rain-soaked lawn. As we reached the garage, a startled thrush fluttered out of the big shrubs, and a few flustered squirrels chattered about our arrival.

Jeremy heaved open the little munchkin door at the back of the garage, and we went up into the schoolroom, half expecting to find Great-Aunt Penelope, Grandmother Beryl and Great-Uncle Roland seated in the small chairs and holding one of their secret club meetings.

But it was still a slightly sad, abandoned children's room, covered in dust. As we walked around peering into various cupboards, looking for a clue to the coded message, all we found were the usual signs of childhood preoccupations—a favorite seashell, a set of miniature horseshoes for children to practice with, and a number of rubber balls of various sizes. Strange to have these little trinkets outliving their owners.

"Okay, Penny Nichols," Jeremy said. "It's your Great-Aunt, so start thinking the way a spunky little kid detective thinks."

I sat down quietly in one of the little school-desks, watching the shifting rays of sunlight casting shadows on the floor, and I listened to the distant, soft shushing of the ocean.

"Penny?" I heard Jeremy saying. "What are you thinking?"

"The Black Rod," I answered. "It's not Great-Aunt Penelope's mind we have to get into. It's Great-Uncle Roland's. If you were a little boy, where would you hide something important?"

Jeremy didn't even hesitate. "Some yucky place where grown-ups and girls would never go," he said.

"The basement of the house," I said instantly. "Even Harriet didn't want to go down there."

"There's a door on the side that leads right in," Jeremy recalled.

"Bring the flashlight," I reminded him. "No electric in there."

We went out of the garage to the house, where a short flight of four stone steps led down to a very solid wooden door. But the place where the lock met the wood framework of the house was rotted from years of rain, so it wasn't that hard for Jeremy to force it open. He shone his light inside and we stepped into the dark cellar. Then he waved the flashlight in a series of sweeping arcs so that we could look before we leaped.

"God, it's more like a cave than a basement," I observed, glancing around apprehensively. "And the ceiling's so low."

The walls were stone, and here and there was a very narrow window that let in weak light. There were vast spiderwebs everywhere—overhead around the supporting beams, and in every dark, damp corner.

There was something so deathly in the musty, underground smell, and I found myself stepping very gingerly across the earthen floor, so I confess that I let Jeremy do the dirty work of feeling along the stone walls for any conceivable hiding place. The cellar was not shaped as a rectangle, but more like a twisting and turning tunnel. We peered about, but it soon became apparent that Grandmother Beryl had used the basement only as a root and wine cellar, and nothing more.

Disappointed, we emerged like a couple of moles, blinking in the light of day. This time, Jeremy used my health-club lock to padlock the door.

It had been so long since the weather was fine that we found ourselves automatically drawn to Grandfather Nigel's garden, with its hedges and rectangular beds of herbs and flowers, and the path leading down to the sea. We could hear bees buzzing where they were busily investigating the rose, hollyhock and bergamot plantings, and the patch of hyssop, and fragrant thyme, lavender and rosemary.

In that dreamy atmosphere, I drifted trancelike through the yard, feeling as if I were walking across a Ouija board, and I myself was the little heart-shaped wood planchette that you put your fingers on to let the spirits guide you to their message. When I stopped, though, I felt I was only halfway there. Jeremy had been watching me quizzically.

"I keep thinking about that poem," I said finally, digging into my pocket where I had copied it out on a sheet of paper. "The bit about resting *where flowers will not grow,*" I said, perplexed, handing him the page. "So maybe it's under the stone path in the garden?"

Jeremy took the paper from me and examined it. "No!" he said suddenly, moving swiftly toward Grandfather Nigel's gardening shed. "It's got to do with this business of I *lie beneath the house of fish*. Remember what Harriet told us when she gave us the tour of this place? She said the gardening shed was originally a kippering shed."

"Yeah, I didn't really know what that meant," I admitted.

"Kippers. Fish. It's where they used to smoke them," Jeremy said, hauling open the door to the shed. I peered over his shoulder as he gazed inside, studying the watering cans and tools to see what else was on the shelves. But there were only some neatly arranged seed packets, garden spades and various clippers.

"*I rest where flowers will not grow*," I repeated.

Jeremy cocked his head a moment, then crouched and ran his fingers along the wooden floor of the shed, until he found a metal ring, similar to the one in the little back door of the garage.

"Look," he said, "this whole piece of flooring picks up. Nigel must have used it as a storage cupboard or something." He grunted as he began to heave up the section of flooring, which was about five feet long.

This gave me a pause. "Gee," I said, "what if your dead-dog theory is correct, after all? I really don't want to recover a lot of old canine bones."

"A bit late for that now," Jeremy said briskly, setting the panel aside and shining his flashlight into the hole. I peered over his shoulder again, and saw a thick wooden box. Jeremy brushed the earth away so that he could read faded letters printed on it.

"It's a piano box," he said. "Well, it's for a piano seat. It's not going to be easy to pull the whole box out. Want me to just break it open?"

A wayward dragonfly came flitting over, landed on the box for a moment, then flew away.

"Yes, open it," I said. Jeremy took a shovel and banged it against the outer edges of the box. The wood split fairly easily, revealing a thick sheet of vinyl, which he cast aside. Below it, something in a distinctly human shape was wrapped, again and again, in white cellophane, like a mummy.

"Oh, God," I said, feeling a bit faint. "You don't suppose they actually murdered some kid they didn't like, do you?"

"Let's hope not," Jeremy said. "Hand me those pruning shears."

He leaned forward and awkwardly managed to cut part of the cellophane away. It had held remarkably well, but it was old, and gave way enough so that he could peel back the layers, as if opening a present.

And then, involuntarily, I let out a shriek.

For the face that stared up at me was a woman's, with round black eyes and pink cheeks and a red mouth, and tendrils of wavy black hair framing her face. She had dark eyebrows and a finely chiseled nose and chin, and a rounded, high forehead. She seemed dressed in a purple, fitted gown that was edged in white lace and cut low to reveal her suntanned bosom.

"It's only a wooden statue of some sort," Jeremy told me hastily. "Crikey, Aunt Pen practically embalmed her," he said, brushing away a scattering of mothballs from all around it.

"Sorry for the scream," I gasped. Gently, very gently, Jeremy lifted the figure out of the box. Something stirred in my memory from years of scavenging props in antiques stores, and I realized what it was.

"It's a masthead!" I exclaimed. "You know, a figurehead that they put on the front of ships for luck. In ancient times they thought it could scare away sea monsters, and for centuries after that, sailors kept using them for good luck. I wonder where this came from? Let me see that poem again."

Jeremy handed me back the paper. I had copied out a bit of the kids' club minutes, too, and now my eyes locked on to it:

*The 21st of August. Officers of the C.S.E.C. discover the Great Lady. Her ghost has haunted these shores for many a decade. We shall give her a proper burial. Only the Black Rod decides where to bring her to her final resting place.*

"Jeremy!" I exclaimed. "All this time, while we've been focusing on the Shakespearean lodger, there's been some other history to uncover here, right under our noses!"

"Well, not exactly our noses," Jeremy said, blowing his now. "Look. Let's put this right back where it was, and bike home and get the car so we can bring the Great Lady out of here before somebody else finds her. Harriet said we could take what we wanted."

"Right," I said, and we hastily rewrapped her and put her back, and replaced the flooring. We even covered it up with the watering can and other tools.

Then we hopped aboard our bicycles and pedaled like mad down the country lane toward the farm and our cottage. The sky was already clouding up again, but it didn't look like it would rain yet.

"Know what I think?" I called out to Jeremy.

"Yes," he shouted back. "You think there's more to this story, and you're hoping it will somehow do the trick and save your grandma's house."

"Aw, c'mon. Maybe Shakespeare didn't sleep there," I said, "but somebody interesting sure did."

We were pedalling side by side now, close to the turn-off for the farm, when there came a sudden roar from behind. A split-second later, a truck was bearing down on us full bore.

"Penny, look out!" Jeremy shouted. The truck aimed itself straight at us, and we had no choice but to drive our bikes right off the road.

I didn't stay up on my wheels for very long. I flew left, and the bike flew right. The ground, although grassy enough, was lumpy and bumpy in a big way, and I went tumbling into a steep but shallow, muddy ditch. It all happened so fast that my mind was like an outside observer, and I seemed to experience it all, oddly enough, in slow motion.

I heard Jeremy's bicycle go crashing off on the other side of the ditch. But I couldn't see where he'd landed, and I got up and frantically crawled along to find him, shouting out his name above the roar of the truck, which had gunned its engine and gone screeching away.

"I'm over here. I'm all right!" he shouted back. "Are you hurt?"

I was still stunned, and completely unaware of my skinned knees dripping blood. So I just said rather idiotically, "I think I'm okay."

Jeremy had gotten up and come stumbling across the ditch to my side. "You are too hurt," he said, looking up furiously for the culprit, who had disappeared, leaving the road dead silent now.

I glanced down. "No, it's nothing," I said. "Just a flesh wound," I joked. Jeremy examined it.

"What the hell was the matter with those guys?" I said indignantly. "They *were* trying to kill us, weren't they?"

"No," Jeremy said shortly. "If they'd wanted to kill us, believe me, we'd be dead. They just wanted to scare us off."

I would like to say that I stoutly refused to be bullied, that I sneered in the face of death. But, the fact is, I *was* scared. However, not so scared that I hadn't already made up my mind about our next move.

# Chapter Twenty-Five

S haken, but not stirred, we returned to the cottage and bandaged our wounds. Then we jumped into Jeremy's Dragonetta and went right back to Grandmother Beryl's, where we retrieved the Great Lady masthead. Jeremy laid it carefully on the rear seat. All the way back, we speculated as to who was out to get us.

"Could be anybody in town," Jeremy told me. "They all hate us, because of the Shakespeare debacle."

"Oh, come on," I said. "Harriet and her Legacy Society? They'd poison our tea, maybe, but not run us off the road," I said jokingly.

"Well, then how about Colin and his Vandals and his Visigoths?" Jeremy countered. "Those kids are always swooping around town on their bikes. Like bats out of hell."

"Right," I said. "Bicycles. Not cars and trucks."

"Colin has a truck," Jeremy pointed out. "Know what those T-shirts say in Cornish? *Death to second-homers.*"

"But it wasn't Colin's truck," I argued. I stared at him accusingly. "You know perfectly well you don't think it's the locals. Right?"

Jeremy was busy fiddling with his mobile. "Hah. An e-mail from Rupert," he announced, looking enormously pleased with himself. "The temporary injunction against the sale of Beryl's house and the surrounding grounds has come through. I can tell you now that I was never entirely sure we'd get it."

"That's terrific! So, what have we gained, exactly?" I asked.

"It buys us time, pending an environmental study," he explained. "This means nothing can be sold until a team of environmentalists have examined it. We can do the whole show—we'll get nature experts in there to comb the area and take tests looking for vernal springs and endangered species and the whole lot—anything that can prove that the land has natural value for conservation purposes, in case we can't turn up anything of historical value. We'll stall as long as we can."

"Good," I said.

Jeremy paused thoughtfully. "I have to warn you, the Mosley brothers don't like to be crossed and they take no prisoners. We are now the biggest thorn in their side, with this injunction."

"So, it *was* the Mosleys who ran us off the road, right?" I asked.

Jeremy admitted, "Anything's possible with those guys. In fact, with their political connections, they may have already heard about the injunction even before I did!"

We had reached the cottage and now we carried our Great Lady masthead inside, where we laid her out on the kitchen table and got down to the business of examining our new find.

"This is your field. What do you make of it?" Jeremy asked.

"Well, most mastheads are sort of whimsical and mythological, you know, like a Grecian sea goddess or a mermaid, with long flowing hair and fish scales and all," I said, as he used his phone to snap pictures of the wooden figure. "But I've never seen one so lovingly rendered, with such finely detailed features. See how beautifully sculpted her eyelids, nose, mouth, jaw and brow are? Just look at the hair—it's all wavy around her face, but tied into a bun at the nape of her neck. From the looks of her hairstyle and outfit, I'd say she's from the mid-1800s."

I moved around the table and peered more closely. "See all the pleats in her gown? And the pattern of the bodice, and the ruffles and layers in her sleeves!" I marvelled. "I mean, you seldom get such a well-dressed lady to adorn the front of a ship! Look at her fingers!" I said, pointing to the left hand, which was raised across her body and rested just beneath her throat. The other arm hung close by her side, with the hand clasping a wide-brimmed hat, so cleverly sculpted that it just *looked* like a silk hat made to match her dress.

I stepped back now, for an overall view. "I think this is actually solid mahogany. It means somebody spent a lot of time and money on it," I concluded. "And this image is so realistic. It seems more like a commissioned sculpture, like a portrait."

Jeremy had been listening attentively, but now he went into the parlor and began busily tapping away at his computer. I have learned to stand back whenever he's on the cyber-trail of something important, for he has an uncanny ability to make connections with unexpected combinations of keywords, to track down whatever he's after.

When he grunted, I peered over his shoulder. On the screen were rows of thumbnail-sized images of nineteenth-century mastheads, which Jeremy was rapidly scrolling through. Suddenly he stopped, double-clicked on a picture that filled the screen, and then he compared it to one of the photos he'd taken of our masthead.

"Look at this," he said triumphantly. "It's a perfect match, right? Which means our masthead is from"—he clacked a bit more on his computer—"a clipper ship. It's from the mid-1800s, just like you said. It was called *La Paloma*."

I stared at the drawing of an elegant ship with many sails. Jeremy reported, "It says here the ship wrecked on its maiden voyage from where it was built, in Genoa. It sailed past Gibraltar but hit a storm somewhere off the Cornish coast where it foundered and split on the rocks. The owner was a man named Prescott Doyle of . . . Port St. Francis!" Jeremy exclaimed.

"Hey. I'll bet there's something about this ship in the maritime museum!" I exclaimed. "Remember, the one in my guidebook that I wanted us to go see? They've got a whole section devoted to ship-wrecks. Why don't we drive out there and take a look after lunch?"

But then, out of the corner of my eye, I saw a shadow flitting in the driveway. I turned my head, thinking it might be a deer coming to nibble at our garden; then I realized that it was a male figure, moving stealthily closer.

"There's a strange man in the front yard!" I exclaimed. My stomach clutched with fear at the idea that whoever had run us off the road had followed us here to finish the job. Jeremy must have been thinking along the same lines, because he picked up the biggest kitchen knife. Together, we hovered near the window watchfully. As the man drew closer, we could finally see his face.

"Rollo," we both said together. Jeremy shook his head, and I opened the front door, stepped out and waved to him. Rollo glanced up, as if he'd been uncertain as to whether he had the right house. Upon seeing me, he flashed a relieved grin.

"Greetings!" he said. He was holding a suitcase. "Just arrived a few hours ago. Whew! What an infernally long drive. That farmer fellow Geoffrey met me in town so I could follow him to the farm, and then he introduced me to his little hippie wife."

I couldn't imagine what our New Age hosts would think of Rollo, and vice versa. People are usually instinctively wary at the mere sight of Rollo; for, despite his basic good taste when it comes to clothes and antiques, he has a tendency to always look a bit rumpled, as if he's slept in his suit overnight on a park bench.

Today, for instance, he had not shaved yet, and the dark stubble gave him a roguish air, as if he'd been at the roulette table all night somewhere. Which was not entirely inconceivable, either.

"Didn't they show you the other cottage Shannon picked out for you?" I asked, surprised.

"Yes, yes, the girl had a perfectly awful hut in mind for me," Rollo explained, lounging in the doorway. "Penny darling, you could hardly call it a cottage. Damned thing is a mere shed, with one of those wretched gas tanks that goes *poof!* every blasted time you turn on the hot water or the stove. I simply can't stay there, my dear girl. Just won't cut the mustard, it's far too rustic. And that cheeky gal actually asked me if I'd like to pitch in and help with the farming and the lambing! Fancy that, *me* shearing sheep! Does she actually expect me to earn my keep?"

I could just imagine Shannon, in all seriousness, inviting Rollo to take part in the farming that she loved so much. I explained to Rollo that Geoff and Shannon believed that everyone should learn about farming, in order to appreciate the food they eat.

"Humph. Always had the utmost respect for those who till the soil. But, really now. Enough is enough. I put her right straight about that one," Rollo concluded. "I say, shall we have a spot of lunch together?" he inquired as we headed into the parlor.

I grinned at him. But Jeremy motioned to me to hang back so that he could whisper warningly to me, "If Rollo actually thinks he's going to sleep on our sofa here, you'd better disabuse him of that notion straight away."

"Take it easy," I advised. "When we go into town this after-noon to check out that maritime museum we can try to find him other accommodations."

"You know there aren't any other accommodations," Jeremy reminded me. "Let's not roast that old chestnut. Rollo is lucky to have gotten any kind of 'private hut' on such short notice."

"Look, he can stay here with us for a couple of days," I sug-gested. "If he even lasts that long. You know how easily he gets bored."

"Whoo-hah!" Rollo shouted suddenly from the kitchen. "Good God!" A silence followed. Then he returned to the door-way, wide-eyed.

"You failed to introduce me to your *other* houseguest, Penny dear," Rollo said, clutching his chest dramatically as he gestured toward the masthead lying on the kitchen table. "Gave me an aw-ful fright! Thought she was a corpse and you were performing an autopsy. What's it all about?"

We lugged the Great Lady into an empty closet. Then over lunch, we informed Rollo of our noble mission to find some his-toric value to Grandmother Beryl's house and the property around it. I even told him about H.R.H., so Rollo understood that we weren't just going off half-cocked out of sentimentality about the house. The funny thing about Rollo is that you can't trust him on ordinary matters—he'll steal a cigarette or an antique trinket—but on huge matters like the cases that Jeremy and I work on, Rollo has proved himself an invaluable, trustworthy agent.

At least, so far.

So, when I suggested he accompany us into town to try to find out anything about Lady Mascot's real identity, he perked up and said, "Delighted, my dear. She does rather look vaguely familiar. I'm sure I've heard of her somehow."

Rollo and I headed for the car while Jeremy printed out extra copies of his best photo of Miss Paloma.

"Nice to be back in the saddle again," Rollo said with a lop-sided smile. Jeremy joined us now, and we all climbed into the Dragonetta and headed for town.

# Chapter Twenty-Six

Once we got into Port St. Francis, we decided to split up so we could cover more ground in our search for the story of the Great Lady. I went to the library to dig out all I could about the masthead; Jeremy went straight to the maritime museum, which was a few miles outside of town; and Rollo . . . well, he followed his nose, doing what he does best—ducking into dark or dubious places where Jeremy and I would never think to go and would in any case stick out like sore thumbs.

At five o'clock, as pre-arranged, Jeremy and I met up on the large outdoor deck at the back of Toby Taylor's restaurant, where drinks and finger food were served for a cocktail hour before dinner. It was so noisy and busy that we could speak without anyone around us caring about what we were saying.

Rollo arrived, out of breath and smelling faintly of beer. "Bit hungry after all this research!" he said, settling himself in a chair and signalling the waiter for a drink. Jeremy gave him a skeptical look, but ordered a platter of appetizers. Rollo surveyed the view appreciatively, for the sun was slowly setting, and the boats were coming into the harbor below, with hungry seagulls cawing and dipping for their own appetizers.

I was bursting to tell Jeremy what I'd found out, for I was sure I'd made the most astonishing find of the day. Now that Rollo had finally arrived, I plunged right in.

"You know the guy who built the ship that our masthead came from? Prescott Doyle? Well, not only is he from Port St. Francis, but he just happens to be the former owner of Grandmother Beryl's house!" I exclaimed. "Can you believe it? This was *after* The Earl's Players lived there, of course."

I opened my portfolio to get the pages I'd copied. "In the late 1700s," I went on, "the earl sold the house to a shipping magnate named Jonathan Doyle. When Jonathan died, the house was inherited by his only child—our Prescott Doyle. And it belonged to Doyle's relatives until, lo and behold, Grandmother Beryl's dad bought it in the late 1800s."

"Did the masthead come with it?" Jeremy inquired.

"Nope," I said emphatically. "The masthead was retrieved from the shipwreck and given to the Port St. Francis library. But later, there was an auction, and Grandmother Beryl's father bought it! They had a little story about this in an old edition of the local paper. Look."

I spread out the copy I'd made at the library from a feature story about the auction:

*Item #24. Ship's Masthead. Carved mahogany study of Paloma, the lady for whom the ship was named. Sold to Thaddeus Laidley for ten pounds. The new owner admitted that he does not possess a ship. When asked what he planned to do with the masthead, Thaddeus replied, "Why, it would make an excellent scarecrow for my garden!" Mr. Laidley is the proud new owner of the summer cottage that belonged to Prescott Doyle.*

"Thaddeus Laidley!" I repeated, pointing at the name on the page. "My great-grandfather! He's the father of Great-Aunt Penelope, Grandmother Beryl and Great-Uncle Roland. No wonder they got their little mitts on it! Do you suppose their dad just gave it to them?"

"Maybe the masthead was a lousy scarecrow," Rollo joked. "Maybe the crows shat on it."

"Well, in any case, that's my report," I said.

"Great! Now it's my turn," Jeremy said eagerly. "I found out all about the ship—and the woman who inspired it! Her name was Paloma Manera. She was known as 'the Spanish songbird', although she was actually born in Madeira, an island which is technically Portuguese territory. Anyway, she was a world-famous performer, who 'took Europe by storm' as they say, with an opera company from Madrid that also toured the English countryside," he explained, reading from the notes he'd taken at the exhibit. "The guy at the museum told me that Paloma's company showed up in Port St. Francis one summer, and performed at the theatre where Harriet and her club have an office now."

"Oh!" I cried, picturing the elegant soprano on that wonderful old stage.

"They say that Prescott fell hopelessly in love with Paloma 'at the very first note that he heard her sing'," Jeremy continued. "According to the museum guy, Prescott chased her all around the globe, courting her until she finally agreed to marry him. Prescott designed and commissioned the ship, *La Paloma*, as a luxury honeymoon yacht for her. It could carry two hundred fifteen passengers!"

"I wouldn't want two hundred fifteen people aboard on *my* honeymoon," Rollo commented. I nodded.

"I saw some of the design drawings of the interior of the ship, in the museum." Jeremy went on. "Incredible. *La Paloma* was constructed in Italy, using the very finest materials. There was an actual theatre aboard, so that Paloma could sing for their guests. The masthead was just one of many fancy pieces on this luxury yacht-to-beat-all-yachts."

"Doyle must have been incredibly wealthy," I commented. "And hopelessly in love!"

"Yeah, the guy spared no expense. Linens, lace, clothing—everything a bride could want. He even hired a French chef to cook aboard, and brought on an orchestra to play for their wedding day," Jeremy replied. "So," he intoned dramatically, "a week before the wedding, the ship sailed out of Genoa for Cornwall, with all those hired people aboard. But a storm drove it against the rocks, and everybody—crew, musicians, chef—perished . . . including Prescott Doyle."

I gasped. "What about Paloma?" I asked. "Was she aboard?"

"No, she was finishing up her tour on the continent," Jeremy explained. "When she got the news, she retreated in shock to her villa on the island of Madeira, and she never performed publicly again. She lived there the rest of her life, as pretty much a recluse, and she died there. The villa still exists. It's a music museum that hosts an annual classical concert every year."

We all fell silent for a moment. Jeremy signalled to a waiter for the check.

Then Rollo cleared his throat. "Well, I must say all of what you've both reported certainly tracks with what the earl told me," he announced. I nearly fell off my chair.

"The *earl*!" I exclaimed. "You talked to the earl?" Rollo nodded sagely.

"Where?" Jeremy asked warily. "Did he invite you into his manor house for tea?"

"Not necessary, old boy," Rollo said. "I nearly tripped over him down at the old Red Rooster Tavern."

I recalled seeing the painted sign down by the docks for a rather sorry-looking dive that might attract sailors, drunks, Rollo . . . and the earl?

"Man has a terrible stutter," Rollo said, "but he likes his ale, and he likes to make a sporting wager on a game of darts. He's a good player," Rollo admitted ruefully. "Emptied my pockets! Once he started winning, he stopped stuttering—and he talked up a storm. When I showed him the photo of the masthead he really got going. I say, Jeremy, couldn't we have a bit more to eat and drink?"

The waiter had just brought us the tab, but Jeremy hastily ordered another round of nibbles and cocktails, looking impressed with Rollo now.

"So what did the earl *tell* you?" I demanded.

"Well, for starters, Penny dear, Prescott Doyle may well have been a shipping magnate, but his *father* was a bit more than that. Jonathan Doyle was more commonly known as Blackstrap Doyle. Because although he owned a shipbuilding shop, he made his real fortune smuggling."

"Not an uncommon occupation in those days," Jeremy observed. "What did he smuggle?"

"French brandy and Spanish lace," Rollo said, looking down at a stained paper coaster from the Red Rooster bar, upon which, evidently, he had hastily jotted down notes while talking to the earl.

"The brandy sold in England for five times what he paid for it!" Rollo exclaimed. "But it was dangerous work, and he had a lot of close shaves with the law. The earl says that Blackstrap Doyle knew these coves like the back of his hand. Among the locals, old Blackstrap was a folk hero—he was generous to his Cornish neighbors, selling his booty cheaper than the going rate—and tax-free."

"But how does the earl know all about this?" I asked. Rollo and Jeremy exchanged a knowing look.

"Blackstrap Doyle couldn't run an operation that size without—shall we say—partnering with the earl who lived in his day?" Rollo explained to me gently. "Both men made tidy profits. Our earl today *wishes* he had someone like that to help him pay for the upkeep of his estate. He doesn't really like the Mosleys any more than you guys do. But, as he says, 'One must live'."

"So tell me more about Blackstrap Doyle," I urged, fascinated.

"Well, he drove his wife to suicide!" Rollo said, awaiting my shocked look. "They say she was a beautiful, dark-haired lass. But that didn't stop Blackstrap from carrying on an affair with a local barmaid. The poor wife plunged to her death from a high cliff. It was recorded as an accident, but the earl says it was definitely suicide. After his wife's death, Blackstrap felt guilty and got more and more careless with his smuggling."

"Did he get caught?" I asked, wide-eyed.

Rollo nodded, reaching into his pocket to pull out another paper coaster from the Red Rooster Tavern, with a whole new set of his scrawled notes. This time I caught Jeremy's eye, and we both worked hard to suppress our grins.

"Yep," Rollo said, "in 1837, Blackstrap's smuggling ship, the *Falstaff*, was captured off the shores of St. Ives, with a full load of brandy from Normandy. Blackstrap was convicted and sent to an Australian penal colony, where he soon died."

"So, did Prescott Doyle continue the smuggling operation?" Jeremy asked.

"Briefly," Rollo chuckled. "But after his father was arrested, the coastal guards were getting more sophisticated and a lot harder to dodge. Prescott knew that his prospects as a smuggler weren't great," Rollo said.

He broke off when the waiter returned with more appetizers. Rollo leaned forward, savoring the choice, and selected three appetizers, putting two on his own plate and one into his mouth.

"But Prescott saw a bright future in those fancy new clipper ships," he continued, still chewing. "The clippers could get to China quicker and carry back tea to England, where, of course, there was a huge market," Rollo explained. "So, Prescott wisely focused on the perfectly legal importation of Chinese tea. He quadrupled his family fortune within ten years."

"Not bad," Jeremy said.

I was gazing down at the harbor, watching the boats unloading their day's catch, and I could well imagine Prescott's crates of tea being unpacked onto these very docks.

"However," Rollo continued, "his personal life was another story. Prescott was rich, he was good-looking, but he was very moody. Everyone in Port St. Francis knew it was because he had a shadow hanging over him from his mother's suicide. The ladies considered him a 'catch' but, try as they might, they couldn't touch his heart. That is, until that fateful evening at the opera, when he first heard the voice of Paloma Manera. And the rest, as you might say, is history."

Rollo sat back in his chair, looking satisfied but not yet done. He reached into his pocket while saying casually, "Oh, by the way, the earl also told me all about a fine antiques shop in town called *The Frantic Antique*."

"The one with all those whale's teeth and ships' wheels in the window?" I asked.

I'd thought it was just a tourist trap, but Rollo, with his compulsive love of vintage doodads, had been right at home there, and he now pulled out a rosewood cigar box whose lid bore a painted portrait of Paloma on it. With her fiery dark eyes and sensual red mouth, she looked as if she were inviting a male guest to avail himself of a highly fashionable cigar. It occurred to me that her dark, good looks might have reminded Prescott of his beloved mother.

"Only cost a few quid," Rollo admitted.

Jeremy peered at it. "That's our Paloma, all right," he said.

"Apparently, opera singers were like movie stars in their day," Rollo explained. "You know, they sometimes did product endorsements. You should see all the stuff she lent her name to—lady's fans, scented soap wrappers, powder puffs, tea canisters, sheet-music scores and music boxes, even the backs of hairbrushes!"

"But Paloma never returned to Cornwall?" I asked, amazed by it all.

Jeremy jumped in, quoting what he'd read at the museum. "Well, according to the locals, there have been a few sightings of a Woman in White trailing her seaweed-covered wedding gown and veil as she 'searches for her betrothed along the shores of the sea, like a bride looking for her beloved'."

"You mean a ghost?" I exclaimed, feeling goose-bumps as I pictured it. Jeremy nodded.

Now the waiters were politely chasing everybody off the dining deck, because the cocktail hour had ended and they were setting the tables for the first seating of dinner. We rose and headed back to the cottage, where we cooked our own meal of freshly caught fish.

Naturally, Rollo stayed with us for dinner. Afterwards, I made up the sofa for him, then I went off to the bedroom, shut the door, and climbed into the big bed with Jeremy, where I put my head on his chest and lay snuggling there.

"Maybe we should let Rollo stay here on his own, and see what else he can learn," I suggested.

"Why? Where are we going?" Jeremy asked suspiciously.

"Oh," I said airily, "I just thought that now would be an excellent time to take a break somewhere sunnier, and warmer, and more helpful to this case."

"Spill it," Jeremy advised.

"I've been all over the Internet to find out about Paloma's villa," I admitted, "or as they call it in Madeira, a *quinta*. You were right—it's now a museum—so wouldn't you think they'd have a Web site listing their exhibitions? And the program for that classical music festival? But the darned place doesn't even have a domain name! Did you ever hear of such a thing? How can you have a museum and a music festival without a Web site?"

"They do that on purpose," Jeremy explained. "To maintain the exclusivity. My grandparents used to go to Madeira," he told me, smiling. "Every year, at the same old hotel. They went for the cream tea and the music and the scenery—and the reason they loved it was because it always stayed the same, year after year. I bet Paloma's museum caters to that crowd. Doesn't surprise me at all that the place avoids advertising. They're not interested in attracting new people. You either know about Madeira . . . or else you don't know."

I had met Jeremy's snobby Grandmother Margery, and I could well imagine the scene. Even on vacation, her type only wanted to see their "own kind."

"All right, then," I said briskly. "We'll just have to go there and find out for ourselves. Because I'm getting one of those spooky feelings that if there's any mysterious and historical story to uncover about Grandmother Beryl's house, it's got to do with Paloma."

I expected Jeremy to object, but he said wryly, "Well, I guess it beats hanging around here and being run off the road, and having eggs thrown at us, and the whole town despising us for screwing up Shakespeare. I'm sure Harriet will be happy to see the back of us. So, hell. Why not?"

# Part Six

# Chapter Twenty-Seven

The tropical island of Madeira is really the tip-top of an underwater mountain range born of volcanoes nearly twenty million years ago. It sits twelve hundred fifty miles north of Africa, and six hundred miles east of Portugal, who has "owned" Madeira for about five hundred years. In all those centuries, many a ship and many a sailor who were blown off course have made emergency landings on Madeira, which to them seemed to rise out of the mists like an enchanted world unto itself.

"They say that Christopher Columbus plotted his voyage for the New World from Madeira," I told Jeremy on the airplane. "Legend has it that he got the idea when a dying, shipwrecked sailor washed ashore and whispered the secret of a new continent to him," I said in delight.

"What was Columbus doing on Madeira?" Jeremy asked.

"Possibly chasing after a girl from a wealthy seafaring family who had lots of good charts and maps," I said.

"I myself am coming here just for the madeira wine," Jeremy announced. At my slightly puzzled expression he said, "You've never heard of it? Then you don't know your American history.

Your Founding Fathers drank madeira in a toast to each other just after they'd signed the Declaration of Independence."

"Really? So, what does it taste like?" I asked, for Jeremy was becoming quite a wine connoisseur.

"It's like port or sherry, only better," he replied. "Supposedly the secret to making it was discovered by accident, back in the early 1700s, when the crew of a ship that docked in the New World forgot to unload a barrel of the wine, and the cask sailed right back to Madeira. They discovered that the wine, after months of gently swish-swishing in the warm hold of a boat slowly gliding along the equator, had matured perfectly. They say it's 'eternal wine' because no matter how old it gets, it's always drinkable."

"Can't wait to see this place!" I exclaimed, and a passing flight attendant smiled at me.

When we landed in Madeira, all my senses were immediately aware that I was now in a lush, tropical world of its own, with mountains, jungle, beaches, prized forests of laurel and mahogany, and a very old, elegant European town. At the airport, the buzz of voices around us were Portuguese, Brazilian, English, Spanish, African. The air was fragrant with flowers, fruit and the salty taste of the sea.

However, I have learned one interesting rule about travel any-where: If you plan to visit a museum, beware of arriving on a Monday. Nine times out of ten, it will be closed. Paloma's *quinta* was no exception. The gate at the foot of the hill was locked, so we couldn't even get near the villa to see what it looked like. A sign with the museum hours posted on the gate said they'd be open tomorrow.

Therefore, Jeremy and I had no choice but to take a day off and enjoy ourselves. First, we went for a swim in the hotel pool. Then, we walked into the main town of Funchal, whose name comes from the word *funcho* for fennel. From there we took a cable car ride and went swaying all the way up a mountain, swinging high over adorable pastel candy-colored houses, ancient churches, and venerable evergreens. Jeremy pointed out fields of sugar cane and vineyards and orchards, interrupted by beautiful, faraway waterfalls spilling silently below us.

Our ride ended at the tiny mountaintop town of Monte, with its centuries-old tropical gardens. We were so high up that I could immediately feel the difference in the air, which was refreshingly cool and gave the whole area a purifying quality.

"You see that church?" I asked Jeremy, pointing up at an amazingly steep staircase that led to a beautiful building made of white baroque stucco trimmed in grey, with a tower on each side.

"It's called 'Nossa Senhora do Monte'," I said. "Let's go look."

"Penny dear," Jeremy objected, "we've just ascended a mountain in a bucket. You can't possibly think that we're going to now climb those stairs. There must be a hundred of them!"

"Just seventy-two," I answered cheerfully, remembering what I'd read on the plane. "Come on, true believers have been coming here for centuries and *they* climb those stairs on their *knees*. I'm not asking you to do that!"

"Okay, okay," Jeremy said, taking the challenge now. And up we went. The basalt steps were old and in some places cracked, sunken and uneven, so I was soon fairly breathless.

"Whew!" I exclaimed when we finally reached the top. "We made it."

I glanced up at the church. Perched this high, it seemed to almost float among the clouds. At that moment, the pretty blue clock on the outside face of the right tower struck the hour, and then the bells in both towers began to toll. The sound reverberated solemnly in the thin air.

We went inside, where we could hear our footsteps echoing in the cool darkness. Jeremy gazed at the gilded woodwork and ornate glass chandeliers, but I led him to the one, more humble item that was the main object of centuries of pilgrimage: a little wooden statue of the Virgin Mary, which a fifteenth-century shepherd girl claimed she'd gotten as a gift from a mysterious lady who appeared to her. To this day, people still believe that the statue has miraculous powers. There was something sweet and touching about this modest item being the true focus for faithful visitors.

Although the painted and carved face on this wooden statue was very different from Paloma's masthead, I was reminded of it in a forceful way. We were in her world now, and I could sense the influences that had shaped her. When we went back outside, blinking in the brilliant sunlight, I said to Jeremy, "I just got the strangest feeling of Paloma's presence."

We were moving along with a flow of other visitors and now we paused at a small park nearby, with flowering shrubbery and some wooden benches. As soon as I mentioned Paloma, Jeremy appeared startled and then nodded toward one of the benches.

"Look," he said, pointing.

There was a gold plaque on the back of the bench, with these words engraved in Portuguese:

*Na memória de meu Prescott amado. –Paloma Manera*

"In memory of my beloved Prescott?" I guessed. Despite the warm sunlight, I felt an eerie shiver. It was as if she had spoken directly to us. "She loved him so much," I mused. "I guess she never went back to Cornwall because she just couldn't face the loss. I think we'll learn a lot when we see her place tomorrow."

We descended the church steps in silence. Finally, still dizzy from the view and the scent of the fragrant flowers, I said curiously, "How do you want to get back down to town? The cable car again, or should we take one of those taxicabs?"

"Hah!" Jeremy said with a mysterious look on his face. "Why go the ordinary way, when you can have a sleigh ride?"

I looked at him as if he'd lost his mind. "Darling," I said. "We are in the tropics. I know these misty mountain peaks are high, but I am fairly certain there is no snow up here."

"Who needs snow?" Jeremy scoffed. "Follow me, my girl."

We were at the foot of the church's stone staircase, and Jeremy walked over to where a group of moustachioed local men, all dressed in white pants and flat straw hats, had been sitting around smoking. But now, when they saw that a bunch of tourists had just been dropped off by the cable cars, they stood up smiling, stubbed out their cigarettes, and gestured at what, to me, looked like a row of big wicker baskets on long wooden runners, with Santa-Claus-shaped seats inside that had white padded cushions.

"Quick, let's grab one of those toboggans," Jeremy said. "You can't leave Maderia without going for this ride."

I glanced about doubtfully. Other people were doing it, including old folks and couples with kids. Jeremy and I climbed into one, and suddenly, two of the men with straw hats pushed our toboggan right onto a steep, narrow road. Then, with a quick shout, they ran madly alongside us, giving the sleigh a great big push down the hill. Once we'd gathered enough speed, the men hopped onto the runners so they could stay aboard and steer us all the way, giving an extra push with their feet if necessary.

And suddenly we were plunging headlong down the very narrow road, with high stone walls on both sides. The road curved so abruptly that at each turn I was sure we'd go crashing into a wall. But miraculously, we didn't. We just kept picking up speed and careening around each stone corner as we flew downward like an arrow toward its mark—our target being the town of Funchal.

Once I settled back and relaxed, it was fun, whooshing past the pastel-colored houses and going down, down, down until we reached the very bottom of the hill, where some flower vendors were waiting there to laughingly toss flowers at us. When the sleigh stopped, my lap was full of roses, violets, the famed fennel, and other fragrant beauties, which Jeremy obligingly paid for.

"What say we head back to the hotel for dinner?" suggested Jeremy. So we walked hand-in-hand along the harbor, which was filled with fishing boats, yachts, and cruise ships.

Since it was still a bit early, we were able to bag a table on the balcony of the dining room, where we had a splendid view of the sheer cliffs, the sea and the mountains. A tall, curly-haired singer was strolling among the diners carrying a very rounded, mandolin-style Portuguese guitar, and singing the dramatic, yearning music that the waiter told us was called *fado*.

When we got our menu, Jeremy insisted I try the grilled sardines (which are big and fresh and fat, not tiny and oily and crammed into little tins), accompanied by a young white wine called *vinho verde*. Then we tasted fresh beef cooked on an open grill and skewered with laurel sticks, which have the fragrance of bay leaf. Everything was soft, scented and dreamy. It might have gone down in my record books as a perfect evening . . . except for one thing.

The mosquitoes. Now, there are two kinds of people in the world. There are those who rarely get bitten, and even when they do, they seldom react to it.

And then there are people like me. Mosquitoes crave us. They mass in the shrubs, they hover overhead, and they speak to each other on their little mosquito walkie-talkies and proclaim, "There she is! Let's go *get* her now!"

And the worst part is, I don't always see and feel them right away. They sneak up on me, they make their snippy little pinches and I absently brush them away . . . until suddenly I realize I'm under attack. By then it's too late.

"Good God," Jeremy said, staring at my arms and legs when we returned to our hotel room, where the maid had heedlessly opened the windows to let in fresh air . . . and more night-biting mosquitoes who may have missed out on me downstairs. I was covered with big red bites that were growing alarmingly more swollen by the minute.

"Why me?" I wailed. "How come they never ever bite you?"

"Your blood is sweeter," Jeremy suggested, unoffended by my question.

"Bosh," I said.

"Well, the other theory is that they are attracted to the warmth and scent of human breath," Jeremy told me. "And you, my dear, are a bit of a chatterbox sometimes. So they adore your conversation."

I was too busy shuttering the windows to comment. Jeremy called down to the front desk and asked if we could have some mosquito netting put over the bed. Apparently I wasn't the first to need it, because shortly afterwards a man came up and strung the ghostly white netting all around the bed.

And there we stayed all night, kissing in the moonlight, sleeping with the scent of pine and roses, and the far-off sound of the sea . . . until the morning light finally woke us.

# Chapter Twenty-Eight

The next day, something about the old-fashioned formality of Madeira prompted both Jeremy and me to get dressed up a little bit before going out. I rummaged around in my suitcase to find an outfit pretty and feminine enough to match the way the soft air made me feel. I'd packed a sleeveless silk dress, but, mindful of the mosquitoes, I chose instead a silk pantsuit with a white, pink and green floral pattern, and a pink halter top.

When I paired this with white leather sandals and a wide-brimmed white straw hat I'd bought yesterday, Jeremy glanced up at me and said, "You look beautiful—the way I always imagined Aunt Pen did in the 1930s on all her exotic travels."

I beamed with delight. "Hey," I said, frankly appreciative of his white linen suit and beautiful blue shirt that brought out the deep blue in his eyes, "you look pretty spiffy yourself. Like you stepped out of that movie *Casablanca*."

"Well, Casablanca is just about a hop, skip and a jump from here," Jeremy noted. "Let's get out and about before the sun gets too hot."

\*   \*   \*

I was very excited when we pulled up to the wrought-iron gates of Paloma Manera's villa, or *quinta,* and found them open. There was a small stone hut for a guard, but nobody was inside it, so we drove past and continued up the steep, curving driveway that was made of irregularly shaped and various-colored flat stones.

When we reached the top of the driveway in front of the *quinta*, there was a dramatic turnaround, in the center of which was a large, round inlaid stone mosaic depicting a compass with its needle pointing toward Madeira on a map of the world. We circled it and went off to the side, where we found a parking area.

In front of the house was a stone lily pond, and as I watched, a small frog hopped off the sunbaked stone and disappeared into the water with a tiny *plop!* The *quinta* was a soft, cotton-candy pink stucco with a russet-colored tile roof and dark green shutters. The first-floor windows were protected with fancy iron grillwork, and the second and third floor each had wrought-iron balconies outside bigger windows.

The front walkway was flanked on both sides with neatly planted palm trees, white orchids and pink-blossomed shrubbery; and the front door had two large stone urns on each side, from which an abundance of red and pink roses spilled out. Standing there in the driveway, we saw that the *quinta* was built on a high hill overlooking terraced farmland, evergreen woods and, beyond all this, the town of Funchal and the sea. The front door was wide open, so we stepped inside the cool, dark interior.

"Look at these beautiful floors!" I said. "The concierge at the hotel told me that there's nothing better than mahogany from Madeira forests."

"Probably accounts for the fine wood that the masthead was made of," Jeremy observed.

We had paused at the front desk, an admissions center with various color brochures advertising the annual classical music festival, and guided tours of the *quinta*.

I perused a flyer, then exclaimed, "Hey, it says that in Paloma's study, there's a framed magazine interview she gave. The last one before her death. *That* we've gotta see!"

At that moment, we heard a loud, rude blast coming from somewhere upstairs. This was followed by what, to me, sounded like a humongous dentist's drill. It was surely just a construction noise, but its shrill whine sent a shudder down my spine.

"That sounds none too promising," Jeremy said, and, as if to punctuate his comment, we heard a sudden loud bang, as if someone had dropped a two-ton brick on the floor above us.

While we stood there uncertainly, waiting for someone to get off their coffee break and come and sell us our tickets for a tour, three workmen came clattering down the staircase. Two were in white but paint-spattered overalls. The third was carrying a tangle of electric wires which were so entwined that they looked like inky black squid-spaghetti.

The painters clattered past us, but the electrician caught my eye, and, I guess because I smiled at him, he spoke, but in Portuguese, saying, "*O museu esta encerrado.*"

"Holy cow," I said in panic. "Does that mean what it sounds like?"

"I think he's trying to tell us the museum is closed," Jeremy said, frowning.

"It can't be!" I exclaimed. "They're supposed to be open all day today."

The man was standing at the front door, still trying to untangle his wires, but he looked as if he expected us to turn tail and leave.

When we didn't, he pointed at the back of one of the open doors, then shrugged and walked out.

Jeremy went to the door and closed it a bit, so that we could read a new sign that was now posted there, just above the old one listing the regular schedule. Since the signs were for tourists, they were written in several languages. The new sign said in English:

*CLOSED FOR RENOVATIONS UNTIL NEXT YEAR*

"No!" I wailed. "It can't be! That damned sign just went up. They've gotta give one last swan-song tour before they shut these gates."

As if in response, the drill upstairs resumed its ear-piercing whine in earnest.

Then I heard the distinct clattering of a woman's shoes, tap-tapping across the back of the first floor.

"Quick," I said to Jeremy. "Let's make a dash upstairs before she spots us."

"Too late," Jeremy warned as a woman appeared suddenly around the curved, carved staircase and marched toward us. Jeremy straightened his shoulders and put on his most charming smile.

"*Hola*," he said to her.

"That's Spanish," I hissed.

"Close as I can get," Jeremy retorted from the corner of his mouth.

"*Olá!*" the woman answered. "It's Portuguese, too," she said in English. "But in any language, the museum is closed." Even in this heat, she was dressed in a severe black suit, which made me think that she was an administrator, not a tour guide.

"Oh, but we've come such a long way!" I said. "Couldn't we at least speak to a guide?"

The woman, who was a tall, thin creature wearing wire-rimmed spectacles which the light danced in, said, not unkindly but firmly, "I am so sorry, but you cannot possibly stay here. It is too dangerous with the workman all about. The guides do not come here today."

"But you see, we *must* have some information about Paloma Manera," I pleaded, and when she shook her head and I felt that I was losing her, I added recklessly, "We are working at the behest of Prince Charles."

Jeremy nudged me sharply, but I continued, heedless. "We need to learn all we can about Paloma. We have been researching her connection to Prescott Doyle, and we know about the ship-wreck tragedy," I said, plunging onward with no idea of where I could go with this. "But we know nothing of her later life here in Madeira, and we want to find out why she never came back to Cornwall."

"Miss, I wish I could help you. Come back next year, yes?" the woman said, edging us toward the door determinedly.

But even as she spoke, a young, handsome Portuguese man in a white suit came out of a little office behind the front desk. He must have been listening to my plea, because now he said, "But Paloma Manera *did* go back to Cornwall!"

Seizing our only opportunity, it was my turn to give him the full wattage of my very best smile. I don't lay claim to being a daz-zler, but this young guy was so sweet and so sorry to see me un-happy, that he was visibly relieved to have made me smile. Now he appeared to make a decision on his own.

He turned to the woman and spoke rapidly to her in Portu-guese. At first, she seemed to be arguing with him. Politely but very firmly, he persevered. The woman, looking slightly annoyed but resigned, now pretended that she didn't care one way or the other. She said something in Portuguese that to me sounded along the lines of, *Well, then, do what you want, it's your funeral.*

But what she actually said to us was, "Afonso is a tour guide. It is only luck that he is here today. He cannot give you a tour. But he will talk to you."

This little speech of hers was obviously a face-saver, and the man politely allowed her to take credit for the decision. Then she turned sharply and walked away with a brisk tap-tapping of her heels.

"She is a very busy person," Afonso said to us lightly, by way of an apology. "Follow me, please."

To my surprise, he led us out the door, past the lily pond and down a side path that crossed the lawn and led farther along the grounds. "Paloma brought these exotic plantings from her travels around the world," he said, and he pointed to the left and right of the path to show us various herbs and flowers that were now fragrant, mature shrubs. Greek oregano, French lavender, Chinese anise, Tahitian vanilla . . . the list went on and on.

I confess, though, that I was barely listening to him. I was racking my brain trying to come up with something I could say to make him turn around and bring us back into the *quinta*.

But now we had reached a white octagonal-shaped pavilion of some sort. It looked like an antique gazebo, yet it seemed more whimsical than that, like a pretty wedding cake. It had iron-trimmed glass windows, some of which were fan-shaped. The roof, too, was made of glass and iron; yet the rest of it was all white-painted wood, which, I now realized, gave it a bridal look; and in a flash of sympathy I wondered if Paloma had this built with her wedding in mind.

"This structure is what you English call a 'folly'," Afonso explained. "They are meant to be fanciful and wonderfully impractical!"

"Follies," I repeated. I had heard of them before, because many of the queenly, historical characters in the movies I'd worked on, from Joséphine Bonaparte to Lucrezia Borgia, had loved follies. So I'd seen pictures of follies that were actually quite elaborate buildings, usually associated with the luxurious gardens of great estates, built purely for fun and ornamentation. Eccentric rich folk who had nothing but time on their hands and loads of money at their disposal—like Marie Antoinette, for instance—had such extravagant ones constructed that they really were whole houses or estates unto themselves.

And because the wealthy often indulged in whimsical, child-like fantasies when they built their playhouses—creating tiny castles, mini Taj Mahals, Hansel-and-Gretel cottages, and even ones shaped like a pineapple or a favorite toy—hence, the name "folly".

"Please to enter," Afonso said gallantly, using a key to open the door and then stepping aside to allow me to go in first.

"Oh!" I said, when I saw that the interior walls, floor and benches were all covered with amazingly beautiful tiles.

"These tiles are called *azulejos*," Afonso said. The ones on the floor were rough-textured and of deep colors—dark evergreen, midnight blue, blood-red and fiery turquoise. By contrast, the wall tiles were smooth white-and-blue and sunny yellow, and these depicted various scenes of lives of the saints, as well as more mythological-looking creatures that resembled mermaids and fauns.

"The tiles on the floor are very old and very Madeiran," continued Afonso. "The wall tiles are more modern—from the Spanish occupation of the late sixteenth century, showing the Dutch influence from the Spanish Netherlands."

Only a European tour guide could imagine that the sixteenth

century was modern, I thought in distracted amusement. Any other time in my life I would have been thrilled to get a close-up, private tour of these highly prized Portuguese tiles, but all I could think of was how I could find out more of Paloma's personal story that lay inside that damned *quinta*.

"Afonso," I said softly, "Was this built for Paloma's wedding?"

A shadow crossed his face. "Yes. The wedding that never was."

"You said that Paloma did go back to Cornwall," I continued. "How do you know this?"

Looking caught, Afonso admitted, "Just before her death, Paloma gave one last interview."

I pounced, as gently as I could. "We really need to see it. Can you please let us in to read it?"

Afonso had such an empathetic, expressive face that reflected what he saw on mine, so now his happy look became grave and sorrowful.

"Unfortunately, no. It is the—how do you say—insurance policy. We cannot take the risk that you and this gentleman might get hurt with all the work going on," he said worriedly.

"We should have introduced ourselves," Jeremy interjected now, having been silent for so long because, as he later told me, he observed that Afonso was "sweet" on me. "I am Jeremy Laidley, and this is my wife and business partner, Penny Nichols. You may have heard of us. We are working on a case of some importance in England, and we would deeply appreciate whatever you can do to help us."

"Because a lot of good people are depending on us!" I exclaimed.

"Please excuse me for a moment," Afonso said, still shaking his head in his regretful but polite way, and he turned and walked right out of the folly.

"Swell," I said apologetically to Jeremy. "I really put my foot in it. Now I've scared him off. Wish I had more finesse like you."

"You don't need finesse," Jeremy said consolingly. "Just being your winsome self is what's kept us here this long."

"So, now that he's shown us the *azulejos* I guess the tour's over, huh?" I asked, for I saw through one of the windows that Afonso had come back out of the *quinta* and firmly locked its front doors. He still wore a grave expression on his face as he came down the garden path toward us, and gestured for us to come out of the folly.

Reluctantly, Jeremy and I stepped aside and watched him lock the folly door as well. Then he walked us along the garden path, toward the driveway. I figured he wasn't going to leave our side until we were back in our car, because he directed us beyond the house and toward the parking area.

But just as we reached the cars, he turned abruptly and led us around the far side of the *quinta*, to a very ordinary side door that he carefully unlocked, after looking over each shoulder as if he were a thief trying to escape being noticed.

"We must be quick," he murmured. "Follow me."

# Chapter Twenty-Nine

Afonso led us up a very simple set of stairs without any embellishment or fine carving. It must have been a servant's staircase, for it was so different from the rest of the house. We climbed one flight, and came out a plain door that opened into the second floor, where Paloma's personal quarters were. Afonso explained that the main level had always been for receiving guests and musical entertainments.

"But alas, Paloma saw no one for many years," Afonso said, as if speaking about his own maiden aunt instead of an historical character.

"Watch your step," he added as we proceeded down the corridor. Everywhere there were signs of renovation, and we had to step over long, thick power cords that lay all along the hall floor. We passed rooms that were draped with plastic sheeting, put up by a restoration crew who was cleaning the murals and walls; but also there were areas where the corridor's ceiling was completely exposed, and from which dangled ominous-looking wires. Occasionally, too, there were clumps of plaster on the floor, and very tall ladders, which I carefully avoided stepping under.

But with all these signs of disarray, there were no workers to be seen anywhere.

"They're on their lunch break," Jeremy guessed under his breath, as if reading my mind.

We reached a big, quiet room at the back of the house, which had a very large, ornate window that overlooked the sea. There was a stunning view, but it reminded me of Cornwall, and I knew in a flash why Paloma had come here to be alone in her sorrow.

Afonso steered us toward one wall of this private room, where a long row of wood-and-glass framed objects were mounted, all an identical size. Peering closer I discovered that each frame enclosed one of a series of printed pages from an old magazine.

"It is Paloma's last interview," Afonso said graciously. "We displayed it because it tells her story so beautifully. Very few people ask to see it now."

I wanted to throw my arms around him and kiss him, but as it was, I just beamed at him and said with utter gratitude, "Oh, Afonso, thank you so much!"

He blushed as if I *had* kissed him, then glanced at his wristwatch. "We haven't much time," he warned. "I must get you out of here before the workers return. Otherwise I could lose my job."

"Okay," I said, and Jeremy and I quickly began to read the framed pages as Afonso left the room and posted himself in the corridor, where he nervously kept a lookout.

The cover of the magazine was displayed first. It was an old and long-defunct English periodical, an elegant but gossipy magazine about the rich and the famous. It reminded me of *Tatler*, but it was called *Visages*.

The interview with Paloma had taken place right here in 1928. The female reporter began her piece by describing how thrilled she was to be invited into the *quinta* after all these years of the great soprano's solitude. The interviewer noted that Paloma, who was eighty-five years old at the time, had a magnetic presence and "retained her astonishing good looks", with hair that was still mostly dark, and dark eyes that flashed with intelligence, and enviably smooth, pale skin, and a regal, proud way of moving through the room in her silk caftan. There was an accompanying photograph, large and lustrous, of the world-renowned diva, and she did indeed have an arresting, timeless aura.

At first, the reporter asked Paloma the usual questions: her favorite roles in the opera, her most memorable co-stars, and what her favorite foods, perfume and clothing were. This took up the first few pages that Jeremy and I squinted at, reading them carefully as we moved down the wall. I began to doubt that we would actually find anything useful here.

But on the third page, the lady interviewer plucked up her courage and dared to raise a subject about which Paloma had been resolutely silent for most of her life: the wreck of *La Paloma*. Apparently, having reached this advanced age, she was finally ready to talk.

And boy, did she. In vivid detail Paloma described her first performance in Cornwall, in the beautiful theatre at Port St. Francis. Prescott Doyle had had his own private box; and by the end of the show, he'd already sent her a dozen red roses, which were presented to her onstage.

This was the beginning of Prescott's flamboyant, persistent courtship. Paloma said she resisted him for a long time, not because she did not love him, as she explained to the interviewer— for she candidly declared that she became Prescott's mistress soon after they met—but when it came to marriage, Paloma demurred because she'd worked hard to become an independent woman, and did not want to end up being a rich man's possession.

Nevertheless, the affair continued, and over time, the pair became closer, with Paloma sometimes staying at Prescott's summer home in Cornwall, overlooking the ocean. Prescott vowed to redecorate it as Paloma's "palace over the sea", if she would only consent to be his bride.

"Listen to this," I said to Jeremy, reading a bit of the interview aloud in which Paloma described how Prescott Doyle relentlessly courted her, right from the get-go.

*"The bouquet of blood-red roses was but the first of many gifts of love bestowed on me by this remarkable man. Every week from then on, he sent me something, big or small, to remind me of his devotion. And so they came, these wondrous gifts: a tiara of the finest diamonds and sapphires; three priceless, snowy-white Egyptian ponies adorned with colored stones from Africa; fine caviar from Persia; a lemon tree from Morocco; silk slippers from China; perfume from India; and the most sacred, treasured gift of all: the Scarlet Knot, this mysterious, magical red stone which his dear mother had given him. Of all his gifts, this was the one I cherished most, for it was such a personal gesture."*

"Wow," I said. "A red stone from his mother! Maybe an antique ruby—just like you and your mum gave me for my engagement ring, Jeremy."

He smiled as I held out my hand, gazing fondly at my heirloom ring. I felt an immediate kinship with the mysterious Paloma.

Eagerly I read on, to where the interviewer asked Paloma to elaborate about the gift. This was what she said:

*While my beloved Prescott was at first reluctant to speak about his boyhood memories, he soon trusted me enough to show me this dearest treasure which his mother told him had magical powers of healing and protection. She gave it to him when he was only a boy, on his way to boarding school, so he took it to please her. Poor Prescott came to believe that his mother would never have died that tragic death had she not given away her lucky stone to him. Having grown up as I did in Madeira I understood the power of such a talisman, and so when Prescott insisted that I keep it for luck, I knew that he was trying to protect me, the woman he loved, from the sufferings of this world.*

*But alas, in giving me the stone, my beloved Prescott lost the protection that his mother had tried to give him. And that is why, I believe, he was killed at sea.*

On this page of the article there was a reproduction of an oil painting of Prescott Doyle, who looked dark and handsome, in a rugged, slightly defiant attitude, seeming more like a Welsh poet than the hard-nosed businessman he'd become.

This was followed by a section where Paloma described how she carried the Scarlet Knot with her wherever she went, and she swore that it did indeed have protective powers. She claimed that on one occasion, for instance, while backstage, a hundred-pound sandbag was accidentally loosened from above, and fell within inches of her head. On another occasion, her horse-drawn coach lost a wheel, flipping the vehicle, and killing the driver. Yet Paloma emerged unscathed. Each of these times, Paloma attributed her survival to the "power of my lucky stone".

I stared at the final illustration in the magazine piece. Paloma had sketched the Scarlet Knot for the interviewer. It did indeed look like an engagement ring, with a single stone at the top, and decorative spiral engravings on the band.

The article went on to describe how Prescott built his ship, *La Paloma*, as the ultimate enticement to convince her to marry him and sail away with him on such a dreamy honeymoon vessel.

Prescott wrote to her from Genoa explaining his plan, and Paloma finally relented. Her note back to him from Paris said: *I do, I shall, I am yours forever.* So Prescott joyfully outfitted the ship with every luxury imaginable, and went aboard it for its fatal maiden voyage.

"This tracks with everything the guy at the maritime museum in Cornwall told me," Jeremy noted, craning his neck to read the next page.

"Yes," I said excitedly, "it says here that Paloma was finishing up her tour at the time, which explains why she wasn't aboard the ship with Prescott. They arranged to meet at Cornwall. But then the ship wrecked in that awful storm."

In the final page of the interview, Paloma confirmed that this was why she returned to Madeira and never performed in public again—choosing, instead, to teach music to children—and she never married nor had any children of her own. Paloma explained that over the years she sought comfort from spiritualists, hoping to "connect" with Prescott, but she felt unsatisfied with these attempts.

"In the late 1800s Paloma made a pilgrimage of some sort, to an archeological site on the eastern shores of Lake Neuchâtel in Switzerland known as La Tène," Jeremy read aloud.

I sidled over to get a view of the page that Jeremy was reading. "It's an old Celtic site," he explained. "In Paloma's day, La Tène was a new find, with excavations and scientists still uncovering it. I've been there once, on a business trip," he told me. "But it's all very modern now—there's conference centers and tennis courts nearby. All you can really see of La Tène is just this glass display case full of metalworks—arrowheads, shields, and swords-in-stones. Very touristy."

"Is it worth having a look, to see what this Celtic stuff is all about?" I asked.

Jeremy shook his head. "You don't have to go all the way to La Tène to see touristy Celtic swords stuck in stones," he answered. "I know a place that's much closer to Port St. Francis."

We heard a slight stir in the house, of voices below. Hurriedly, I took one last look at the final page of the printed interview, hastily trying to memorize it before Afonso came in to tell us that time was up.

"Here's what I've been looking for!" I exclaimed. "It says that Paloma went back to Cornwall one last time, in the 1920s, the year before this interview," I noted, pointing to the reporter's final question, in which she asked to see the Scarlet Knot. This was Paloma's answer:

*I did not keep it. I could not but feel that the Scarlet Knot was sending me a message in the form of strange impulses that I wished to understand. And soon I learned why, for I felt that I was being haunted not by Prescott, but by the spirit of Prescott's mother, who wanted me to restore the gift to its rightful place. And this I did. And that is how I found peace.*

"What's that supposed to mean?" I said aloud.

"Dunno," Jeremy said. "She isn't really telling."

"Why would she return poor Prescott's engagement ring?" I said, feeling sad. "What on earth did she do—bury it at his mother's grave? That seems rather ghoulish."

"Guilt makes people do strange things," Jeremy commented.

Now Afonso hurried in, saying urgently, "*Por favor!* We must go now."

Quickly, we followed him back down the servants' staircase, and out the side door to the parking area.

"Did you find it helpful?" Afonso asked hopefully.

"Oh, yes," I said gratefully. "Thank you so very much!" He

smiled warmly at me, and shook hands with Jeremy, then hurried back to the *quinta*.

It wasn't until we drove past the front gate that I remembered to ask Jeremy, "So what's all this stuff about some Celtic place in Cornwall with swords in stones?"

"Tintagel," Jeremy said. "The birthplace of King Arthur."

"Of course! He was a Celt too, wasn't he?" I queried.

"Yes, he was a legendary king," Jeremy said. "But the Celts were a very mysterious crowd, and they go back even farther than King Arthur. They came from the European continent and migrated all over Cornwall and Wales and Ireland."

"Tintagel," I repeated, remembering all the signs I'd seen for it on the drive through Cornwall. "That's a hot spot on the tourist trail, isn't it?"

"Yep," Jeremy said. "Big ruined castle on a rock. Saw it when I was a kid. It's practically a stone's throw away from Port St. Francis."

# Chapter Thirty

I must say that when we drove through the village of Tintagel I was utterly horrified. Of course, it was high tourist season now in perhaps the most touristy town on the coast. Throngs of day-trippers who'd been disgorged by buses were walking six abreast, flapping around in flip-flops, all with a vague, distracted look in their eyes as they sought the next attraction while holding bags of cheap souvenirs, and eating candy, fudge, sausages—and large hamburgers from a cart that advertised them as "Excaliburg-ers".

Jeremy had to stop the car abruptly to let some of these push-carts cross the street.

"Excali-burgers?" I asked. "Is that a pun?"

"King Arthur's sword was called Excalibur," Jeremy reminded me with a wry look. "And you'd probably need a magic sword to cut one of those huge burgers."

"Oh, yes, I remember. Didn't the young Arthur have to pull a magic sword out of a stone to prove that he was the rightful heir to the throne?" I asked.

"Either that, or he got the sword later, from the mysterious Lady of the Lake," Jeremy said.

I recalled that Jeremy, in his boyhood, had been fairly obsessed with such adventure stories. He went on, "The stories of King Arthur evolved down through the ages by Irish, French and English troubadours. According to Tennyson, King Arthur was fair-minded and brave, trying to create a perfect kingdom that performed only noble deeds. You know, the Knights of the Round Table, where everyone was equal, and chivalry reigned," Jeremy explained.

He parked the car and we got out, weaving our way through the crush of people who'd emerged from guest houses and bungalows carrying Styrofoam surfboards and beach balls. Many of them were brandishing plastic Arthurian swords, and they seemed to be heading in the same direction.

"Where are they going?" I asked.

"To see the castle, of course," answered Jeremy. "The home of King Arthur. Hope you're wearing good walking shoes. Follow me, milady," he commanded, leading me past several signs that pointed in the direction of a looming, isolated island just outside of town. But Jeremy knew an off-the-beaten-path way of getting to the castle via a coastal trail, so we bypassed the hordes of tour groups waiting outside a nearby Camelot-themed hotel.

From afar, Tintagel Castle looked dark and foreboding, like a blackened, lost kingdom atop a rocky island; and in fact, as Jeremy explained to me, it had been abandoned for a long time, having nearly washed into the sea by the sixteenth century. Nowadays it was connected to the mainland by a narrow bridge.

"This way," Jeremy said. "Watch your footing."

Once we were on the island, the castle itself was reached by a series of formidable stone and wooden staircases, and wooden platform-bridges with high railings, all erected for modern-day visitors. As we climbed, I avoided looking down, for it felt as if one false step would indeed send us tumbling to our deaths.

When we finally reached the top, and stood there with the wind tearing at our hair and clothes, Tintagel truly did seem to be a nearly impregnable site. On one side, the castle reigned over a sheer, steep drop to deep, rocky gorges. On the other side, the castle towered above the churning sea that was violently crashing far, far below.

"Boy," I said, panting with exertion, "this place would give any marauding Viking or Vandal a pause before trying to breach it."

But time itself had overtaken the castle, for now only its broken remains stuck up out of the mossy, flat-topped peak. Fragments of its high stone walls stood in bleak relief against the skyline; and cracked sections of centuries-old stone flooring lay open to the elements. Although it all looked so tumbledown, like an estate that's perished after fire and flood, I could still make out the shape of castle towers, battlements and other signs of a long-ago fortress.

Walking around these impressive ruins, I felt awed but still a bit confused. "This looks medieval, like it's from the thirteenth century," I observed.

"It is," Jeremy replied.

"But, King Arthur would be much earlier," I objected. "Isn't Arthur a fifth-century Celtic king?"

"That's the prevailing wisdom," Jeremy agreed. "See, the bits we're looking at are indeed from a medieval castle—but this was built atop the ruins of something much older. Nobody knows for sure what the underlying, original structure was; there's a theory that it could have been a Celtic monastery from the fifth century."

"Or else it was an ancient 'Homecoming Inn' for bygone tourists," I teased him. "Can't beat this view!"

Jeremy grinned. "Let's go back down. There's something else you'll want to see."

We began our descent, and once we reached sea level, he led me to a viewing area where I could glimpse a stunning sight that lay at the foot of the castle. Tucked into the cliffs was a dark, mysterious cave that looked like a great black hole impossibly carved out by glaciers many eons ago. The roiling, swirling sea seemed to rush in and out of the rocky grotto with formidable power.

"That's Merlin's cave," Jeremy said. "Legend has it that he was a magician who transported the stones of Stonehenge all the way from Ireland, in order to create a sacred place to properly bury Celtic heroes who'd died in battle."

"So that's how those strange big rocks got to Stonehenge," I joked. "I always heard that it was built by aliens from another planet."

Jeremy ignored this. "They say that when King Arthur was an infant, he was put in Merlin's care, for safety," he continued, just like a kid who wants to tell you a story he read at summer camp. "And when the boy Arthur pulled the sword out of the stone, it was Merlin who proclaimed him king. In some stories, Merlin actually became a member of the court of King Arthur, where his job was to protect the kingdom by fighting off the bad spells of evil witches."

"But poor Merlin lived down there in that cave?" I asked. "Geez, you'd think that Arthur would have given him a proper room in the castle."

Yet for all my teasing, and despite the touristy nonsense, I must admit that there was something compelling about this windswept island that made it all seem believable and real—the great and noble King Arthur, the good Knights of the Round Table, the gifted Merlin and the magical sword.

But later, as we came away from the quiet, moody place, and walked back to our car, I admitted, "I don't think this helps us much with Paloma, though." It had been my idea to come here, and now it was looking like a dead end.

"Well, at least you can say you've seen the birthplace of Camelot," Jeremy said philosophically.

"Hey, lady," said a vendor with a pushcart that was blocking our path to the parking lot. "Wanna buy a sugar-coated magic wand?"

"Nope," I said wearily.

Undaunted, the guy said, "How 'bout a crystal ball, luv?"

"I can already tell you what's in your future if you don't step out of our way," Jeremy said in a light but firm tone. The man shrugged, moved on and turned his attention to other potential customers.

As soon as I entered the car, my mobile buzzed in my purse. I picked it up and squinted at it.

"What's up?" Jeremy asked.

"E-mail from Rollo," I said, showing it to him: *Hullo Pen, Dogged out something rather amazing. Could have important implications for The Case. Essential that you and Jer meet me back at the cottage ASAP. Yours, Rollo.*

"Wonder what he's been up to while we've been away," Jeremy muttered suspiciously.

"With Rollo's bar-room acquaintances, you never can tell," I said. "He just might be on to something. Let's go!"

# Part Seven

Part Seven

# Chapter Thirty-One

Just when I hoped we might make some progress on this case, fate threw us a curve ball. Well, maybe not fate. As my old friend Will Shakespeare said, *The fault is not in our stars but in ourselves.*

The first sign of trouble was the outside of the cottage. It was splattered with a series of concentrated pink and orange blobs of paint that looked as if they had been hurled like water balloons against the house.

"We've been paintballed," Jeremy said, steering away from where he would normally park, because the driveway also had puddles of the pink and orange paint.

"Who did this?" I said indignantly. Jeremy shook his head.

Once inside the cottage, we noticed that Harriet had delivered the items from Grandmother Beryl's house that we had asked for: the rocking-horse, the croquet set, the teak credenza and the beaux arts lamps.

"But what on earth happened to that rocking-horse?" I asked incredulously. One handle was broken off and lying on the floor; and the back ends of both its wooden runners were cracked and splintered.

"It looks as if some grown-up fat-ass sat on it," Jeremy said. We just gazed at each other.

"Rollo," I said.

"So where the hell is he?" Jeremy asked.

I didn't have an answer to that. But a short while later, you might say that the other shoe dropped. It arrived on our doorstep in the form of a white envelope, mysteriously unmarked. No address on it, no postmark, no sign of having been delivered by the mailman or any other courier. No noise, either, so I can't even say when it arrived.

As I picked up the envelope lying at my feet, I got a queer feeling of foreboding in my stomach. Nobody sent us mail here. People who knew us either phoned or e-mailed.

"What's that?" Jeremy asked, observing my wary expression as I handed it to him. There was only one sheet of paper inside, and the message was made of cut-up newspaper letters, which I thought people only did in movies. It spelled out, plain and simple:

*Your cousin Rollo for a million pounds. Fair trade?*

What a question.

"This must be a hoax, right?" I said nervously, handing it to Jeremy. Before he could answer, the cottage telephone rang. Jeremy picked it up on the third ring.

"Hello?" he said. Then he held the receiver out so I could hear, too.

"Jeremy?" It was Rollo. He initially sounded relieved to hear Jeremy's voice, but then he went on, in the most sober, scared tone I've ever heard poor Rollo use, with a message that sounded rehearsed:

"Jeremy, old boy, did you get the ransom letter? Well, they want me to tell you it's no joke. Listen carefully. You will receive further instructions shortly. Do not involve the police or I'm a dead man. Please talk to my mum and make her get the million pounds together for you in small bills. I assure you, these fellows mean business. You will hear from them when you hang a red kerchief on your car door handle and park it in town, to signal that you got the money. Please don't wait to do this. There simply isn't going to be any time to waffle about it."

This last bit sounded pleading and desperate, and touchingly frightened. A second later, the phone went dead.

"Damn it," Jeremy said, looking both concerned and exasperated now.

Worried as I was, I can tell you that the mind does funny things when you're in a situation like this. While Jeremy was talking about what to do next, some part of my brain was wondering where on earth I was going to get a red kerchief on such short notice to signal the kidnappers.

"Who would want to kidnap poor old Rollo?" I wondered.

"Could be the same weasels who've been threatening us out here in Cornwall. Or, it could just be some gangster in London that Rollo has a gambling debt with. Doesn't matter," Jeremy said shortly. "We still have to deal with whoever's got him. I can get some police advice from Denby in London, before we go back to the local coppers. Denby might know somebody out here who can be trusted to keep it quiet."

"Rollo said not to involve the police," I reminded him.

"Just for advice, quietly. But in any case, we're going to have to get some money together, and at least appear to do what the kidnappers want," Jeremy said. "It's quite possible that we can successfully make an exchange. But that means we're going to have to go to London today and pay a little call on Great-Aunt Dorothy. She won't believe it unless she hears it from us in person."

At the thought of visiting Great-Aunt Dorothy, I felt even more trepidation than facing down kidnappers. "God, no," I said. "Not that."

"You want to tell her we're coming?" Jeremy said, scrolling his mobile for the number.

"If we call her, she'll duck us," I warned. "I say we just land on her. The element of surprise is essential."

I'd been in Great-Aunt Dorothy's apartment only once in my life, and at the time, I'd been fairly certain I'd never return voluntarily. It was when Jeremy and I first came into our inheritance. And to give you an idea of the kind of person she is, Great-Aunt Dorothy had summoned me there with the intent to convince me that Jeremy was a nefarious character trying to rob me and Rollo of our share, when, in fact, it was she and Rollo who were the ones scheming to do that very thing to me and Jeremy.

So, when I now found myself once again standing outside that slightly spooky, tall, dark apartment building with its black wrought-iron fencing that ringed it with arrow-like, spiky tops—like rows of medieval spears ready to impale us right there in the street—I think I can be forgiven for inwardly cursing Rollo for putting me in this position again.

Jeremy reached for the heavy iron handle of the front door, but apparently the building had new security, so we had to first buzz an intercom to talk to the guard in the lobby. I explained, in my most earnest Little-Red-Riding-Hood way, that I had come to surprise my old Auntie on her birthday. I made this up on the spot. Jeremy just grinned and went along with the ruse.

It worked. The ancient, wizened old doorman buzzed us in without bothering to ask Great-Aunt Dorothy if it would be all right. He must have figured that a crotchety old bird like her was lucky to have any young relatives come calling.

We entered the lobby, which smelled vaguely of mothballs, and we walked toward the very same elevator operator I'd seen last time—an elderly guy who was still dressed in his navy blue uniform with gold braid. It took all his strength and concentration to haul open those heavy wooden elevator doors and the old-fashioned iron grate, and then close them again, before the elevator lurched upward.

It is the slowest elevator in the history of the world. Upon finally alighting on Dorothy's floor, we had to walk down a long, gloomy dark corridor where her apartment was the last one on the end.

This trek probably gave the doorman time to phone Great-Aunt Dorothy and let her know we were on our way. Which is probably why, just as we approached her door, the maid opened it before we could knock. She was that same tall, gawky woman I'd met last time, and, with her goosey neck and slightly bulging, staring eyes, she resembled a kind of greying, aging Olive Oyl from the *Popeye* cartoon.

"Hi," I said boldly. "Penny Nichols here to see my Great-Aunt Dorothy. And of course, you remember Jeremy Laidley."

The maid just gawked at us, but she didn't try to detain us at the doorway, which I considered a good sign. We walked right into Great-Aunt Dorothy's parlor, a huge, dark lair decorated in baffling, depressing tones of brown, beige and a mustardy yellow.

And there she sat in her favorite high-backed gold-and-brown chair as if it were a throne, surrounded by all those expensive islands of opulence that still couldn't fill up such an enormous room—the antique sofas and chairs, the urns and lamps and knick-knacks and tall, potted plants. She peered at us from the shadows of this gloomy parlor, which was always kept darkened by heavy, dusty velvet curtains.

Great-Aunt Dorothy herself was a petite, birdlike lady with silver-white hair. Even at her advanced age she sat straight and rigid, dressed in a dove-grey silk dress. Her thin fingers were like little bird-claws clutching her favorite walking-stick at her side, the only evidence of her frailty when it came to getting in and out of chairs and walking about.

"It's not my birthday," were the first words out of her mouth as she eyed us suspiciously.

"You're looking well, Dorothy," Jeremy said neutrally.

"What do you want?" Her tone indicated that relatives only showed up unannounced when they wanted money. Normally she'd be wrong about us. But thanks to good old Rollo . . .

Although she did not invite us to take a seat, Jeremy calmly and easily plunked himself in one of those overstuffed armchairs. The nearest one to him was a good three feet away, and I took it, realizing that to remain standing would give the appearance of a supplicant easily dismissed.

Jeremy, who knows Great-Aunt Dorothy better than I do, must have decided that the best course of action was to be as blunt as she was, for he said unceremoniously, "Rollo has been kidnapped."

"Bah!" Dorothy waved her bony hand in the air as if she were talking to Rollo himself and would brook none of his shenanigans. "He's probably made the whole thing up, just to trick me into increasing his allowance. Well, when you speak to him again, tell him he's fooling no one and I won't fall for this deception!"

In fairness to her, I must say that her son had a definite history of periodic crises where he had to pay off loan sharks and worse. She must have grown weary of Rollo's constant, desperate attempts to wheedle money out of her; nevertheless, Dorothy had seldom given him tuppence, which is why he would beg, borrow, or bully Grandmother Beryl and Great-Aunt Penelope into helping him. But Rollo had been trying to reform lately. Surely that counted for something.

"He's really in trouble this time," I said.

Jeremy explained to Dorothy that he'd quietly consulted both the London police and a local cop in Cornwall for advice. The Cornish cop made discreet inquiries, and a few eyewitnesses reported seeing Rollo outside the pub last night, where he apparently was hustled into a car with a strange man at each side. Not much more could be offered in the way of clues, except that the men escorting Rollo had worn long black raincoats and dark glasses and hats.

Jeremy concluded this recitation by looking Great-Aunt Dorothy in the eye with a firm expression and saying, "So, we do believe that Rollo is an innocent victim. We think he was just in the wrong place at the wrong time, and got picked up by some thugs out in Cornwall."

I had been watching Dorothy's face as she listened, and her expression remained impatient and annoyed throughout.

"The fool!" she spat out now, with, I must say, a surprising tone of triumph. "I *told* Rollo not to go visiting you there this summer. I *told* him times had changed since he was a boy. Why, *nobody* goes to the seaside anymore. There's nothing but riffraff out there now."

"Except for royals like Prince Charles," I couldn't resist saying to her. She turned to me with a beady-eyed glare.

"Exactly," she said evenly. "His *mother* doesn't go there anymore."

Only my Great-Aunt Dorothy could conceive of Bonnie Prince Charles as riffraff.

"You have to listen to us!" I exclaimed. "Jeremy and I drove all the way here from Cornwall without stopping, because time is of the essence. Don't you understand? These kidnappers are serious, and they say they're going to kill Rollo if you don't—"

Jeremy jumped in, apparently thinking I was heading for the breakers. "We heard him with our own ears, Dorothy. Rollo was forced by his kidnappers to plead for his life," he said crisply. "They have instructed you to put up a million pounds in cash so that we can make a trade. For your son's life."

"Ridiculous," Dorothy said. "Let your police handle it. They do this sort of thing all the time."

"The cops advised us to bring money to make the exchange," Jeremy replied. "Of course we'll try to do it with the minimum of risk, and yes, the police will back us up, so that quite possibly we'll be able to recover the money once we get Rollo back. But we still have to go through with a convincing swap, and in order to do that, we have to have the cash."

Dorothy scowled. "This is a matter for my lawyer. He's on vacation. Come back next week."

"We can't!" I interjected, totally exasperated now. "If we don't do this within hours, Rollo will be dead."

There was a short silence. I would like to say that Great-Aunt Dorothy finally broke down, and wept for her son, and said of course, we must do as the police advised. I would like to say that she clutched my hand with those birdlike talons and begged me to do everything in my power to see that no harm came to Rollo.

But, alas, she did none of the above. Rather, what she did was lean forward with a smile I can only describe as evil, and say to me, "Well, you two are rich now, so why don't *you* pay it?"

Now here I must explain something that Jeremy, and our accountant, and countless other people have divulged to me over the years. When it comes to money, there are those who are luckily well-heeled, then there's the veddy-rich, and then there's the *veddy*-veddy-rich, which is the top of the aristocratic pyramid. On a parallel track are those whom Great-Aunt Dorothy dismissively calls "people in trade" who actually work for their money, and these are divided into the wealthy, the super-wealthy and the obscenely-wealthy.

Where do I fall in all this? They tell me that, despite my pathetically modest upbringing, my inheritance from Aunt Pen has catapulted me into being one of "the luckily well-heeled". Jeremy's mum's family is veddy-rich. But Great-Aunt Dorothy, sitting here in her parlor like a spider in her web, actually falls into the *veddy*-veddy-rich category.

So imagine how hard it was to sit there that day and watch Dorothy putting on the air of an elderly pensioner who's counting her food stamps. She actually said, rather defensively, "I'm an *old* woman, you know. I must look ahead to my last years, when I may require assisted living. I simply can't be throwing millions about as if it were paper for the loo."

Nice metaphor. I really didn't know what to react to first. I mean, how much longer does she think she's going to live? If she lived to be a hundred and thirty—perish the thought—she still couldn't spend all she's got. And with a butler, a driver, a maid, a doting attentive son, a cook, a hairdresser, masseuse, plus the best personal, high-end, concierge-style medical care, a slew of lawyers and accountants—how much more "assisted" does this woman plan to get?

Worse yet, it was clear that, of all the people in her entire attentive entourage, Dorothy actually believed that Rollo was the most dispensable person on her team. Rollo, the only one who truly loves her. I felt indignation rising in my throat.

"How can you be so cold to your only son?" I gasped. "He lives for you. Last year when you got sick, he was absolutely beside himself with worry. Don't you know how much he loves you?"

Dorothy looked amused for the first time all day. "Dear girl," she said petulantly, "what romantic notions you have. But we all must accept life as it is, not simply as we want it to be. And I have always known that I might one day outlive my son."

Having dropped this final, astounding bomb, she took the tips of her fingers and tapped her own chest in the place where a heart should be, and said slyly, "I am touched, truly touched Penny dear, that you care so much for my foolish son. I leave it entirely in your capable hands. I'm sure you and your Jeremy will make this all turn out for the best. Now, I am sorry but I have a dental appointment and must prepare for it. Clive will show you out."

The butler, I'd noticed, had been hovering in the doorway for some time now. Dorothy must have pressed a button somewhere to summon him, but I didn't even see her do it. I glanced inquiringly at Jeremy, who was gazing at her now with undisguised disgust.

"Dorothy, you will simply have to put up half of it," he said briskly. "Call your bank and arrange to have it ready for us. Otherwise your son's blood will be on your hands, and I will be sure to inform everyone who knows you about your unconscionable actions here today."

Dorothy had grabbed her cane and risen to her feet, but now she took a step forward so that she was right in Jeremy's face as she leaned on her stick. I'd seen her wield that very cane as a weapon before, and I moved forward, too, not really knowing what I'd do, but perhaps to show her that I was prepared to clonk her right back with her own weapon if she dared assault Jeremy.

"My friends—very nearly all of them—are *dead*," she said levelly, as if, having outlasted most of the people she knew, she believed that God had done it on purpose to show that he was on her side, rewarding her for being a superior human being. "But, were they alive, my friends would applaud me, for they knew what a burden this son of mine has been, and they always thought that he would one day come to an end like this."

"Crikey," I said to Jeremy when we were back out on the street, "she's got Rollo dead and buried in a pauper's grave already. I can't believe she didn't offer a single brass farthing. Not one!"

Jeremy sighed. "I figured it would go this way," he said, "but it was worth a shot."

"So now what do we do?" I demanded.

"We go back to Cornwall, and find out who's got Rollo," Jeremy said decisively. "Otherwise you and I are going to be out of a lot of money."

# Chapter Thirty-Two

I must say it really looked like it was curtains for Rollo, no matter what we did. We managed to scrape together thousands of pounds in small notes, all marked by the bank so that, if the kidnappers took them and then spent them, the bills could be traced. The real money was then wrapped around packets of counterfeit bills (provided by the police). The fakes were just bundled in there to pad them out, so that it looked like we had a suitcase full of a million pounds.

We were banking—if you'll pardon the pun—on the hope that the kidnappers wouldn't take the time to closely examine every single bill in the suitcase before making the exchange.

"But what if they *do* see the fakes?" I asked Jeremy, looking apprehensively at the open suitcase full of bundled bills.

"Hopefully they won't notice before the cops are able to move in and grab Rollo," Jeremy said, adding cheerfully, "assuming the kidnappers don't simply shoot us all dead immediately."

We drove into Port St. Francis with the red scarf dangling from Jeremy's car door. (In case anybody wants to know, I bought the scarf in London from a sidewalk vendor just outside Harrods.)

I kept a lookout for any pedestrian who seemed to stare intently at the scarf.

Well, the fact is, they all did. I mean, it looked fairly ridiculous. And in a small town, any little thing out of the ordinary seems to capture the attention of the bored locals. Plus, the sidewalks were still teeming with tourists who gawped at everything, since they weren't quite sure what they should stare at.

"Look, there's those creepy Mosley brothers," I told Jeremy when he pulled over to pick up two cups of takeout coffee from Toby Taylor's. "They've got the longest, blackest limo I've ever seen. I thought it was illegal to have dark windows. I bet the Mosleys are behind this kidnapping!"

"Well, if they are, then our goose is cooked, because those guys would surely know how to pull off a professional kidnapping," Jeremy commented.

As we sat there drinking our coffee, I watched Toby Taylor come out of his restaurant, hop into the blue Ferrari that a valet brought him, and go roaring off. Suddenly my mind snapped into gear.

"Jeremy!" I cried. "Follow that Ferrari!"

Startled, Jeremy put down his hot coffee in the coffee-holder slot on the dashboard, and started up the car, saying only, "What's up, Pen?"

"Toby's tires!" I exclaimed. "They have a streak of that orangey-pink paint on them. You know, just like the paintballs that somebody shot at our cottage. So, the only way a car could have that kind of paint on its tires is—"

"If someone drove their car through those paint puddles in our cottage driveway," Jeremy said, pressing his foot to the pedal to speed up. "Why should Toby have trespassed there?"

Toby's sports car had gotten pretty far ahead of us, but we could see him veering off the main road now in the direction of the older part of town.

"Do you suppose it's been Toby Taylor all along who's been behind these threats?" I wondered. "Why should he care if we halt the sale of Grandmother Beryl's house?"

"Because it would stop the condo development," Jeremy said. "Think of all the customers Toby stands to lose if we prevail. Why, with an influx of that many visitors, he could open three or four more restaurants; it's what he's publicly said he wants to do."

"Does he want it enough to go out and hire kidnappers?" I asked speculatively.

"Darling," Jeremy said, "restaurant owners can sometimes have links to unsavory characters who are known to get things done when all else fails. And it's quite possible that Toby has ties to the Mosleys or anyone else who'd be a natural ally on this issue. So yes, Toby could be part of this."

"And to think we ate his Dover sole!" I said indignantly.

"Well," Jeremy admitted, "it was pretty good."

"I've had better," I said stoutly.

By now Jeremy caught up with the blue Ferrari. Toby had led us to the old warehouse area, not far from Ye Olde Towne Pub where Colin and his band played. But Toby didn't pull up to the pub.

Instead, he tore around the corner, down a road so narrow it seemed more like a driveway, which led us farther into the labyrinth of shuttered warehouses, over by a section of the docks that was largely deserted, since the fishermen had already sold the day's catch and gone home.

Jeremy slowed his car a few feet away, so that Toby didn't notice us tailing him. Toby seemed preoccupied anyway, as he parked his car, locked it, then went up to one of the boarded-up warehouses and knocked at an unmarked, nondescript door. I watched in fascination as the door was opened by someone I couldn't see. A second later, Toby went inside.

Jeremy expertly backed the Dragonetta into an alleyway between two of the warehouses that were across the street from the one where Toby had disappeared.

"Now what?" I whispered.

"We sit here and scope this out," Jeremy said in a low voice.

"Oh, good!" I said, reaching for my coffee. "I always wanted to go on a stake-out."

"Be quiet," Jeremy said tensely. "This is not a game."

"Woo, excuse me," I muttered. At least the coffee was still hot. In all my excitement, I hadn't drunk any yet. "Well," I said after a few sips, "the guy makes a good cup of coffee, I'll say that for him."

"True," Jeremy agreed.

"What do we do when he comes out shooting?" I asked.

"You *will* keep chattering," Jeremy commented.

"You only scold when you're worried," I retorted.

"Quiet," Jeremy answered, gesturing ahead. "Looks like we've got more company."

A swarm of young men on bicycles had come swooping down the road. The bikes—and the kids on them—looked pretty scruffy. I'd seen these kids in town before. They all wore black, unmarked helmets and dark sunglasses. Their bikes were old but seemed souped up, enabling the riders to do daring stunts in the deserted streets. They acted as if they were on skateboards, and they rammed the bikes up against a curb, to fly in the air and yet land miraculously intact.

They were imitating motorcycle stunt drivers, I realized. They kept shouting at each other in hoarse voices, and there was something anarchic about the way they operated, making sudden, risky moves that could easily end in disaster.

"I guess these must be the vandals I've been hearing so much about," I said in a low voice.

"They could be Colin's friends," Jeremy noted. "Some local 'eco-warriors', see? It's on their T-shirts."

I saw that they were all wearing similar black T-shirts with gold and red lettering; and most of the kids had cigarette packs rolled up in the sleeves.

"How can they be eco-warriors and smoke?" I murmured distractedly.

"You're mixing apples and oranges," Jeremy commented. "One does not necessarily follow the other."

The bikers were still swooping around us like bats, but their group had already thinned out, and only a few diehards remained. They didn't notice us because Jeremy had shut off his engine.

At that moment, Toby came out of the warehouse, followed by a guy in fisherman's clothes who was hauling a big crate. Toby unlocked the trunk—excuse me, the "boot"—of his car, and the man obligingly put the crate inside. The man then locked the warehouse door, and climbed into his own nearby truck.

Toby scowled at the few bikers who swooped past him. Then he got into his car and drove off.

"Well, that's all there is to Toby," Jeremy said with some irritation. "The only deal that went down with him today was a wholesale fish buy."

"That still doesn't explain the pink paint on his tires," I pointed out.

"For all we know, these stupid kids could have paintballed him with their environmentally-correct paint, just like they threw eggs at my windshield," Jeremy said.

"I still don't think those kids threw the eggs," I insisted. "Farmers' kids know the hard work that goes into gathering eggs."

"Forget the eggs!" Jeremy said. "Who cares? Got any other bright ideas?"

"I'm as exhausted as you from our little visit to Great-Aunt Dorothy," I replied huffily, "but you don't see me blaming you for every dumb idea you came up with."

"That's because I don't come up with dumb ideas," Jeremy said maddeningly, drinking his coffee as if we had all the time in the world now.

"You certainly do! Threatening Dorothy with ruining her rep among her snotty friends. Even if she hadn't outlived them all, couldn't you figure that her friends despise Rollo as much as she does?"

Jeremy winced. Then he nudged me. "Look. One of the eco-warriors is still hanging about, and he's going into that call box. Think the old phone in there could possibly work?"

I glanced up with mild interest. Because of mobile phones, English call booths are a vanishing species. This one looked as if it had been erected in the 1950s. As for the phone, I could see that it was the kind that starts your call for you, then, a few seconds later, requires you to jam a large, thick coin into it really fast, or else the call cuts out. I sat there idly waiting to see if the kid actually succeeded in making a call on one of those dinosaurs.

And then, all of sudden, my mobile phone rang.

For a moment I just stared at it. I saw that my incoming call was from a local number. I answered it on speaker mode, so Jeremy could hear it.

"Penny Nichols?" came the voice, sounding as if someone were talking through a sock. I looked up, and I saw that the kid in the booth had indeed put a cloth over the mouthpiece. Jeremy waggled his eyebrows to indicate that he saw it, too, and that I should respond.

"Who is this?" I asked cautiously. Jeremy was busy trying to e-mail the local cop he'd talked to.

"Your cousin Rollo is safe . . . for the time being. Bring the money to the abandoned railroad station tonight at midnight. It must be only you and Jeremy who make this drop. Don't bring anybody else, or the deal is off."

My phone clicked just as I saw the kid hang up. He rapidly hopped onto his bicycle and drove away. Jeremy set off after him. But it was impossible to tail the kid, because he disappeared through alleyways between the warehouses where a car couldn't fit. Jeremy and I tried to figure out which street he would come out on, but in the end, we lost him.

"Damn!" Jeremy exclaimed. "It looks like those kids really have kidnapped Rollo. If that's true, then Colin has a lot to explain."

# Chapter Thirty-Three

Well, we ended up assembling our own SWAT team. First, of course, we had to get the local cop, Alfred, on board. He swore that he would bring only a select group of cops with him for back-up, and most of them would be in plainclothes. Jeremy made him promise that the cops would hang well back, out of sight.

Of course, when Geoff, Shannon and Colin learned that a few renegade eco-warriors were behind the kidnapping, they were aghast. Colin wanted to interrogate his younger brother and "punch out his lights" but the cop said that would be foolish because he would surely tip off his buddies.

Colin insisted that he must accompany us. "You might need a hostage negotiator to talk to those little punks," he explained.

"Not you, you hot-head!" Shannon said firmly. "Geoff will go."

Colin glanced at Geoff, who wore his usual mild expression, and, with his hair tied in his ponytail, looked like the sort of fellow who'd try to make peace, not war. "They won't listen to him," Colin said briefly.

"We don't need any of you!" Alfred said sternly. He was a very lanky man with slicked-back hair and a thick, bushy moustache that curled up on both ends. "I know how to talk to those kids," he said. "The main thing is to get this Rollo person out of their hands safely."

"Aw, please, Alfred," Shannon said. "Don't go shootin' my kid brother. No matter what he's done, he's not to be killed."

"Of course not," Alfred said. "But don't expect me to handle him with kid gloves, either. If those fools have weapons, well, it's their funeral."

"Great," Colin muttered.

"Let's go," Alfred said briskly. "Jeremy, you and Penny drive ahead. We'll be behind you, even if you can't see us."

"I don't want Penny to do this," Jeremy said unexpectedly.

"Why are you throwing me overboard?" I asked, insulted. "The kid phoned me, not you."

"So what?" Jeremy said. "He probably found your number on Rollo's cell phone. If these kids *do* have weapons, I don't want my wife getting caught in the crossfire."

"How dare you call me a wife at a time like this!" I said indignantly. "If I don't show up they'll know something's wrong. Don't be absurd. I'm going, and that's that." The cop grinned.

"Fine!" Jeremy exclaimed, pretending he didn't care anymore. I knew from his face that he was just annoyed at having me push back at him in front of the guys. But it was his own fault.

"There's just one thing," I said hurriedly. "We have to stop by the Actors' Home so I can drop off those books and biscuits that I promised I'd bring to Simon."

"You have got to be kidding," Jeremy said.

"I have to, Jeremy. He'll worry about me if I don't show up. I've put it off for weeks now. I can't cancel on him again. The Actors' Home is on the way, anyhow."

Jeremy just looked at the cop, who glanced at his watch, then shrugged. "We've got time," he said. "If she makes it snappy."

I hate when people say *She* when you're standing right there in front of them. However, since Alfred had sided with me, I didn't comment.

So Jeremy drove me right up to the front door of the Actors' Home, and I went running inside like a madwoman, tearing down the corridors past all the elderly actors and actresses who were moving along like slow beetles; but, since none of them had lost their flair for the dramatic, they all looked up at me with arched eyebrows and an exaggerated salute as I raced breathlessly by.

I found Simon sitting in his room by the window, his hands folded in his lap. A shaft of sunlight came through the window-pane, falling on his high forehead and nodding, bald head. I stopped rushing, and began to tiptoe in, thinking I'd deposit the books and the biscuit tin on his night table. But as I approached he stirred.

"Penny?" he whispered, still sleepy. "Darling girl, won't you stay awhile and tell me what's going on in the world at large? Have you solved your case yet?"

"Nope. And the world at large is going to hell in a hand-bucket," I said breathlessly. I knew I couldn't stop and chat. Jeremy and Alfred would have my head.

"I must go, Simon," I whispered regretfully. "Rollo got himself in trouble and I have to bail him out of a really bad jam this time."

Simon's eyes widened. "Will it be dangerous?" he whispered back.

"Maybe not," I said unconvincingly. "I'll come back to see you when it's over, and tell you all about it."

"Fine, Penny dear," Simon said, staring down at the tin of biscuits. He normally would have opened it right then and there and popped one in his mouth. But now he put a hand on my arm and said, "Do be careful, won't you, dear?"

"Sure," I said hastily.

I gave him a kiss on the cheek, then ran out of the room and tore down the corridor again, nearly colliding with a lady in a walker. She had long grey hair down to her shoulders, and a slick of red lipstick across her mouth, and rouge in two spots on her cheeks, and a purple scarf around her shoulders. "Adieu!" she called out with a theatrical wave of her hand, even though we didn't really know each other.

A laundry truck collecting linens had forced Jeremy to move his car away from the front door, so I had to run all the way down the long, curving pebbled drive. Just as I reached the car and was about to climb into the passenger seat, Trevor Branwhistle came rushing toward us, waving his cane in one hand and his hat in the other.

"Thank heaven I caught up with you!" he said broadly, and before either one of us could object, he had already climbed into the back seat. "Give me a ride into town, will you?" he said. "Go ahead, Jeremy, drive on," he instructed, as if Jeremy were his chauffeur.

Knowing how much we owed Trevor for taking Simon in, Jeremy had no choice but to do as Trevor instructed. When we reached town, Jeremy slowed down in front of the theatre, but it was dark.

"Trevor, there's nobody here tonight," I said.

Trevor replied, just a shade too innocently, "Oh, really? Foolish me, I must have the wrong date. Ah, well. I'll just stay with you until you're ready to go home."

Jeremy glanced up into the rearview mirror and stared knowingly at Trevor, who blushed a little but soldiered on.

"Don't waste time, dear boy," Trevor said crisply. "Are we doing a 'rescue op' or not?"

And before Jeremy could object, Trevor said to me quickly, "You know, Simon was worried about you, Penny darling. He asked me if someone could keep an eye on you. And as we are shorthanded right now, I thought, what better person than myself?"

When we pulled up to the deserted railway tracks, there was nothing but some fractured shafts of moonlight to show us the way. That, and our headlights. No train would come through here; this was a disused section of the railway that ran below the Old Town, not far from the pub where Colin and his band had played.

Jeremy turned off the motor and waited for instructions from Alfred, who was parked a few blocks away, out of sight. Trevor Branwhistle obstinately refused to leave the car, even when Alfred telephoned us and demanded to know why we'd brought Trevor along.

"We don't need complications," the cop said, exasperated.

"Is that Alfred? I know him," Trevor intoned; and he added severely, "Tell him I was playing Hamlet when he was still in diapers. Tell him I'm here because I made a vow to a friend to keep an eye on you two, and I intend to keep my vow. That is all there is to be said on the subject."

"Then tell Hamlet to duck down in the back seat and keep his big mouth shut," Alfred said, having overheard it all. "So as not to get his head shot off. Otherwise he'll be playing the corpse in *Julius Caesar*."

When Jeremy relayed this message, Trevor said, "Well!" in exaggerated outrage, but I noticed that when Jeremy hung up, Trevor did exactly as instructed—scrunched himself on the floor of the back of the car.

"Penny," Jeremy said quietly, "I wish you'd do the same." He checked his watch. "Time to make the drop," he said, opening the car door. "Don't follow me, Pen, until I'm ready for the money."

"Okay," I said after a pause.

I sent Alfred a frantic e-mail. *Jeremy going out alone. Please make sure nobody kills him!*

It is a terrible moment to sit and watch the man you love go out and do a brave and crazy thing. I remained transfixed as Jeremy walked in front of the light of the car's headlamps, moving with a measured, purposeful stride toward the tracks. He had gone only about three feet when a voice came out from ahead, somewhere in the darkness.

"Halt!" It was a young voice, but it sounded edgy, scared, and I knew that this was dangerous, because the kid might be unpredictable.

"Where is Rollo?" Jeremy called out. There was a silence.

Then the voice replied challengingly, "Where is Penny Nichols?"

I really didn't like hearing my name taken in vain like that, echoing across the empty rail yard.

Neither, apparently, did Jeremy, for he retorted, "She has the money. But you won't see her until I see Rollo."

I thought I heard whispers echoing across the tracks, which meant that there was more than one hooligan on this mission. My heart sank. Maybe we should have taken Colin and Geoff with us, after all.

"Jeremy!"

It was Rollo's voice, and then I saw his figure shoved out onto the tracks from behind an old platform that, Jeremy told me later, was in such disrepair that the wood was simply collapsing in sections from rot.

"Freeze!" somebody ordered from behind the platform. Poor Rollo stood there, blinking in the glare of the car headlights, uncertain what to do next. The voice from behind the platform said, "Now. Let's see the girl and the money."

Jeremy turned and signalled me. He had instructed me earlier that if it came to this, I should take only a few steps, then hand over the suitcase to him and get back in the car as fast as I could.

"Penny, what's happening?" Trevor whispered from the back seat.

"Rollo's out there," I whispered back. "I have to go and give Jeremy the money. If I'm back soon with Jeremy and Rollo, it's fine. If I'm not, it could mean trouble, so stay put."

I opened the car door and slipped out, with the suitcase in hand. The sound of my own breathing seemed scared. I made my way toward the tracks. I held the suitcase out, so anyone could see it, and I was all set to hand it to Jeremy, when the voice that was calling the shots commanded, "Place the suitcase on the tracks and back off, both of you."

So I walked a bit farther, then gingerly laid the case on the tracks. Weeds were poking out between the rail ties, and even though I knew it was a disused track, I kept expecting some ghost train to come roaring along and mow me down. My hand shook a little as I let go.

Jeremy had already come to my side, and I could tell that he was trying to use his own body to shield me from anyone's aim from the platform. We backed off together, until the voice said, "Stop there!"

Rollo was still standing uncertainly near the derelict platform. The suitcase was in the middle. And Jeremy and I stood on the other side of the tracks. Now another figure was moving toward us.

He was dressed in black jeans and a black hooded sweatshirt with the hood up so that it was impossible to really see who it was. He moved swiftly toward the suitcase and opened it.

And then, to my horror, he picked up only one of the packets of money, and began to examine each bill. I saw that he had a small but strong flashlight dangling on a cord around his neck, which he now aimed at the money. He wasn't counting it, I saw. He was studying it closely. Then he looked up sharply.

"Hey," he began, "what's going on here? I—"

"Young man, don't be GREEDY!"

This new, booming voice seemed to come right out of the suitcase. It sure scared me, and I wasn't even holding it. But the kid quickly dropped the bag involuntarily, and began to run with fright.

Later, Trevor Branwhistle would tell me that he had peeped out the car window just after I'd left, sized up the situation, and, as he said, "My theatrical instincts kicked in, and I automatically went into Ventriloquist Mode."

Now everyone was shouting and running in all different directions. Jeremy called out, "Rollo, run this way!" and Rollo bolted toward us.

Trevor's booming voice then seemed to be coming at the kidnappers from another spot—the sagging platform. "FREEZE, villains!" it said, then intoned, "You are surrounded. You cannot escape. Don't use a weapon or you will be in bigger trouble than you are now."

"Who the hell is that?" Alfred the cop asked me, having just appeared at my side. I could hear the squeal of truck tires as the kidnappers tried to escape, prompting Alfred to snap into high gear, shouting into his cell phone, "Okay, boys, move in on the north side of the tracks, MOVE in, NOW!"

I heard police sirens as Alfred's back-up cops swung into action. Rollo hurriedly came panting up beside me and Jeremy. "Got the suitcase," Rollo gasped.

"Get in the car, everybody," Jeremy shouted. Rollo, Trevor and I dove into our seats. Jeremy put his pedal to the metal and off we roared.

Soon we reached the street where the police had cornered the truck with several squad cars whose lights were flashing. We slowed down to watch as eight kids were dragged out of the truck and herded into three police cars. Alfred came into view, with one kid in tow, and, right in front of us, Alfred gave the kid a cuff on the ears.

"Wow. That's a bit harsh," I said. Alfred shoved the kid into the police car, then looked up and saw us. He must have realized that we had just witnessed what he did, because he came over to Jeremy's window and leaned in.

"These kids won't bother you anymore," Alfred said. "They got the bright idea to kidnap Rollo when they heard him talking in the pub about how much money was on the table for your grandmother's house. They were afraid you guys had decided to back off the case and maybe profit from the sale. Stupid gits. We'll keep them in custody overnight, but I hope I can persuade you to let us reduce the charges."

"Why the hell should we do that?" Rollo demanded from the back seat.

Alfred looked embarrassed. "Because my asshole youngest brother was the mastermind," he confessed. "And I promise you that I will punish him in a way more fitting than the law allows."

I had been watching the "eco-warriors" and they looked scared as hell, and ashamed. Without their helmets and dark glasses, they appeared younger than I expected. Two of them even stepped forward to apologize to me and Jeremy as they were being led toward the squad cars.

"They're just kids," I said to Alfred. "Can't you have them do community service or something?"

Alfred grinned. "I sure can," he said. "Any time you need an army of workers, you just let me know."

# Chapter Thirty-Four

So everyone got back into their cars—the cops and "warriors" driving off together—and that left me, Jeremy, Trevor and Rollo in our car. For a few moments we drove in silence.

"Jeremy, old boy," Rollo said suddenly. "Damned sporting of you to raise the cash and come out here tonight. I'll probably never hear the end of it from Mum."

Under the circumstances, we thought it best not to tell Rollo about Great-Aunt Dorothy's refusal to pay her own son's ransom. Jeremy just mumbled, "Don't mention it."

"Rollo," I said after a moment. "What was it that you discovered about the case and wanted to tell us? Did it have to do with these kids?"

Rollo shook his head vigorously. "No, no. It's about that rocking-horse."

"Did you sit on it?" Jeremy could not resist asking.

Rollo coughed, embarrassed. "Always wanted one when I was a boy. Bad idea to give it a gallop, obviously. Damned thing buckled, and I can tell you, it would have been unsafe for anybody. It's just too old, I suppose. Dry as kindling wood. Anyway, I found something odd twisted up inside the handle when it fell off."

He thought for a moment as if trying to recall where he'd put it; then he reached into his breast pocket and pulled out a piece of yellowed, lined paper that was all curled up in a narrow roll. Rollo flattened it on his knee to smooth it out, so that I could read it.

At once, I recognized the paper and the handwriting. It was Great-Aunt Penelope's childhood scrawl, and the page looked as if it had been torn out of the notebook of her Explorers' Club minutes.

"Extraordinary thing," he said, handing it to me. "Signed by Beryl, Aunt Pen, and my father . . . and some bloke named Basil!"

I leaned forward in the dim light and squinted at the page. It said:

*Upon this day our pact we seal,*
*Our secret never to reveal.*
*The magic stone has shown the way,*
*A hidden world from a faroff day.*
*Await the time we meet again,*
*The Keeper holds the Stone till then.*

> *Signed, in ink and blood,*
> *on this day of our Lord, 5 September 1927,*
> *Penelope Laidley, the Exalted President*
> *Beryl Laidley, the Esteemed Treasurer*
> *Roland Laidley, the Loyal Sergeant-at-Arms*
> *Basil Parnell, Honorary Member, Keeper of the Stone*

All around the poem were more of Great-Aunt Penelope's funny little doodles. But now, all those swirls, whorls, and spirals looked familiar for another reason.

"Jeremy!" I exclaimed. "Look at these drawings on this page—

don't they look a lot like the illustration that Paloma drew of the
Scarlet Knot?"

Jeremy glanced over at it. "Yeah, they do," he agreed.

My mind was reeling suddenly, because words and images that
had been fragments in this case were now coming together like
bits of a jigsaw puzzle. "Could it be that Aunt Pen's 'magic stone'
and Paloma's Scarlet Knot are one in the same? Did the kids' club
find the ring?"

Rollo had been scrutinizing the signatures. "Who the bloody
hell is this Basil Parnell?" he asked. "They call him the 'keeper of
the stone'."

Jeremy pondered this, then said, "Obviously some friend of
theirs. I wonder if he's still alive." He picked up his phone and
called for information.

"You're kidding," I said. "He can't still be here. I mean, we're
talking about a little boy from the 1920s. Why, by now he'd have
to be . . ."

"In his mid-nineties," Jeremy said briskly. After a few moments
fiddling with his mobile over the information, he said, "Well, if the
guy is still around, he's either not listed or doesn't have a phone."

"Shannon and Geoff know every local on the coast," I suggested, and I phoned them, knowing they'd be awake because of
Shannon's younger brother being involved in all this. I had to
waste precious time going over the whole kidnapping with Shannon because by now she'd heard the news and wanted to know
how Rollo was doing. Finally I asked about Basil Parnell.

"Basil? Oh, sure," Shannon said easily. "He's lived here all his
life. His family's been around for ages. They're all fishermen. He's
the last of them. He lives all alone in a shack by the sea." She gave
me directions, which I relayed to Jeremy.

"It's nearly midnight. Let's go there first thing tomorrow morning," Jeremy said.

"Do me a favor, old boy?" Rollo asked. "Drop me off at my car back at the farm, will you? I'm going to drive straight to London tonight. I've had all the excitement I can take. And I hope I never see Cornwall again!"

# Part Eight

# Chapter Thirty-Five

Now, as I've said before, there are cottages and there are cottages. Basil Parnell's home really *was* what you'd think of as a genuine, fairy-tale cottage—the kind a little elf would live in. In fact, with its weather-beaten brown roof and its greyish-white-shingled sides, it looked more like a mushroom that had sprouted up in a sandy patch between the rocks of the cove.

This was not a cottage-by-the-beach; it was a cottage *on* the beach, just beyond the horseshoe-shaped rock near Grandmother Beryl's cove. It was so close to the sea that Jeremy and I could barely hear each other speak over the roar of the crashing waves as we approached the front door the next morning.

We knocked, but I didn't see how anyone inside or out could hear us above the cacophony of ocean, gulls and wind. Yet neither one of us wanted to just walk right in. We stood there uncertainly, until I saw the stooped figure of an old man on the beach making his way toward us along the shore.

He seemed to appear right out of the mists, having just come round the bend. He moved with slow, deliberate steps, and he wore a fisherman's hat and sweater, with his pants' legs rolled up, so that the waves that rushed toward him and away again didn't soak him.

As he drew nearer, I observed that he had a long white beard, and long white hair that hung down his back. He was carrying a bag made of fisherman's netting, which had shiny silver-backed fish inside. When he saw me, he smiled and revealed that he had several teeth missing.

"Penelope?" he shouted above the roar of the sea. "You can't be Penelope, can ye?"

"My great-aunt was Penelope Laidley," I shouted back at him. He put a hand to his ear and shook his head. I leaned closer and called out, "Are you the Keeper of the Stone?"

He looked up at me sharply, then at Jeremy. Slowly, he walked into his house. Jeremy and I glanced at each other, and followed him in. He didn't tell us not to. He just went up to a small, chunky wood table and started to clean his fish.

The cottage was basically one big room that appeared to serve as parlor, bedroom and kitchen, for it had a bed, a rocking-chair and a table with a lamp in one corner; while the opposite corner was occupied mainly by a sink, a cupboard, table and an icebox. In between stood a black wood-burning stove, which had a kettle on top. From the bedroom area was a partial view of a curtained alcove containing a closet-sized cubbyhole with a tiny bathroom.

"Basil," Jeremy said, "you do know what we're talking about, don't you?"

Basil looked up, then went back to his fish. "I'm an old man," he said finally. "I forget lots of things, all the time."

"Come on, Basil," I coaxed. "We know you know."

He looked me in the eye now. "You be always full of tricks," he said sulkily. "You trying to trick me again?" He sounded plaintive, like one kid afraid of the wrath of another. "You know I wouldn't tell. You made me swear. In blood."

"He thinks you're Aunt Pen," Jeremy murmured to me out of the corner of his mouth.

I saw with a pang of amused sympathy that Basil, after all these years, was still afraid of breaking the blood oath of the little Explorers' Club. I tried to think of what Great-Aunt Penelope would have sounded like as a kid.

"Oh, stop being such a baby. I'm not trying to trick you," I said in my best imitation of a formidable, bossy English girl. "I only want my friend Jeremy to see it. I'm going to let him join our club. So come on. Where is the stone?"

The knife that was scraping the scales off the fish and slicing through the silver skin stopped suddenly. Basil looked at me keenly now, as if trying to make up his mind. Slowly, he put down his knife on the table. He went to his little sink and washed his hands, and dried them carefully on the worn-out towel that looked as if it had hung there since the beginning of time.

Then he turned slowly to face us, and reached into the pocket of his trousers, which were baggy on his wiry frame. He held out his hand in a fist. But he didn't open it yet.

"You won't tell the Lady that I took it, will ye?" he asked plaintively. "She be a ghost bride. She walked in the cave and put it there. Her gown be all wet. She went away and never come back."

I glanced at Jeremy, who just shrugged. "No, I won't tell the Lady that you took it," I said.

Basil studied my face closely, then, quite suddenly, he opened his fist.

But what lay there was not a ring. Nope. It was a doughnut-shaped stone with a reddish bump at the top like a knot. I recognized it instantly from the picture in the magazine for Paloma's interview. But what I hadn't realized was that when Paloma said "stone" she did not mean "gem", she meant "rock". I knew this was right, however, because the ring-like "band" of this stone had all those swirls, whorls and spirals carved right into it, just the way Paloma had sketched it, only these were all blackened now, and weirdly fascinating to behold.

"The Scarlet Knot," I breathed. I looked at Basil and said, "You found it in a cave?"

When he nodded, I said, "Let's go back there where you first saw it. Can you lead the way?"

"G'wan. You know," Basil said cagily, putting the stone back in his pocket. "I showed it to you the day I found it. That's why you let me join your club. You told me to hold on to this stone, till you came back again."

And he told us that when Great-Aunt Penelope, Grandmother Beryl and Great-Uncle Roland returned to school in London that autumn, they swore Basil to secrecy before making him the "Keeper of the Stone". And then, as kids do, they all moved on to other pursuits in the next summers . . . chiefly romantic interests in little picnicking and kissing parties.

"Been a long time. Thought I'd never see you again," Basil said, charmingly shy. I think he must have been a little in love with Great-Aunt Penelope. He hesitated. "I like the stone. It be lucky for me."

"Basil, please take me to the cave," I said. "I forgot the way there. And I want to show it to my friend. You can tell him the whole story of how you found it."

Basil had finished with his fish, and now he put it on a plate and into the tiny icebox. Then he sighed and took the fisherman's hooded rain-jacket from a peg on the wall. He slowly, methodi-

cally pulled on a pair of rubber boots. Then he picked up a flashlight and gestured for us to follow him outside.

"I thought you be the smugglers at first," Basil confided as we
walked along. "They war bad men."

"What's he talking about?" I muttered to Jeremy.

"Maybe he thinks I'm Blackstrap Doyle," Jeremy grumbled.

"The Great Lady war walking on the beach in her fine white
gown here," Basil told us, having to shout above the roar of the
ocean as he directed us along the jagged shoreline beyond his cottage.

With a sure-footed gait, Basil showed us how to get around the
craggy rocks that we waded past, splashing knee-deep in the sea,
where pockets of water, left behind by the tide, collected in large,
deep puddles and ponds that the locals call "rock pools".

I was wearing my little plastic beach shoes today, but I still had
to move slowly to avoid slipping. Jeremy climbed ahead of me,
then turned back to help me make my way across the slippery
rocks, until we reached the next beach, which was more pebbly
than sandy.

After this, the beach narrowed considerably, up against sheer
cliffs and caves. The wind blew hard and noisily now, and the sea
came banging in against the rocks, leaving behind a thick white
mist like a little fog-cloud who'd wandered too close to earth. Just
around the corner, I could see the earl's headland thrust out over
the sea, but the manor house was shrouded in fog.

Basil had already stopped. We were in an area of steep, formidable cliffs that towered over us. Basil squinted out to sea, and,
following his gaze, I saw that about twenty feet from the shoreline
there was a big, jagged black rock, sticking up out of the swirling
tide and resembling, to my mind, a gigantic Hershey chocolate kiss.

This rock seemed to be a marker to Basil, for he suddenly

veered left now, and approached a cleft in the cliff wall, which I would not have noticed on my own. This opening in the cliffs was like a narrow, six-foot-tall keyhole. Basil fished around in the voluminous pockets of his seaman's oilskin rain-slicker, and came up with his high-powered flashlight.

"She war in thar," he said, beaming the light inside to show us that we were at the mouth of a cave. We squinted to look in. But already it was flooded with seawater.

"Her dress be all wet," Basil said matter-of-factly. "She be the ghost bride." He backed away from the cave opening, then glided toward it as if in a trance, to mimic the Great Lady's actions.

I could picture it vividly now; Paloma walking on the beach, dragging her wet dress across the shore, hence the myth of the ghostly "bedraggled bride".

"She left the stone in the cave?" I asked quizzically.

He nodded. "But she war afraid of the tide coming in," Basil said.

Jeremy looked at Basil keenly now. "Did she see you when you were watching her?" he asked.

Basil actually blushed. "I be behind the rocks," he admitted.

"And when she left, you went inside the cave and took the stone?" Jeremy asked.

Basil only nodded, then looked at me and said, "You said it was alright for me to keep it, as long as I didn't tell anybody else about it."

But now there was a sudden rushing sound as the tide came crashing in on us with an alarmingly aggressive roar. You didn't have to be an experienced Cornish fisherman to guess what that sound indicated.

"Run this way! Tide's coming in," Basil said warningly. "We must go, else we drown."

# Chapter Thirty-Six

"**D**o you think Basil's telling the truth?" I asked after we left him.

Jeremy shrugged. "Maybe. The guy's half-barmy," he said. "But somehow he managed to get his hands on that stone."

We were late for our meeting with Jeremy's environmentalists, who had begun scouring the property around Grandmother Beryl's house while we were in Madeira. They'd scheduled this meeting just to give us a preliminary report on what they'd learned so far.

Jeremy warned me that this pow-wow was nothing unusual, but still, I was hopeful that they'd tell us they'd found some rare natural species of animal, vegetable or mineral that required protection and could therefore stop the Mosleys' development plans permanently.

When we arrived, the environmentalists were tromping through the eastern meadows across from Grandmother's house. The team consisted of a man named Peter who was the leader, and several students who were working for him over the summer.

Peter, a tall, lanky dark-haired fellow dressed in jeans and a tan shirt open at the throat, shook hands with us both as soon as we arrived. "Normally, I'd be walking you through all the flora or fauna," he said immediately. "But there's nothing of real significance on that score so far. However, I did call in Barbara, an archeologist advisor whom I've used many times in the past. I'll let her explain why."

He jerked his head toward a woman standing farther away in the field, near the low, stone farmer's wall that separated this property from the earl's. Sitting on the wall a few yards away were Harriet and Colin, so deep in conversation that they didn't notice when I waved at them.

And just as Jeremy and I were crossing the field to meet Barbara, I saw another figure emerge on the other side of the low wall, and he leaned across to speak to Barbara. I recognized the newcomer instantly.

"Jeremy!" I whispered. "That's the earl!"

We drew closer, and as Peter made his introductions, I couldn't take my eyes off the earl, for his face, up close, was more weather-beaten than I expected; and his eyes were a bright, lively green. He had shaved this morning, though, and he removed his hat when he spoke to Barbara. I saw that the earl was younger than he first appeared; somewhere in his thirties, just as Harriet had told me.

"But s-s-surely those arrowheads d-d-didn't w-w-walk over h-here on their own!" he exclaimed.

Barbara shook her head, then glanced up at us, and Peter said, "Barb, can you bring Penny and Jeremy up to speed on this?"

Barbara was what you might call a handsome woman, with light brown hair, a squarish jaw, and a high, intelligent forehead. She was dressed in a safari shirt and khaki shorts. "Well, the long and the short of it is this," she said in a clear, strong voice. "Peter's team thought they found some ancient arrowheads on this property this morning, which is why I was called in."

I felt ready to whoop with delight, but the expression on her face stopped me.

"However," she said, and that one word made my high spirits immediately plummet, "I can say with certainty that these arrowheads are neither Roman, nor Celtic, nor Anglo-Saxon nor Norman. They are not even Germanic or Iberian. What they are, are Chinese."

This gave me a pause. "Furthermore," Barbara said, rather severely now, "they are made of a hard-grain plastic meant to mimic bronze. See the dye marks and seams? Authentic bronze from antiquity don't have these imperfections. These arrowheads are fakes."

"Fakes!" I exclaimed. Then I wished I hadn't spoken. Because Barbara was looking at everyone as if we were all in a police line-up.

"Right," she said, studying me closely. "Which means somebody planted them here. That's not lawful. That's not good."

Peter looked at Jeremy and said, "Any idea who might have done this?"

"No," Jeremy said shortly. The earl simply turned away abruptly and retreated into the thickets of his private property.

But Harriet and Colin had edged closer to us now, and Colin was so red-faced, looking quite ashamed, that it was very clear who the culprit was.

"I don't know what to say," Harriet said in a wounded voice.

"It wasn't Mum," Colin said shortly. "She knew nothing about it. Nobody else is to blame." But he could not resist adding, "Except the asshole who sold me the arrowheads."

"You bought them," Peter said. "That makes you the . . ." He didn't have to finish.

Barbara glanced around the group, her attitude softening a bit

at all the disappointed, stricken faces. "This is not the way to protect a property," she said crisply.

"It was all in a good cause, truly," Harriet said in a small voice.

I glanced up and saw that Jeremy had a grim look as he gazed
off toward the road, where a thuggy-looking man in a black suit
and sunglasses was standing, with his arms deliberately folded
across his chest, in a mute but unmistakably threatening manner.

"The Mosleys' man," Harriet muttered. "He's acting as if the
property is already theirs. Won't be long now before they make
the final *coup de grace*."

# Chapter Thirty-Seven

The phone was already ringing when we got back to the cottage. It was Simon.

"Tonight's the night!" he exclaimed, sounding really juiced up.

It took me several moments to remember what he was talking about. Then I realized that it was the Shakespeare fête; that performance at the old theatre by the residents of the Actors' Home to raise money for the hospital.

"Be there with bells on!" Simon was saying. "And don't be late! Trevor got his friends from the BBC to cover it!"

"We have to go," I told Jeremy when I hung up the phone. "We've got to dress nice, too. This is a big deal."

"Fine, fine," Jeremy said absently, heading for the shower. "It's the least we can do, considering that this case is rapidly going south."

"What a doofus thing Colin did," I said. "Poor guy. I guess he's been crazed with worry, seeing that his mum is so desperate."

"Well, he's set us back considerably, and he may have even given the Mosleys plenty of ammo against our whole case," Jeremy said shortly. "Do one dishonest thing, and everything's up for grabs."

This thought depressed me. But for Simon's sake, I put on my best summer dress and my best smile.

And actually, it was all very exciting, because when we arrived in front of the theatre, the streets around it were jammed with cars and TV trucks. Not only was the BBC there, but also the local news and, I suspected, some newspaper reporters from London, judging by their slightly imperious attitude as they fired off questions at Trevor, who clearly enjoyed the spotlight and was more than up to the task of master-of-ceremonies.

"Some of the very finest names in theatre, film and television will be on that stage tonight AND in our audience!" he proclaimed as he stood before the microphones that had been arranged in front of the theatre. A new red carpet had been rolled out on the entrance path. Trevor looked especially spiffy tonight in his elegant tuxedo, and his face had that wonderful, highly animated quality, which good actors always manage to summon in the teeth of an important night.

"We sold out this morning!" said Harriet's Legacy Society friend with the tortoise-shell framed eyeglasses.

"They're even scalping some of the tickets," said a young man who at first I did not even recognize. It was Colin, in a rented dinner jacket. His spiky hair had been slicked down. Harriet was wearing a bright red dress and lipstick, totally uncharacteristic of her. Shannon and Geoff were right behind them, and Shannon was wearing the most beautiful embroidered silk floor-length dress I'd ever seen.

"She made it herself," Geoff told me, looking distinguished in a purple dinner jacket.

Toby Taylor showed up next with his entourage from the restaurant, which included a few fashion models and sports figures.

"Oh, yeah, it's been really great working with the locals and getting our supplies straight from the land and sea," Toby was telling a reporter.

"And a warehouse," Jeremy muttered to me. "Probably got his fish from New Zealand."

Meanwhile, as Trevor fielded questions from the press, he was periodically interrupted whenever a celebrity's fancy car rolled up to the red carpet and somebody important got out. Jeremy and I stood with all the other gawkers to watch the parade of politicians, film actors, and other worthies who'd been spending their summer vacation in Cornwall, and were now making a big show of arriving to claim coveted seats for what was shaping up to be *The* Event of the season.

A popular young actress who'd played a girl ghost-hunter in a successful movie series now alighted from her limo in a long gown and high heels, and obligingly posed on the red carpet with her trademark toothy grin for the photographers and fans who screamed out her name. Another limo pulled up, and out stepped a young actor with long blond hair who was a heart-throb from a recent blockbuster action movie. And then came the older, more venerable actress who'd recently picked up an Oscar award for her stunning portrayal of Mary, Queen of Scots.

"How on earth did Trevor assemble this cavalcade of stars?" I asked Jeremy in a whisper.

But just then, the car-to-beat-all-cars arrived bearing the guest-to-beat-all-guests. I didn't recognize the auto, but the press certainly did, and they abandoned the other celebs and flocked to the curb there. The driver parked and moved hurriedly to open the back door for the guest of honor.

A male passenger stepped out. He wore a bemused expression,

and he seemed completely unruffled when the cameras and lights were all suddenly turned on him with a force that would have stunned any mere mortal.

"It's Prince Charles!" I breathed to Jeremy.

"There's your answer about Trevor's roster of luminaries," Jeremy said wryly. "They all heard that the Prince was coming tonight."

Everyone pushed forward as the rest of the royal entourage emerged from their cars and followed H.R.H. up the red carpet. Prince Charles acted as if he had all the time in the world, even while he and his group kept moving quickly and smoothly forward. From time to time he paused momentarily to shake someone's hand or say a quick word; and I just stood there, drinking it all in.

But I certainly did not expect what happened next. A man accompanying the Prince—no doubt a palace associate—whispered something in his ear, causing His Nibs to pause, then glance up straight at me and Jeremy. With a more intense look, Prince Charles just gave us one brief but significant nod. Then the whole group continued on.

"Good God," I heard Jeremy mutter behind me.

"At least he doesn't seem to hate us," I said weakly.

Now a long black limousine shaped like a barracuda pulled up to the curb, but the crowd scarcely noticed it, still enthralled with the passing parade of royalty. And so the Mosley brothers, upon making their big entrance, were at first completely ignored. No reporter, no gawker approached or noticed them. But I sure did.

"What are *they* doing here?" I hissed indignantly to Jeremy.

"Show of support for the community," Jeremy said dryly.

"As if!" I responded.

But now everyone was rapidly hurrying to get through the lobby, and soon we were all directed by young usherettes to take our seats. Jeremy and I got nice box seats upstairs, to the left of the stage.

Glancing below, I saw that most of the bigwigs were led to the front rows. And, some residents from the Actors' Home who, like Simon, were wheelchair-bound, were also given special seating in the orchestra section. In the orchestra pit, a local group of musicians were tuning up. In the balconies directly across from the stage, there were lots of younger people who had come to see their friends that were performing with the elder thespians tonight.

Suddenly, the chandelier lights dimmed. The chattering dropped to a murmur, then stopped completely as the crimson curtain with the gold Tragedy and Comedy masks on it rose slowly. From deep in the orchestra pit, a lone trumpet sounded. Then an elderly actor entered the stage. The spotlight made his whitened face look eerily compelling. In a rich, well-modulated voice, he spoke:

*"Now, my co-mates and brothers in exile,*
*Hath not old custom made this life more sweet*
*Than that of painted pomp? Are not these woods*
*More free from peril than the envious court?"*

These, I noticed, were timeless words for an environmentally-conscious crowd. The actor boomed his lines out across the stage, with perfect pitch and control, and the audience was raptly attentive.

As more players joined him, I could not help feeling real pride at the sight of all those old troupers, now coming to incredible life onstage. The faces were painted, the expressions highly dramatic, but I could recognize, here and there, the very same folks I'd passed in the hallways of the Actors' Home, or seen lying in their beds, or eating quietly in the Priory dining room, or nodding in lawn chairs on the terrace.

But tonight each of them had special power and grace; they seemed to glow from within, and even when they occasionally stumbled on a line or made a slightly wrong exit, they were still amazing to behold. The young actors moved with less confidence but more vigor and excitement, so there was a nice symmetry in the way that old and young performed their vignettes from various scenes of Shakespeare.

One verse hovered in my mind long after I heard it:
*And this our life, exempt from public haunt,*
*Finds tongues in trees, books in running brooks,*
*Sermons in stones, and good in everything.*
*I would not change it.*

It seemed to sum up all that was good about the Cornish countryside. I wondered if Trevor had deliberately selected this passage to resonate with his struggle to protect Port St. Francis. I sighed contentedly, allowing myself to get lost in the drama of it all.

But about forty-five minutes into the show, out of the corner of my eye I saw a figure directly across the theatre, coming through the door at the back of the special box where the Mosley brothers were seated. It was that thuggy guy who'd shown up at Grandmother Beryl's place today; the one who stood in the road with folded arms and a menacing attitude. Tonight he'd managed to enter the theatre quietly and unnoticed, for the lights were low and the audience was gazing steadily at the stage.

I watched as the thuggy guy bent over to whisper into the ear of the taller of the Mosley brothers, who inclined his head without turning it. Even in the dim light, I could see his expression change, only slightly but significantly.

I nudged Jeremy and whispered, "Look! Something's up with the Mosleys!"

Jeremy watched closely as the shorter brother checked his flashy wristwatch, which set off a sharp gleam in the dark theatre. Then the thuggy guy retreated behind the curtains at the rear of the box; and in the next moment, the two Mosley brothers rose quietly, and stealthily stole out of their box.

There had been something urgent and sneaky in the way the Mosley brothers slithered away, despite their deliberate attempt to appear unmoved and casual.

"They're up to no good, I just know it," I whispered.

"Right. I've had it with those bastards," Jeremy replied in a low voice. "I'm going out to see what they're on about."

"I'm going with you," I said.

"No way," he said.

"Yes, 'way'," I said, "or else," I added dramatically, "I'll scream this place down."

"Oh, for God's sake," Jeremy said. "Let's go."

# Part Nine

# Chapter Thirty-Eight

The Mosley brothers and their thuggy driver got into the limo and sped out of town. Jeremy and I were very careful to follow at a distance. Luckily, a farm truck got in between us, so the Mosleys weren't seeing our car directly behind them.

When they turned onto the country road that led to Grandmother Beryl's house, I said suspiciously, "Where are they going?"

The answer was soon apparent, for as the road curved away toward farmland, the Mosley limo instead pulled right into Grandmother's driveway and stopped; whereupon the Mosley brothers and their driver got out on foot and headed toward the house. The farm truck continued on the road that climbed up along the farms and meadows, and Jeremy followed it, bypassing Grandmother's house.

"Where are you going?" I exclaimed.

"Just parking farther away," Jeremy said as he maneuvered into a small, dirt area off the road. He turned off the headlights and cut the engine.

"We'll have to go out on foot if we want to see what they're up to," he explained. "You'd better stay with me. I don't think you'd be any safer sitting in this car alone. We'll cut across the meadow and come down by the earl's stone wall. From behind Grandfather Nigel's garage, we should get a decent view."

It was a good plan. When we reached Grandfather's garage, we sidled up along the wall near the earl's property line, until we came to the back of the garage, where we were able to crouch in the overgrown shrubbery. From that vantage point, we could see quite clearly that the Mosley brothers were standing at the far edge of Grandfather Nigel's garden, peering over the stone staircase to the little cove below. The thuggy driver was already making his way down the staircase, carrying a flashlight.

The Mosleys remained above, smoking cigarettes. I could see the red dots of the ends of their cigarettes, and from time to time, when the clouds passed away from the moon, I could make out the two pairs of Mosley eyes momentarily glinting in the moonlight.

Jeremy nudged me and nodded toward the horizon line, where a boat had suddenly appeared. As it came closer, it looked like any other yacht that might have been heading for the Port St. Francis harbor. Except that this one stopped here, parallel to Grandmother Beryl's cove, beyond the rocks, and anchored. Then it did something very odd indeed—it turned out all its lights.

A moment later, one strong signal light could be seen flashing on-off, on-off, on-off.

I watched as, from the cove, the Mosley driver raised his flashlight and echoed the message: on-off, on-off, on-off.

A dinghy must have been lowered from the yacht; for when the moon shone briefly again through the moving clouds, I could see that a little boat was now coming away from the big boat and moving straight toward the shore of Grandmother Beryl's cove. Two men were in it. They brought their little boat right up on the shore, and beached it there.

"Boy, these look like bad men," I whispered to Jeremy. Then we both realized we'd heard somebody say this before.

Jeremy murmured, "That's what Basil told us! He wasn't raving about Blackstrap Doyle or some smuggler from years ago. He was talking about the Mosleys in the here and now!"

While the Mosley brothers looked on, their driver stepped forward and examined the cargo on the small boat. This appeared to be a stack of packages that looked like large, flat white bricks.

"What are they doing?" I whispered.

"Smuggling drugs, from the look of it," Jeremy said in a low voice. "I'll bet that's another reason why they want to control all this property out here."

He reached for his mobile, then swore under his breath. "No signal," he said. "We've got to get out on the road and call Alfred. Fast!"

But it was already too late. Because now a truck had pulled into Grandmother Beryl's driveway. Before we had time to realize what was happening, two more tough-looking guys had popped out of the truck, and were heading toward the garden. They had guns in holsters visible under their open jackets. Meanwhile, the men from the beach were already making their way up the stone staircase with their contraband cargo.

Well. To this day, Jeremy blames me for what happened next. All I did was scrooch a little closer to him. Can I help it if men keep their mobile phones in their pockets? And is it my fault that those damned mobiles are so touch-sensitive that the minute I bumped into Jeremy, his dumb phone started to talk in that mechanized female voice?

"Say a command!" the voice chirruped loudly. Before Jeremy could hastily turn it off, the impatient fembot spoke again, this time, I swear, in a more annoyed tone. "Say a command!" she repeated.

Now all three thugs, plus the two Mosleys, whirled in our direction, just as the moon decided to peek out again through a pocket in the gauzy clouds, thereby shining a most unwelcome light on us. Suddenly, the Mosleys' motley crew dropped everything, and they all began to run toward us.

"Come on, Pen!" Jeremy exclaimed, grabbing me rather roughly, I must say, and dragging me off in the only direction we could possibly go to get away from the bad guys: down the slope of land toward the sea, where the horseshoe-shaped rock stood as a portal to our escape. But if you think this is an easy thing to do in your nicest evening shoes and dress, guess again.

When we hit the beach, we tore off as fast as we could go, with the Mosley crowd in hot pursuit. First we ran past Basil's cottage, which was locked and dark. God knows where he was tonight. Fortunately, having just been down here with Basil, we had a better sense of the strange terrain than the Mosley guys did. We knew how to weave our way around the rock pools and cliffs in the dark . . . whereas those other guys stumbled in an attempt to keep up.

We rushed onward, where the wind and sea were rougher, but I knew what Jeremy was thinking: if we hurried, we might reach that cleft in the rock and vanish into it unseen; and in the dark the Mosley guys would never even guess that it was there.

I heard a loud popping sound and realized that someone had fired a shot. The sea was swirling across my ankles and the jagged rocks that we picked our way around; the wind whistled up against the sheer wall of the cliffs. Jeremy had a flashlight but didn't dare shine it. He just felt his way along the cliff, until his fingers found the keyhole-shaped opening.

"This way, Pen," he said softly, darting inside and drawing me in with him.

It was a leap of faith. Well, a squish of faith. We were, after all, banking on Basil's crazy story that he'd seen Paloma go into this opening and yet live to come back out again, so many years ago.

We soon discovered that this unassuming cleft in the cliff wall led into a deeper cave than we'd realized. It was more like a narrow tunnel, about five feet wide and barely six feet high, with a curved but very jagged ceiling and walls. So we had to be quite careful not to scrape our heads or hands against them. The ground beneath our feet was sandy and rocky, with little eddies of water here and there.

Only scant minutes later, we could hear the Mosleys' men thumping around just outside the cave. They ran right past it, so there was silence for a moment, during which we watched from inside. A short while later, the men returned, angrily walking up and down the shoreline and gazing out to sea, as if waiting to see if we'd tried to swim for it.

"They can't hold their breath forever," I heard one of them say.

We backed off, and stood quite still. One of them struck a match, but only to light a cigarette. Smoke wafted in the air. We could hear their voices as they stood there trying to figure out what to do, but I couldn't make out the words. I started to get the feeling they were going to camp out for awhile and roast marshmallows or something.

Jeremy sensed this, too, and very carefully he pulled me deeper into the cave with him.

"How long are they going to stay there?" I whispered, trembling.

"Depends on how big their operation is tonight," Jeremy said quietly, "and how badly they want to catch us."

We decided to retreat even farther, following the cave-tunnel, which abruptly turned left and continued. As soon as we'd made that turn, Jeremy was finally able to switch on his flashlight. After we'd walked about twenty-five feet, the tunnel opened into a much wider chamber. Sharp rocks jutted out everywhere from the walls, and without our light, the cave would have been treacherous indeed.

Cautiously we made our way deeper into this larger chamber. Jeremy shone his light dead ahead so we could watch where we stepped, until at last we reached the very back wall.

I gasped when I saw it. For, flat against the wall was a big, life-sized rock construction, which, clearly, human hands had made. It resembled a huge doughnut with a knot at the top, so that it looked like a giant engagement ring mounted against the back of the cave.

"Look!" I whispered, stepping forward to trace my fingers around the strangely familiar carvings decorating it—that very same mesmerizing pattern of swirls, whorls and spirals which I recognized from three places—Paloma's sketch, Basil's Scarlet Knot stone, and Great-Aunt Penelope's doodles in her notebook. What we were now standing in front of was a nearly six-foot tall replica of the Scarlet Knot.

"Jeremy," I whispered, "remember what Paloma told her interviewer? She said she was haunted by the ghost of Prescott's mother, so she believed she had to return the stone to its source. Prescott must have shown her this place when they were courting."

"Which is why she came back here toward the end of her life to return it," Jeremy agreed.

"Right," I said. "It all matches up perfectly with Aunt Pen's minutes about the Great Lady. Do you think Basil took Aunt Pen in here to see this?"

"Of course," Jeremy replied. "No wonder she let him into her club."

After what I guess was about a half hour, Jeremy went back to check on the tunnel where we'd come in. I had turned on my little pencil-sized flashlight and waited hopefully.

Very soon though, Jeremy retreated back to the chamber where I was waiting.

"I can't tell if the Mosleys' men are still out there, because the tide's coming in, fast. I couldn't get far enough to see outside. The tunnel is filling up with seawater," he said grimly. I saw that his shoes and pants were wet. "It's too late to try to swim for it. This whole place is going to be flooded soon," he warned.

I glanced around wildly, looking for some escape, but already the seawater had been seeping into the inner chamber itself. I watched, horrified as the tide now came swirling in rapidly with sudden force, already lapping around the giant-sized Scarlet Knot.

But then Jeremy noticed something interesting. "Look!" he said, pointing to where the rising tide was sloshing up over the bottom curve of the "wedding band" of the Scarlet Knot. The water seemed to spill over the stones and disappear.

"It's acting almost like a drain," he said, examining it. "There's got to be some place behind that rock where the water is going."

"What are you going to do?" I asked in alarm when Jeremy shone his light between the Scarlet Knot and the actual wall of the chamber, then began to wedge himself in there.

He didn't answer at first, just kept feeling around with his arm and leg. "There's a narrow opening back here!" he announced. "I'm going to try to get through it and see what's on the other side!"

Before I could even object, within seconds, he disappeared. I waited for what was probably only a moment but seemed interminable. Then I heard Jeremy's voice calling out to me.

"Come through, Penny!" he said. "Hurry! There are two steps down, once you get in."

I flattened myself against the crevice where he'd vanished. The area was worn smooth here. I held my breath and pushed forward, and for a moment I found myself wedged between two rock walls. I pushed again . . . and then popped out on the other side.

# Chapter Thirty-Nine

There is an old saying, that when you're in a situation where there's no way out, the only answer is to go deeper in. And so, in we went.

Behind the Scarlet Knot was a labyrinth of well-constructed tunnels that was truly astonishing. The first one where we'd just landed was about fifteen yards long, with stacked stone walls and a corbelled stone roof shaped in a curve overhead. The floor was hardened earth. Although some of the seawater had indeed seeped in at the mouth of this tunnel, the tunnel itself was built on an upward slant, so that as we walked up it, very soon we were on higher and drier ground.

"Look at how the walls and roof are stacked. They're different from the first caves we came through. These are man-made," Jeremy marvelled. "So it's got to lead somewhere, right?"

"Unless it's a burial chamber," I said gloomily. But since the tunnels continued, so did we.

"We should keep moving until we're far enough away so that the high tide won't reach us," Jeremy said. "Then, when the tide goes out again, maybe we can go back out the way we came."

"Wish we'd managed to call Alfred before all this hit the fan,"

I said, glancing at my phone's diminishing battery power, and turning it off to save whatever spark of life was left in it.

"Well," said Jeremy, "we can hardly expect to get Wi-Fi in a prehistoric tunnel."

"You don't think we're going to run into lions and tigers and bears in their lair, do you?" I asked, shuddering from the chill. Jeremy gallantly took off his jacket and put it around my shoulders.

"No, all the woolly mammoths are long gone," he assured me. So, we soldiered on.

We moved through another stone tunnel to the left, which took us to higher ground still, and then a sharp right, where the new tunnel widened slightly.

Now, let me just say that when it comes right down to it, you'd really be hard pressed to find a nice soft landing in a cave. I mean, look. Rocks are not really made to be beds or easy chairs. But we knew we had to hunker down, so we did the best we could. Jeremy finally found a very wide, flat rock, and sat down with his back to the dry wall.

"I hope they didn't sacrifice virgins on that stone slab," I said apprehensively.

"Come on, babe," he said, opening his arms wide so that I could sit in his lap and rest my head against his warm chest. "I always wanted to go camping with you."

At first, I found myself dropping off to sleep, but then I awakened suddenly, as if I'd heard an unfamiliar noise but could not recall it. It was probably the deep silence that was so eerie to me. Finally, though, we both fell into a deep, undisturbed sleep.

I knew it was morning for one reason only. Light. Not much, but, as any miner will tell you, whatever shaft of sunlight you can get is paradise when you've been stranded underground. This was a long, thin ray of sunshine that came down like a laser from a tiny sliver between the rocks in the ceiling over our heads. Jeremy awoke when he felt me turn my head, and now I pointed at the light. We got up carefully, and nearly stumbled on something rectangular that we had not seen in the dark of night.

It was a crate of three dusty, black, unmarked glass bottles, stoppered and sealed, and filled with a mysterious liquid. The bottles were blank. Only the box itself bore the name of the wine: *Napoleon madeira.* "Wow," Jeremy said. "If this actually is what it says it is, then it's probably the best madeira ever made. They still talk about it at wine auctions today, as if it's the Holy Grail."

Dimly I remembered, from my work on a ridiculous TV biopic called *Joséphine, Queen of the Romantics,* that Napoleon, who suffered from a stomach ailment, was, at the end of his life, unable to quaff the barrels of wine that had been sent to him. So it was divided up into bottles, and afterwards it was unclear what became of them.

"There are legends far and wide of discoveries of these lost bottles," Jeremy explained.

"Is this that 'eternal wine' you told me about, that never goes bad?" I asked in awe.

Jeremy nodded. "Do you realize what it could mean?" he said. "We may have just stumbled onto Blackstrap Doyle's smuggling caves. Which would make sense, because Prescott gave Paloma the little Scarlet Knot that must have originally come from here!"

"Ohh," I said. "But, this tunnel was surely built long before Blackstrap arrived on the scene."

Jeremy was still gazing upward. "The ceiling here is flatter than the others. Maybe we should see where that crevice overhead opens to. We might be able to get out of this cave, right here and now."

"But how can we reach the ceiling?" I asked.

Well. Let me tell you what my caveman did. He started gathering stones. And he labored on his little construction site until he'd built me a staircase of my own that went all the way up to, if not heaven, at least to the light. Jeremy climbed first, to test it with his own weight. Once he reached the top, he then had to heave and ho and push and shove with all his might against the section of the ceiling where light was peeping through. At one point he very nearly lost his balance, and I feared that he would topple and fall. But he hung on, and he finally broke open a piece of the roof above us.

"Let's go!" he said triumphantly; and then he, and I, popped through it.

I somehow imagined that we'd end up in a meadow, or at least at the mouth of an above-ground cave. And indeed, at first, we did seem to be in just another cave, albeit one with many shafts of light streaming in. But then Jeremy swept his flashlight around, and I saw that we were in a place so familiar, I simply couldn't believe it.

We were in Grandmother Beryl's basement.

# Chapter Forty

"Fuggy-holes," said Barbara the archeologist. "That's what the Cornish call them. But in archeological terms they are known as *fougous*."

She pronounced it "foo-goo", which, as far as I was concerned, was as funny and unscientific-sounding as fuggy-holes.

You can imagine how shocked she and the environmentalists were when Jeremy and I came tearing out of Grandmother Beryl's house, still dressed in our evening attire from the previous night, albeit smudged with cave dirt. My face looked as if I had been playing in a coal scuttle. Jeremy's hair was full of white powdery dust, from the way he'd shouldered those roof-stones just like Atlas.

We had run across the fields where the environmental team was doing their morning survey of the western section of the property. Jeremy paused to phone Alfred the cop, to inform him about what we'd seen of the Mosley brothers' operation, while I began to explain our adventure to Barbara and Peter.

"Caves?" Barbara asked immediately. "What caves?"

Jeremy quickly joined us, and brushing off his jacket, he described the peculiar construction of the network of tunnels from which we'd emerged. At first Barbara's expression was hard to read. I fully expected her to dismiss those tunnels as old, disused copper and tin mines, which no doubt had been a boon for Prescott Doyle's smuggling operation.

But while everybody else was marvelling over the Napoleon madeira, and conjuring up stories of smuggling, Barbara moved thoughtfully closer to me and spoke in a low voice. "Take me there, right now," she said. "I want to see the tunnels for myself."

So Jeremy and I brought her into Grandmother Beryl's basement and we retraced our steps. We began with the spooky far end of it where we'd popped out. With a ladder we all managed to lower ourselves down, and Jeremy led the way back through those elaborate stone-roofed tunnels with their sharp turns. Barbara was silent at first, as we all beamed our flashlights around for her to get a good look. And that was when she told us what she believed they were.

"*Fougous* are tunnels built by the Celts," Barbara explained, as she wandered around in growing delight. "Nobody really knows why they built them. Maybe to store food, or to have a hiding place from the enemy, or to store their weapons. They are all over Cornwall, but I've never seen a network of them quite like this."

We continued onward, until we finally reached the area behind the giant replica of the Scarlet Knot. We showed her how we'd squeezed in, and we all went through that narrow passage until we got into the main cave chamber. The tide was out now, so we stood there awhile, gazing at the remarkable stone formation that looked so much like an engagement ring.

Barbara stepped right up to it, shining her light at various spots, staring with a new intensity.

"It looks to me like a megalithic Celtic entrance stone," she said slowly. "Hmm, you can quite clearly see that very interesting pattern of a *triskele* design."

Jeremy and I waited for her to explain further. It took Barbara a second to notice that we weren't familiar with the term.

"Three spirals together, and then another three, and then another three," she explained, moving her fingers reverently over all those swirls, whorls and spirals that were carved into the stone. "The Celts loved the number three, believing that everything important happened in three's. Birth-life-death. Sun and moon and stars. Land, sea, sky. Et cetera. I'm thinking that this find is from the Neolithic period, which is from 5000 B.C. to 1000 B.C. I'd say we're talking early Iron Age."

"Wow," I said. Then I asked, "You called it an entrance stone?"

"Yes," answered Barbara. "They are usually connected to a ceremonial site of some sort; you know, it's a gateway to something. Obviously this one leads to all the *fougous* behind it, and ends at the property we were inspecting. So, there must be a reason that all these tunnels lead there."

Now Barbara made us take her outside, via the cleft in the cliffs, exactly where we'd originally entered from the beach. We walked along the shoreline, back past the rock pools and Basil's cottage. Basil himself was out in the water in a little boat, fishing. He waved to us, and we waved back, then we passed under the horseshoe-shaped rock, until we got to Grandmother Beryl's cove and the steps leading upward to her house.

When we reached the western property, Peter, the team leader of the environmentalists, had more news for us. "We uncovered a few stone markers," he told Barbara. "Think you're going to want to take a look."

We hurried across the field, where we saw the stones he'd found, which were flattish granite rocks, all about four and a half feet tall; and each were shaped like a rectangle topped with a head-and-shoulders, giving them a bit of personality. They lay in a neat row on the ground.

"We left them lying flat, but exactly where we found them," Peter said. "They seem to have been arranged on a diagonal line."

Barbara spoke to no one, and instead began circling the field, sometimes kneeling, sometimes standing on tiptoe.

"She looks like a Native American scout," I said. "What's she after?"

"Not sure," said Jeremy, fascinated.

When she returned to us, Barbara, who initially did not strike me as a particularly excitable person, now looked highly animated, her eyes glinting.

"I have to call in my team," she said, as if her fellow archeologists were the only ones who'd really understand how truly fantastic this all was. So she got on her phone and conferred with her pals at her office. When she was done, she spoke to Jeremy, me and Peter in a low voice.

"Look, here's what I think," she said. "We need to excavate this area, and find out if there are more stones like this. Thanks to Peter, we already have a permit to do so. But once we begin, it's going to be hard to keep it quiet. And if news about this find hits the press, then all the antiquities dealers and looters will descend on us."

My ears picked up the word "find", which she'd used before. Barbara must have noticed the expression on my face, because she smiled conspiratorially now.

"I can get the geological survey going today," she said, "but after that, we need to clear the site of grass and stuff before we can start a proper dig. That's going to take a bunch of interns to help."

She probably meant she wanted to hire some posh grad students from universities in London.

But I had a better idea. "Hey, if you want to keep it quiet, then deal with the locals, not the London crowd," I said. I turned to Jeremy. "Let's call Alfred and bring on the eco-warriors."

"You mean the ones that kidnapped Rollo?" Jeremy asked incredulously.

"Why not?" I said. "They're supposed to do community service. I can't think of a better service to Port St. Francis, can you?"

And that's how Colin and Alfred were put in charge of the very penitent eco-warriors. Over the next few days, they were like an advance army, carefully clearing and assisting under Barbara's team leadership. And every evening, Alfred posted twenty-four-hour police guards around this new "historical site of interest", which included Grandmother Beryl's house.

Then the dig began in earnest, and over the next few weeks Barbara uncovered more marvels as her team dug trenches, and sifted, and dug some more. I looked at the newly excavated stones that the archeologists were re-assembling, standing them up now in the rows where they'd been discovered. Apparently over time the stones had fallen and sunk, but Barbara believed that they once stood in a very distinct and formal arrangement of lines that emanated outward like the spokes in a wheel.

On one bright, sunny day, even I could see that what the archeologists were reconstructing was beginning to look like a miniature Stonehenge. The dig had expanded slightly into Shannon and Geoff's farmland, so they came to watch and help out when they could.

Shannon paused to talk to me about it. She said, "Look. Geoff was right about the ley lines. See how this row of stone markers forms a line that goes straight through the farm? Remember he told you that for some reason the crops grow taller here? Energy," she said, her eyes shining. "The ancients knew how to channel the best energy."

By noon that day, the earl had come to the edge of his property to check on the progress of the dig. Barbara now told him that the team needed to expand their work into his property as well.

"C-c-certainly," he said uncertainly. But then, being a nature and history aficionado himself, he sat right down on the ground and sketched their finds.

Harriet had stopped by, and she perked up now. "All of this could change everything," she said meaningfully to the earl. "Can you imagine the kinds of house tours you'll be able to have when people find out about this Celtic site?"

The earl looked as if he'd wakened from a dream. "What a l-l-lovely turn of events!" he said, sounding vastly relieved, and smiling not only at Harriet but at anyone who caught his eye. I had to smile back when he gave me a grin of such childlike delight.

By the end of the day, Barbara had more news for us . . . and the earl. She took us all tromping over to see a spot where Geoff's farm met the earl's property and the town property. This was the "hub" of the wheel from which all other lines of stones emanated. Barbara's team was now carefully digging and cataloging whatever items they turned up there.

"I don't want to say for sure," she said, looking like the cat that swallowed the canary. "But, judging from what we've found so far, this could be the site of an ancient Celtic holy well with hidden springs beneath it," she continued, gesturing at smooth round stones being piled up neatly. "If so, it may explain the other markers, because the Celts might have erected the big stones to guide people in a ceremonial procession, from both land and sea, to converge here at this sacred spring."

For a moment we all stood there gazing silently, visualizing the hordes of ancient Celts clad in animal skins—elders, children, men and women from all around—making perhaps a once-a-year pilgrimage to their sacred site, just like the pilgrims who visited the church in Madeira.

"Incredible," I sighed. "But, what does it all mean now?"

Jeremy gave the answer.

"It means the Mosleys are toast," he said triumphantly.

# Part Ten

# Chapter Forty-One

I am happy to report that, as the summer season was winding down, the archeologists did indeed uncover a hidden spring and enough artifacts to make a lot of people very happy. Already the impact of the discovery was becoming more clear. The area that needed protecting from development was the western corner, where Shannon and Geoffrey's farm met the town land and the earl's. No new building could possibly be done here now. However, building could occur on the eastern, outlying land opposite the dig, exactly where Harriet had planned . . . but even so, it would be unthinkable to embark on a scale of development with an impact such as what the Mosleys had in mind.

The earl had already declared that he had no intention of selling "a single blade of grass" to the Mosleys or anyone else like them. "Why, I will show them the door . . . with great pleasure, madame," he told Harriet. "I do not do business with criminals!"

For indeed, it looked as if the Mosley brothers weren't going to be doing an awful lot of property development anywhere for awhile.

"Alfred gave me a little call this morning," Jeremy confided as we were having breakfast at our cottage on the farm. "He agrees that part of the reason the Mosleys were so keen to develop this area of Cornwall was the elaborate security system they intended to build, ostensibly for their wealthy tenants, but actually so that they could expand their nasty little racket with impunity. But now, Alfred says they're in deep jinx with the law for drug smuggling, because he got Scotland Yard to catch up with the Mosleys' truck in London. It was loaded with the kind of stuff we saw them carrying off the boat. The cops impounded everything."

"What were they smuggling?" I asked, not sure I wanted to know.

"Cocaine, mostly," Jeremy said. "Stuffed to the gills. Not only that, but the coastal guard raided the Mosley yacht. They found more stash, probably for the Mosley brothers to use as deal sweeteners for special clients."

I shuddered to think of what Port St. Francis might have become if the Mosleys had had their way. And right then and there, I knew that everything we'd been through was worth it.

On the weekend that we were scheduled to leave, Harriet insisted on throwing us a party. Trevor let her hold it at the old banquet hall in the Priory. Some of the elder residents weren't quite sure exactly what we were celebrating, but it didn't matter because the champagne was flowing. Colin's band played ancient Cornish or Celtic songs, I couldn't say which. But everybody was singing and dancing.

"To the earl!" said Trevor, holding up his glass, and everyone *hoo-hah*'d to that.

"To Harriet!" said someone else, and the glasses clinked again.

"To Penny Nichols and Jeremy Laidley!" said a voice in the crowd, and I saw that it was Simon, sitting in his wheelchair with a glass in his hand. I had to kiss him, he looked so sweet.

Everyone clinked again, and the music started up as they sang, "For they are jolly good fellows." Jeremy actually blushed, and I ducked behind him.

But for me, the best news was delivered by Harriet when she proclaimed that funds were already flowing in from new donors, to make the Legacy Society become the permanent custodians of the house and all the protected land that the town had bought. What's more, she assured me that Grandmother Beryl's house would not only be saved from the wrecking ball, but would be restored to its former glory, just as she'd originally promised us. She seemed especially proud of being able to make good on that.

As the festivities began to wind down, Jeremy murmured to me, "I say we get out while we can go on a high note."

"Right-O!" I agreed.

But, I have to admit that I felt kind of sad when we hugged and kissed everyone goodbye. Geoff and Shannon presented Jeremy and me with two beautiful, handmade sweaters from the farm. I said *au revoir* to Simon and Trevor and the Priory; and gave Colin and Harriet a big hug. Harriet handed us our own personalized Cornish pasties for the ride home; and I said a fond farewell to sweet old Basil, and the earl, and Barbara and the whole team of eco-warriors.

On the way back to the cottage, we stopped at Grandmother Beryl's house, so I could have a special, private moment. I walked inside the parlor one more time, while it was still quiet with my family's history-dust, just to whisper, "Well, Grandma, I hope this is what you had in mind. But I bet even you had no idea what you were protecting."

As we drove away from the house, I found myself also giving silent tribute to the Scarlet Knot and the caves and the sea below; and to Paloma and Prescott, who surely must have found each other by now; and to Tintagel and Merlin and Arthur and the whole noble dream of a perfect kingdom.

When we went back to our little cottage on the farm to pack up the car, we realized that Rollo had already taken the broken rocking-horse out of the closet where we'd stored it, and brought it back to London. He'd left us a note, swearing that he would have it "carefully restored" for us.

"Hah! That's the last we'll see of that pony," Jeremy commented.

"He earned it!" I said loyally. We'd arranged to have the lamps, credenza and croquet set trucked to our town house in London. We had already donated the masthead to the maritime museum. I somehow felt Paloma would surely approve.

The drive home out of Cornwall seemed to go a lot faster than our arrival had, months ago. In fact, I felt as if Jeremy and I were whooshing through all those layers of history at warp-speed. For awhile we drove in silence.

Then Jeremy said, "Hey, hand me those Cornish pasties that Harriet gave you."

I unwrapped them. Each was a pastry shaped like a half-moon, crimped on the edges, kind of like an apple turnover. Both pasties had initials carved into them, one saying *PN* and the other *JL*.

"Wow, personalized Cornish pasties," I said.

"Yeah, that's an old tradition," Jeremy explained. "They used to make pasties for the miners, and they put their names on them so the miners wouldn't mix up each other's lunch."

I bit into my pasty, which on one end was filled, essentially, with a delicious chicken stew and vegetables. But as I ate my way down, I reached a pastry divider. Beyond it was my dessert, where the pasty now became a fruit tarte.

Munching his, Jeremy explained, "See? It's a whole meal-in-one. So those miners could eat it all with one hand, and not get it dirty from handling it too much."

"Mmm, tastes great," I commented, enjoying every bite.

"That's because Harriet made sure we got a real one, made in a good Cornish bakery," Jeremy answered. Gently I picked up his napkin and touched it to his lips.

"You're my knight," I said.

"Still?" he teased.

"Still," I affirmed.

We drove onward, and, when at last we reached the hub of roads around London, I got an e-mail from my father. I scanned it quickly.

"Dad says the house in Antibes is ready and waiting for us," I reported.

"Great," said Jeremy. Then his phone rang. All I heard him say was, "Yes? Uh-huh. Right."

"What's up?" I asked when he rang off.

"Well," he said, "it seems we must first make one little stop in dear old London-town."

# Chapter Forty-Two

The leaves of the silver maple trees along Buckingham Palace were green with just a touch of September's royal gold at the edges when Jeremy and I came careening around the corner in the slightly mud-splattered but heroic forest-green Dragonetta. We pulled right up to the entrance, where two palace guards in full regalia had come out of a little booth and now approached us rather warily. One peered into Jeremy's window, the other in mine.

Jeremy rolled down his window. "We have an appointment with Prince Charles," he said, looking like an English schoolboy who's been called to the headmaster's office.

"Name?" asked the guard on my side.

"Give him your card," Jeremy murmured out of the side of his mouth.

Hastily I fished around in my purse for something I thought I would never use in my life—a fancy little antique calling-card case made of ebony and edged with gold trim and tiny opals, which Rollo had given me as a wedding present. I had filled it with formal, engraved calling cards that, in a burst of nineteenth-century nostalgia, I'd purchased at an old-fashioned Parisian stationery shop while ordering my wedding invitations last year. The cards matched my bridal invitations, for they were of the same cream-colored Italian paper with a hand-crafted burgundy monogram.

Now, trust me. Back then I had no inkling that I'd ever end up paying a fancy afternoon call on any royal personages. Yet at the time, I thought that if I bought the cards, then surely fate would chuck me a glamorous opportunity to use them. And, if there's one thing I've learned about life, it's that if you just put one foot on the road you'd like to travel, pretty soon you find yourself arriving there. Only, it's never quite the way you pictured it . . . and, you could get into trouble.

So now I nervously handed the guard this card:

> *Madame Penny Nichols*
> *of Nichols & Laidley Ltd.*
> *has called upon you today*
> *for the pleasure of your company*

I suppose I could have told the French printer to leave off the "Madame" before my name. But hell, I was in Paris. And I was getting married. So, I couldn't resist the idea of officially becoming "madame" instead of "mademoiselle".

The guard took the card and, seeming slightly dubious at our windblown appearance, he and his fellow guard retreated into their little station behind the gate.

"It looks like the kind of booth you go into at an amusement park, to pose for a row of pictures while you're sitting in each other's lap," I noted. "What do you suppose they're doing in there?"

Jeremy leaned forward and craned his neck. "They're on the phone," he reported. "They're holding up your card and reading it aloud."

He sighed heavily. For, despite all the English bluster about the royal family being obsolete and irrelevant to modern times, when you're right there at the palace with all the costumed attendants, you do sort of feel as if you've been summoned to a higher calling . . . and you could get hanged if you somehow manage to piss off the Queen.

"What say we high-tail it outta here while the going's good?" I suggested.

But suddenly, without any pomp or circumstance, a white-gloved hand emerged from the booth to vigorously wave us in, and Jeremy's sleek little Dragonetta glided forward as we were directed where to leave the car.

When we walked into the front door of Buckingham Palace—or, Buck House, as we chums of the royals like to call it—we entered a reception area containing the Grand Staircase. And it was grand indeed. Trimmed with elegant wrought-iron rails, it swooped and curved in arcs overhead, which made it look as if it were awaiting the arrival of Eliza Doolittle of *My Fair Lady*. The walls were a dreamy cream color, trimmed in gold, and there really was red carpeting underfoot.

"Jeremy Laidley and Penny Nichols? Follow me, please. You are expected."

This came from a youngish yet slightly bald man in a neat dark grey suit, who never bothered to tell us his name. Nor did we ask. He began walking at a fast, purposeful pace, so we hurried along, past several huge reception rooms with names that invoke *Alice in Wonderland*: the Green Drawing Room with framed portraits of stern-looking people staring back at us as if to inquire disdainfully, "And *who-oo* are *you-oo*?"; followed by the Blue Drawing Room (which they tell you was originally red, and frankly it still looks mostly red to me, so I don't know why they changed its name, except, I suppose, for the blue-seated chairs everywhere); and then the White Drawing Room with its mirrored walls which disguise a secret door to a hidden inner chamber.

I caught my own image flickering by in those darned mirrors in the White Room, and I saw that my brown eyes were wide with sheer, undisguised terror. My hair looked as if it had been blown dry by a Mad Hairdresser, because of all the previous hours riding along the highway in a convertible that had chosen this day to get its top stuck permanently down. But when you are summoned by H.R.H., well, you drop everything and show up on time.

"Please wait here," said our guide, allowing himself a slight smile of amused sympathy at my trepidation as we approached a new suite. "You may sit down." And suddenly, he was gone.

So there we were, standing in a breathtaking set of rooms with walls trimmed in so much sun-reflecting gold that the effect was like being inside a jewel box. The big, tall windows were framed in stunning deep fuchsia-pink draperies. Throughout the room were golden tables and pedestals for black-and-gold urns, and some black-and-gold cabinetry, and various other works of art; and gold standing lamps with pale shades on golden branching arms like gilded trees. Here, instead of red carpeting, there was beautiful parquet flooring and antique carpets in delicate soft tones of pink and blue. The soaring ceiling was a radiant gold that had a gigantic sparkling crystal chandelier.

Gingerly, I parked myself at the edge of a gorgeous fuchsia sofa, whose pillows had gold tassels that matched the tassels on the dramatic draperies. Jeremy sat beside me and we gazed out of the attractive windows, which gave such a peaceful view of the splendid grounds, with their ancient leafy trees and the milky-blue sky. I felt as if I ought to be wearing a white powdered wig and a fancy dress with crinolines.

I smoothed my hair and my dress carefully, and had just begun to calm down when I heard the distinct sound of approaching footsteps.

"God, I bet it's him," I whispered, stricken. "You know, I never did learn to curtsey."

"Too late now," Jeremy said in a low voice, as the door opened—and the heir to the throne of the United Kingdom walked in.

And, he had his mother with him.

I gulped. However, I discovered that I am enough of an American to admire but not genuflect to royalty. Even if I knew how to curtsey according to protocol, I don't believe I would have done it. I just couldn't. I mean, you simply can't ignore an entire revolution. That's what happens when a Connecticut Yankee like me ends up in Queen Elizabeth's court.

Did I imagine it, or did the Queen's eyes note my insubordination and was she, as they say, "unamused"? Prince Charles seemed unruffled, and he just moved things along, speaking graciously.

"On behalf of our mutual friends in Port St. Francis, we wish to thank you for your good works," Prince Charles said, looking each of us directly in the eye. He went on to speak in a calm, modulated tone; and I must say that Jeremy handled himself beautifully, managing to nod and respond intelligently to even the most ordinary questions, such as, "And how has the weather been in Cornwall?"

As for me, I think I managed to answer every question the Prince directed at me. Jeremy says I did fine. But the whole time I couldn't help wondering what the Queen was thinking. Her gaze was alert and attentive, and occasionally she nodded, yet she hadn't spoken a word.

Finally, Charles said with a twinkle in his eyes, "The Legacy Society has asked our advice on a gift for you."

This seemed to be the Queen's moment, for she snapped her fingers in the direction of the doorway, and I wondered what palace flunky was awaiting her orders outside the door to this room.

I didn't have to wonder long. On those beautiful, royal floors I suddenly heard the pitter-patter of paws echoing in the room, and a moment later a beautiful black long-haired field spaniel with dark, silky long ears and a round, highly intelligent head came bouncing into the room toward us; then, rather regally, he stopped a foot away and sat down, with only his wagging tail indicating anything other than royal reserve.

"He's been highly trained," was what Prince Charles said.

Then the Queen spoke.

"He shall be called," she said firmly, "Sir Francis."

# Chapter Forty-Three

"**S**peaking of smugglers," Jeremy said unexpectedly, "I have a little something to mark the end of this case with."

We were sitting by the pool in Great-Aunt Penelope's villa in Antibes. September is, after all, a lovely month to be here. The sun was still shining warmly, and the pool reflected the puffy clouds in the serene blue-and-white sky of Matisse. Sailboats were gliding peaceably across the Mediterranean Sea, which sparkled in the soft yellow sunlight.

Aunt Pen's villa was a peach-colored affair with bright blue shutters at the windows, and a wrought-iron balcony that ran along the entire second floor. Jasmine and honeysuckle vines twined against the wall. I gazed up at this pleasant sight while we lounged in steamer chairs on a patio flanked by big terracotta pots containing blooming flowers. The air was filled with the heady scent of all these plantings, and I sighed deeply and contentedly.

Jeremy rose, went inside the house, and returned with two brandy snifters and a familiar black bottle, still coated with Celtic dust. "You've gotta be kidding," I said, fascinated. "We can't actually *drink* that old Napoleon madeira . . . can we?"

"Well, we could sell it at auction," Jeremy answered, sitting down next to me. "But that's just money, my girl. If we did that, we'd never, ever know what this stuff tastes like. Now, wouldn't a fine historian like yourself owe it to Napoleon, and to the hands that made this wine, to sample it?"

How could I resist that? "Okay," I whispered. "Open it."

With remarkable reverence, Jeremy carefully removed the black, waxy seal. Then he opened the bottle just as he'd been instructed by a wine expert he'd consulted in Cannes. I watched in awe as, after centuries of waiting in that cave for us, the bottle opened with a small, dignified *pop!*

A second later, we heard a car crunching in the gravel drive. Then it came to a stop alongside the vintage blue Dragonetta that Aunt Pen had bequeathed to me. Presently, I heard the unmistakable, hearty voice of Rollo calling out, "Halloo! Anybody home?"

"Good God, hide the madeira!" Jeremy groaned, but Rollo had already come around the side of the house, and he now appeared on the patio.

"Heard all about the grand finale of our latest case out in Cornwall!" he said jovially, taking a seat. "Thought we might drink a well-deserved toast to another job well done."

Jeremy was still trying to hide the bottle, but I reminded him, "Don't forget, the Celts believe in the luck of the number three."

"Right," said Jeremy. "You, me and the dog."

"Get a third glass," I advised. And we poured it, and I would tell you all about it, except for an odd thing that happened just as we were sipping our madeira.

Sir Francis, our royal spaniel, had been lying indolently on the warm stone patio, with his silky black ears and tail neatly laid out, and his beautiful paws posed regally in front of him. He was oh-so-elegant, and perhaps even a bit of a snob, having rather disinterestedly allowed Rollo to enter and even to pet him.

But suddenly, Sir Francis raised his head alertly. I thought of what Prince Charles had said about this dog's elite training. It now appeared that Sir Francis considered himself a staff member of the firm of Nichols & Laidley, for he got up and trotted over to the door, and looked back at us quite significantly.

And then, Sir Francis barked.

Apparently, we had a new visitor.

But, that's a tale yet to be told . . .

## THE END

*Catch up with Penny and Jeremy in the other "Rather" novels!*

**A RATHER LOVELY INHERITANCE** is where it all began, when an American art historian—Penny Nichols—meets British lawyer Jeremy Laidley, in London at the reading of Great-Aunt Penelope's will. Penny also meets Rollo, a ne'er-do-well relative, and other "vultures" in the family tree who want to keep the loot all to themselves. Who can she trust? Bickering and bantering all the way, Penny and Jeremy team up to uncover family secrets on a chase from London to Paris, Cannes, Antibes and Rome. If you've ever dreamed of having the perfect apartment, auto, wardrobe and loved one to jaunt around the French Riviera with, then go for the ride!

**A RATHER CURIOUS ENGAGEMENT** follows Penny and Jeremy as they become real partners, in love and in work. They decide to sock away their inheritance, except for one splurge—a vintage yacht that they win at auction on the Côte d'Azur. This soon leads to their first official "engagement"—a new mystery to solve that leads them to the world of Beethoven. Meanwhile, Jeremy's ex-wife is trying to steal him back. Can Penny and Jeremy's relationship survive the test? If you want to know what it's like to cruise the Mediterranean on a yacht, and visit Lake Como, Nice and Corsica, then climb aboard!

**A RATHER CHARMING INVITATION** finds Penny and Jeremy trying to plan their wedding while balancing the demands of Jeremy's English family, and Penny's mysterious French relatives, who invite the couple to an ancient ancestral château near the fragrant perfume fields of Grasse. When a family heirloom loaned to Penny and Jeremy for the wedding goes missing, they must solve the theft before it's time to say "I do." If you've ever experienced a family tug-of-war while planning a wedding, or if you just love the idea of travelling to Provence, Paris, Lake Geneva and Monte Carlo with the one you love, well . . . here's your invitation!

# A Rather Remarkable Homecoming

## C.A. Belmond

# A CONVERATION WITH
# C.A. BELMOND

**Q.** *In this fourth novel of your "Rather" series,* **A Rather Remarkable Homecoming***, Penny and Jeremy's new adventure takes place at her grandmother's house by the sea in Cornwall, England. What made you choose this setting?*

**A.** Actually, the seeds for this novel were planted back in the very first book of the series—*A Rather Lovely Inheritance*—when my American heroine, Penny Nichols, is summoned to England for the reading of her Great-Aunt Penelope's last will and testament. On her flight to London, Penny tells us that she'd been to England only once before, long ago during a childhood summer visit to Grandmother Beryl's house-by-the-sea in Cornwall. This is where Penny met her glamorous Great-Aunt Penelope, for whom she was named, and she also met a boy named Jeremy whom she really liked and connected with. In *A Rather Lovely Inheritance* the adult Penny is reunited with Jeremy, and together they must solve a family mystery that brings them to Paris, the French Riviera, Italy . . . but Penny never gets a chance to return to Cornwall. Yet all along, through the first, second and third "Rather" novels, the memory of the childhood summer at Grandmother Beryl's house lingers vividly in Penny's mind.

So somehow I always knew that I—and Penny and Jeremy—had to go back to explore Cornwall again. Now in this new book, *A Rather Remarkable Homecoming,* it just seemed right and natural that the time has come for Penny and Jeremy to return to that important place where they first met.

**Q..** *Most people can really relate to the deep connections and powerful memories of a grandparent's home. Why do you suppose a grandmother's house has so much resonance?*

**A.** I imagine it's because our earliest childhood memories often revolve around grandparents. Going to see them is a bit of an adventure for a kid, like the Thanksgiving Song that Penny sings, "Over the river and through the wood . . ." Everything looms large in our memory—the backyard seems boundless, the rooms strange and enormous, and our elders sometimes tend to be more indulgent than our parents. The occasion when you visit a grandparent is usually a holiday, like Christmas or summertime, so there is a festive atmosphere about it. The world of adults seems odd and mysterious, and as a kid you scamper about like a squirrel, climbing trees and existing in a world apart from the grown-ups.

Then, when you yourself grow up, these childhood memories can lie dormant for years. But the moment you go back to revisit Grandma's place—even if your grandmother no longer lives there—you can be surprised by the powerful impact the house still harbors. It's not just that you're going through the scrapbook memories of childhood; the place now takes on a symbolic importance as well. As you walk around exploring your own past, the terrain is at once both familiar and strange.

**Q.** *But Penny doesn't go back to Cornwall simply out of nostalgia; it turns out that her grandmother's house, and indeed the entire village of Port St. Francis, is in peril of being demolished, so the locals hire Penny and Jeremy to solve the case.*

*This new assignment seems to come from Prince Charles himself! What made you decide to make this royal personage a player in this novel?*

**A.** Well, Prince Charles is the Duke of Cornwall, and he has for many years been deeply and passionately involved in protecting the English countryside for future generations. So he was just the perfect new "client" for Penny and Jeremy! I really loved the idea of Penny and Jeremy being given a rather royal and noble task to perform, just like the knights of Camelot going off on a special mission. Cornwall is, after all, the birthplace of King Arthur and the knights of the round table, who were all willing to fight bravely against formidable enemies and nearly impossible odds. Penny and Jeremy have certainly had to slay quite a few "dragons" before, while working on a case, and this one's no exception!

**Q.** *Does the town of Port St. Francis really exist in Cornwall, England?*

**A.** No, there is no actual town called Port St. Francis in Cornwall. But although this is a fictional place, it's very much based on a real coastal area. I had in mind a composite of the various fishing villages perched above harbors on the northern coast of Cornwall. In the novel, Penny is pretty specific about where it is, when she tells us that Port St. Francis is "not as far east as the castle town of Tintagel, but not as far west as fancy Padstow with its trendy gourmet restaurants."

**Q.** *What prompted you to create the Shakespeare connection to the story?*

**A.** That was a really fun element to play with. Whenever you delve into English history, sooner or later the Bard figures in. I discovered that the Shakespeare element in my story tied together a lot of the "supporting" characters—Simon Thorne who is an elderly actor that befriended Penny in the first "Rather" novel; Prince Charles and his quest to protect the natural world; and all the eccentric locals like Harriet and Colin—in a manner that allowed everyone to interact in their own quirky way. I don't want to spoil the surprise here, but the twists and turns that occur when Penny and Jeremy pursue the history of Grandmother Beryl's house are really what propel the story. As in life, you often find the answers in the least likely place you expect.

**Q.** *In addition to the regular characters in Penny and Jeremy's world, you introduce some fascinating new characters in this novel, some historical and some modern. Where do they all come from?*

**A.** The supporting characters that Penny and Jeremy meet, and the historical ones that they investigate, all seem to "grow" naturally right out of their physical locale. So in this novel, I couldn't help seeing a bird-watching English earl and a Shakespearean actor and a TV chef just springing out of the Cornish landscape like wild, indigenous plants and mythological creatures. In my previous novels, I just "saw" a German count in his castle on the lake for *A Rather Curious Engagement*; and in *A Rather Charming Invitation* I couldn't help imagining the French perfume-makers in that lavender-and-rose-and-jasmine world of Grasse, where the world's greatest fragrances come from.

**Q.** *There are other dazzling locales in this novel. What made you decide to set some scenes of* **A Rather Remarkable Homecoming** *in the Portuguese island of Madeira?*

**A.** Madeira is such a very mystical place, where, in Columbus' time, seamen that were blown off course accidentally landed their ships on Madeira, sometimes telling strange tales of a New World to explore across the Atlantic Ocean. In a sense, Penny and Jeremy get temporarily "blown off course" in solving their case, so they must map a new direction. Also, in this novel, the juxtaposition of Madeira with Cornwall represents the love affair between the historical characters of Paloma, the tempestuous opera singer, and Prescott, the dashing smuggler. Cornwall is such a rugged, masculine place, and Madeira contrasts so nicely with its warmth and tropical lushness representing the feminine side of the story. The moment that Penny and Jeremy arrive in Madeira in pursuit of clues to the case, you just know that you're in another world, and that the story is ready to take a very different turn.

**Q.** *Speaking of love affairs, Penny Nichols and Jeremy Laidley have just returned from their honeymoon, and it's clear that they are a highly compatible couple, whose mutual affection and playful banter have caused reviewers to dub them "a modern-day version of Dashiell Hammet's Nick-and-Nora and Agatha Christie's Tommy-and-Tuppence". When you began the series, did you plan to create a sleuthing team?*

**A.** Yes and no. Actually, it all began with Penny's vintage auto, which I call a Dragonetta. Long before I'd written a word of the first novel in the series, I imagined an attractive couple in a beautiful vintage 1930s convertible, tootling along the corniche roads of the French Riviera. I wondered, "Who are they, and what are they doing here?" I toyed with the idea of jumping right in and writing about this married couple, but something made me put the idea aside to simmer for a few months.

So, while I had this "couple-in-a-car" image tucked into the back of my mind, I went to work on what I thought was a completely different idea: a sort of Henry James story of an American girl working and living abroad, seeing Paris and London and Monte Carlo and Rome for the first time, living modestly until her whole life is turned upside down by an unexpected inheritance. I knew that my heroine, Penny Nichols, would be what I call a "sincere seeker": someone who starts out struggling, and you root for her because, on the one hand she's earnest and idealistic, but she's also very human and down-to-earth, and she's nobody's fool, so she's funny and self-aware. As I followed Penny through her first adventure in *A Rather Lovely Inheritance,* I just naturally came upon her English hero, Jeremy Laidley, who's a perfect match for her. Over time they decide to pool their resources and create their brand-new investigative business called "Nichols & Laidley".

And lo and behold, as I went from the first book to the second and the third, suddenly Penny and Jeremy, quite on their own, became this attractive couple tootling along the French Riviera in a vintage car. That's how my "back-burner" idea had almost subconsciously merged with the "front-burner" idea. On days like that, the writing life can be a great pleasure!

# QUESTIONS
# FOR DISCUSSION

1. Penny and Jeremy have just returned from their honeymoon, and they are clearly still in love. What is it that makes them so compatible? What do they have in common? How do they deal with their differences? Jeremy seems to know when to protect Penny; and Penny understands what motivates Jeremy. How do Penny and Jeremy balance each other? Do they take turns being positive and negative?

2. Penny and Jeremy are also running an investigative business, Nichols & Laidley, where they research estates and art treasures. They work together and apart, but usually in harmony. Penny's area of expertise is historical research, and Jeremy's is estate law. How do these skills merge? Where do they diverge? Think of various turns in the story, and discuss which member of the team seemed to be in charge of the situation. How do they back each other up as they move forward? Why does Penny go on the house-tour of the Earl's estate? What does she find there? How does she manage to work together with Jeremy, even though he's in London at the time?

3. The character of Rollo, who is a slightly disreputable cousin of Penny's mother, has returned in each of the "Rather" novels. He is very fond of Penny, and she of him. Jeremy, though tolerant, is more doubtful of Rollo. How do the three of them work together and play off each other? What does Rollo symbolize to Penny and Jeremy? What are Rollo's skills? His foibles and liabilities?

4. Penny discovers that when her Grandmother, and Great-Aunt Penelope, and Rollo's father were children they had a secret summer club in which they explored the very same area of Cornwall that Penny and Jeremy are now investigating. How does this element weave through the story? Discuss the various points in the novel when the kids' club contributes to the investigation. How do these clues unfold?

5. Discuss how the people in the town of Port St. Francis either hinder or help Penny and Jeremy in solving the historical mystery. Harriet and Colin are friends of Prince Charles, but Colin has some eco-warrior pals; how do they figure in? Do they make things worse or better? Where does the Earl line up in the battle to save the town? What is Trevor Branwhistle's role? Where does the chef, Toby Taylor, line up? What part did the old fisherman Basil play?

6. Discuss the significance of the discovery of the masthead from the ship *La Paloma*. How does it affect the turn of the plot? Why does it change things so profoundly? Was its importance evident right away?

7. Discuss the tragic story of Paloma Manera and Prescott Doyle. They are both superstitious about the Scarlet Knot. Have you experienced the effect of superstition in your life? Do you know

people who believe in lucky charms? What happens when they lose the charm and things go wrong?

8. How does Nature figure into the story? What are "rock pools"? How does the landscape reflect Penny and Jeremy's situation as it changes? What happens when the weather turns bad? Does it stop Penny and Jeremy from making progress, or does it create an opportunity that they otherwise might have missed?

9. Simon Thorne is an old friend of Penny's from the first novel, *A Rather Lovely Inheritance.* Simon was Great-Aunt Penelope's old singing-and-dancing partner from the 1920s and 1930s. How does Simon figure into this new story, *A Rather Remarkable Homecoming?* How does Simon repay Penny for her kindness?

10. What were the various clues to the Shakespeare connection? How do all the research and discoveries about Shakespeare unfold? Discuss the town meeting when Jeremy and Penny present their findings. In your own experience, how do people respond when they get news they don't want to hear?

11. In King Arthur's time, the knights often had to go off to solve near-impossible riddles, or to fight formidable foes. How does the task given to Penny and Jeremy fit into this? Have they been given an impossible task? What mythological elements arise to help out when the task seems as if it can't be done?

12. Have you ever visited a childhood haunt as an adult? How did it feel to go back and see the things you cared about? Were they as you remembered, or were they different, and how so?

## About the Author

**C.A. Belmond** has published short fiction, poetry and humorous essays. She was awarded the Edward Albee Foundation Fellowship and was twice a Pushcart Press Editors' Book Award finalist. Belmond was a writer-in-residence at the Karolyi Foundation in the South of France, and her original screenplays were short-listed at Robert Redford's Sundance Institute and the Eugene O'Neill Playwrights Conference. She has written, directed and produced television drama and documentary, and has taught writing at New York University. Her debut novel, *A Rather Lovely Inheritance*, launched the original story of Penny and Jeremy. The second book in the series is *A Rather Curious Engagement*, followed by the third novel, *A Rather Charming Invitation*. And now, the fourth and newest novel is *A Rather Remarkable Homecoming*. For news of upcoming works and events, visit the author at her Web site, www.cabelmond.com.